'I AM AN INDEPENDENT AND QUITE FREE INDIVIDUAL. I DO AS I CHOOSE AND WILL CONTINUE TO DO SO.'

She lifted her chin with a suddenly hard expression on her face, which vanished at once as she became aware of their somewhat startled expressions ... 'So do tell me, dear aunt, may I be one of your paying guests? I would like it above all things.'

'I am not sure,' Tilly said, aware she was stammering and wishing she were a good liar. If she could look this girl in the eyes and announce she had every room full it would be so much easier, but the second floor back on the far side of the house was empty ...

'Oh, please, Aunt Tilly!' Sophie jumped up and became all at once a pliant, charming half-child, half-woman that only the hardest of hearts could resist ... 'Please let me come home, Aunt Tilly. For that is what it would be like for me. Coming home.'

ABOUT THE AUTHOR

The author of numerous works of both fiction and non-fiction, Claire Rayner wrote her first novel in 1964. Her successes include the twelve-volume *Performers* series and the six-volume *Poppy Chronicles.* Signet publish *First Blood* and *Second Opinion,* the first two books in a series of medical mysteries featuring Dr George Barnabas. *Paying Guests* is the sequel to *London Lodgings,* which introduces the character of Tilly Quentin and is also available in Signet.

Claire Rayner is Britain's best-known advice and medical columnist. Born in 1931 she worked as a nurse for several years before starting her successful career as a medical journalist and agony aunt, writing for several national newspapers and magazines and appearing on national TV and radio. Claire Rayner is married with three grown-up children and lives in Middlesex.

CLARE RAYNER

Paying Guests

A SIGNET BOOK

SIGNET

Published by the Penguin Group
Penguin Books Ltd, 27 Wrights Lane, London W8 5TZ, England
Penguin Books USA Inc., 375 Hudson Street, New York, New York 10014, USA
Penguin Books Australia Ltd, Ringwood, Victoria, Australia
Penguin Books Canada Ltd, 10 Alcorn Avenue, Toronto, Ontario, Canada M4V 3B2
Penguin Books (NZ) Ltd, 182–190 Wairau Road, Auckland 10, New Zealand

Penguin Books Ltd, Registered Offices: Harmondsworth, Middlesex, England

First published by Michael Joseph 1995
Published in Signet 1996
1 3 5 7 9 10 8 6 4 2

Printed in England by Clays Ltd, St Ives plc

For Geoffrey Ring. With gratitude.
For making assurance doubly sure.

Chapter One

'HOW MUCH?' TILLY QUENTIN said and stared at the man on the other side of her little desk with horror. 'How much did you say?'

'Sixty-five pounds all together,' Mr Collins said with gloomy relish. 'Twenty guineas to Colonel Nichols for sundry items of gentleman's tailoring, fifteen to Jerrison the jeweller in Brompton and the rest to various merchants in Kensington. I fear that you are liable, Ma'am.'

'I liable for those debts as well as the more direct ones to me?' Tilly was wrathful. 'How can that be? Is it not enough that he mulcted me of seventeen guineas for his rent and board? Why should I have to take on the burden of these other debts as well, and –'

'I am afraid he used your name as guarantor, Ma'am, and that was why he was accepted as a customer so readily. I dare say you could indeed refuse to pay on the grounds that he acted criminally in not consulting you and obtaining your consent, but I am not sure that this would be wise. It would cost you far more in goodwill and reputation than it would save.' The lawyer shook his head dolefully and stared at her for all the world, Tilly found herself thinking crossly, like a mournful dog with his red-rimmed eyes and shaggy head of grey hair. She could have shaken him in her frustration, but instead she took a deep breath and tried to compose herself.

She had to face the fact that once again she had been baulked in her plans. Running Quentin's Guest House was not, as she had once fondly imagined it would be, a matter of simplicity. Two lady schoolteachers had been her financial salvation long ago when, as a young widow with an infant son to support, she had first taken paying guests. The thought of opening her home to strangers had been repugnant, but at least it had been an answer to her problems. Now, seventeen years later, when she had managed to add the adjoining premises to her original establishment and make the pair of high-fronted terraced houses into a harmonious whole by means of judicious rebuilding and rearrangement of the interior, it should have been much easier. All she had to do was let her twenty rooms, provide care and food for the various people who occupied them and tuck away into the bank the money she earned to build a snug fortune for her dear son, Duff, now so close to leaving school and embarking on adult life.

But over and over again, matters failed to proceed as smoothly as they should. There had been the time when, owing to the widespread building work being done in the neighbourhood, together with the construction of new sewers and water supply pipes, a section of Quentin's back garden had fallen into a crater and the cost of shoring it all up again and replanting the garden had been considerable. She had found herself liable for that because she had neglected to supply herself with adequate insurance cover. Then there had been the matter of the drains, which one resident had insisted had been the cause of her severe attack of fever five winters ago, and which had needed costly repairs, not to speak of the constant expense of painting the exterior of the building and keeping the interior as handsome as persons paying as much as three guineas each week for their rent had a right to expect. And now this! In spite of paying a sizeable sum in insurance premiums each year to protect her establishment from the sort of depradations she now realized were horridly commonplace for even the most careful and hard-working of proprietresses, she had to face yet another loss.

She lifted her head and looked at Mr Collins. 'Could I not claim this loss from the insurance company, Mr Collins?' she said hopefully. 'After all, I pay considerable sums for their protection and –'

'No, Ma'am.' He shook his head regretfully. 'It was decided, do you not recall, that the cost of paying for such cover would be prohibitive. No one can guard against wicked dishonesty. I suggested to you then that the only way of guarding yourself against unscrupulous persons of Mr Greenwall's sort was to insist that your guests pay you in advance rather than in arrears.'

She shook her head, her old stubbornness rising in her. 'No, sir, that I cannot do. These are my guests, remember, and I wish them to feel that they are – that they are more than mere customers. In none of the shops from which I buy my necessaries do I have to pay before I receive the goods – it is my right, after all, to be sure that I am suitably supplied before I agree to pay. I cannot treat my guests in a less honourable manner. I am sure you will agree.'

'Then you must take your chances, Ma'am, that one of them will cheat you as Mr Greenwall did, running off in the middle of the night.' He said it with an air of self-satisfaction that made Tilly's hackles rise, but she did her best to control it. He spoke only the truth, after all. He had, she remembered, tried to warn her that people might cheat her, and she had dismissed his lugubrious words almost airily. She would choose her guests with such care that it could not happen, she had told him. And now look at what had happened!

Though she had to be fair; this was the first time she had suffered the experience of having a guest sneak off, complete with luggage, leaving a sizeable bill unpaid. He had requested only three weeks ago to change his arrangements from paying at the end of each week to paying monthly and since he had been her guest for almost six months, and she had found him agreeable (he had been a good-looking young man and full of wit and Tilly enjoyed the company of amusing people), she had stifled any doubts she might have had and agreed. And now she had paid for her own trusting heart.

She got to her feet in a flurry of dark green sarsenet, pushing her skirts to one side with a pettish gesture, finding some relief of her irritation in the physical action, and he stood up politely and bowed in a vague sort of way.

'Is there nothing more, Ma'am?'

'Since you are so adamant that nothing more can be done to

recompense, then I suppose not,' she snapped and then softened as the old man blinked at her. 'It is not your fault, Mr Collins. I should not be so – well, I am sorry.'

'It's understandable,' he said. 'None of us likes to be cheated.' He sighed then. 'It is so difficult to find the right people to deal with, is it not? Here I am, well ripe to step back a little, and take some ease as I grow older – I am past seventy, you know. Oh, yes, seventy. You must not look so surprised, for although I am hale and hearty, I was born in the last year of the old century, indeed I was – 1799, that was my birth year, and I am not ashamed to say so!'

Tilly, who had not been at all surprised, for she had always regarded him as exceedingly elderly, composed her face and tried to look impressed.

'Indeed, sir, I would never have thought it,' she said politely.

'Well, there you are, you see, there you are! Healthy living and a tranquil life, that is what does it. But what was I saying? Oh, yes – as to being cheated – I have been looking for some time now for a new young lawyer to work with me and take some of the burdens from me, since my son was lost to me you know, yes, lost in the Chinese wars, and he but a young man, but there you are, you see – as I say here I have been searching for a new young lawyer to work with me this many months and no success have I had of it, for they are all only interested in lining their own pockets, don't you know, and that is not the idea at all, no indeed. So I –'

Tilly, who had enough problems of her own to think about, interrupted the flow of language crisply.

'I well understand the problems you have, sir, as well as I understand my own. You tell me that there is no possibility of insuring against any such future losses as this Greenwall one?'

'It would be very costly,' he said heavily, a little sulky at having been treated so by such a chit of a girl; Mrs Quentin she might be, but not a day over thirty, he'd be bound. And then he remembered about the boy being seventeen and amended it in his head; she must be thirty-five, but she looked little more than a chit. And she should have had better manners than to interrupt him as she had.

She continued, unaware of his disapprobation. 'So, I must go on as best I can, choosing my guests as carefully as may be and ensuring also that I store all portmanteaus and trunks and suchlike in the attics. Mr Greenwall preferred to keep his in his room, he told me, and I should have been suspicious, but – well – in future, all such items will be taken and put away behind a locked door.' She patted the keys she had on a chatelaine at her waist. 'Then any future would-be absconder will realize that they must leave their baggage behind if they choose to flit. That way at least I will have some recompense.'

'Indeed,' he said, still a little sulky. 'And get them to pay in advance, at least for a month or two until you are sure they are reliable.'

She ignored that, moving towards the door of her small morning room to persuade him that the interview was over.

'Well, as to that, I have told you my views. This means, I fear, that I am no nearer making you an offer for the house next door, which has been empty so long that I am amazed some other person has not taken it. It has long been my hope that –'

'Well, Ma'am,' he bent his head towards the maid out in the hall who, at a gesture from Tilly, had fetched him his hat and stick, 'as to that, I cannot say. It is available to anyone who makes a suitable offer, as you know. Perhaps the reason it has not yet found a buyer is its proximity to a guest house. Not all householders wish to live in an area where private residences and trade establishments stand cheek by jowl, as it were. Good morning, Ma'am!' With which shrewd parting shot he marched out of the hall and on to the top step where he stood for a moment with his hat clutched in his hand and his grey hair lifting in the warm summer breeze that filled the street, looking at her. 'I hope, Ma'am, that this will be the last of your misfortunes. I will, as you directed earlier, ensure that all your insurances are reviewed and checked. Good day to you.'

She watched him go with a twinge of conscience as well as irritation; she could have been kinder to him, perhaps, but she had every right to be in a disagreeable frame of mind, and she moved back into the house and snapped the front door closed behind her, her face marred by a frown which sent the maid scuttling for the kitchen out of her way. Absconding guests or no, Tilly told herself firmly, she had other guests to consider and that meant she had to shop for them. She lifted her skirts and ran up the stairs to fetch her bonnet, ready once again to take on the daily business of running Quentin's.

Another week or so, and Duff, her dear Duff, would be home from school for good. Then life would be a great deal more agreeable and she would be able to work more happily and be less angered by the bad behaviour of a guest. When Duff was about, life was altogether a sunnier business, and she was able to be grateful for her good fortune. She might have been much worse off, after all, she assured her reflection as she tied her bonnet strings in front of her dressing-table mirror; lacking any man to care for her and with no other family connections to support her, she could have been quite indigent, and what would have happened to Duff then? As it was, despite the many vicissitudes of her early life, she was now snugly established.

And, she reminded herself as she settled her light summer pelisse over her shoulders, there was always Eliza, once the tweeny in Tilly's father's household, now peacocking a little as the Quentin housekeeper, but above all Tilly's prop and stay and, within the bounds of the servant–mistress situation, her good friend. Life was tolerable after all. All she had lost with Greenwall was money, and that she would soon earn again.

And she hurried downstairs to see Eliza in the kitchen and collect her list of requirements and promised herself she would never think about the wretched Greenwall ever again.

Chapter Two

THE TURBOT IN the centre of Mr Jerryman's slab looked back at her blankly, its indigo stare accusing and insulting at the same time. 'It must have been something you said or did,' it seemed to imply. 'How could it be otherwise when he has always been so sweet and biddable before?' She stared back at the turbot, denying its accusation deep inside her mind. It can't be due to my behaviour in any way. I have always cared for him more than any other person in this whole world. How could I possibly cause him any distress? And anyway, he isn't distressed precisely. He's just –

'Perhaps the cod, then, Mrs Quentin?' Mr Jerryman's voice intruded on her reverie. 'If you're not sure about the turbot – though I has to tell you, it's as fine a turbot as was ever pulled from the briny. A good six-pounder, that is, lovely. Be any bigger and it'd be nasty and stringy. This one'll be as tender and firm as a young nut, believe you me. I could have that dressed for you in a trice, Mrs Quentin, and your Eliza, she'd see it cooked up as delicate as may be and you'd not regret it. But if you feel it's a touch more'n you want to go to, why then the cod's as sweet, if not so 'andsome.'

'I shall take the turbot, Mr Jerryman,' she said briskly, pushing away all thoughts of Duff and banishing any fanciful notions of turbots communicating with her. 'And a second like it, together with three pints of shrimps to make a sauce for them. That should serve twenty and a little left over for the kitchen.'

'I'll give you some 'errings for the kitchen, Mrs Quentin, Mum.' Mr Jerryman was scandalized. 'That there turbot runs out at ninepence the pound, Mum! You don't want to go feeding that to your servants, or they'll be getting as uppity as may be. A few penny 'errings'll do them very nicely.' And he bustled about his sea-scented marble-slabbed emporium, picking up handfuls of slippery silvery fish and tossing them into his scales with the dexterity of a stage magician, and Tilly was content to let him do so. Two turbot, now she thought about it, would just be sufficient for the dining room, since she had a full complement of guests at present, so the herrings for the kitchen were no bad idea; and she pulled on her gloves and turned to go.

'Send it up at once, Mr Jerryman,' she instructed. 'And some finnan haddock for the breakfast table. Oh, and Eliza requires some extra bones for her fish stock, if you please.'

Mr Jerryman escorted her to the street from his premises with as much dignity as if his open-fronted shop had been a palace and she a queen, and she nodded at him and made her way further along Brompton Road towards number one hundred and five, very aware of the bustle and noise about her.

The road had changed in more than just its name in the past few years; what had once been an ordinary row of shops called Middle Queen's Buildings was now one side of a handsome thoroughfare with some elegant establishments. Colonel Nichol and his wife, once Miss Elizabeth Harvey, had extended their ribbons and lace shop into a most handsome emporium well supplied with the latest in silks and chiffons as well as ribbons, and Jem Leland's place with its new, wide shop front was bidding fair to overtake its neighbour in style. But she did not wish to speak to Jem today; tomorrow would be soon enough to discuss with him the provision of new linen to replace some of the worn sheets at Quentin's. Today she had promised to go and see the progress at number one hundred and five Brompton Road, lately number eight Middle Queen's Buildings, and she had never been one to fail a promise.

The noise, when she reached Charlie Harrod's shop, doubled and redoubled. The thudding of hammers and the clatter of chisels and screwdrivers as well as the shouts of workmen at the rear of the premises made her head ring and she said – or rather shouted – as much to Charlie when she found him at the front of his shop with his bowler hat on the back of his head, as usual, and his shirtsleeves pushed up. He would have been mortified had any of his assistants – he had a dozen of them now – been seen without their proper calico jackets, but for himself, shirtsleeves were permissible.

'Don't I know it!' he said and his face shone with pleasure. 'I keep 'em at it! I won't have any humbugging when they're working for me! Oh, it'll be handsome, really handsome, when it's all done. Come and see, do.' And he almost pulled her further into the shop and led the way towards the back.

The shop was busy, in spite of the noise from the rear, with ladies at every counter earnestly poring over the new catalogue – a typical piece of Charlie Harrod's forward-looking ways, she told herself as she passed them – selecting their teas and coffees, and in many cases the daring new foods Charlie was now importing from Italy, notably preserved olives and raisins of a very superior quality. Everywhere there were piles of neat packages and deep boxes of biscuits, jars of jellies and essences on the mahogany counters and, of course, bottles of wine and oil and vinegar. The smell of cinnamon and cloves, mace and pepper and sugar hung in the air, mixing not unpleasantly with the scent of good ham and other preserved meats, and altogether made the atmosphere of Harrod's stores its usual agreeable self; she took a deep breath of pleasure and followed Charlie to the far back.

'You see?' he said eagerly and took her arm in a way that would have seemed shockingly familiar in anyone else, but in Charlie Harrod was not, being simply an expression of his excitement of the moment and his trust in her as one of his oldest friends as well as customers. 'That's where my old kitchen and parlour were – it's as well my Caroline can't see what's happening, or it'd break her heart, much as she likes living in Esher in that fine new house, but there it is. You can't blame her for being sentimental, seeing this is where we first set up together. Now, over *there* I shall be selling patent medicines. Yes, I shall – there's a big call for them and I don't see why the apothecaries should have it all their own way. And here on the other side, stationery and the like. And perfumes – that was young Will's idea, and I don't deny a good one. He'll turn out to be the best of 'em all yet, for all he's my sister's boy, and young as he is –'

'Not as young as you were when you first started in the shop,' she said and smiled at his eagerness. He had changed a great deal in the past dozen or so years, being now a solid, and it could not be denied, slightly paunchy thirty-two year old with a big round face, a tendency to look sour when not smiling but a permament twinkle about the eyes. She thought of the boy he had been, all lanky boniness, rumpled hair and impudence, and smiled even more widely. The impudence of those days had become a breezy self-confidence, but he was still Charlie. A good man.

'Oh, well, as to that, I was thirteen when I started working for my old father, but I had advantages Will don't have. He ain't as quick in the understanding as I was, but he'll shape up, you see if he don't. Good as a son he could be to me.' Suddenly his face lost its beam and Tilly spoke quickly to distract him.

'I saw Caroline only last week, at the church bazaar and thought she looked uncommonly well.'

'Oh, she's well enough,' Charlie allowed and the moment passed. The repeated loss of Caroline's pregnancies were clearly as much a sadness to her husband as to Caroline herself. 'But I shan't let her see what we're doing here till it's done. Going to have another floor, you know! Yes, another floor, one flight of stairs up! Won't that be capital!'

'Capital indeed,' Tilly said. 'You will need more assistants, I imagine.'

Charlie beamed. 'I will indeed. I shall take in four more to start with and see how we do.'

'And will you start to dress your windows with your goods?' Tilly said, knowing herself to be teasing him and laughed aloud when he bristled.

'Indeed I shall not! Vulgar ostentation, that's what window displays is. Fine enough for linen drapers and the like but not for me. I'll keep 'em the way they are, and no one shall make me change 'em!' He glared at her as sternly as if she had volunteered that moment to set about putting goods in the window with her own hands.

She laughed again. 'I agree with you, Charlie. They look very fine as they are.' They both looked over their shoulders at the great plate-glass windows which were Charlie's pride and joy, with the simple arrangement of wire blinds bearing his name in gold letters: C.D. Harrod.

'I've got it all worked out, you know,' he said then in a confiding manner. 'I shall set the perfumes right in the far corner of the first floor, so that customers have to go past all the other goods to reach 'em. They'll spend more that way – they'll all go to the far corner, for what lady can resist a perfume display?'

'Ah,' said Tilly. 'Then a display of goods *inside* the shop is not vulgar and ostentatious?'

He looked at her sharply and she looked back at him with a wide-eyed, limpid gaze and after a moment he laughed.

'Well, you was always one to tease me, Mrs Q!' he said. 'And I wouldn't have you any other way. Now, tell me, did young Duff enjoy that ham we sent round? The best Bradenham it was, as succulent as could be. I chose it myself for him. I'll bet he tucked in!'

Tilly had forgotten, just for a moment, her worries about Duff, but now they all came flooding back. She felt her face go a little pink and was glad of the dimness of the shop interior.

'I am afraid he has had none as yet,' she said as lightly as she could, and turned away, ostensibly to look closely at a pile of jars containing preserved peaches. 'He – oh – he was very tired and did not take dinner with us last night. And this morning I was out and about my affairs before he rose.'

'Well, that's natural enough,' Charlie said heartily. 'A lad just released from school – why, he must feel like a prisoner newly out on parole! He'll be wanting to take life as easy as may be for a few days yet. But that ham'll improve with keeping, and he'll try it soon enough, I dare say. As long as your guests don't get there before him and wolf the lot!' He laughed even more heartily and picked up one of the jars of peaches. 'Do you take one of these, Mrs Q. They are a new line I'm trying and I'd be glad of an honest opinion. You've got the most taste of any customer I have and –'

'Fiddlesticks,' she said and shook her head at him. 'You are always giving me extra items and it really must stop. It cannot be good business to give away your goods in such a manner.'

'It is when it's you I give to, Mrs Q,' he said, and lifted a finger at one of his assistants who came rushing over at once. 'Put that in Mrs Q's order,' he instructed and then turned back to Tilly as the man obediently hurried away. 'You're one of the best customers I have, you know. Why, if you like a new line and choose to buy it, look at how much you buy! How many guests have you at present?'

'Twenty,' she said.

'Then there you are! That's a big household and no error. And what with Eliza and her four girls to feed as well – I'd be a fool to myself if I didn't treat you special!'

She shook her head, amused and irritated at the same time. 'Nonsense, Charlie. You must do business with much larger households than ours! I have but the one son and no husband, while there are other houses where there are so many children and cousins and aunts and uncles besides, and far more servants, that they must surely outnumber my total greatly. You must not give me goods, but put them on my bill. I am willing to try new lines, as well you know. I do not need such coaxing. But I always have and always will pay my way.'

'It was you that taught me the value of not allowing credit, Mrs Q,' Charlie said. 'I owe you for that, as well you know. I've never been held back by bad debts like some I could mention. Poor old Jobbins.' He shook his head sadly but with an air of suppressed satisfaction. 'I warned him he'd come a cropper and a cropper he came. And the man as took his shop ain't doin' no better. You mark my words, Mrs Q, I'll be taking over his premises and all when I'm ready, and the one alongside him too, come to that. He's losing money fast, for he's as poor a saddler as ever I came across. By the time I'm ready they'll be glad to sell to me.'

'Well, as long as you don't run too fast, Charlie,' she said and reached into her reticule for her shopping list. 'I wouldn't wish to see you fall over your own feet in your hurry.'

'I won't,' he said, supremely confident. 'Any more'n you would if you did the same, Mrs Q. You've got twenty guests? Why, you could take that house alongside yours, what's been up for sale these last ten months or more and improve your business by fifty percent.'

'I have quite enough to keep me busy as it is, Charlie,' she said firmly and held out her list. 'Now, let me see, I require pudding rice – it had better be a half sack, I think – and sago and semolina. Then some curry spices – Eliza is heart set on making more curries since we've had a retired officer from India among our guests – and raisins, and almonds, and loaf sugar and –'

For the next half hour they were heads together over her extensive list and when at last she buttoned her gloves ready to venture back into the street and her last call of the morning, at Mr Spurgeon's the butcher, she was once again in full command of her own thoughts. Duff, she told herself as Charlie saw her to the door and on her way (with a further reassurance that the peaches would be sent, no matter what she said and were to be regarded as a gift of the establishement, at which point she gave up arguing; Charlie Harrod could be amazingly stubborn), was just tired. She had imagined his remoteness and unwillingness to be part of the company at dinner last night. He had been her own sweet Duff, as usual, of course he had. It must have been a megrim of her own that made her think him aloof and impatient.

She made her way along the street, automatically weaving through the strolling shoppers, towards Mr Spurgeon's shop and yard, which was making its presence felt on this warm August morning: the farmyard smell of his animals waiting to be killed for the table wafted across the hot pavements in a way that was, while far from agreeable, at least not as unpleasant as it might be, because of its overtones of the countryside. She ignored it, and walked with her head up and her step springing. The important thing was that Duff was home. That he would never again go away to school.

She bit her lip as, against her will, the memory that had plagued her all through his schooldays came wafting back to her: the small Duff, his face white and pinched beneath his pertly tasselled cap, staring at her wide-eyed and brave as he struggled not to let the tears show; her own aching desire to snatch him back from the train on which he was to travel with the other boys dressed as he was all the way to Dorset and how Miss Fleetwood and Miss Knapp had held her back, one on each side, and stopped her from doing anything so foolish.

'It is for his own good,' they had assured her earnestly. 'He is a clever boy, a most intelligent lad. If he remains here with you, even if he does go to a day school, he will lack the benefits that attendance at such a school as Sherborne must give him! He is a boy without a father, dear Mrs Quentin! He needs the company of men and boys, you must see that. If it were not so he would not be so tearful now, and he eleven years of age! He is too old to be so attached to his dear Mamma – you must let him go if you want a man made of him.'

Since they had had the teaching of him since his infancy and had indeed made a splendid job of it, imbuing him with the rudiments of Latin and Greek as well as a good understanding of the use of the globes and natural philosophy and some theology, she had deferred to their opinion.

But it had hurt. Every holiday had been a mixture of delight and misery; starting with the huge excitement of his return home at the end of the term and culminating, as always, with the dreadful pain of parting. But the school had been the making of him, she had to admit. Each year that passed had seen him taller, more muscled – for he played many games and played them well at Sherborne – and more clever. He would talk to her sometimes on long winter holiday evenings and amaze her with the breadth of his new knowledge of such matters as chemistry and physics and mathematics. He enjoyed history and geography too; altogether, she took a pride in him that almost made her burst. She had looked towards with such eagerness the end of his schooldays.

And now it had come. Nearly eighteen, he had completed his studies at Sherborne and was home for good. She had been in an ecstasy of excitement when he had arrived yesterday in a flurry of trunks and boxes fetched from the station in two cabs, since one was not large enough for it all; and he had refused to let her meet him there, telling her in an earnest letter that, at his age, it would be demeaning to be greeted like a boy of the first or second years when he was a swell of the Sixth.

But then as the afternoon had worn on, and she had stopped gasping at the way he had grown in this past term (he was fully four inches taller than when he had left Brompton after the Easter holidays, and much more solid) and at the fact that he now clearly shaved (she had suffered a pang too as she remembered the downiness of his infant cheeks but had managed not to speak of it to him), the feelings had changed. He had been uneasy, remote, not like himself at all as he had gazed round at the little changes she had rushed to show him in the house: the new seat covers in the dining room which the guests so much preferred and the extra chairs in the drawing room that made it possible for so many more of them to spend time there in the evenings if they wanted to. He had been quiet, not at all as interested and excited as once he would have been; she saw him off to bed early, as he had insisted he wanted only a sandwich on a tray for dinner, with her feelings in a turmoil. She had slept little, still worrying over the change in him and her concern had stretched itself into this morning.

But now, she told herself, it was all a hum. She had been a foolish, over-excited woman, allowing her anticipation of her only son's return home for good to overshadow her normal good sense. She must give the boy time to catch his breath and be comfortable again and then all would be well. She was sure of it.

At Mr Spurgeon's shop she spent a half hour in close colloquy on the subject of the proper hanging of beef and the chining of mutton chops. Mr Spurgeon was an excellent butcher, or always had been, but now as he grew older and his son Walter took a more active part in the working of the business, standards seemed to have slipped a little. Last night's steaks had been less than perfect, she told Mr Spurgeon severely, and he was mortified and talked to her for some time of the way sons meddle in matters they didn't understand and assured her that in future he and only he would deal with her order. She came out again into the street, having left with him a full description of all the meat she needed until the end of the week, well satisfied.

Outside the street was beginning to thin of passers-by and she glanced at the clock set over the jeweller's on the corner and lifted her brows. A quarter before noon. Close to time for luncheon. She must hurry home and see how Duff was, now he was up, as surely he must be at this hour of the morning. And, she thought fondly, ravenously hungry I'll be bound. We must see what is available in Eliza's larder for a special luncheon for him. The ham, perhaps.

She saw him before he saw her: on the other side of the road, with another young man who looked much the same age as he was. Standing taller than his companion, Duff was wearing a glossy top hat tilted at a somewhat rakish angle over his eyes, so that his long side-whiskers, curled and very elegantly trimmed, were clearly visible. They were the first thing she had noticed yesterday afternoon when he had stepped out of his cab in Brompton Grove and it had made her heart contract then as it did now. The length of the side-whiskers, which reached almost to the point of his jaw, made him look so very adult and elegant, and now, seeing him in a high-buttoned fine worsted frock-coat in a deep blue with the most elegantly tied of octagons, and narrow trousers in silver-grey checks over spatted patent-leather shoes, she was amazed. He was exceedingly good to look at; and again she could have burst with pride.

She stood at the side of the road, impatiently waiting for a gap in the traffic as great lumbering carthorses plodded by dragging their loads, and faster stepping cabhorses tried to overtake them, her skirts held high above the dust, hoping to catch his eye before he moved away. It would never do to shout across at him, for that would be the height of vulgarity, but she could hold her head high in the hope he would glance her way and see her; and she did, craning above the traffic towards him.

And he did see her. He had half turned to speak to the young man at his side who had stopped to look into the jeweller's window, and he glanced across the road and saw her. She was certain he had;

she could tell by the way his eyes widened and his face half froze. Automatically she lifted one hand in a half wave, but he seemed not to see it. He turned his head away, his face still blank, and spoke to the young man at his side, who at once turned towards him, looked up at the clock above their heads and moved away with him at a sharp pace.

She had not imagined it, she told herself as she stood there at the side of the new Brompton Road, staring across at the space where he and his friend had been. He had seen her and cut her dead. She, his own mother, had been totally snubbed.

Chapter Three

BY THE TIME she reached home, walking as quickly as she could through the dust of the summer-dried streets, she had almost convinced herself that she had, once again, misread the signs. He hadn't seen her; he could not have snubbed her – not her Duff. And with that thought firmly in her mind she let herself into the coolness of her entrance hall and stood there for a moment as she removed her gloves and her wrap, glad to be out of the glare of the sun, and made one last effort to compose herself before going to speak to Eliza.

Around her the house was quiet and yet had an air of being occupied with purposeful people. The hall stand was draped in coats, hats and umbrellas which were reflected in the high gloss of the black and white squares of the tiled floor, and the mahogany table at the foot of the stairs bore a few letters awaiting collection. The arrangement of dried grasses and flowers in the tall floor vase which stood beside it had a slightly rumpled look, as if someone had brushed past it in a hurry. Above stairs she could hear the faint sounds that meant Rosie and Dora, the housemaids, were finishing off the cleaning of the rooms up there, and from the dining room came the clink of cutlery and china that showed Lucy was at work. She could smell the beeswax and lavender used to polish the drawing-room furniture, the bowls of roses from the garden that were everywhere, and beyond that the shadowy scent of hot bread. Eliza baking, she thought; that will be for Duff. He adores her doughnuts and she only makes them when she bakes bread. So, she would be baking an extra batch just so that she could make doughnuts for Duff.

Absurdly, Tilly's spirits lifted. She was the most foolish woman alive. Duff must be down in the kitchen with Eliza, in the old comfortable way, and the young man she had seen in Brompton Road hadn't been him at all. She caught up her dark green surah skirts and went hurrying to the back of the hall and the green baize door that led down to the kitchen quarters.

She stood for a moment at the top of the stairs that led into the kitchen, staring down into its familiar comfort. Ahead of her the stairs sparkled with clean white paint on each side of their runner of dark red drugget; the brass stair-rods that held the drugget in place glittered with the rich polish given them by Mrs Cooper, the woman who came in by the day to do the roughest of the housework. The well scrubbed floor of the kitchen itself looked, in the midday light, as though it were made of a dish of rich cream instead of humble sandstone and the many coloured rag rugs that were scattered across it winked brightly back at her. Everywhere there was a gleam and glitter from the copper pans that hung across the beam in the centre of the whitewashed ceiling and the blue and white dishes on the great Welsh dresser and the glow of the fire in Eliza's highly polished black stove.

Eliza was at the table, itself scrubbed to warm amber by years of loving attention, slapping bread dough rhythmically from side to side with regular turns of her muscled wrists which showed clearly under a dusting of flour, for her black housekeeper's dress sleeves were rolled back. Her face beneath the neat white cap she liked to wear over her carrotty hair was scarlet with the heat and the exertion of her work, and she had unbuttoned her dress at the throat so that her neck was clearly visible too, in a way that made her look vulnerable. Tilly felt a wash of affection for her. All these years of building up Quentin's that she and Eliza had shared had formed a bond between them that no amount of trouble could strain.

She moved on down the stairs and Eliza looked up and grinned, splitting her wide freckled face into its familiar creases. She was still a young woman, barely thirty, but the long years spent over cooking stoves had permanently reddened her cheeks and dried her skin. But she was still good to look at.

'There, and I thought I could be done with this before you got home!' she said comfortably. 'You must have gone like the wind, Mum, to be back this soon.'

'I've ordered turbot for tonight, Eliza,' Tilly said. 'And shrimps for a sauce.'

'And there's a nice bit of cold beef to make a platter of beef cakes,' Eliza said, and gave her dough one last thump before putting it under a clean white cloth in a yellow pottery bowl to rise beside the stove. 'And I got a dish of macaroni for Mr Geddes all planned – poor man, to live on such sorry stuff! – and a couple of nice fowls that'll boil up lovely. And the last of the lettuces from Mr Morton's market garden together with a few of his late tomatoes fit for baking. We shall contrive an excellent dinner, and economical too.' She laughed richly. 'It do add to the pleasure, Mum, to know I've done a dinner as'll protect your cash box.'

'As long as we do not keep them on short commons, Eliza,' Tilly said, a little absently. She was trying to think of a way to ask about Duff that would not be too pointed. She was almost ashamed of her thoughts, and could not have shared them even with Eliza, or at least not at present.

'As if I would!' Eliza said indignantly. 'Does anyone ever have cause for complaint?'

'No, Eliza, of course not.' Tilly settled herself in the chair on the far side of the kitchen table, not wishing to overheat herself in the fireside rocker, comfortable chair though it was. 'I just meant –'

'Well, never you think it, Mum.' Eliza was genuinely ruffled and stood there with her hands on her hips, looking down at Tilly with her face crumpled with concern. 'It's one thing to be economical and quite another to be mean. Like it says in my new *Englishwoman's Domestic Magazine*, the art of kitchen management is to –'

'Yes, indeed,' Tilly said hastily, anxious to stave off the torrent of information that Eliza liked to give her from her favourite weekly reading. 'Indeed, I meant no reproof, and I am very happy you are so thrifty. Ah, have you planned anything special for the pudding course? Perhaps a damson tart?' The fact that such tarts were great favourites with Duff she did not mention for there was no need to do so. Eliza knew it perfectly well.

'Oh, yes, Mum.' Eliza was diverted at once. 'I've the fruit already steeping in a sugar syrup, and I'll add the pastry directly. And an Exeter pudding too – rich as may be, it says in my receipt book, with its rum and cream and jam and lemon and all – Duff'll like that as much as the damson tart.'

'I'm sure he will.' Tilly was elaborately casual. 'Did he take much breakfast?'

'Oh, that he did, but ate it that fast I told him as he'd hurt his digestion, but he paid no heed, and why should he, young as he is?' She smiled fondly. 'And it was very good ham and ate as sweet as butter. One of Charlie's best offerings, that is.'

'Yes,' Tilly said, still being as casual as she could. 'Er, is he in his room now, then? Or perhaps –'

Eliza chuckled. 'Not he! Dressed himself up all elegant and was away like a shot from a gun at eleven on the dot. Said he wouldn't want no luncheon, on account he was meeting a friend. I must say he looked very well. Such clothes! I never thought to see him so fashionable! Not when I remember how scapegrace he used to be, ripping his breeks and his coats to shreds with his rushing about! He has grown up smart, and no error.'

'Well, young people you know, like to be in the first stare,' Tilly said, and tried to hide how wretched she felt. It must have been Duff she saw in Brompton Road after all, she thought miserably. With his friend. But why, oh why?

'Is there something amiss, Mum?' Eliza said and Tilly glanced at her and managed a smile. She had forgotten just how sharp Eliza's understanding was.

'Oh, no, I am just sorry not to have seen him today,' she said. 'But I dare say I can last till he returns for dinner. I assume he will do so?'

Eliza looked a little puzzled. 'Well, as to that, Mum, I can't say. I didn't ask him, like – I just sort of took it he would be. I mean, he knows everyone always eats together, don't he? And he knows the Misses F and K'll be all agog to see him too, so I never thought to *ask* him.'

'Quite right, Eliza,' Tilly said as heartily as she was able, and got to her feet. 'Why should you? He is home now and is free to do as he chooses. It must have been irksome for him as he grew older to be under the constant direction of schoolmasters, after all. We must be patient with him while he feels his freedom. I am sure he'll settle down in a day or so.'

'Yes, Mum,' Eliza said, looking somewhat puzzled, but Tilly did not notice. She just made for the stairs.

'I must deal with the household books, Eliza,' she said as she picked up her skirts and began to climb, 'before I take a little luncheon. Are yours on my desk?'

'Yes, Mum,' Eliza said and watched her go, a small frown between her eyes.

In her own private room, which had been the morning room of the original family house in which she had been born, Tilly was able to busy herself about her work and push away her concerns about Duff, which, she assured herself yet again, were exaggerated and foolish. It was as she had herself told Eliza: the kicking over the traces of a young colt newly free to trot and canter at will. He would be here at dinner time and she would be able to discover that he had not even seen her this morning. The traffic in the road and all – of course he hadn't.

Dealing with the household books absorbed her for a half hour, and it was a very agreeable half hour. She set herself careful budgets, month by month, seeking always to give her guests the best of care and provisions while at the same time ensuring she made not only her costs but a respectable profit as well. The past twelve years had made her adept at it, and she totted up her figures and wrote totals in her neat round handwriting – not copperplate but easily legible – and closed the books and her cash box tolerably satisfied. Eliza was managing her staff exceedingly well and she had avoided the necessity to employ another housemaid, for which Tilly was deeply grateful. Young housemaids needed not only their wages but also a good deal of feeding and Tilly could never bear to keep her servants ill fed, which was the way some housekeepers made their ends meet – so that had helped the budget greatly. Maybe one day she would indeed be able to contemplate purchasing the empty house next door and so make Quentin's into a larger establishment, an ambition she had felt growing in her this past two years, though she would never admit it to anyone, not even Eliza. Yet.

She put the books back in her desk drawer, set the cash box on top of them and locked the drawer with her special key, worn on the bunch at her waist, and then sat with her elbows on her desk and her chin resting on her clasped hands as she looked about her room.

It was the only one she had never redecorated. Every other part of the house gleamed with new white paint and enjoyed the comfort of good Axminster carpet underfoot or, at the very least, oilcloth; there were new water closets created out of slices cut from rooms, of which she was very proud. Each had, in addition to their modern high cisterns and mahogany-handled pull chains, a wash-hand basin in tasteful blue and white bird designs to match the pedestal of the water closet itself, and in the house's three bathrooms, an amazing number for so modest a household as hers, there were equally tasteful furnishings. The bedrooms with their polished mahogany wardrobes and bedsteads, tallboys, dressing tables and wash-stands were the last word in modernity and her drawing room and dining room, everyone agreed, were the *dernier cri* in well chosen ornamentation, drapery and furnishings.

But in her own room nothing had been changed. The carpet on the floor was the old Turkey carpet her mother had put there when she had come to the house as a bride. It was almost threadbare now and its original red could just be discerned here and there, but its familiarity made it possible still for Tilly to see it as she remembered it, in all its glorious intricacy of pattern. The furniture was still the light fruitwood chairs and tables of seventy or more years ago, and her desk was even older, with its curved cabriole legs and sadly scratched, sloping front. But she loved it just as she loved every bit of the room as it was, only ensuring that the walls, which were covered in very faded Chinese paper, were brushed down occasionally with bread to remove stains, and the windows and fireplace well polished. It was the one room in the entire house where she felt totally at ease. When she had been a small child, afraid of her booming, ill-tempered father, it had been here she would hide, close to her mother, a gentle soul who had, in those baby days, been able to make the small Tilly feel safe. Some of that feeling lingered still, so that now not even Tilly's bedroom, which was as well appointed as that of any of her guests, gave her the serenity and quiet sense of comfort that this room did.

Everyone knew, almost from the moment they came to Quentin's that this room was out of bounds. Only Eliza ever tapped on the door to speak to her, and it was well understood among the guests that if they wished to speak to Mrs Quentin and could not find her elsewhere in the house, the answer was to ring for Eliza who would tell the mistress she was required. And Tilly would emerge from her happy fastness, her features composed and her hands folded neatly against her skirts to deal with whatever it was.

So when there was a tap on the door now she did not even lift her head, but remained staring a little vaguely at the window and its view of the garden, saying only, 'Come in, Eliza!' and sighing a little because she had been disturbed. She knew what it was Eliza wanted, though, and she turned her head to assure her she need worry herself no further; she would come directly to the dining room and take a little luncheon so that Lucy could clear the table and prepare it for its most important role of the day, the setting for dinner at Quentin's.

But it was not Eliza who stood framed in the doorway, but the tall figure of her most recently arrived guest, Mr Silas Geddes. He looked at her with his brows a little raised and she stared back, startled. Not that he was disagreeable to look at in any way. Indeed, when he had first come to see her and discuss the matter of her large back room on the second floor she had thought him a most interesting-looking man; clean-shaven in spite of the current fashion for whiskers, with hair that was dark, did its best to curl but failed because it was cut short and brushed back firmly, and wide, oddly coloured eyes, a sort of deep amber. He was well dressed without being extravagant in his appearance and smelled pleasant, with an aura of bay rum but no tobacco about him.

'Oh dear,' he said. 'I suspect I have strayed where I should not have done. I was looking about for a newspaper, you know, and thought perhaps – I do apologize.' At once he bent his head and drew back, closing the door behind him.

She was embarrassed and annoyed with herself at the same time; but perhaps she shouldn't have looked so forbiddingly at him. She must have done so, for why else would he have withdrawn so precipitately?

She was on her feet at once and reached the hall to see him halfway up the staircase, and she called a little breathlessly, 'Mr Geddes!'

He stopped and turned towards her and she managed a smile. 'I am so sorry, Mr Geddes!' she said. 'I did not mean to seem unwelcoming.'

'I did not mean to intrude,' he said and came down the steps to walk back to her and make a small bow. 'I realized as soon as I saw you sitting there so pensively that I had strayed beyond where I should have done, and I do apologize.'

She set her head to one side and looked at him consideringly. 'It is indeed true that that is my own room and people don't usually disturb me there, once they know.'

'I know now,' he said gravely. 'I will never trespass again, you have my word.'

'Heavens!' she said 'Such a fuss over a minor matter. Now, what was it you wanted?'

'A newspaper,' he said at once, accepting her control of their conversation without demur. 'I am the last to take any luncheon so I must eat alone. I thought I would read over Eliza – Mrs Horace's – excellent plate of cheese pastries.'

'Oh,' she said and laughed. 'You may call her Eliza! Everyone does. I believe she prefers it. A newspaper, you say? There is one here.' She darted across to the hall stand and reached into the space on one side just beneath the table section. 'There are always newspapers here for any of our guests who require them. Should you wish for your own use every day, then we will gladly –'

'Not at all.' He lifted both hands in protest. 'I am happy indeed to share. Thank you so much.'

He returned to the staircase, with the newspaper tucked neatly under his arm and then turned back and looked down at her a little tentatively. 'Er, I suspect, you know, that you have not taken luncheon yet either.'

She was a little surprised. 'Oh! Why should you – well, you are quite right. I haven't.' She laughed. 'I had quite forgotten.'

'That is not good for you,' he said. 'When a lady works as hard as you do, she needs her sustenance if she is to retain her health.'

She felt her face go a little pink. 'Oh, come, I don't work that hard.'

'Oh, yes you do. I've watched you ever since I arrived. I know I've only been here a few days, but I have noticed.' He nodded with an air of sagacity. 'Oh, yes, I've noticed.'

'Well, I am well enough, I do assure you,' she said briskly, shy now that he was looking at her so directly with those oddly sharp eyes. She wanted to look away, but felt it would be impolite. 'There is no need to concern yourself.'

'Well, all the same, I am concerned,' he said and then, suddenly, held out one hand towards her. 'Perhaps you would do me the honour of joining me in my light luncheon? I shall not eat too much, because I know that the good Eliza will have prepared some special dish for me tonight. I do appreciate her concern for my welfare, although I suspect that if she understood why I need her special efforts she might be less sympathetic. She thinks I eat so for my health, you know.'

'Oh!' She was surprised again. 'Don't you?'

'Oh, not at all!' He laughed and it was a pleasant sound, low and rumbling and it made his eyes vanish into slits of pleasure that made her smile too, for the look it gave him was so droll and merry. 'But I need time to explain it properly. So, perhaps you will take luncheon while I do? Please do.' He still looked merry, if less comical and she looked back at him, her lower lip caught between her teeth. Then, as a little gurgle of sound came from her middle to remind her just how long it had been since breakfast, she made her decision.

'Why not?' she said. 'We shall ring for some fresh coffee, for I am sure the pot will be quite cold by now, since it is close on two o'clock, and you shall explain to me why it is Eliza has to make you special food.'

'And you shall explain other matters to me,' he said and crooked his arm so that she could tuck her hand into his elbow. 'If you will.' And he led the way to the dining room.

Chapter Four

HE WAS SUCH very agreeable company that she found herself talking more easily and freely than she had for many years (if indeed she ever had, as she was to tell herself later). He sat on the other side of the dining-room table, watching her as she ate and refilling her coffee cup from time to time, and by dint of asking sympathetic and quite inoffensive questions, persuaded her to tell him all about herself.

That she was a widow, and indeed had been widowed twice before the age of twenty-five. That she had just the one, much-loved son, Duff, whose name was really Francis, for he had been named after his dead father, Francis Xavier Quentin, but had been given his nickname because he looked so like a sweet round pudding as an infant. That after her father's death, which led to a complete loss of income for her (but she did not tell him of the machinations of one Mrs Leander, which had led to that loss), she had been driven to earn her own and her child's subsistence by means of turning her home into a respectable lodging house for paying guests, which had been enlarged by the legacy of her second husband, Frederick Pomfret Compton, who had owned the house next door. She almost told him of her ambitions to extend even further by taking a third house, the one next door in the row, but bit her tongue in time. It was none of anyone else's concern, least of all this strange young man's.

It was at this point that she realized she had been doing all the talking and made a strong effort to change the direction of the conversation. She found aid in the fact that he ate so heartily of Eliza's cheese pastry but refused Lucy's offer of a slice of Charlie Harrod's black-skinned Bradenham ham.

'I had understood that you did not eat meat on doctor's orders,' she said as Lucy removed herself back to the kitchen, together with the remains of the mushroom soup with which they had commenced their luncheon. 'But you said before –' She stopped invitingly.

He smiled. 'I often find it simpler to let people make that assumption.' He was very relaxed and comfortable, seeming not at all put out by what must have seemed an implied criticism of his veracity. 'The truth of the matter is that I have made a definite choice to abjure the eating of dead animals.'

She stared at him. 'What a very unpleasant way to describe the eating of meat!'

'But isn't it true?' He seemed all gentle sweet reason. 'Is not that there –' and he indicated the ham, resplendent on its silver dish, its thick skin glistening with the black treacle and spices that had been used in its dressing, and the meat succulent and pink. '– is that not the hind quarter of a pig that not so very long ago was snuffling happily for acorns in some wood, or trotting along beside its mate in search of its cosy sty? Just as the collops of lamb which appeared at table last night, dressed with mint and green peas and new potatoes – which vegetables, by the by, I ate with great enjoyment – just as those collops, as I say, were this very spring gambolling in the fields and bleating for their mothers.'

'Oh, really, Mr Geddes!' Tilly protested. 'You can't speak so! It is true undoubtedly that the food we eat was once live animal or bird or fish, but that is the nature of the world. One creature feeds upon another. And anyway, these animals we breed for the table are not thinking creatures, are they? And wasn't mankind given dominion over the beasts of the field and the birds of the heavens and so forth, so that we might eat? I learned that in my infancy.'

'Ah!' he said gently. 'If the things they taught us in our infancy about God and the Creation and so forth were strictly true, then of course it would be a different matter.'

'True?' she stared even harder, amazed and rather excited. She had never heard anyone speak so. 'But how can it be otherwise – oh –' and stopped.

He looked at her closely and then laughed. 'So! You too have had your doubts, I see!'

'Doubts? I cannot say –' She floundered and then bit her lip. 'I have to say I have doubted the true goodness of some people who profess to be religious, but show themselves to be less than compassionate.'

'Oh?' he said. Again she found herself telling him more than she had intended.

'It was – after Francis died. Before Duff was born. I was very anxious about – my father had died, you see, and I had no money that I knew of. I feared I might even lose the roof over my head, and with the baby coming, I – well, I went to our curate at the church where I had always attended and had been married and he –' Her face hardened. 'He had no help for me. None at all. I have not been to that church since, but chose another to take Duff to, and to attend. When I am able, that is –'

'When you feel embarrassed at how long it is since you showed yourself there,' he said softly. 'Am I right? Not because you feel any loss of virtue, or any draw from the Divinity. Simply because it is a social affair, because successful people must display themselves at church if they are not to lose the respect – and the pecuniary benefit that accompanies that respect – of their neighbours.'

'Really, Mr Geddes!' She got to her feet, more ruffled than she would have expected. 'You go too far!'

'I apologize,' he said at once and also stood up. 'I meant no impertinence. But you were asking me about my reasons for not eating meat and suggested I was flying in the face of Divine Law in behaving so. And I needed to explain to you that it is possible to live a good and thoughtful life without being unduly concerned with – um – the opinion of the Deity.' He looked at her silently for several seconds and then went on, 'I did not think I had misread you. In watching and listening to you in the few days since I joined this household I had judged you a thoughtful person who would be interested in the new ideas that are now abroad.'

'New ideas?' She knew she should have gone by now, that this conversation was becoming amazingly intimate on so short an acquaintance, but she was curious and, she had to admit, a little excited. No one had ever spoken to her as seriously as this man was speaking to her; most men with whom she had dealings assumed her to be like all other women and interested only in the fripperies of daily life, clothes and children, servants and suchlike, and even though she had for this past many years been earning her own and her son's living – a rare enough occupation for women of her class – they continued to treat her so. Yet this man had no qualms about implying that he lacked religious belief and even suggesting she might share his views!

'What sort of new ideas?' she went on cautiously. 'I have little time, I am afraid, to read the latest books or sit and discuss weighty affairs.'

'They are not so very new, after all. Thomas Paine expressed some of them before the start of this century – the rights of the individual, you know, and especially those of women.'

'But he supported revolution!' Tilly said. 'I am not as educated as I would wish to be, but I do know that. Did he not support the French Revolution and all its blood *and* the American one? I can recall my father speaking very slightingly of the ideas of Paine.'

'Oh, many people believed that he was only about revolution without understanding why he felt so. But many of the new ideas of today are more scientific in nature. Mr Huxley says –' He stopped, and laughed a little awkwardly. 'Mrs Quentin, I must beg you to stop me if I seem to become so enthusiastic in my manner that I grow tiresome.'

She shook her head. 'You are not tiresome, Mr Geddes. Surprising, perhaps, but not tiresome. Do explain.'

'Well, there is a scientist for whom I have a great admiration – Dr Thomas Huxley. Perhaps you have heard of him? He created a considerable stir a few years ago when he and Bishop Wilberforce defended Darwin in an Oxford debate. Anyway, he is, I am proud to say, a friend, and I have learned from him that it is impossible to have true knowledge without science. The ideas of religion and some philosophers cannot be tested rigorously by the scientific method, so must be regarded as – well, it is better to be silent than to speak of what you cannot truly know.'

'Ah!' she said, enlightened. 'I understand now! *You* are a scientist, Mr Geddes!'

He looked a little uncomfortable. 'I am interested in the subject,' he said, 'but I am not an active – an – I do not work in a laboratory, you understand, I am just interested.'

'Oh?' She felt on surer ground now. 'Then do tell me, Mr Geddes, how you do occupy your time. What is your career?'

'I have to confess that I am little more than a dilettante, Mrs Quentin, most interested in science and the new thinking that is so exciting at present. I edit a small and rather select magazine –' He flashed a sudden smile. 'That means we have only a few readers and organize meetings and discussions from time to time.'

'It cannot be –' She paused, seeking to be delicate. 'It is not a lucrative occupation.'

'I am fortunate in not needing to worry about that,' he said and looked down at his hands. 'I have a private income.'

'Ah!' She said no more but, puzzled, looked more closely at him from beneath lowered lashes. Generally her paying guests were drawn from the middling levels of society, people who needed to earn their own livings and who sought a place to live that was comfortable and respectable without bringing down on them the high costs of running their own homes. Schoolteachers like the Misses Knapp and Fleetwood and their special friend, Miss Cynthia Barnetsen; Mr Oswald Gee who was an articled clerk to a lawyer in Kensington; and retired couples like Mr and Mrs Grayling who had sold their grocer's shop and therefore their home over it, and now planned to live frugally with Tilly to ensure their savings lasted their lifetimes. To have a man with a private income and a tolerably large one at that, going by the costly appearance of his clothes, was surprising.

He seemed to understand her surprise and smiled disarmingly. 'I dislike the loneliness of life in a house of my own or in bachelor chambers,' he said. 'I have long been seeking the sort of accommodation where I might be comfortable and well cared for and yet have the pleasure of agreeable company when I require it. I think my search is now over.'

'I am glad if that is so, Mr Geddes. It is our hope here at Quentin's always to ensure that our guests are the centre of our concern.'

She crossed the room to ring the bell and let Lucy know that she could come up from the kitchen to clear the dining room at last.

Mr Geddes remained standing by the table, looking at her. 'I – perhaps you might be interested, that is, that you might enjoy, well, I am organizing a meeting next week to explore the meaning of Mr Darwin's newest book *The Descent of Man.* Dr Huxley will be speaking and it should be very interesting. Perhaps you will permit me to offer you a ticket?'

Lucy appeared at the door and Tilly nodded at her, and she bobbed, came in and began to clear the table, and as Tilly led the way out of the room, Mr Geddes had to follow. She was thinking hard, and was in something of a fluster by the time she reached the hallway.

'You are very kind, Mr Geddes. I will indeed think about the possibility – but I cannot be sure whether or not I will be engaged.'

When he seemed about to try to persuade her she said, 'My son is home from school, you know, and I intend to spend as much time with him as possible.'

'Of course,' he smiled at her as she reached her morning-room door and turned to stand with her back to it, so as to make it very clear that she had no intention of inviting him in. He had confused and excited her simultaneously and she needed time to think. Indeed, she now felt as though she needed to escape from him. 'So, we shall see,' she ended a little lamely.

'Well, I shall ask you again!' He was suddenly jovial, and took her hand and bent over it politely. 'The meeting is next Friday at nine o'clock in the evening, so that people have time to dine first. It will be at the meeting hall of St Ethelburga's Church in Kensington, so it is not too far away.'

'At St Ethelburga's?' She was diverted. 'A meeting about Mr Darwin in a church hall? You surprise me.'

He chuckled. 'Well, as to that, they do not know the subject of the meeting. It was arranged by me as a private affair. It will not be advertised, you see, since we have many members of our magazine subscription list who buy tickets in advance. So there need be no difficulty.'

'It seems wrong to use a church hall,' she ventured, wanting still to escape but drawn back to the argument almost against her will, 'since there is much opposition to Mr Darwin in religious circles.'

'Perhaps. But it is also amusing,' he said and again bowed. 'I shall speak of this again, Mrs Quentin. Until then, thank you for your company at luncheon.' He turned and went, running lightly upstairs; as she watched him go, she found herself thinking that attending meetings even about the highly dubious Mr Darwin might be amusing, and there was little enough in her life to amuse her, after all. And then she too turned and went into the haven of her morning room and closed the door.

She was just coming downstairs, dressed in her new dinner gown in the latest mode of two colours, emerald green and very pale blue, when the front door opened and Duff came in.

She stood there, still buttoning her gloves, which were pale blue to match the underskirt of her gown and looked at him, her pulses thumping a little loudly in her own ears. She had been fretting over him all afternoon and now he was here she didn't know what to say to him.

'Oh, don't you look fine!' he said and took off his rather rakish top hat and flung it at the hat stand where it managed to find a hook and remain, albeit swinging rather wildly. 'That's a new gown, isn't it?'

'Yes,' she said. 'Yes. I thought I'd indulge myself a little. I'm glad you like it. I wasn't sure of the colours.'

He looked at it, his head turned consideringly to one side and his hands thrust deep into his trouser pockets, so that his coat-tails bunched up behind him. He looked debonair, a little flushed with the freshness of the air he had left outside, and his hair was slightly flattened where his hat had controlled it. Almost involuntarily she smiled widely; he looked so very well and she was so very proud of him.

'I tell you what, Mamma, it's as handsome a gown as any I've seen. Bang up to the minute without being foolish, like some there are about. Why, I saw a lady t'other day in a gown that had a blue faille underskirt and a ruched green overskirt in, I think, taffeta, and to top it all, a great train in ruby velvet. She looked like an explosion, to tell the truth. You look most elegant, however. And I do like your cap. Very charming.'

Tilly touched her cap which had been appallingly expensive for such a trifle of Chantilly lace and silk and smiled again. 'Well, I feel I must make an effort for my guests,' she said. 'It would not do to come to the dinner table looking unkempt. They are all dressing at the moment, I was about to check in the kitchen –'

She left the question in the air, unasked, but he heard it.

'I thought, Mamma, that tonight I would dine out. I have an invitation from a friend.'

She couldn't help it. Her brows snapped together and she said, 'Again? But you lunched with a friend. I thought now you were home we might see something of each other.'

He seemed to lose some of the glow that had been about him, and certainly became less relaxed. He pulled his hands from his pockets and shrugged out of his topcoat and tossed it over one arm.

'Dear me, Mamma, it is not as though you have always been so anxious for my company.'

She stared at him, nonplussed. He was looking quite different now, hard and enclosed in just the way he had seemed yesterday when he had first come home, and she said impulsively, 'Dear Duff! Whatever is the matter? Why are you so angry with me? What have I done that you are so – strange? I have been so worried! Yesterday you were so – well – as you are now. Angry. And this morning when you snubbed me in Brompton Road – I don't understand it!'

He went brick red and for a dreadful moment she thought he was going to shout at her. What had happened to her dear, sweet boy to make him so? She began to be more and more frightened.

'I – am just as I have always been,' he said then, and his colour subsided a little. 'Less biddable, perhaps, more able to speak my mind.'

'But why should doing so cause so much – I mean, what can there be in your mind about me to make you behave so unkindly? You were always such a sweet child and –'

'Mamma! I am not a child! That is the trouble. You and Eliza were behaving yesterday as though I were the same age now I was when you sent me away.'

'Sent you away – but you had to go to school!' she cried.

'I could have gone to school here in London and never left home,' he said. 'And if I had, then perhaps you would have seen that I am grown up now and not a child. As it is, you have not watched me change and can't understand me now that I'm not a boy any more, but a man.'

'At seventeen?' she said and again his colour rose, clearly to his own fury.

'It is not the same as seven!' he snapped. 'Or even ten or twelve. It is as near being full grown as may be, and I take leave to live like a man now I am one. I want to do what I want to do, and not what others tell me I should.'

'Dear Duff, I would not try to stop you ever from following your own bent!' Tilly said. 'I love you too dearly to wish to make you unhappy! It is not as though we've even talked about what you will do now you've left school, though I suppose some thought must be given to it some time. I mean, you cannot look to any sizeable income unless you have an occupation and that must be decided. But I have said nothing of that and I don't understand why you are being so unkind to me now, I really don't!' To her horror she felt her eyes fill with tears as her voice wobbled and she had to swallow hard to keep it under control.

It was that as much as anything that seemed to finish him. He stared at her with his eyes very bright and his mouth in a tight line and then shook his head and, pushing past her, fled up the stairs.

'I shall be out for dinner,' he called down from the top. 'I shall return before midnight so please not to lock me out.' And then he disappeared and she heard his bedroom door slam shut.

Chapter Five

THE DINING ROOM looked particularly fine tonight. Eliza had gone to the trouble of finding more roses from the garden (I must tell her to be less vigorous in her culling, Tilly thought. I shall have none left for the drawing room at this rate) and had arranged them prettily at intervals down the long table. Usually this was one of Tilly's own tasks, but clearly Eliza had realized that her mistress was preoccupied with other matters and had dealt with it for her. She had added trails of fern from the far bed, quite in Tilly's own style, and made it all look very dainty. 'If only Duff would –' But she lifted her chin and looked determinedly at everything else there was to see. She would not think about Duff, she would *not*.

The linen was not the only thing that was perfect. The glass and the china and silver sparkled with Lucy's loving attention and the three housemaids themselves, ranged along the wall beside the sideboard waiting to be told when to commence serving dinner, were as clean and shining as any of the objects in the room, with perfect crisp aprons and hair tucked well away under their caps. Tilly was suddenly very aware of the way she had dressed her own hair, in the current modish manner, with a frizzed-out fringe over her forehead, and wished she had not done so. She must look frivolous in the extreme, and she didn't feel at all frivolous.

The guests were coming in to take their places as the gong, which Eliza had banged with her usual gusto in the hall, shuddered into silence. First, as always, the Misses Knapp and Fleetwood, with Miss Barnetsen close behind them. The older ladies were rather plumper than they had been when they had first come to 17 Brompton Grove, but Miss Barnetsen, who had arrived as thin as a tent peg and with eyes as bulging as any frog's, had not changed an iota. She still behaved like a flibberty bit of a girl, though she must be forty if she were a day, flirting with a fan and teasing her two friends outrageously as they vied for her attention. It was an odd trio, and Tilly had long given up wasting any energy in trying to understand them. Their emotions and their relationships with each other and Miss Barnetsen were none of her affair.

They were followed in swift succession by Mr Oswald Gee, who was always punctual for his meals and devoted all his time in the dining room to eating, never deigning to waste his energies on any conversation apart from a brisk 'G'd evening, Mrs Quentin' to his hostess and 'Yes please' to the serving maids; and Mr and Mrs Grayling who, in contrast, never stopped talking. They managed to eat a considerable amount, however, never missing either a word or a mouthful, and were sprightly company who saved the table from ever falling into silence. Not that it was likely to do so when Mr Hancock and Mr Cumming were dining; the former was eating his dinners at the bar and the latter was a young surgeon walking the wards at St George's Hospital up near Apsley House, the Duke of Wellington's home. These two were great jokers, and much enjoyed teasing each other over the shortcomings of their respective professions, with Mr Hancock accusing Mr Cumming of smelling quite disgusting (and indeed the young doctor did seem sometimes to bring the horrid air of the sickroom into the house with him) and Mr Cumming telling his tormentor with equal attack that he clearly had ink in his veins instead of blood and obviously no heart at all.

Tonight they made a beeline not for their usual places, but for those opposite the most recent arrivals at Quentin's, a group of visitors from abroad. The party included two young ladies who, though not of the most immediately pretty sort, had the advantage of being much the same age as the two young men, which made them seem a great deal more attractive than they were. Tilly watched them greet each other with sly giggles (the girls) and bluff compliments (the men) that were clearly to be the order of the evening, as their elders, the aunt of Miss McCool and the parents of Miss Lampeter, watched them cautiously. They would need no attention from their hostess tonight, Tilly told herself with relief, and turned her attention to the remainder of her table, calculating who was present and who absent as they took their places.

Miss Baker and Miss Duke, the rather dim and very quiet schoolteachers who had been recommended to Quentin's some five years ago by the Misses K and F and yet who never spoke to their sponsors (not that they spoke much to anyone else either, Tilly had to admit) arrived next, bringing the total to – she counted them with swift glances round her table – fifteen. Just Mr Hunter and Mr Graham to come: they were young men who taught at the St Aloysius College for Boys in Kensington and who had been living at Quentin's this past two years and showed every sign of intending to stay as long as the female teacher guests, much to Tilly's relief. Regular guests were far easier to deal with than drifting occasionals like the visitors from America now so busily flirting with Charles Hancock and Melville Cumming. But just as she wondered whether to wait any longer for them, Mr Hunter and Mr Graham arrived and took their places, and she lifted her hand to signal to Lucy that the service could begin. The table was complete, since Duff was not to dine. ('Don't think about that,' a secret voice whispered in her ear. 'Don't think about Duff!') So they could start dinner.

Lucy looked blankly at her signal and Tilly was a touch irritated; it was not like Lucy to be so obtuse. She lifted her hand again and still Lucy looked dumbly back at her and did not move and then the door behind her opened again and Silas Geddes came in.

'Oh, dear, am I last?' he said. 'I beg everyone's pardon. I heard the gong but was not quite ready. Good evening, Mrs Quentin.' As he slid into his place down the table she bent her head to acknowledge his arrival, hoping her embarrassment didn't show. She had managed to forget him completely in her checking of her guests; how very remiss and how inefficient – and how very odd, since she'd spent so much time talking to him earlier.

She looked again towards Lucy to signal to her yet again, but Lucy hadn't waited. She was already moving around the table with

Rosie and Dora, in well drilled concert, in their places too serving the Brown Windsor soup. A faint 'ahem' behind Tilly's chair told her that Rosie was there waiting for her to move her shoulders so that her plate could be set in position; she obeyed, glad to know her staff were so well trained, but feeling herself flustered and irritable as well. She who was usually so calm and sensible to be thrown into confusion because she had forgotten one of her guests? How absurd she was being.

The clatter of dishes and the sound of desultory chatter gave way to a contented silence as soup was taken with gusto by all (except, perhaps, by Tilly herself, who found her appetite oddly capricious tonight). Eliza's Brown Windsor was a soup of rich depth of flavour as well as being most nutritious, unlike the sort peddled by some less careful establishments, and was a great favourite. It was not until they were all well into the next course and were eating Mr Jerryman's excellent turbot, which had come to table most elegantly dressed with its rich shrimp sauce and smelled delectable, that any of them had the time for much real conversation. But as the level of the flasks of Chablis which Tilly had chosen to accompany the fish went down, the noise of chatter and laughter rose to match.

The four young people laughed a great deal and showed small interest in their other neighbours, not that that mattered since the the elder Mrs McCool and Lampeters senior were happy enough talking to each other in low voices ('probably comparing what we do with what they do at home,' Tilly thought a little sharply as she looked at them, for she had already been treated to some of their animadversions on the British as compared with the American way of plumbing) and in turn ignored their other neighbours.

But here again this caused no offence, for they were the Misses Baker and Duke, who never spoke in more than monosyllables anyway. Opposite them, however, the Misses K and F were in sprightly conversation with Mr Hunter and Mr Graham.

'I cannot see,' Miss Priscilla Knapp said, 'why young ladies should not study biology. If it is suitable for the young male mind, then the young female mind can encompass it too.'

'It is not the female ability to comprehend the subject to which I object.' Mr Hunter was a thin man with a drooping eyelid on the right that gave him a totally unjustified rakish air. He was the soul of probity and very concerned always to be completely *comme il faut*. 'It is the effect on their more delicate constitutions that concerns me. Botany is enough for the female, I am convinced. When other higher life forms are being studied there is no need to disturb them with it. As for the study of human anatomy –' He almost shuddered. 'I would prefer if that were studied only by those young men who have to, in order to be doctors. Though I have to say,' and he looked across the table sharply as Melville Cumming let out a peal of even louder than usual laughter, 'that I fear it has a sadly coarsening effect on them. I never yet met a doctor who was also a gentleman of refinement, and so I tell you.'

'Then you have been unfortunate.' Silas Geddes lifted his head from his plate on which Lucy was setting a serving of macaroni, somewhat to the surprise of his immediate left-hand neighbour, Mrs Grayling. 'I know of several who are excellent ambassadors for their vocation. And one in particular who is a gentleman of the highest probity and sensitivity, though I have to admit he is not a doctor of medicine. He is a true scientist, however, and has studied all aspects of life in great detail. His knowledge, far from coarsening him, has refined his mind and his conversation to a degree that is quite remarkable.'

Mr Hunter looked at him and his drooping eyelid seemed to twitch. 'Indeed,' was all he said, and he looked away towards Miss Priscilla Knapp again. But she had switched her attention across the table to Mr Geddes.

'Do tell me more, Mr Geddes. Who is this paragon of virtue? And would he agree with me that there is no reason why young ladies should not pursue the same studies as young men?'

'I would be amazed if he thought otherwise. Indeed I think I can speak for him and say I am sure he would agree that all young people should embrace study of all the sciences in great depth. He is Dr Thomas Henry Huxley, Miss Knapp.'

He said it with a sort of pride and lifted his chin with an air of defiance; and it was needed. Several of the other diners turned to stare at him and the talk died away, even that between the four young flirtatious ones.

'Dr Huxley?' It was Cynthia Barnetsen who spoke first and she trimmed her speech with a trill of breathy little giggles. 'Isn't he that dreadful man who said Darwin is right and that we are all descended from the monkeys? How can you regard such a one as being anything but thoroughly coarse?' And she giggled again.

'Cynthia, I beg you not to speak of matters you do not comprehend,' Miss Fleetwood said briskly and smiled a wide yellow-toothed smile at Silas. 'So you know Dr Huxley, Mr Geddes? That must be a considerable privilege. I am a great admirer of both him and Bishop Wilberforce.'

'Oh, of course Mr Wilberforce is a good man,' Cynthia Barnetsen said with another foolish giggle, 'for all I have heard – did he not end slavery?'

'That was Mr William Wilberforce,' Silas Geddes said and, to his credit, Tilly thought, there was not a flicker of amusement on his face. 'He died a great many years ago, Miss Barnetsen. This is Bishop Samuel Wilberforce. He is also a good man, and a supporter of Mr Darwin together with Dr Huxley.'

'Well, for my part I cannot understand how any person of refinement can ever say we are descended from monkeys,' Mrs Grayling burst out, looking as though tears were about to appear in her round, rather foolish eyes. 'I am sure the very idea is quite disgusting, don't you agree, my dear?'

'Indeed,' Mr Grayling said, not lifting his head from his turbot. Since he always agreed with all his wife said, this was of small surprise to any of the company.

'And I can't believe that any bishop could ever support such a shocking notion,' Mrs Grayling continued. 'Why, it is quite –'

'I do assure you it is so.' Silas sounded a little sharp, Tilly thought and began to wonder if she should try to deflect the conversation. Generally she left her guests to their own conversational devices unless there seemed to be problems brewing and she certainly had no wish to join in this discussion. Her own views were not yet fully formed, and she could make no decision either way, but to say as much would offend everyone at the table. Mrs Grayling would think her monstrous for not agreeing with her, and the Misses K and F would despise her for her poor support.

But she did not need to intervene. A rescue came from a most unexpected quarter. Mr Melville Cumming, at last distracted from his flirtation with Miss Lampeter (who to tell the truth did little more than giggle at his sallies, which made it difficult for him to get very far), raised his voice.

'I think there must be much in what Mr Darwin says,' he offered. 'I have his book – his new one, don't you know – *The Descent of Man* and hope to start reading it properly soon, but what I have seen – I have skimmed it a little you know, just skimmed it – he says there's little to choose between us. And I have to tell you that when I have done dissections on animals I, too, have found there is little to choose between 'em for their internal arrangements, and now I am dealing with human subjects, why I have discovered the same is true.'

'Oh!' Mrs Grayling leaned back in her chair and began to fan herself with great vigour. 'Do give over, Mr Cumming! You make me feel quite qualmish, indeed you do, with such talk! It isn't proper at the dinner table, now is it, Mrs Quentin?' And she looked appealingly at Tilly, who sighed and glanced at Mr Cumming.

'I think perhaps this might be left for another time,' she murmured. 'Now, Mrs Grayling, Eliza, I know, would warmly welcome your opinion of her baked beef. She told me herself that she much admires your understanding of culinary matters and would be most grateful for your consideration.' She glanced at Lucy who collected her silent instructions at once and hurried round the table to offer Mrs Grayling some baked beef.

Silas glanced at Tilly with his brows slightly raised and, without meaning to, she shook her head at him in the most minute of signals and he let his lips quirk in a half smile and subsided. Oh, the wretched man, she thought. Wretched man. He has made me into his supporter and conspirator with that look. And there was I, trying to remain impartial. I shall have to tell him.

'Tell him what?' her secret little voice jeered. 'That you rather like the look of him and would enjoy more conversation with him? For you would and you know it. He is interesting and amusing and anyway, he stops you thinking about Duff. Is that not why he interests you?'

She ignored the question and concentrated on the meal, as the boiled chickens went round and then the lettuce salad and the baked tomatoes together with sundry other vegetables, and everyone became more relaxed and contented. Not another word was said about Mr Huxley or the propriety or otherwise of teaching young ladies about biology, and Tilly drew a breath of relief. The last thing she needed was controversy at her dinner table.

When the dishes had been cleared for the third course, Eliza arrived at the dining-room door, very handsome in her black housekeeper's dress (not for the world would she have been seen above stairs in an apron) bearing in her own hands the tray on which rested her own special offering, the puddings. The damson tart was large, golden and glittering with the sugar on its crust, and the Exeter pudding was magnificent, sending tendrils of butter and rum-scented steam into the warm atmosphere of the dining room, where the candles had lifted everyone's cheeks to a bright rosiness and some of the men to an actual dampness about the brow, which they mopped with large white handkerchiefs. How the women managed to escape the same fate it was impossible to say.

She was greeted with approval by all, especially the young quartet, and even the collection of schoolteachers made it clear that they admired Eliza's efforts. The remainder of dinner passed harmoniously with a great deal of the tart and the pudding vanishing, though Tilly noticed that Eliza had quietly kept back a sizeable portion of the former, once she had made a swift study of the people at the table and realized that Duff was not among them. Her darling wouldn't miss his special treat, Tilly thought, not if Eliza could help it. Would he love me better if I made the damson tart, I wonder?

Again she dismissed the thought and signalled with her eyes to Lucy, who nodded and set out for the kitchen to fetch the tray of coffee with which, in the daring modern manner, Tilly chose to end her dinners. It was not customary at Quentin's for the men to sit over port after dinner, and not because Tilly was meagre in her provision of wines. She was not. They had enjoyed an excellent claret as well as the Chablis with the turbot and sherry with their soup. It was simply that she had never wished to separate her male and female guests, feeling that to do so would smack of over-fashionable behaviour. Quentin's was a good solid lodging house for people of the middling sort, not the private home of a member of the aristocracy, and she was never going to pretend otherwise.

So now her guests followed her out of the dining room, some to accompany her to the drawing room where the coffee would be served, and others, like Mr and Mrs Grayling, to repair to their own rooms, where they would be fetched a tray of old-fashioned tea which they preferred, and could rest with their feet up and, in Mrs Grayling's case, their stays comfortably loosened. The American visitors went too, somewhat to the chagrin of Mr Hancock and Mr Cumming, to go to a theatre, and the two young men, after a little disconsolate hanging about also went out, clearly intending to spend their time in more convivial company than that of the clutch of schoolteachers now clustered in the big drawing room, where Tilly dispensed coffee.

Mr Geddes was one of those who remained, however, and he settled to a long and quiet conversation with the Misses Knapp and Fleetwood, at which Miss Barnetsen took some umbrage and flounced off to her room. Usually they would have gone after her to coax her out of her sulks, but tonight they stayed with Mr Geddes, quite entranced by his conversation; and Tilly was left to sit over her coffee tray watching Mr Hunter and his companion Mr Graham playing piquet and listening to the buzz of the others' voices.

She was content enough, she told herself. It would have been better still had Duff been at dinner and had come to sit here with her afterwards, but that was not to be. She must accept what he had told her, that he was grown up now and had different needs and different activities to those that she chose.

And then the drawing-room door opened and Duff came in. He was wearing a well cut evening suit and looked very dashing. He smiled around at the company, then at Tilly and said simply, 'Hello, Mamma, I am back early and thought I might take some coffee with you. I hope there is some left for me?'

Chapter Six

THERE WAS AN embarrassed silence for a moment, because it was quite obvious to everyone that Duff was decidedly bosky, not to say positively inebriated. He stood at the door with one hand in his pocket, his eyes very bright and bulging a little in a flushed face. His hair was rumpled and there was an air of danger about him and Tilly felt her belly tighten with anxiety as she looked at him.

After a moment the chatter started again, but only for a short while. By the time Duff had come to sit beside his mother and her coffee tray, Silas Geddes was on his feet.

'It is remarkably late, is it not?' he said to Miss Sophia Fleetwood. 'I had not noticed the clock move round so fast! I declare I am quite tired out.'

Miss Fleetwood, who had relaunched herself into an account of her trenchant views on Mr Darwin's first and now notorious book, *The Origin of Species*, looked a little startled and then pulled at the fob watch on her considerable bosom and peered at it.

'Oh,' she said, looking up at Silas. 'It is not so very –' and then stopped. Quite how he had communicated with her Tilly was never to know, but that he had was undoubted. Miss Fleetwood glanced swiftly at Duff and then surged to her feet.

'You are quite right, Mr Geddes,' she said. 'Come along, Priscilla. It is time we were up the wooden stairs to Bedfordshire. Tomorrow is to be a busy day, with the bishop coming to school, drat the man – oh, I mean every word of it, Mr Hunter! You should not look so shocked. And I dare say you have a busy day too? We must still bid

Mrs Quentin goodnight – and you too, dear Duff. So good to see you home again.'

It took a matter of moments. She went sailing out of the room carrying Miss Knapp and the two men in her wake, like the tide going out and cleaning the beach of its detritus. Silas Geddes lingered a moment more at the drawing-room door and said in a neutral voice, 'I shall see you tomorrow, Mrs Quentin, I hope, so that we may continue our most interesting discussion. Good night to you,' managing to make the banal words sound like a promise of concern for her well-being. She flashed a glance at him and nodded, and then sat there staring at the door after it had closed and left her cocooned with Duff in the warmth of the big drawing room.

''S funny,' Duff said after a while. 'Most people I know say that the rooms and houses they knew when they were children have shrunk when they go home for the hols, but not here. Here the rooms get bigger an' bigger.'

'It is because of the use of this house, Duff, as you know perfectly well,' she said and passed him a cup of coffee, taking care not to fill the cup too full in case he spilled it. He smelled powerfully of brandy and cigars and she could have wept, remembering suddenly the round downy head that had used to tuck itself in under her chin after his childhood bath times, filling her nostrils with the scent of soap and tooth powder and the sweet essence that had been his own special smell. 'It took a few years to have enough money to consider the conversion of the drawing rooms of the two houses and to make this big room as well as the two extra bedrooms.'

'Oh, I know, I know.' He laughed then, a high pitched sneering little giggle. 'Haven't I grown up in the trade, hearing of nothing but the costs of this and that, and how much money the guests bring in and –' He caught his breath and then bent his head to his cup and drank thirstily.

She looked down on his rumpled crown and said sharply, 'You do not need to speak as though it were so very boring, surely? I don't recall you ever speaking so slightingly of my endeavours before!'

'Didn't know any better,' he mumbled.

'And what does that mean, precisely?' She was sitting very straight now, and knew her voice sounded flinty. She was shaking inside; he had never spoken so to her, had never shown by any word or action that he was uninterested in the house and her work in it, and to hear the contempt she now heard in his voice was painful in a way that she could never have imagined.

'It means that it's a bit hard on a chap to have to see his mother taking in lodgers to live! Worse'n runnin' a shop, almost. I mean to say –' His voice was high and shrill and he stared at her petulantly.

She leaned forwards and took his cup and saucer from his hands and set them down on the tray with a little clatter. And then she took him by the shoulders and shook him. He seemed to make no resistance, letting his head roll from side to side as he stared up at her still with that sneering look in his face.

'You are drunk, Duff, I am disgusted with you. You go out to dine and come back to me here in a state that is – that should fill you with shame as it does me. I will be charitable and put your comments down to the drink. But I tell you –'

'Well, it's true!' He pulled away from her pettishly and then sat with his arms round his knees, staring at her over them with slightly swimming eyes. 'It's been damned hard for me there at school to hold my head up sometimes! The way they went on at me – well, I learned pretty fast, I can tell you, to say nothing about my home or about you for it wasn't worth the ragging they gave me! Why else did you think I begged you never to visit me there? Thank God for Lord Patrick. Dear old man, best pal a fella ever had.' And to her amazement tears rose into his eyes and remained trembling on his lower lashes.

'But – but you never said! I thought you were – I thought you liked school and were happy there and only kept me away to protect yourself from pangs of homesickness! Why did you not say? You could have come home, no matter what anyone else said.'

'Oh, pooh!' He sniffed hard. 'School's all right. It's home tha's the trouble. Tol' you. But I got Paton to make up for it all – good ol' Paton.' He sniffed again and this time the tears seemed to settle and he looked pugnacious rather than lugubrious.

'But this is the first I have ever heard –' She was wretched and knew that she too was barely controlling tears. 'I would not have had you unhappy for the world. I sent you there because it seemed better for your future, to give you an education that would take you to university and perhaps –'

'I'm going to no university,' he said then. 'That's for swots.'

'But,' she shook her head, still bewildered, 'to be so ashamed of your home and – and of me –'

It was more than she could bear and now tears did come, and she reached in her small reticule for a handkerchief and scrubbed at her wet cheeks in a fury of shame. Not to be able to control herself in front of Duff was dreadful.

He stared at her, and then it was as though the years had rolled backwards and left him the vulnerable eleven year old he had been when she had first sent him away to school, six long years ago. 'Oh, Mamma!' he wailed. 'Please don't cry, oh *please* don't cry. I cannot bear it – I really cannot bear it! I am so sorry to have vexed you!' and he hurled himself into her arms and clung to her, and she held on to him, feeling his tears on the hand he had grasped to hold to his cheek, aware that her own face was equally wet.

The tide receded at last until he was reduced to occasional gulps and sniffs, and after a few more moments she mopped her own face dry with some ferocity and then raised his head between both her hands and looked at him.

'You silly boy,' she said unsteadily. 'Do, I beg you, blow your nose.' And she smiled, unable not to, for his nose was running copiously and he looked piteously like his junior self.

He took the damp handkerchief, blew vigorously, mopped his face with his shirt cuffs and sat back.

'I am sorry, Mamma. I could not help it. I am a little merry you know, though why they should call it merry when it makes one feel so wretched, I can't imagine.' His eyes threatened to fill up again but he controlled himself and managed to speak again. 'I did not mean this to happen, truly I didn't. But he makes me so – so, oh, Mamma, it is so hard!'

'What is, my love?' she said gently and then held her arms in the air so that he could do as he had when he was small, and sit with his head on her lap. It had been a wordless invitation he had never been able to refuse and he did not refuse now.

He lay there for a while, his eyes fixed on the last tired flickering of the flames in the grate and sighed, a deep gusty and slightly tremulous sound, and carefully she began to stroke his hair. He'd always liked that.

'I tell you what it is, Ma, I just don't know what I feel and that is the truth of it,' he said suddenly. 'I used to laugh at the others, you know, when they did it, and when I was a sprig in the first form, why, we all used to think them quite absurd. Except those that liked it, don't you know. There're always a few of *them*.' He wriggled his head in a sort of moue of distaste that sent the frills on her skirts dancing. 'I believe there are always a few of the young ones who egg them on, but for my part, I thought it all a hum. But when it happens to you, you just –' again he produced that big gusty sigh, '– you just don't know what to do.'

'I am, perhaps, being very stupid,' she ventured. 'But I am not sure I entirely understand what you're saying. Would it be better to wait until the brandy you have clearly had is less –'

'If I do, I won't talk at all, I think,' he said with a flash of commonsense and sat up. 'It's because I've had so much that I feel able – oh, Ma, have I been hateful to you?'

She thought for a moment about what form her response might take and then knew what it had to be.

'Yes,' she said simply.

'Oh, Ma, I'm so sorry!' And again he hurled himself at her, weeping, but this time she did not feel he needed to have a burst of it, and gently pushed him upright again and firmly set her handkerchief back in his hand.

'Now, that is enough of that,' she said. 'Tell me what it is that is distressing you. I had no idea that you suffered at school because of my occupation. Is that the problem?'

'It was the start of it,' he said after a moment and discarded her handkerchief for his shirt sleeve again. 'If they hadn't been so hateful, some of 'em, taunting me about being in trade and so forth,

I'd never have paid any attention to him, you see. But because some of them did, and it got worse – I was so afraid they'd torment you too if you came to school, which was when I begged you not to, for I could not have borne that – when Patrick came along and defended me, well it was natural, was it not, that I should come to – to – regard him so highly?'

He looked appealingly at her, begging her to say something that would make him feel better but her puzzlement deepened.

'But my dear boy, of course if someone is kind to you and stands as your friend against those who are not kind – but who is this Patrick? I am very confused.'

'Oh, I explain badly.' He sniffed again and closed his eyes as though he were willing himself to lose the effects of the brandy, and indeed his speech was becoming clearer as the time passed. 'He is Lord Patrick Paton. He is a little older than the rest of us, for he remained in the Fifth Form for two full years, you know, since he could never master his Latin and because his papa – he is the duke, do you see – insists he must go to his old college at Oxford, he made the school keep him until he could pass the exams. He's been in the Sixth for two years as well so he is quite old – past twenty, don't you know.' He smiled then, a sudden glimmering grin of reminiscent pleasure. 'And such fun! He cares nothing for the masters, you know, and what they say, and does such things! I know it is because his papa will always deal with the school, but it is still brave of him, for his pa has him beaten at home for every bad report he gets, and sometimes he says he is quite raw meat and fit only for the hounds to breakfast on. And he came to rescue me! He was still in the Fifth Form then, and I was but thirteen – and after that they left me alone, or at least when he was about. Anyway that was the start of it.'

He bent his head and looked at his hands, and she said, 'Please, dear Duff, the start of what?'

'I do love him, you know,' he said suddenly. 'I mean, it is not just that he is a lord and so rich and brave and, well, all those things. I just admire him so – it is so painful not knowing what to do.'

Tilly leaned back in her chair and tried to collect her thoughts, which had begun to whirr about her head like demented bees. She was not a woman of the world in the sense that the term was generally used to denote those who were knowledgeable about such matters as other people's lovers and the latest crim. con. cases and the doings of the high and mighty, which were such enthralling subjects of gossip for many of the ladies she knew in Knightsbridge, but for all that she was not totally innocent. She knew that men and women sometimes behaved in ways that were regarded as less than proper by people of pure mind and life, but it was not a matter to which she had ever given much thought. When her acquaintances on morning calls or at meetings or parties in the neighbourbood started talking about such things she tended to find a good reason to wander off, if, that was, she could not change the subject of the conversation. So, now she was at a disadvantage.

But not completely. She knew how some men were with boys and her heart contracted as she looked at her son, sitting there with his square face and troubled grey eyes and rumpled brown hair. Was he growing up to be such a one? Had his lack of a father to guide him and to emulate made him the sort of sissified young man her neighbours had been known to giggle and whisper about behind their fans?

'You had better tell me all there is to tell me, dear Duff,' she said carefully. 'I cannot – I can't help or advise you if I do not know all the situation.'

'I love him,' Duff said again, and now his mouth was set in a mulish line that was all too familiar to his mother. 'I did not think at first I did, that it was just friendship, but I have learned to find him – well, if I do not see him I am wretched and when I do he can tease and torment me to his heart's content and know I will do nothing to retaliate. And anyway he had been so good to me when I was a sprog! I used to be his fag, you know, doing all he demanded of me, with his boots and cleaning his study, and so forth, and I was so grateful to him for never seeming to care about my coming from trade. But now, when I have found how much I love him he is so – so capricious. He torments me more about you and this house – the way we live – than any of the others did. He wanted to come here, you know, but I did not dare to let him and would not even tell him where we lived. I know he would say something cruel to you and you would be mortified, and I could not bear to think what you might say to him. So I meet him out and hope we can be comfortable together, but he torments me and – and tonight he said I must keep march with him while he drank, and I did and then when I said I felt sick and could drink no more he got horrid and went off with Garston and everyone knows what *he* is like. All I could do was come back here and – oh, Ma, what shall I do? I love him so, you see! It hurts so to see him with that creature Garston, for he peacocks about and mops and mows like some – it makes me puke and so I tell him! But he will do it – how could Patrick be so hateful to me?'

Again he wept, throwing himself down to use her lap as the recipient of his misery; she sat staring over his head as mechanically she stroked his hair and tried to think. She could not question him in detail, of course and yet, 'Duff,' she said at length, 'has he ever done anything to – to hurt you – um – bodily?'

Duff lifted his head.

'How do you mean?' he said, looking at her with eyes which were a little sleepy, but certainly no longer swimming.

'Oh, Duff, you must help me. It is very hard for a mother to know in such a situation what to do or say. But I feel I must. I would not wish to pry into your – um – private life, you understand.' She stopped, defeated and looked at him imploringly. 'Oh, Duff, you must know what I mean! Have you done anything that you might feel is shameful or –'

He stared at her for a long moment and then went a rich crimson. 'Oh, Ma, don't you understand *anything* of what I've said to you?' He almost shouted it, so that she looked anxiously at the drawing-room door to check it was closed and that no one else in the house could overhear them. 'It is what he *wants* me to do and which I feel I cannot. I love him, of course I do, but not in the way he wishes me to love him and he gets so angry with me about it! I wish only to be his dear friend and to be close to him in heart and mind. I am not interested in the sort of games they play, he and the others. Half the school does it, but the other half does not and I have never been one of those who did, for I think it stupid, to tell the truth. And now I think perhaps I have been a fool to be so – so old-fashioned and childish, for I do love him and want him to be happy. But he says that he cannot care for me if I am so namby-pamby and won't play their games and the next that he admires me the more for being as I am and – and – I don't know what to do!'

'If you were to ask me I would say you should never see this Lord Patrick again,' Tilly said firmly and clearly. 'He sounds like the sort of very bad influence every caring parent most fears and had I had the least idea there were such boys at your school I would have removed you at once and sent you elsewhere.'

'Oh, Ma!' he said and laughed. 'D'you imagine other boys' schools are any different? These things go on at all schools. I have met any number of chaps and they all agree that – you can always count on it. I suppose I'm just a prig the way Patrick says I am and should know better.'

'You are not a prig!' Tilly said, fired to sudden anger. 'And I will not have it said by anyone of you. You may not even say it of yourself! If you choose to live your life in a particular way, then that is your choice. It is not priggish to –'

'Oh, Ma, do stop!' he said and suddenly, incongruously, yawned hugely. 'My head is going round enough without more lectures from you. I have said too much.'

'Not at all,' she said. 'Not at all too much. It is better for me to know. Oh, Duff, I wish I could help you to be happier. It is all I want for you, the chance to be happy.'

'Me too,' he said and then stood up and tried to tidy his clothes; she looked at him and then frowned sharply.

'I have wanted to ask you – these very fine clothes you are wearing. Did you manage to buy all of them out of your allowance? I did not think I was able to be so generous, and I would be most distressed to hear you had gone into debt.'

He reddened again. 'No debts,' he mumbled.

'Patrick? You foolish creature!' she jumped to her feet. 'Letting him buy you costly gifts when he is trying to persuade you to – oh, Duff, where is your sense?'

'I wish I knew,' he said with a sudden glint of humour. 'I think I had more when I was a sprog than I have now.' He shook his head ruefully. 'It was so easy to be little, well, most of the time it was.' He looked over her shoulder into the past and his eyes glazed a little.

'Do you know, Ma, I hadn't thought of it before but now I recall those days, it occurs to me Patrick reminds me of someone – in his colouring and his tricks of movement and so forth.'

'Oh' Tilly said and stared at him. 'Reminds you of whom?'

'Oh, that little girl who used to visit. From next door was it? She stayed here for a while, I seem to recall. We played together a lot and she was such fun! I remember that very well, though – anyway, her. I forget her name.'

'Sophie,' Tilly said after a pause and bent her head to look down at her fingers, interlaced on her skirts. 'Sophie Oliver.'

'Yes –' Duff lifted his chin and stared at her. 'Sophie Oliver! I had quite forgot till now. Heavens, what a tease she was! And now I think of it, Patrick is just such another. In his way, I mean – quite different really, he is a man and she was just a child, but all the same –'

'Well, whatever the likeness, it is not really important now,' though she was thinking quite otherwise as a confusion of memory and anxiety filled her. 'I have to say I think it is high time you were in bed. You are still a good deal more affected by that man's brandy than you realize, and tired by all this – well, all this talk has not been easy for either of us. It is time I went to bed too!'

She went closer to him and lifted one hand to touch his cheek. 'For all it has been so painful to hear the things you have said, my dear boy, it is not so painful as being cut by you in Brompton Grove.'

'Oh, I am sorry about that, Ma! I didn't know *what* to do. He was being so very difficult at the time and I was so afraid of what he might say if I noticed you that I just hurried him away.'

She managed a crooked smile. 'Hurried him away? Indeed you did. I recollect that fact perfectly well. But all is forgiven. As I say, that we have talked is better than silence. Promise me you will not be so remote with me ever again? I almost broke my heart over it.'

'I won't,' he promised and bent and kissed her cheek. 'I suppose you're right. Bed would be nice.'

'I shall come and –' she began and then stopped. 'I'm sorry. You are too old to need my help to get to bed, are you not? It's not easy to remember. Goodnight, my dear. I shall see you at breakfast I hope, thick head or not.' She nodded briskly. 'I expect you to make an effort in the morning, remember – and we shall talk some more.'

'Yes,' he said with sleepy obedience and went to the door, dragging his feet a little. 'Goodnight. I'm happier too – though I'm still absolutely wretched of course.' And he left her staring after him with her hands twisted against her skirts still and her mind in a hubbub.

'Sophie Oliver,' she said aloud then. 'Sophie Oliver,' and closed her eyes to try to escape from the thoughts that had come into her mind. But of course she couldn't.

Chapter Seven

SILAS GEDDES HEAPED his plate with devilled mushrooms, added a lavish spoonful of scrambled eggs and sat down in his place as Tilly poured him coffee and sent the cup down the table to him. The remains of the breakfasts of the four schoolteachers were being cleared by Rosie, for they had long gone, as had Mr Cumming and Mr Hancock. The American party had breakfasted in their rooms and only Mr and Mrs Grayling remained at table, loitering over their last slices of toast and cups of coffee.

Tilly sat at the table head, a little tense as she waited, very aware of time ticking on. There was work to be done at her desk and below stairs, where Eliza would be waiting to discuss the day's menus and have their usual gossip about the work of the house in general, and Tilly also had intended to go out to buy linen to make new bed sheets this morning. And still there was no sign of Duff, though it was almost half past nine and the sounds of the busy street came in through the open window, as well as the scent of the dusty street and the faint linger of roses from the garden.

'I trust you are well this morning, Mrs Quentin?' Silas Geddes said and looked at her with his head on one side, as he chewed his mushrooms with obvious enjoyment. 'You seem not to have eaten any of this excellent breakfast yourself, and I do recommend it!'

She looked down at the coffee cup that stood beside her clearly unused plate. 'I am not very hungry this morning,' she said. 'But I am very well, I do assure you.'

'I am happy to hear it. I wondered if perhaps this afternoon you might care to come to one of my meetings? It is on Darwin's new book. The speakers are not as eminent as Dr Huxley or Bishop Wilberforce, but they are knowledgeable men and it might make an introduction to the subject for you – and you seemed to be sufficiently interested when we spoke of the possibility.'

He stopped invitingly and looked at her with raised eyebrows and she was irritated, as well as a little embarrassed. She had been listening to him with only half her attention, the other being set on listening for Duff, and she was not at first quite sure what he had asked her. As she hesitated, seeking her memory for guidance, the door of the dining room opened.

'Sorry t'be late,' Duff muttered and came to sit at the table, ignoring the sideboard and its silver covered dishes. Tilly looked at him anxiously and then nodded a little distractedly at Silas.

'I doubt I shall be able to, Mr Geddes, but I do thank you for the thought,' she said. 'Duff, my dear. Good morning.'

She poured a large cup of black coffee for him.

'I think this will be to your liking,' she said and pushed it to him and also the sugar basin; he dropped several heaped spoonfuls into the cup, stirred and drank, clearly very grateful for it.

'Some more toast for Mr Duff, please Rosie,' Tilly instructed. 'And you may clear the sideboard, if Mr Geddes has had sufficient?' She looked at him inquiringly and at once he nodded. 'And some more coffee please.'

Rosie bobbed and went, bearing a trayful of dishes with her, and Silas Geddes threw one more glance at Duff and then with some ostentation picked up a copy of the *Morning Post* from the centre of the table and opened it and held it in front of his face so that he was quite obscured from view, while managing to eat the rest of his breakfast with just a fork in his right hand. Mr and Mrs Grayling, having finished their breakfast at last, with much fussing got themselves to their feet and out of the room, and Tilly relaxed her shoulders and looked at Duff.

'Not too bad, I hope,' she said in a low voice, and he glanced at her with lacklustre eyes and a hang-dog expression but said nothing. Tilly could not help it; she chuckled.

'You will take more water than brandy in future, I hope,' she said. 'Too much brandy makes one feels dreadfully ill, I am told.'

Duff did not reply, but his glance said it all.

'Now, this morning I thought I would suggest that you might accompany me on my shopping expedition,' she went on, lifting her voice a little. 'We have hardly had a chance to talk yet, and although buying linen might not be your idea of an agreeable occupation, still –'

'Oh, Mamma, must I?' Duff looked at her almost piteously. 'I really feel the need to return to my bed for a while, you know. No thank you, no toast – and –'

'I insist on the toast,' Tilly said, as she took the fresh supplies from Rosie and began to butter a slice, adding some of Eliza's best cherry conserve. 'You will feel better for it, I'll be bound. As to returning to bed –'

Along the table the newspaper rustled, then rattled and at last was put down and Silas emerged, looking as though he had heard not a word of the discussion, because of his absorption in his reading. Tilly, however, was not beguiled by this display. He had clearly heard every word and made a decision to join in.

'Mr Quentin,' he said. 'I wonder if I might trespass on your kindness if you have the time to spare? I am told that it is possible to get a horse from a livery stable and ride in the park. It is now some time since I had the chance to take such exercise and I feel the need for it. If you, as a local man, you know, have any suggestions for a good livery stable, I'd take it kindly.'

Duff looked at him a little blearily, and frowned. 'Stable?'

'Why yes. I imagine you have ridden in your time?'

Duff looked a little affronted. 'Of course. We all ride at school. Some huntin' too.'

Silas laughed merrily. 'Well, I doubt we can draw a covert in Hyde Park, even at the proper time of year! No, I just thought I'd enjoy a gentle hack about the park, don't you know, on such a fine morning, and I'd be uncommonly glad of company, to tell you the truth. I know no better exercise than a little canter on a well mannered nag, don't you know. It quite shakes the liver up and blows away one's megrims.'

Tilly looked at him gratefully, her irritation with him now quite banished, and smiled brilliantly at Duff. 'My dear boy, I'm sure you can take Mr Geddes to Cope's Stables, in Bolney Mews? Their animals for riding are excellent, I am told, Mr Geddes, and I have never had cause to complain when I have had one of their carriage and pairs. And you will benefit greatly from the exercise, Duff?' She addressed her son apparently in enquiry, but there was a steely note in her voice.

He looked back, opened his mouth to protest and then closed it again as his mother smiled even more brilliantly. 'I am sure you will do this for Mr Geddes,' she said. 'It would be much appreciated.'

'Indeed, glad to be of help,' Duff muttered and drank some more coffee and Silas folded his paper immediately and stood up.

'That's most kind of you, m'boy, most kind,' he said heartily. 'Give me a few minutes to change into more suitable clothes and I shall be with you directly.'

'I shall check your own riding clothes, Duff, shall I?' Tilly said and got to her feet to follow Mr Geddes from the room. 'If you wish?'

'Eh? Oh, no need, Ma – well, to tell the truth I've not fully unpacked yet.'

'Oh, you probably didn't notice, but Eliza saw to all that yesterday,' Tilly said. 'I shall put your riding clothes on your bed.' And she led the way out of the dining room as Duff, a little gloomily, addressed himself to the remainder of his coffee.

'I am much obliged to you, Mr Geddes,' Tilly said as they reached the staircase. 'It is clearly no secret that my foolish son overdid his entertainment somewhat last night.'

'I would think less of him if he had not,' Silas said heartily. 'It's not every day a boy leaves schooldays behind him and becomes a gentleman of leisure. At least for a little while. I imagine he will have some future occupation?'

'As to that, we cannot be sure yet,' Tilly said. She set her foot on the lowest step. 'I really must go and deal with those riding clothes. Will you be here for luncheon?'

'I will indeed.' He smiled at her cheerfully. 'I would not miss one of Eliza's collations for the world. Perhaps then we can speak of your attending my meeting?'

'Perhaps,' she said. 'But at present you must forgive me –'

'Of course.' He came up the stairs behind her. 'In the meantime, if your son feels the need of a man in whom to confide his anxieties –'

She had reached the top landing and at this she stopped and turned to look at him, a faint frown between her brows. 'I am not sure I understand you, Mr Geddes,' she said stiffly, trying not to give credence to the thought that had come into her mind; that he had listened at the door to her conversation with Duff last night and was, for his own reasons, trying to involve himself in her affairs.

'Oh, please,' he said. 'I'm not trying to meddle in what does not concern me. It's just that I'm not so old that I can't remember what it's like to be growing up and to have anxieties that need a man's opinion! I was reared by my maiden aunt, after my parents' death, and there were times when, excellent lady though she was, I positively ached to find a sensible male ear into which I could pour some of my words. I found such a one in the son of our local vicar, and I much appreciated his friendship. I see certain parallels for your son in my own case. My aunt, like you, was a dear, caring lady who wanted only the best for her boy and who showed a most admirable delicacy of character. She never pried into my private thoughts, but was always there should I need her. I imagine you are like that. And that being so, it is harder for your son to tell you of those worries he might have of which he is not proud – and at seventeen or so we are all ashamed of the thoughts that beset us – than to tell someone else. He will be concerned to protect his own reputation in your eyes, d'you see? I am offering to be that someone else. Should he choose me for that task, of course. I would not impose myself on him for the world.'

She looked at him for a long time, uncertain what to say and after a while he laughed and shook his head. 'I try too hard, I fear,' he said ruefully. 'Never mind, Mrs Quentin. Give it no more thought, I beg of you. I was but seeking to be useful. Ah, Duff!' for downstairs the dining-room door had opened again and Duff had emerged.

'You see, I gossip. But I shall be ready directly!' And he nodded at Tilly and went off to his own room with a rapid lope, leaving her to help Duff find his riding clothes and prepare for his morning in the saddle.

She walked to the shops, thinking hard as she went. Mr Geddes certainly seemed to have a wise head on his not-so-old shoulders. How old was he? She hadn't thought about the matter before. It was hard to tell, because he was not entirely like other men. He did not use tobacco, for example, so his face was never screwed up against rising smoke and that, she knew, made men's faces line more swiftly than they might. Also he ate abstemiously, which would encourage his neat youthful figure. He might be older than he appeared, however, and she thought, Perhaps thirty five? and smiled to herself. The same age as I am. Yet because he had the impulsive eagerness of a youth he seemed younger. Why is it that women are so much older in so many ways? she asked herself as she lifted her skirts high to make her way across the dusty cobbles to the safety of the pavement on the far side. Why do I feel so much older than he, when we are probably the same age?

'Because I have a son of seventeen,' she murmured aloud and then bit her lip, amused, as an elderly lady bustling by on her way to Colonel Nichol's shop threw her a sharply enquiring glance. But it was true. Nothing, she told herself a little bitterly, is more ageing than fretting over an errant child, and then as the thought came her spirits lifted, for wasn't she going to buy linen for new bed sheets? And did that not mean she must see her old friend Jem? She could think of no one more suitable in whom to confide her worries about Duff.

She was so determined that Jem's conversation was what she most required that she broke her own careful housewifely rule and didn't go first to all the other linen drapers' shops to check their prices. She knew really that Jem was never undersold, and that if she told him she had seen the same goods elsewhere at a lower price than the one he was asking, he would have no hesitation in reducing his charges especially for her.

She stood for a moment staring sightlessly into the window of his neat shop where swatches of good cloth were pinned up to show their quality and ribbons had been displayed in such great bows and swirls and stripes that the whole window seemed to shimmer with colour. Dear Jem. To have stood her friend so many years, when she had been so captious with him.

There had been a time when she had seriously considered marrying Jem Leland. He had loved her dearly and made no effort to hide that regard and had continued to love her unswervingly all through the difficult days when she decided to get married again, to poor dear Freddy, when Duff was but a little boy of four. Jem had stood foursquare her friend all through the long months and years after her second widowhood, when all had seemed so confusing and difficult, and she had been so busy growing her home into the handsome guest house it had now become. He had never asked her for anything for himself, except, from time to time, to repeat his offer of marriage.

I have been unfair to him, she thought as she went on staring sightlessly at his ribbons, and I must tell him that he should find himself someone else. He seems content enough, but it is not good for him. He needs a wife and child of his own, not this half-hearted attempt to pretend that Duff is his own boy, though he loves him as though he were, I swear. And I must also tell him that I will never be more to him than what I am now. I will never marry again. I know that. I am well past that stage of life and all my efforts now must go into Duff and, of course, into our property. For it was for Duff's need for property that I married Freddy, after all, and changed my plans to marry Jem –

Her reverie was broken into sharply as the door of the shop opened with a melodic jangle of the bell that hung on a spring just inside it, and Jem appeared beside her. She looked up at him with genuine pleasure.

He was, in fact, some five years her junior, not that that had ever worried either of them particularly, for unlike Silas Geddes, there was a somewhat staid air about Jem that made him seem older than he was. He was ageing now, too, in a rather obvious way. Even though he was only thirty, his thick dark hair was receding on both forehead and temples, giving his square face a most serious air, and his blue eyes were well surrounded by lines because of his tendency to narrow them when he looked at fabrics, in order to sharpen his vision. He had tried spectacles, he had once told Tilly, and couldn't be doing with them. 'I shall settle to 'em well enough when I have to,' he had said and laughed. 'Till then I'll fettle along well enough as I am.'

Now he stood squinting at her in the bright sunshine and she smiled warmly at him.

'Good afternoon Tilly! I saw you from inside.'

'Good afternoon, Jem. I hope you are well?'

'I am very well,' he said and held out a hand and they shook cordially. There had been a time when they had greeted each other with kisses on the cheek, but they had been considering marriage then. All that had changed, but the handshakes were as warm as ever the kisses had been, and indeed warmer, for there was an easy friendship in them that, to Tilly at least, mattered far more than anything more intimate. 'Is this but a social visit? Or –'

'How well you know me! It is, of course, an *or*. I need some new linen for bed sheets. I find that the laundress is very heavy-handed and I need to add a further half dozen pairs to my store. A hard-wearing linen, now, one that will see me well over the next few years. It is so laborious making the sheets that it's poor economy to buy cheap stuff for them.'

'Whenever would I sell you cheap stuff, Tilly?' he said and led the way to the shop door, holding it open to invite her in. 'You really know me better than that! Cuthbert! A chair for Mrs Quentin, if you please.'

The shop boy darted forward from between the piled bolts of cloth and the long mahogany counters and cutting tables and pulled a high chair out invitingly, and gratefully Tilly sat down. It had been a long walk on a hot day and her boots were on the tight side. She sighed contentedly and pulled off her gloves.

'I think a glass of some of that excellent lemonade Charlie Harrod sent over,' he said. 'I've been keeping it in the cellar to be cool. Cuthbert, a tray and jug and glass, if you please – bustle about!'

Cuthbert duly bustled and brought the lemonade and she and Jem settled to a cosy prose over the relative merits of Irish as opposed to English linen, Lancashire as opposed to Sea Island cotton and the various available weights of cloth on offer and at last settled on the amount that would be needed, so that Jem could cut it.

'Six pairs of sheets, with three-inch top hems and a narrow turnback at the foot,' Jem muttered, pulling a pencil from behind his ear and making jottings on his cuff. 'That'll be – let me see – plenty of hem, under and at the sides – hmm – full width, then – hmm. Twenty-six yards, I make it, Tilly, and I shall throw in the hem bindings as a discount. There. Measure that up, Cuthbert, and be quick about it. And if there are faults in the bolt, then start a new one. D'you understand me, boy?'

Cuthbert indeed understood and Jem was at last able to relax. His other more senior shopman was busily occupied in dealing with a brace of ladies buying ribbons at another counter and clearly set to spend the whole morning at that delectable occupation, much to the shopman's obvious boredom, and that meant Jem had time for her. He settled himself against his counter comfortably, leaning over it so that they could talk easily.

'How is he, then?' he said. 'You've not said a word, so I supposed all is well.'

'Not entirely,' she said after a moment, knowing there was no need to ask him of whom he spoke. 'He has had some troubles at school and they bid fair to be brought home with him.'

He stiffened. 'Oh? And what might those troubles be? Nothing much I'll be bound and no fault of Duff's. That boy could never be anything but all he should be.' Jem's loyalty to Duff was fierce and now Tilly smiled at him gratefully for it.

'You can't cast him as an angel, you know, Jem. He's a boy after all, and boys are prone to scrapes. He is far from perfect.'

Jem looked carefully at her. 'What has he done?'

'Nothing, to the best of my knowledge.' She kept her head down, twisting her gloves between her fingers. Even with Jem, her good old friend Jem, it was difficult to be honest about what Duff had said and she certainly could not have voiced her own fears for his virtue. She could not even be sure herself what Duff had done or not done. His speech had been so elliptical and her own understanding of such matters so patchy, how could it be otherwise?

'It is what might happen that concerns me,' she said, in a rush of confidentiality. 'I cannot pretend I fully understand the way boys think and behave, but last night –' Her voice dwindled.

'Well?' Jem leaned over the counter in his familiar manner and she felt a little stronger; being physically close to him like this made it easier to speak honestly.

'I'm not sure that I am not misunderstanding – but let me assume I am not. He told me he has developed a *tendresse* for –'

She stopped, and bent her head and Jem smiled, slowly and a touch bitterly. No one knew better than he did what it felt like to yearn for a person who remained stubbornly unavailable, except as a friend. 'He has found himself a pretty lady to admire, has he?' he said and grinned.

'I wish he had!' Tilly said in a burst of anger. 'That would be no problem!'

There was a long silence and then Jem said a little woodenly, 'I see.'

'I wish I did,' Tilly said bitterly. 'I find it hard to comprehend, but you are a man so perhaps you –'

'I find such emotions as strange as you appear to do,' Jem said, clearly uncomfortable now. 'I am told it is a natural stage in the life of a boy, but to tell you the truth, it never appeared in mine.'

'So, you cannot advise me.' She felt bleak.

'As to that, I may – well, let us both think. There must be a remedy.'

'I have thought long and hard,' Tilly said, 'and I believe there is an obvious way to distract his attention from this tiresome schoolfellow. I think that he needs to widen his acquaintance. He has spent too much time with boys, do you see, all these years.'

'Too much time with boys,' Jem repeated and was silent. So was

Tilly and they both sat there in the sweet-smelling shop, the scent of new linen thick in their nostrils, in a silence broken only by the giggles and chatter coming from the heaps of ribbons on the other side of the shop.

'So,' Jem said at last, clearly unable to deal with the silence any longer. 'A dancing class, perhaps? I hear Miss Hodgkins over at Kensington Gore runs very good classes for young ladies and gentlemen.'

'Well, now, I wasn't thinking of that precisely,' Tilly murmured and then looked at him very directly. 'Jem, do you remember Sophie Oliver?'

'Sophie –' Jem straightened his back and stared at her. 'Remember Sophie Oliver? I should say I do! When I remember the way her mother behaved, when she lived in your house, and how hard she tried to ruin you – well! How could I ever forget the Olivers? Mother or daughter? Dorcas or Sophie, it's all one.'

'Well, it has been some time now,' Tilly said. 'Twelve years.'

'Not so long that I can forget the – the deviousness that Dorcas –' Jem's voice rose, and Tilly looked over her shoulder at the other customers, and shook her head warningly.

He subsided and said in a gruff undertone, 'So long as you forget her too.'

'I cannot blame Sophie for what her mother was,' Tilly said. 'She was but a small child, after all. The thing is, Duff *adored* her. He still has fond memories of her – and said as much to me yesterday. It seemed to me that part of this Patrick – this schoolfellow's charm was that he reminded Duff of Sophie. Quite powerfully, it appears.'

'So what are you suggesting?' Jem was watching her closely, clearly anxious.

'That we – that he sees her again and so forgets this school friend,' Tilly said simply. 'I am sure it would serve very well. If she is half as pretty a young lady as she was a child, she will entrance him. It will be natural that he – you see what I mean, Jem? However tiresome she might be, it is so *proper* for a young man to love a girl. Even a difficult girl would be preferable, I am convinced, to Duff following this present bent! I could not – I –' She bit her lip to control the sudden desire to weep which had risen in her. 'Whatever Sophie is like, she cannot be as wrong for Duff as this Patrick. He is not a good influence. He is older, and – well, I am not comfortable about him.'

'Will you be any more comfortable with Dorcas about you again?' Jem said bluntly. 'She caused you much unhappiness in the past.'

'I doubt she means me any harm now,' Tilly said. 'She could have come to visit any time this past twelve years, for I have not budged. Yet she has not! And anyway, I am older and wiser now. I can deal well enough with Madam Dorcas should she still be interested in tormenting me, which I doubt.'

'And you think it is worth risking turning over their particular stone in order that Sophie – who might be as devious as her mother, remember, for apples do not fall far from trees! – in order to –'

'To make life better for Duff? I will do anything and risk anything to make life better for Duff,' she said. 'Oh, Jem, say you will help me! Please? I do have need of you!'

'Hmph,' he said and glowered a little. And then sighed. 'Just what is it you want of me, then, Tilly?'

'Oh, Jem – ' she said and then stopped yet again and he managed to twist his mouth into a sort of smile.

'You want me to find her, don't you? Oh dear, oh dear, you want me to find her. And if I do, we must both be quite mad, for you know the trouble that happened when she was last around and –'

'I know,' Tilly said. 'But I am thinking of Duff, you see. And Sophie and Duff, you'll remember –'

'Yes,' Jem said heavily. 'I remember. So I suppose I'll have to go and seek her, shan't I? When could I refuse you anything? But I pray we won't both live to regret it.'

Chapter Eight

TILLY SAT IN her kitchen, surrounded by baskets of damsons waiting to be boiled into pots of damson cheese, and pears to be seethed in syrup to preserve them, wondering whether they would need to make extra plum jam to enhance their winter supplies. There were already several dozen pots of redcurrant and raspberry jelly which they had made in July and as many of blackcurrant jam but they might still need to make some greengage jam and quince jellies if they were to avoid the ignominy of having to buy ready-made preserves from Charlie Harrod.

She gave herself a little shake then and made a conscious effort to fix her attention. Eliza would look after all that perfectly well, she told herself a little scoldingly; no need to fret over it. All she had to do to help her, as she had promised she would, was to pick over the fruit for blemished parts and to ensure that no unwanted caterpillars and the like lurked in it. A simple enough task, after all.

Perhaps I am thinking of the fruit as a way of not thinking about other matters? she wondered then. Though again, perhaps those matters are not so pressing as I feared. And again she tried to concentrate on the job in hand. But it was no use. All she could think of now was not damsons, but Duff, and her concern for and about him.

She had returned from her visit to Jem's shop, via the seamstress's little house where she had left the linen, together with clear instructions on how the sheets were to be made up, and thinking all the way of Jem's unease about her plan. That he had agreed to do as she wanted was no surprise; he usually did. But that he should have been so very hostile to Dorcas and her daughter Sophie puzzled her.

It was true that Dorcas had been a very difficult and selfish person all the time that Tilly had known her, ever since her earliest childhood in fact, when Dorcas had been a backstairs resident in the house in Brompton Grove as the daughter of the housekeeper, Mrs Leander, and had teased the small Tilly unmercifully. It was true that Dorcas had tried hard to cheat Tilly in many ways as the years had gone by, their many years together culminating in a painful scene when Tilly had had to banish Dorcas from her house, where she and her child had lived for some time. But was all that enough to make Jem so very unwilling to seek out Sophie for Tilly?

And then Tilly remembered and smiled to herself. Of course, there had been a time when Dorcas had shown a marked interest in Jem on her own account, and he had found that very difficult to deal with. It must be that which had alarmed him. It could not be simply because of his forebodings about Dorcas re-entering her, Tilly's life, but because she was trying to become reacquainted with Jem himself.

Or so she thought, trying to batten down her own doubts; and she had been much comforted when Duff and Silas Geddes had returned from their morning ride, for Duff had looked so much like his old happy self that she had been almost overcome at the sight of him. They had come into the house through the kitchen, 'since our boots are so dusty,' as Duff said and she had looked up, alerted by the clatter of their feet on the area steps, to see him standing in the doorway looking rosy cheeked and a little tousled but clearly feeling so much better that she had felt her eyes smart with tears of pleasure and relief.

'We had a capital time, Mrs Quentin!' Silas Geddes said, coming in behind him, grinning at her. He too looked tousled and had a good deal of dust on his riding coat. 'We cantered along Rotten Row at such a speed that we positively sent up dust clouds! We quite wore out our nags.'

'It was not difficult to wear out yours!' Duff said. 'You chose a sorry excuse for a goer. I told you I'd selected by far the more mettlesome beast.'

'Well, well, we won't argue further on that,' Silas said good-naturedly. 'Mine, indeed, was more for show than go, in the event. But I still greatly enjoyed the exercise.'

'You look as though you did,' Tilly said, but she was looking at Duff. 'It must have been agreeable under the trees in Hyde Park.'

'Very agreeable. And so many fashionable people marching about – it looked like a gossip's paradise,' Silas said.

Eliza, who had been in the kitchen at the time and who had, at the sight of Duff, gone immediately to her cool larder to find a jug of her fresh lemonade and was now bustling out with it, pricked up her ears.

'Who was there?' she asked. 'Did you see any of the great people? And were the ladies wearing any of the newer fashions?'

Silas laughed. 'As to the fashion, I can't say whether it was new or old, Eliza, since I am sadly ignorant in that area. I can tell you we saw Mr Sheridan Knowles, with a most remarkably handsome creature on his arm.'

'Mr Sheridan who?' Tilly said.

'Knowles. Sheridan Knowles. Writes plays, Mum. Got one at the Lyceum with Mr Bates's company this very month. Got Henry Irving in it, too! It's a very lavish piece, Mum.'

'Dear me! I didn't know you knew about such matters. Eliza!' Tilly said. 'I did not think you went to the theatre.'

'Oh, no, Mum, I don't. Too far for me to go traipsin' up to London and gettin' home's such a fag, but that don't matter – I can still take an interest. Why, I could tell you of all the actresses what's in the company as well.'

'Not now, Eliza,' Tilly said hastily and Silas laughed.

'You should have been with us, Eliza, for then you could have told us who the pretty lady was, hmm?' And he looked at Duff, who grinned back.

'It was you noticed her first!'

'I could hardly not. I never saw so many frills and fancies on one back in my life. And I swear she had painted her face – yet it was a very handsome face.'

'It was a delightful face,' Duff said. 'And she had quite the most elegant hat, Mamma, you ever saw. All – well, birds' feathers and flowers and fruits and heaven knows what else besides.' His hands fluttered up near his head in a demonstration of a very fussy bonnet. 'You would have hated it.'

'Oh dear, am I such a dowd?' Tilly asked. 'I would be sad to think so.'

'No,' Duff said and came and kissed her cheek. 'You are just more tasteful than any actress I ever saw. I must go and change, Ma. I feel quite filthy. Thank you for your company, Silas.'

'Thank you for yours,' Silas said warmly. 'I'm most grateful to you for arranging it with Cope. We might do it again.'

'With pleasure,' Duff said and clattered away up the stairs to his room, and Tilly watched him go, glowing with gratitude to Duff himself for being so resilient and recovering so quickly, to Mr Geddes for being so kind to the boy – and that warmed her deeply towards him – and with Jem for having been so sensible this morning. Perhaps she shouldn't let him seek out Sophie after all; perhaps he was right . . .

Now, alone again, for Silas Geddes had followed Duff upstairs to change and Eliza too had gone off to some upstairs task, she found herself thinking once more about Sophie, and the memory of her came up before her mind's eye.

A small, beautifully compact child with a great deal of dark red hair spread on her shoulders and eyes which were wide and dark and carefully considering. A little rosebud of a mouth which she kept pursed in such a way that it seemed she knew how delectable it made her look. Long lashes that she liked to sweep down on her cheeks and a skin as pale and rich as new cream. Even at seven she had seemed to know how well she looked and had managed, without obviously posing, to ensure that she was always seen to her best advantage.

Was she still the same? If Jem went ahead and found her, how would she look? Tilly tried to imagine her, but all she could visualize was a larger version of a seven-year-old child, not an adult at all. Yet an adult she was, just as was Duff. They were almost of an age, with Sophie just seven or eight months the older. And Duff had loved her so much then!

It was inevitable of course that thinking about Sophie would lead to memories of Dorcas. How could it not? There was no doubt that Sophie had inherited her mother's good looks, together with something more from her father, the soldier Walter Oliver, who had died in skirmishes in China when the army had gone there to put down people they chose to regard as 'Chinese pagans' – and as though it were yesterday she could hear the officer at Knightsbridge Barracks who had told her of Walter's death, explaining to her how he had been part of that force. So long ago, and yet as fresh in her memory as though it had been yesterday.

Dorcas. She tried to concentrate on damsons in an attempt to keep Dorcas at bay but it was no use. There she was, grinning, laughing, looking at her, Tilly, with those calculating stares of hers, veering in a matter of moments from warm and lovely, friendly Dorcas to the most vitriolic and cruel of tormentors. She had used to talk, too, such outrageous stuff, about how unjust the world was to such as she, born into a low family and kept under for ever by the selfishness of those who called themselves her betters, but were nothing of the sort. She had told Tilly over and over again that she cared nothing for any man's opinion and would live her life as she thought fit. That she saw no reason why a woman should not concern herself with business matters – and indeed, Tilly thought then, don't I occupy myself in a business? What else is my guest house but a money-making enterprise? 'And a successful one at that,' a wicked little voice somewhere deep inside Tilly crowed. 'A most successful one.'

But Dorcas's idea of how a lady should live has not been at all like mine, Tilly protested inside her head. How could they be the same? Dorcas was a housemaid, the daughter of a housekeeper who had once been – well, never mind that. Tilly veered away from memories of Mrs Leander, Dorcas's mother and Sophie's grandmother, whose history had been a most unsavoury one. Her part in my life was such that I never wish to consider her again and I won't, I won't, she told herself, and made a determined effort to think again about Duff, remembering how much happier he had been when he had returned from his ride with Mr Geddes than he had been at breakfast time, and certainly last night. Had those anguished and alarming outpourings been entirely due to brandy? Had she asked Jem to seek Sophie for no purpose? I must speak to Jem again, she thought anxiously. Perhaps ask him to delay. And then sighed as another thought came bubbling up. Whatever Duff had said last night had to be true. He had found none of those problems he had described at the bottom of a bottle. They had been there all the time and were simply uncorked when the bottle was. There was still need for a mother to be concerned.

She stood up, leaving the fruit at last ready for Eliza, for all through her musings her hands had been busy, and made her way upstairs. There was work to be done that could not be ignored. She would find time later today to think again about the request she had made of Jem. Perhaps she would withdraw and perhaps she would not; but at least she felt better than she did when she had started the day. And when she heard Duff whistling as she passed the bottom of the stairs, she let her lips curve contentedly. There were trials to being a mother, undoubtedly, but there were great blessings too.

Chapter Nine

THERE WAS NO doubt in Tilly's mind that Duff had chosen his time with deliberate skill. They had passed three very agreeable days and evenings, during which he had seemed quite his old comfortable self, and spoke not a word about his schoolfellows or any difficulties he might have with them, and Tilly had been lulled into a sense of security. So much so, in fact, that she had made a point of walking down to Jem's shop, ostensibly to assure him that the sheets as sewn by Miss McCrasky, the seamstress who came by the day to do such work, were coming on very well, but actually to tell him not to seek out Sophie after all.

'I have decided it would be a mistake,' she said, sitting beside the main mahogany counter of Jem's shop, as other customers milled about and the two men and the shop boy took care of them. 'I have recalled in greater detail how tiresome Dorcas was and I cannot but wonder, if we tried to find Sophie to entertain Duff, would it mean that I will have to entertain Dorcas? And I don't think I wish to do that.'

'I didn't think it a good idea at all, and I did say so,' Jem said. 'If not in so many words, but I thought you understood.'

'I understood,' she said and briefly touched his hand with one gloved finger. His own hand closed around hers for a moment and swiftly she withdrew. She must do nothing to encourage Jem; it was not fair to him. And she stifled the notion that perhaps seeking his help in matters that worried her was in itself a form of encouragement. 'But the thing of it was I was so anxious about Duff, I felt he was choosing his friends – well – injudiciously. But now he has not spoken of this particular one for days and seems perfectly happy again, so let us leave things as they are, shall we?'

'It mayn't be so easy,' he said bluntly. 'I've already started to make enquiries. You asked me to do so and so I did. When questions have been asked of certain people, you understand, and feelers put out, it's possible that – well, such efforts once started are not easy to stop.'

'But you must!' she said, irritable suddenly. 'You cannot refuse to –'

'Of course I'm not refusing! I'll make no further efforts, I do assure you. I'm happy to leave such sleeping dogs to lie as far and as silently as they may. But I have asked people to look for me – and if the word gets out and to Dorcas's own ears, well then –'

'Oh.' She caught her breath. 'I see what you mean.' She brooded for a while and then said with a bravado she did not actually feel, 'Well, we must hope for the best. I am sure all will be well if we make no further shifts to seek Sophie. And thank you for your kind help, Jem. It is much appreciated.'

'You don't have to thank me,' he said gruffly. 'You know that for Duff I'll do all that is ever required.'

'I know,' she said. 'But Duff is now in no need of any further aid so – well, I cannot help but thank you.'

And now, Duff had started the whole wretched business again. She sat in her drawing room, the backgammon board in front of her, and stared at Duff with a sharp line between her brows. On the other side of the drawing room the American party and Mr Hancock and Mr Cumming were playing a noisy game of spillikins and the sound of the guffaws, giggles and whoops had made it necessary for Duff to speak rather loudly; so loudly that everyone else in the room was made aware of it: the Graylings, the Misses K and F and Miss Barnetsen, and Mr Gee and Mr Geddes who had been playing a hand of bezique.

So the whole drawing room heard and was interested. The evening had been a pleasant one, for Eliza had quite surpassed herself at dinner, giving them a dish of grouse that was quite delicious, cooked with ham and vegetables and sherry with spices to a glorious salmi, as well as a handsome dish of crimped skate, served in a caper sauce. Eliza took a great pride in offering always those dishes that were in season and both grouse and skate were at their best now at the height of August. Her usual attention to the first course, providing excellent collops of mutton with fresh spinach and a great dish of eggs *à la tripe,* that is cooked with a bechamel sauce and garnished with bread croutons, especially for Mr Geddes's pleasure (for she had taken a great liking to him and put herself out for him and his strange ideas about diet) together with the usual range of puddings, not least of which was a West Indian confection of cream, green ginger and the best loaf sugar and sponge cakes, which Duff adored, had left them all deeply contented. They had turned to an evening's agreeable entertainment in a high good humour. And Duff had dropped into the pool of warmth and light and sense of goodwill his casual statement and request.

'I have been invited to spend a week at Paton Place, with Patrick's family in Leicestershire, Mamma,' he said. 'It is for the start of the partridge season, you know – the birds will be good this year, he says, for they have new coverts and an excellent gamekeeper. I trust I might go?'

Mrs Grayling lifted her sharp little nose and peered across the room at him. 'Paton Place? Is that not the seat of the Duke of Mowbray?'

'Indeed yes,' Duff smiled at her. 'He is Patrick's papa, don't you know.'

'And you are asked to spend – well!' said Mrs Grayling, quite dumbstruck with admiration.

'There!' said Miss Fleetwood in high satisfaction. 'Didn't I tell you that his going away to school would be the making of him? Duff would never have met such people as dukes' sons had he gone to a London day school, Mrs Quentin. It will help him further his way in the world admirably to have such a noble friendship.'

'I believed that in recommending he go away to school you set more store by the quality of the education there than by the social standing of his fellow pupils, Miss Fleetwood. I hardly think that merely being the friend of a lord will be of great value in making his way in the world,' Tilly said sharply.

'Then I fear you think wrongly, Mrs Quentin. I do indeed set high store by a good education, but I am not so foolish as to deny the value of friends in high places who may be of aid.'

'Oh, you are right, Miss Fleetwood, you really are!' Mr Gee was at last stung into conversation. 'I know in my own profession – the law you know –' he uttered the word with great reverence – 'It matters greatly that one should be well connected. Not that I suggest Mr Duff enters the law,' he bowed politely towards Duff, 'for it is an arduous world and does not suit all. But I am sure things are ordered in much the same way in other professional fields. I do congratulate you on your most gratifying invitation, young man.'

Duff knew as well as everyone else that Mr Gee, despite his somewhat grand references to his profession, was in fact only a very overworked and far from highly regarded lower grade clerk in a somewhat seedy set of law chambers. But he smiled at him and said easily, 'Indeed, Mr Gee, you may well be right. But I was not concerned with furthering myself in considering this invitation. It is simply that Patrick is my friend and I would enjoy visiting his family.'

'It is the only reason for wanting to go,' Mr Geddes said. 'I for one would think the less of you if you were using the acquaintance merely as a tuft hunter and not because you liked your school-fellow. Do you like him, Duff?'

Duff looked serenely back at Mr Geddes and smiled. 'Indeed I do, as I explained to you. So, may I, Ma?'

'Is there any reason why he should not go, Mrs Quentin?' Mr Geddes asked after a pause, for Tilly did not answer, and she became aware that the entire room was holding its breath, waiting for her to do so. And she was deeply angry with Duff. How could he have been so devious as to ask her in everyone's hearing like this? These people were her guests, albeit paying ones, and not members of the family. The question of Duff and his friendships was surely one for herself and her son alone.

All this and more ran through her head as she sat there with her eyes down, looking at the forgotten backgammon board, trying to think. All she could visualize was Duff in this very room, sitting with his head on her lap and gulping out his misery about the young man he said he loved. And what precisely did that mean? Duff, now fully in control of himself and with no brandy fumes to make him lachrymose, showed no anxiety about his friendship at all. Had things changed between them in some way in the interim? That Duff had not seen Patrick was clear to Tilly. He had remained either at home or at her side almost all the time since that last conversation, so there had been no opportunity. And yet –

'He wrote to me, do you remember, Mamma?' Duff said, as though he had read her thoughts. 'I received three letters this morning – the others were from Edward and Hubert, who are spending the rest of the summer as tutors to spoiled little horrors, poor things, before they return to school. Patrick's letter was the only cheerful one in the bag.'

'Well, we must talk about this, Duff,' Tilly said at length. 'Later, perhaps. Now, is it my turn to play, or yours?'

'Oh, Mrs Quentin, you cannot be so unkind as to refuse him!' Miss Knapp cried, and looked archly at Tilly. 'It is no pleasure for a boy to be so cooped up in London when the hot weather is upon us, surely? The streets are so hot and dusty, and I am persuaded that Leicestershire at this point in August will be quite perfect. When does the shooting season start, Duff?'

'I believe it is September the first,' Duff said. 'For partridge, that is.'

'I thought it was the Glorious Twelfth,' Mrs Grayling ventured. 'I read about that in the newspapers, you know, and –'

'Not at all, my dear!' Mr Grayling had superior knowledge and was happy to display it. 'That's for grouse and *August* the Twelfth – that is why Eliza gave us that splendid salmi of grouse tonight, is it not Mrs Quentin? We can always count on Eliza to feed us as though we were the sort of people who had family seats in Leicestershire and went shooting birds on the proper dates.'

'Poor little birds,' said Miss Barnetsen, sighing lugubriously. 'Such dread must fill their dear little feathered breasts as the evil date approaches!'

'I doubt that game birds keep calendars in their nests, Miss Barnetsen,' Mr Cumming said from the far side of the room, where the American party had been quizzing him and Mr Hancock about the niceties of English sporting traditions, and everyone laughed (much to Miss Barnetsen's discomfiture) and broke into cheerful chatter, all seeming to assume that the matter had been settled and Duff would indeed be going to Leicestershire to shoot partridges.

'That was too bad of you, Duff,' Tilly said in a very low voice as the noise from the spillikins game rose high again to mask her. 'I would not have had so general a discussion as that for the world.'

'I'm sorry, Ma. I meant no harm.' He looked at her with his face quite devoid of any guile and her anger began to subside. If he had been deliberately trying to get his way by devious means there was no sign of any such thought on his countenance now. He looked his usual open and cheerful self. 'You've been so busy all day I hardly had time to talk to you, and I thought that by this evening, once dinner was over, you'd be able to give the matter some thought. Had I asked you earlier when you were heads down with Eliza over that receipt for the grouse, I doubt you'd have been best pleased! And later in the afternoon, when you were with Miss McCrasky, it was impossible. So I asked you this evening. I'm sorry it got everyone else's interest in the way but –' his face cracked into a grin, 'it is rather swish, isn't it? No wonder they're all so agog! I mean, me shooting on a duke's estate!'

'*Can* you shoot?' Tilly said, suddenly distracted by the thought. 'You're hardly a countryman and have not had the sort of education in these matters.'

'Oh, we did at school, you know. Patrick used to lend me his guns for target practice and anyway I don't care if I make a cake of myself trying at a real shoot. It should be fun – if I may go, that is. I shall need extra money, do you see. I've spent all my allowance and there will be expenses.'

He looked sulky for a moment. 'If only I had my own income the way Patrick does!' he said. 'It would be so –'

'Patrick is a rich man's son, Duff.' She said it as carefully as she could, not wanting anyone to overhear her, and that care took some of the sharpness from her words; certainly Duff heard no reproof in them.

'Oh, I know that, Ma,' he said. 'I know, too, that one day I must seek an occupation. But until I must, is it so dreadful to want to take pleasure? I won't be the only one of our set at Paton Place – he has asked several of the other fellows, he tells me in his letter. Please Ma, mayn't I go? And if so, may I have the cash to make it easier for me? There are tips, you know, for the beaters and gamekeeper and so forth, as well as the house servants.'

'Oh, I think money is possible,' she said and leaned a little closer. 'But, Duff, I would not have hesitated had you asked me this a few weeks ago. I would have seen this as an opportunity for you to have an enjoyable new experience amongst agreeable people who – and much as I find it distasteful to discuss such things, I won't deny that knowing good families is of importance in a young man's life – who could be of help to you in future times. But that was before –'

'Yes, Mamma?' He looked at her cheerfully, as though the boy who had wept on her and talked so wildly of his confused emotions had been a total stranger of whom he knew nothing.

'Before you drank too much and told me so many unpleasant things!' she snapped and Mr Gee lifted his head momentarily from his hand of bezique and looked inquisitively across the room, and at once she lowered her voice again. 'I understood you to be miserable about this Patrick and –'

'Oh, Ma, you mustn't pay attention to what a chap says in his cups!' Duff said. 'Silas will tell you that! The oddest things appear in a man's speech when he is full of brandy.'

'Oh!' She was taken aback. 'You have talked to Mr Geddes about – about Patrick?'

'Oh, yes.' He leaned back in his chair and stretched a little, clearly comfortable and at ease with himself. 'One morning, riding – I found I was telling him how captious Patrick can be, and how fickle a friend, but he assured me that I was fretting foolishly, for all aristocrats are like Patrick, he says. It comes of being bred from their cradles to too much deference. They expect everyone to do as they wish and don't know how to behave when people stand up to them. Well, Patrick will have to learn from me that it is no bad thing to be baulked occasionally. Silas said I could be the best friend he ever had if I am able to rub off some of his grandeur and bring him to the level of ordinary mortals. Of course he will one day be the duke, but that does not mean he cannot learn now to tolerate the views of others. That's what Silas said and I agree with him. So I was glad when the invitation came, for it will give me another chance to show Patrick how to behave and Silas said that could be the most useful thing I could possibly do.' And he looked over his shoulder at Silas at the bezique table and grinned, and Silas grinned companionably back and said to Mr Gee, 'My trick, partner, and I think my game. And I have honours too.'

'So you win,' Mr Gee said philosophically. 'And I must go to bed if I am to be fit for tomorrow. Big day in court, you know.' He looked self-importantly at Silas, trying to imply he would be in court personally rather than scribbling furiously at his desk as usual, and got to his feet. 'Thank you for the game, sir. Good night to you all.'

He bowed to the company and went, and it seemed a signal for the rest of them for the Graylings got to their feet, Mrs Grayling wrapping up the *petit point* that she carried about with her and fussed over but never seemed to finish, and were followed by the Misses K and F and Miss Barnetsen, talking in furious whispers with their heads close together. Miss Barnetsen went off in an apparent huff, the other two close behind her, and then the American elders yawned widely and insisted that their young ones also made an end to the evening, greatly to the chagrin of Mr Hancock and Mr Cumming. So the room emptied until only Tilly and Duff remained, together with Mr Geddes who was sorting the bezique cards into their separate packs rather slowly. That he was waiting to talk to Tilly alone was quite obvious to her.

It seemed to be obvious to Duff too, for he reached over and swept the pieces off the backgammon board. 'Enough for tonight, I think, Ma, hmm? You've been very busy today and must be tired.

I shall be away to my bed, then. I have a new book I want to read and it's more pleasant to read in bed than anywhere. Good night, Silas. Shall we ride as usual, then?'

'Indeed we shall,' Silas said heartily. 'Goodnight, Duff.' They exchanged a glance that Tilly saw as conspiratorial and Duff bent and kissed her cheek and was gone.

'Mr Geddes, I wish you would not encourage Duff in – in the things in which you encourage him,' she said sharply and he smiled.

'Oh? And what might that be? Riding? But he enjoys it so and so do I. I thought he was benefiting in his health from the regular exercise – I know I am – and he seems to enjoy discussing matters of interest with me. He is so taken with the new ideas that interest me, Mrs Quentin, that it is a pleasure to talk to him. A wise head on young shoulders, your son.'

'That's as may be,' she said. 'But –' How could she explain what it was that was worrying her about Duff? She could not find the words. No woman could.

'If your fear is that his attachment to this schoolfellow is an unnatural one,' Mr Geddes said in a quiet voice, 'do let me assure you that such anxieties are groundless.'

Her head shot up and she stared at him with wide eyes. 'Sir?'

'Oh, come. Let us behave like friends and discuss the undiscussable. Which is an absurd notion in itself for how can any human behaviour be undiscussable? Silence causes all of us more anxiety than honest talk ever could. So let us be direct, not to say blunt about it. You fear unnatural vice has touched Duff. I can assure you it has not. He has talked to me easily while we have been riding and has come to regard me perhaps in the light of a much older brother. I understand the state of his mind and feelings, for I was a boy too, of course. A while ago now, but I remember it well enough! He is simply going through the experience of hero-worship, my dear Mrs Quentin, and all the horrors of jealousy and yearning that go with that. To make too much of it might well convert it all into something more than it should be. I would most earnestly advise you to stop worrying. You have a fine lad there in Duff, and he should give you no anxiety.'

She had been staring at him throughout his long speech and now she said a little unsteadily, 'Indeed, Mr Geddes. You *do* espouse the new ideas! To speak so easily of such matters is – is –' She stopped, lost for words, and he came a little closer and smiled down at her.

'My dear Tilly – and I hope we have reached that stage of a friendship wherein it is possible for me to speak to you so intimately – my dear Tilly, surely I have sufficiently explained myself to you in the past days while we have come to know each other? I have made it very plain that I value liberty above all, and liberty includes – indeed is rooted in – freedom to speak one's mind, however different a mind it might be from that of the majority. I believe that silence in such matters as these most intense of mankind's emotions is more than illiberal. I believe it actually shackles us cruelly and causes much unhappiness. See how distressed you are because Duff is invited to spend a wholesome holiday with his friend! You would deprive him of good country air and country sport for fear of some unspeakable emotion. But once speak of that emotion and does it not diminish its apparent horror and become ordinary and indeed fully natural?'

'Hero-worship, natural?' she said, still uncertain, quite unable to collect her thoughts into any coherent argument against him, for he was standing so close that she could smell the bay rum on his shaven cheeks and feel his breath warm on her forehead. She quite liked both sensations and that in itself was disconcerting.

'Of course it is,' he said firmly. 'Did I not tell you that I too experienced it?' He laughed reminiscently. 'A rather swaggerish fellow called Hackforth as I recall. He was known at school as Chopper, of course, and how we young ones adored him! Like them, I dreamed of his attentions and yearned for marks of his interest – but I assure you now that I am anything but unnatural.'

It seemed as though he had moved even closer to her, though she had not seen him move, and she found herself breathing a little more rapidly and decidedly unevenly. 'Indeed, Mr Geddes?'

'I wish you would call me Silas. I am surely your friend by now? We have spent so much time talking so agreeably – please to call me by my name. It would give me much pleasure to hear it on your lips.'

'Very well. Er – Silas,' she said and felt herself redden. 'So – so you think I should let Duff go to Leicestershire?'

'Of course.' His voice was low and soft and she could not take her eyes from his face, and he smiled and bent a little closer, and this time she did see the movement and managed, somehow, to galvanize her muscles and pull away. It must have been her imagination, of course, but it had seemed to her he was about to attempt to kiss her. A foolish notion, naturally, but still –

'Well, if you are sure, Mr – Silas, I will tell Duff so and make all arrangements. I must thank you for your interest in Duff.'

'I am as interested in his mother,' Silas said, still in that low voice, but this time she did not look at him and felt herself able to pull away from his spell, as she now found herself describing it. How could she have allowed herself to be so close to him that she had the notion he might actually kiss her? She scolded herself inside her head, even as she collected her reticule from her chair and turned to make her way to the door.

'I thank you for your interest,' she repeated and somehow managed to escape, leaving him in the drawing room, standing looking after her as she went towards the stairs with as steady a step as she could muster, trying to look her usual unruffled self.

It was not at all easy.

Chapter Ten

BY THE TIME Duff had been fully equipped for his visit to Leicestershire – an operation that took three trips to the best gentleman's outfitters in Regent Street and rather more of Tilly's sum set aside for his clothes than she would have expected – everyone was quite exhausted.

Despite her lingering uncertainty about the advisability of the visit, which had been only partly assuaged by a charming letter of invitation sent by Patrick's older sister, who, she said, always dealt with her father the duke's hospitality, Tilly was determined that her boy should not be at a disadvantage among the people with whom he would be spending so long a time. She worked hard to ensure that he had precisely what he would require in terms of a shooting jacket with leather shoulders, a pair of breeches with leggings and shooting boots together with a game bag, and a set of guns which she hired from Purdey's in South Audley Street, while Eliza, in a fever of activity, set about laundering his linen. She would not let Mrs Skinner, their usual washerwoman, do it, any more than she ever let her wash Tilly's chemises and shifts; as far as Eliza was concerned this was far too delicate a job for such a person, and so she set to with boiling copper and blue bag, starch and goffering iron and worked wonders in terms of snowy shirts and perfect collars and cuffs.

Duff, in the middle of it all, seemed sublimely unaware of how much extra work his holiday was creating, and went riding each morning with Silas as usual, an activity which both now regarded as an essential part of their day, and spent his afternoons lounging in the garden on a bath chair reading one of the many books which Silas lent him.

Tilly was reading too, or trying to, at the end of each day, when she went wearily to bed. The excessively warm weather of these dying days of August left the air still and exhausted after dinner, and few of the guests chose to spend much time in the drawing room once the coffee and tea trays had been cleared. They went for strolls in the dark blue twilight to get the breath of coolness that came at last when the sun went down, and went early to their beds, and that was a relief for Tilly. To be sociable each evening was part of the work of a guest house hostess, she knew, and generally she had no objection to it, but at present, she was glad to be free of it.

She would settle down with one of Silas's books, stretching out on her bed with only a sheet to cover her and wearing her thinnest muslin nightgown unbuttoned at the neck, and direct the light of her oil lamp so that she had the greatest possible illumination with the least possible heating from the chimney. She would try to concentrate on what she read, for she knew that Silas would be eager to discuss the book with her as soon as he had the opportunity, but it was almost impossible. Within a very short time she would doze off and wake at two or three o'clock in the morning to find herself lying with her neck twisted awkwardly and the lamp streaking its glass chimney black with soot; and would blow it out and then lie awake, wondering why she could not recapture the delicious sleepiness of earlier in the evening. And then would doze off at last, to wake as the light crept into her room in the early morning, as weary as she had been when she went to bed.

The truth of the matter was that however hard she tried to convince herself that there was no harm in Duff's visit to his friend Patrick and that he would enjoy it and return happily, there was still this lingering worm of doubt that crept in and out of her thoughts each day. It was all very well for Silas to assure her that her boy was like all other boys and that she had no need to fret over him. He had not sat in the drawing room and listened to Duff and watched him sob his heart out.

What was it that he had said? 'I do love him – he can tease and torment me to his heart's content and I will do nothing to retaliate.' And when she had asked him if he had done anything shameful, he had blushed scarlet and told her she understood nothing.

And it was true, perhaps. Her memory of their conversation was getting confused now. She had gone over it in her mind so often. What had he actually said? All she now knew for sure was that she had been left with the conviction that the young lord with whom her son was so infatuated wanted Duff to do something he didn't really want to do. And it was that which worried her. She had considered inviting Lord Patrick to visit Brompton Grove, but the mere suggestion had put Duff into an agony of embarrassment, so she had desisted. And, anyway, she had thought, even if I did meet him, what difference would it make? He would no doubt put on a mannerly show for me, and I'd be none the wiser.

But under pressure from all sides she had agreed that Duff could go to Leicestershire and she could not now renege on her promises; so doggedly she went on with the preparations for his visit and tried to make the best of it.

Strangely enough it came as something of a relief when at last he went. His neat luggage had been packed and he was dressed precisely as he should be to make such a journey, in a light cheviot Chesterfield topcoat, complete with velvet collar and silk facings, and a pair of perfect sponge bag trousers over buttoned patent boots and a rather rakish high hat, and was put into the cab that would carry him to the magnificent new railway terminus at St Pancras.

It was obvious that he was very excited at the drama of it all. His eyes glittered with it as he chattered of how splendid it would be to see the new station and hotel that had just been opened, and how much he would relish the journey, for he was to be met at his destination by one of the duke's growlers and carried directly to Paton Place. Tilly was touched by that. He seemed so like the small boy he had been, jumping up and down with glee because they were to visit Cremorne Gardens in Chelsea, or the Pantheon in Oxford Street, and that, oddly, made her feel less anxious on his behalf. No one could possibly hurt so charming a boy, she told herself as she stood on the steps and waved at the back of his departing cab, with Eliza at her side waving even more furiously. How could they?

'Don't he look marvellous, Mum?' Eliza said as the cab at last turned the corner and vanished. 'Fair brought a lump to my throat, it did, to see him so grown up and all. He'll be a fine catch for some lucky girl he will, one day.' Her eyes gleamed. 'Just imagine, our Duff a married man with babies of his own, no doubt! Wouldn't that be something!'

'My dear Eliza, you're running far too quickly!' Tilly said. 'Will you live our lives in a matter of minutes? Let the years move at their own speed, I do beg of you.' She led the way back into the house and Eliza followed.

'Oh, Mum, I wasn't wishin' our lives away, course I wasn't. Just saying, like, how nice it'd be.'

'We shall start the second batch of preserves, I think, Eliza,' Tilly said, determined not to follow this line of talk any longer. 'We have been very lax this past few days, with all the extra work of organizing this visit, so we must get on with it. Did the fruit come this morning?'

'Oh, yes, Mum. I told him we was ready to put it all up and he said as how he's had a real glut of stuff in – there's the last of the raspberries and some lovely magnum-bonum plums that'll dry a treat he said, or we could bottle 'em.'

'I think the bottled will stand us in best stead, don't you? Have you the bottles ready?' Tilly went down the stairs into the kitchen and pinned on the apron she kept in the kitchen drawer for such occasions as this as Eliza came clattering down behind her.

'Indeed I have, Mum, three dozen of them and all with handsome new corks as tight as you like, and a fine big piece of resin to melt for the covers. But, Mum, you don't need to worry yourself over this. I can get Rosie to lend me a hand and deal with it fine. You go and take a rest.'

'But you won't finish in time if you do it with just Rosie's aid,' Tilly said. 'Is it not the meeting of your association tonight?'

Eliza had last year joined a reading circle for young females run at St Paul's Church in Cottage Place, a little further along the Brompton Road, and seemed to enjoy her weekly forays there, returning always with an armful of new novels to read, for the members ran a lively lending service. Eliza liked nothing better than to spend her free time with her head in a really exciting story, especially one with mad monks and wicked squires and innocent country maidens.

'Well, it won't be the end of the world if I miss one, Mum,' Eliza said. 'And I'd as soon you put your feet up.'

'Nonsense, Eliza,' Tilly said crisply. 'You concentrate on the dinner, and I shall set to work on the bottling. And I will brook no argument. Now, where is the fruit? In the second larder?'

'Yes, Mum.' Eliza sighed, knowing she would be wasting her breath to argue. There were times when Tilly would not be coaxed into the sort of life of leisure that Eliza so strongly urged on her. 'A big basket of the magnum-bonum plums, another of raspberries and a little punnet o' peaches. I got out the ones I wants to use fresh tonight for the dessert, and there's enough there to put up a couple of nice bottles we can save till Christmas – oh, and the very first of the Beauty of Bath apples. I thought to use them for the dessert tonight, too.'

With Eliza chattering busily as usual and Tilly responding with occasional nods and murmurs they set to work. The bottles were standing ready in the back scullery, set on trays, and the copper had been filled, a big jug ready beside it. Rosie had laid the fire beneath the brick container where the copper was fixed and it wanted only a match and Tilly was grateful yet again to Eliza and her forethought. Clearly she had all this prepared some time ago, waiting for the opportunity to do the work.

With Eliza to help her, preparing the fruit didn't take as long as it might have done. Moving methodically, they checked the fruit for dryness, wiping each plum carefully in a clean white cloth, making sure there were no bruised pieces that might set the whole lot to rot, and packed them carefully into the quart glass bottles, as Tilly weighed out the pounded loaf sugar – something else that Eliza had ensured was prepared in advance – dropping a quarter pound into each jar. Then all they had to do was cork the bottles, wrap them in wisps of hay and set them neatly in the copper which they filled from the jug up to their necks in cold water. Eliza lit the fire, and when it was drawing nicely, set the wooden cover on the copper and brushed her hands together contentedly.

'There, Mum! It'll take an hour or so to boil up, then once the boilin' starts, you just need to check the bottles ain't knocking together, though the hay wisps'll protect 'em well enough, you'll see. I'll see to it the fire's doused half an hour after the boilin' starts, and then we can leave the jars there till tonight. They've got to get right cold in there before we takes 'em out. It'll not take me above ten minutes to melt the resin and seal the corks when I gets back from my meeting. You don't need to worry yourself one bit. I'll put them away tomorrow. We can do the jam, now.'

Making jam was one of Tilly's most favoured tasks. She loved the detail of picking over the fruit and making sure it was all wholesome and unbruised, of measuring the sugar to match the weight of fruit pound for pound. She loved standing over the broad shallow copper pans, flattening the fruit with a big wooden spoon over a hot fire, releasing the scent of it to wreath around the room and make her drowsy with it, and then stirring the sugar in till it began to bubble and spit a little and the scent became even more intense.

'I could put in some redcurrant juice, Mum, to sharpen it a little and to make sure it sets,' Eliza said. 'But it says in my magazine as the juice of a lemon answers just as well and I must say as I think it tastes better.'

'As you wish, Eliza,' Tilly said dreamily, still stirring. She was happier than she had been for some time, now Duff was safely on his way. For good or ill the die was cast, she thought, and that is why I feel so much better. It's also because I know now how foolish I have been to fret so. He is a sensible, good boy. There is no need for anxiety.

The lemon juice went into the fragrant crimson mass and still she stirred as the boiling went on, and then skimmed busily to ensure that the jam would be clear. It took a full hour before it showed itself ready to set, which they tested by dropping a little of the jam on to a cold plate Eliza fetched from the dresser and checking it for wrinkles.

And then what for Tilly was the best part: taking the prepared hot jars from the oven and ladling them full and noting that the fruit was well distributed and did not sink to the bottom; a sure sign that they had succeeded with their careful boiling. Then came a tedious but still enjoyable task; each pot had to be covered with a slip of paper over which they had brushed the best olive oil, and after that with larger covers of tissue paper which they brushed over on both sides with white of egg. It was a sticky, tiring job, but satisfying too as one after another the finished pots were set in rows waiting for their labels.

Halfway through this operation Eliza broke away to see to dinner, which tonight was to be a cold collation. She had already dealt with her salmon from Mr Jerryman's shop, which she had dressed in a chaud-froid, the aspic and mayonnaise mixture setting to a perfect gloss on the poached fish, and garnished with radishes and the last precious cucumber of the summer together with hard-boiled egg wedges, and now she had to prepare a number of salads. A chicken one and another of duck, together with a small array of lobster patties and another of cheese puffs. There was to be a side of good roast beef and a cold raised pie of grouse and mutton which was a concoction of Eliza's own and much admired by the guests, who had clamoured for more when she had last offered it, so although none of the food might be hot, 'all will be toothsome', as Eliza put it. The custom of serving a cold collation one night a month to allow Eliza her evening off was a well established one at Quentin's and no guest had ever complained about it.

By the time Eliza, Rosie and Lucy had set the dining room ready and arranged the dishes on the table as well as the sideboard, it was almost a quarter before six o'clock. Eliza's meeting commenced at half past six, and she went off happily to her room alongside the kitchen to get ready. She put on her best bonnet which was in a most handsome Dolly Varden style, a forward tilting ellipse of yellow straw decorated with flowers which looked, when set over Eliza's rather red face, a touch incongruous to tell the truth, and her summer mantle, a much fringed garment in a rich yellow faille that made her look somewhat larger than she was. But she clearly admired herself greatly in the ensemble and came out of her room for Tilly's inspection.

'You look most elegant, Eliza,' Tilly said approvingly and, indeed, despite the fact that the fashions were a touch extreme for Eliza's colouring she had an air about her that made her very pleasant to look at. 'It seems a pity there are only other females at your association to admire you!'

'Oh, as to that, I wouldn't be too sure,' Eliza said saucily. 'Several of the meetings are attended by men as guests, you know, for not all men are empty-headed ninnies who never read a word! Not that it is to meet the men that I go there, you understand.'

'Of course not,' Tilly said. 'Well, enjoy yourself – and we shall see you later.'

'I've doused the fire under the copper, now, so there's no need for you to do anything else there. I'll see to the waxing of the corks when I get in. As for the peaches, I'll see to them tomorrow. Give over, Mum, do. You've worked hard all afternoon and you should take some rest before dinner, now you know that.'

'Well, I shall, Eliza, so don't keep on at me! The raspberry jam looks very fine, does it not?' And she nodded her head at the dozen or so pots that stood like rubies capped with snow in rows on the kitchen table.

'They do indeed, Mum. We can label them tomorrow. Now, you be away upstairs, please.'

'I will,' Tilly promised and at last Eliza went, taking herself out of the back door and up the area steps in a little wash of parma violet scent and a flurry of her taffeta skirts.

Tilly stretched and sighed and took off her apron and took it out to the scullery to put it in the big hamper which contained the laundry awaiting collection by Mrs Skinner. Then she went back to the comfort of the kitchen and she stood still for a moment on the rag rug that spread its vivid colours over the stone floor beside the fire, as she pulled down her sleeves and rebuttoned them.

The place breathed warmth and peace at her, from the great dresser and its displays of blue and white china to the brindled cat asleep on the rocker amid Eliza's crumpled old cushions and she felt her shoulders relax with the sheer comfort of it all as the cat woke, stretched and mewed.

She bent to stroke him and as she did so a bell rang and she peered up at the row of them above the kitchen door. The dozen or so that hung there on their coiled springs were labelled with their source; and it was the front door bell that was dancing madly; she lifted her head to listen and heard footsteps going across the hall upstairs. Good. Rosie or Lucy had heard it. She wondered briefly who it might be, for all the guests had their own keys, and then smiled. Probably Mr Cumming, she thought. He was always forgetting to take his keys to St George's with him, or left them there when he came home at the end of his day; she really would have to scold him for making so much extra effort necessary for her housemaids.

She bent and stroked the cat again, who purred, rubbed himself against her hand and looked blissful, and then straightened as the door at the top of the stairs swung open, and she looked up.

'If you please, Ma'am,' said Rosie, sounding a touch startled. 'It's a lady as wants to see you. Says it's important but wouldn't give me no name, Ma'am, so I thought I'd set her in the hall and come and –'

'You need not concern yourself further,' a voice said and Rosie looked over her shoulder, even more startled, as someone came past her and set her firmly, though not at all roughly or rudely, aside. 'I know my way here.'

Tilly stood staring upwards, her hand still on the cat's head as it rubbed itself against her, purring loudly. She couldn't quite see who was there in the shadows at the top of the stairs. The voice was unfamiliar and yet had a ring about it that she knew, she thought, and then wanted to laugh aloud at such a contradictory notion. Either it was strange or she knew it, she told herself, and peered again into the shadows. It couldn't be both.

The person on the stairs came forward and began to walk down; a tall, slender figure, which moved with considerable grace, and wearing one of the newest of tight tied-back skirts and close-fitting bodices, all in a tasteful shade of deep gold, trimmed with copper-coloured braid. She was wearing a Leghorn bonnet, very like Eliza's Dolly Varden but infinitely more chic, in a golden straw that matched the gown exactly and which showed off to perfect advantage the hair beneath it.

Dark red hair, thick, curly, twisted into the most handsome of coiled tresses and plaits to form a great chignon above the back of the slender neck. The face beneath was small and pointed and the skin was the colour of fresh cream.

'Sophie,' Tilly heard herself say, a mere breath of a word and the vision on the stairs arrived in front of her, tucked under her arm the lacy cream-coloured parasol she was carrying and extended both hands towards her.

'How clever of you to recognize me, Aunt Tilly! And after so long, too! How are you?'

Chapter Eleven

TO SAY THAT Miss Sophie Oliver was self-composed was to put it at its very least. She sat at her ease on the kitchen chair beside the table as though it were a satin *chaise longue* in the most handsome of salons, her thread gloved hands, small and very neat, crossed comfortably over each other on the crook of her parasol and smiling at Tilly with what seemed to be practised charm.

Now that Tilly could see her properly, she realized how much the child she had known had changed. However, she did remember the colour of her hair, which really was remarkable, and the timbre of her voice. It was similar to that of her mother, Dorcas, with the same faint twang of an accent, but in Sophie's case it was greatly disguised. She had, Tilly thought fleetingly, gone to a lot of trouble to cultivate a sweeter voice with thrilling low tones as well as a silvery laugh, which she had already demonstrated when she had observed how amazed Tilly was to see her.

But the rest was very different. The small pointed chin was still there, admittedly, but with a more pronounced cleft in it than Tilly remembered and the dark eyes seemed to have enlarged amazingly. The lashes were long and swept over the cheeks most appealingly and the nose, small, straight and surmounting a charmingly short upper lip that kept her mouth slightly open to reveal perfect little white teeth, was the sort that most girls yearn to have. She was altogether bewitching to look at, and the more she looked, the more Tilly felt her heart sink. What had she done in asking Jem to seek out this girl? What *had* she done?

'You have not asked me why I am here, Aunt Tilly!' Sophie said at length. 'I may so address you still, I trust? I remember I used to.'

'Do you remember so much?' Tilly said. 'You were very small when you left this house.'

The perfect little mouth curved, so that the cleft in the chin became a mere dimple, though still a pretty one. 'I have an excellent memory, Aunt Tilly. I can recall so much! That sad man in the basket chair, for example, when we were at the seaside, you know, and the way you and Mamma –'

'Yes,' Tilly said hastily, not wanting at all to discuss Freddy, who had been so ill when they had met him on a summer visit to Brighton, and certainly not wishing to discuss Dorcas. 'I have heard that sometimes people have great recall of their childhoods. My own is less –'

'Well, you would not recall as much as I do of the times when I was here,' Sophie said kindly. 'After all, you were already a grown up lady and I was but a child.'

Tilly blinked, suddenly feeling extremely old compared to this vision of lovely youth, and then straightened her shoulders.

'I have always had much to think about,' she said tartly.

'Yes, of course,' Sophie said soothingly, and she looked around the room with a faint smile on her lips. 'How charming it is to see the old kitchen again. I can recall sitting here with darling Duff, eating our bread and milk for supper, and dear Eliza bustling about – is she still with you?'

'Indeed she is,' Tilly said, watching her carefully. What was the girl up to?

'She was so kind to us. And I remember how excited she was when the new range was put in – we watched the men do it and she was so – well, cock-a-hoop is all I can say. And there the range still is, and there have been no changes. It is so comforting to find all is the same as I remember it.'

'Not quite,' said Tilly, stung. 'We have much more that is modern. New taps and sinks in the scullery and the great chopping board is there as well as a cold larder to supplement the ordinary one.' The girl was reminding her, and clearly deliberately, that the cooking range that had been put in the kitchen all that time ago had been paid for not by Tilly, but by Dorcas. It was not a comfortable reminder; those had been the days when Dorcas had been plump in the pocket, with a tendency to try to exert some control over Tilly in consequence.

'How exciting,' Sophie said, stretching her eyes and smiling again. 'And what else, Aunt Tilly? I saw when I came in that the house looks quite different. Where there was a small hall there now seems to be a vast one and the stairs are wider.'

Tilly let her shoulders loosen. 'Yes, that is so. We – the two houses were knocked together. The hallway is double width, therefore, and the drawing room doubled in size upstairs. The dining room too.'

Sophie looked at her sharply and this time her admiration seemed genuine. 'Then you have a considerable establishment, have you not? It must be – why, I cannot guess how many bedrooms – a dozen and a half, I imagine?'

Tilly's brows tightened. This girl had a shrewd ability to assess space. 'Twenty,' she said a little stiffly. 'Not including the family's rooms of course.'

'Well, that is indeed a considerable establishment,' Sophie said. 'It is almost as big as a provincial hotel – bigger in fact.'

'It is not an hotel,' Tilly said shortly. 'I offer my guests the comfort of home on a – on a more permanent basis than an hotel does. I prefer it that way.'

'Oh yes, paying guests,' Sophie murmured. 'It is so much more genteel, is it not? One cannot be sure who will come into an hotel and demand accommodation, but if they are regarded as guests –'

'Precisely. I am able to be very selective about whom I will accept to join our – well, we regard our guests as a large family. We are all on excellent terms.' She suppressed awareness of the occasional irritations she had with Mr Cumming, and the way Mrs Grayling's chatter made her sometimes want to snap at her, and looked directly at Sophie. 'We prefer it that way.'

'I am sure you do,' Sophie said heartily. 'And so should I! Now, before we say any more, do please tell me how Duff is. I remember him with such delight. My dearest little playmate –'

'He is well enough,' Tilly said and then looked at her closely. 'You haven't yet said why you are here.'

Sophie raised her brows. 'Why, you make that sound as though you would prefer I was not! And I am so happy to see you again and to see the dear old house. It is, I have to say, like coming home to me – that is why I begged we might stay here in the kitchen rather than repair upstairs. Just yet.'

Tilly let the last words go by her, and went on looking closely at Sophie. 'But why now? Did you – well, why now?'

Sophie shrugged. 'I cannot say – was it an impulse? Perhaps. It was just that my carriage was going along the Brompton Road, where I have not been for such a long time, and I saw Mr Harrod's shop and how enlarged it was and thought – surely I have a recollection of that shop as being much less grand? And I got down to look around in there. He was about to close but he remembered me and stayed open to show me all his new departments! So charming – and of course asked if I were to come and visit you and I said it was a splendid idea. So, here I am!'

Tilly shook her head. 'And no one told you that – no one else asked you to come and see me?'

Sophie set her head to one side and looked at her for a long moment and then slowly smiled. 'Now, what a strange question, dear Aunt Tilly! Why should such a thing happen? Unless you set out to find someone who could ask me? Someone who knew where I might be found?'

'Uh – not at all. I mean – not precisely – I mean –' Tilly floundered, furious with herself. Why on earth had she asked so stupid a question? This might be just what Sophie had said it was, a minor coincidence. But by asking the question she had alerted the girl.

Sophie was still gazing at her with that wide, limpid look and now she laughed, 'Oh dear Aunt Tilly, I do remember you so well! So gentle and kind and so – well, to be truthful I could always tell what you were thinking by looking at your face. You are not at all as I am, naturally given to hiding your inner thoughts, are you?'

'As to that,' Tilly said bravely, trying to salvage some of her composure, 'I really cannot say.'

'Well, never mind. Let me just confess that I had perhaps heard a distant murmur that you had asked after my welfare. There! Is that better? I will not pretend it was a coincidence that I took my carriage down the Brompton Road. To tell the truth, I had not thought about Brompton or the time I lived here for – well, for such a long time. If I ever did think of it at all, in fact. I am not one who looks back over her shoulder, you know.' She looked down at her hands and smoothed her gloves thoughtfully. 'No, I am one who enjoys the present and looks to the future always. And I had not thought about the old days at all – until I heard from a friend that enquiries had been made for me, and I thought – now, I wonder why? And it suited me well enough at present to retreat a little from – well –'

She smiled delightfully. 'Let me take a leaf from your book, Aunt, and speak frankly. It will suit me very well at present to withdraw a little from public view. So hearing that someone in Brompton – and who could it be but you? – had an interest in seeing me again – well, here I am!'

Tilly sat and looked at her. The light of the sun was coming in long, low beams now through the area window as the afternoon slid away into evening and it lit Sophie to an almost unbelievable gold; her gown, her bonnet, her gloves and, above all, her hair. The tips of the curls and the tresses and plaits were outlined in gold dust and the effect was totally beguiling. Tilly almost gawped at her. And was only brought out of her state of bemusement by the sound of footsteps overhead and then a clatter at the top of the stairs.

'Tilly, are you there? May I come down, if you please?' a voice called and Silas came down, taking two steps at a time, and then stopped as he reached the bottom one. 'Oh, I am so sorry – I did not know you were occupied.'

Sophie had lifted her head at the sound of his voice and now turned her head so that she looked at him over her shoulder, and Tilly could not help but notice what a smooth and careful move it was. Not the half turn that most people would have made to ensure a clear view behind them, but a sweet and somewhat coquettish turn of the chin that left her peeping up at Silas, who was just behind her. She must have presented a charming picture, for Tilly saw his eyes widen as he looked down at her and his jaw seemed to slacken slightly. And suddenly she was angry.

'I really do not intend to entertain in the kitchen any longer,' she said firmly and got to her feet. 'We shall repair upstairs, if you please. To the drawing room. Come along.' And she swept past them to the stairs, not looking round to see if they were following her.

But they did. She went surging up the stairs, holding her skirts well clear, and suddenly was absurdly glad that she was wearing her lilac sarsenet in which she had always looked very fine, having put it on specially to bid Duff goodbye, and even more glad that she had managed not to cover it with specks from boiling raspberry jam, and went straight into her drawing room.

She noted at once with relief that Rosie and Lucy had been in and tidied all for the evening. The cushions had been plumped up and the tables checked for dust and the fern arrangement in the dead fireplace carefully fanned out. There were flowers in the big glass bowls on the low tables and it all looked very welcoming and charming. That will show her, she thought absurdly as she swept to her favourite seat and with a rustle of her skirts, sank into it.

Silas and Sophie came to stand in front of her and she looked up at them, feeling very much in command of the situation.

'Do sit down,' she said graciously to Silas, who bobbed his head, looked round at Sophie and then with some ceremony indicated a chair for her. She bent her head and accepted it with the air of a queen allowing a commoner to pay her his obeisance and also sank into it but without any flurry of skirts. In her case the needs of her tied-back tight skirt demanded a sinuous movement when she sat down that she executed with a practised ease, much to Silas's obvious pleasure. He took a chair close beside her, but between her and Tilly.

'You wanted me, Mr Geddes?' Tilly said and he looked at her, a little puzzled.

'Mr – why are you so – oh.'

'Miss Oliver, may I present Mr Silas Geddes,' Tilly said frostily. 'Mr Geddes, Miss Sophie Oliver.'

Sophie held out her hand. Silas touched her fingers and honour was satisfied. He turned back to Tilly.

'My dear Mrs Quentin,' he said with some emphasis. 'I am so sorry I interrupted your tête-à-tête with Miss Oliver. I would not have intruded for the world.'

'Oh, it was no intrusion,' Sophie said merrily. 'I am an old friend of the family, Mr Geddes, you understand. Calling on a sudden whim after many years of silence. Aunt Tilly was quite *bouleversée*.'

'Aunt – ' Silas skewed his head round to look at Tilly. 'Your niece?'

'No,' Tilly said shortly. 'The daughter of – the daughter of someone I used to know.'

'Indeed yes,' Sophie said, still sunnily. 'I lived here in this house for some time, you know, Mr Geddes! When I was a very little girl, of course, and dreadfully naughty, I recollect. I used to tease darling little Duff so much.' She laughed reminiscently, a sweet tinkling sound. 'One quite blushes when one remembers the sins of one's infancy, don't you find, Mr Geddes?'

'Oh, I never look back!' he said. 'Too distressing for words to look back.'

'My own sentiments entirely!' Sophie cried and clapped her hands together softly. 'Why, you are a man after my own heart, sir.'

'I am glad to hear it. And will you be coming to stay in this house again, Miss Oliver?'

She opened her eyes wide and stared at him and then looked at Tilly. 'Why, Mr Geddes, I had not even – well, what a thought! Dear me!' She looked quite nonplussed and turned her head to Tilly and lifted both hands in a pretty gesture of confusion. 'Does that seem a good notion to you, Aunt Tilly? That I should visit for a while? It would be so agreeable to see dear Duff again.'

'He is away,' Tilly said in a dampening tone. 'He has gone on an extended visit to Leicestershire. He went this very afternoon.'

'But he will be –' Silas began and Tilly turned her head to look at him and he stopped at once, seeming to realize that he had made a *bêtise*. She turned back to Sophie and spoke as smoothly as she could.

'It is a charming idea of course, Sophie, but I doubt it will be practical for you. I am, I'm afraid, running a profitable enterprise here.' She shook her head in what she knew to be mock regrets. 'The pleasure of inviting people simply to be personal guests is one I must deny myself if I am to take proper care of my establishment. It is only *paying* guests we have here at Quentin's, you see. I am indeed sorry to have to seem so inhospitable but –'

'Not at all!' Sophie said heartily. 'I fully understand. And I am glad you have been so honest with me, Aunt Tilly – not that you could ever be anything else, of course. As I told dear Aunt Tilly downstairs, Mr Geddes, she is the most honest creature alive with the most speaking of countenances. I could always tell what she was thinking, even as a tiny child.'

'I know Mrs Quentin to be the soul of probity and goodness,' Silas said and looked at Tilly with a smile. It was as though he was using his eyes to beg her pardon for speaking out of turn, but she refused to look at him with equal directness.

'That's as may be,' she said a little sharply. 'But as to staying here –'

'But of course I shall!' Sophie said. 'I can think of nothing more delightful! I have taken a dislike to my present lodgings since they are in a part of town where the ambiance is most depressing. To come here to the outer parts of town will be most agreeable.'

Tilly almost gaped at her. 'You live in lodgings alone?' she said.

'Why yes.' Sophie smiled, with an unreadable glitter in her eyes; was she being brave or brazen? Tilly could not tell. 'I am not able to have my own establishment just yet, Aunt Tilly, though I hope to one day – a house, you know – a pretty little house, somewhere agreeable and quiet where I may have a garden.' She sighed. 'I cannot see my way clear to it just yet, but I will, one day. But in the meantime,' she brightened, 'I think the idea of coming to room here is enchanting. I recall how very comfortable this house always was. To come back would be a delight.'

'But – I am not sure,' Tilly said and then gathered strength. 'What of – your mother? Do you not live together?'

There was a sharp little silence and Silas looked from one to the other, his eyes intent, and then back at Sophie who was sitting once again smoothing her gloved fingers in what was clearly a characteristic gesture for her.

'No,' she said at length, lifting her chin to look steadily at Tilly. 'That was not possible.'

'Why not?' Tilly was blunt. 'You are after all very young, Sophie. Not yet eighteen.'

'Turned eighteen,' Sophie said and a glimmer of a smile flickered over her face. 'I am getting quite old, compared with Duff, who is, as I recall, my junior by some months. I am well able to live in my own lodgings, I do assure you. And I am able to pay my way, you know!'

'Oh, you have an allowance then? Your mother –?' Tilly stopped, aware again of Silas's curiosity. Had he any manners, she thought with sudden warmth, he would have made his excuses and gone before this. But he is clearly far too interested for his own good.

'I have sufficient income,' Sophie said calmly. 'I depend on no one but myself. As to my – any other persons, suffice it to say I am an independent and quite free individual. I do as I choose and will continue to do so.' She lifted her chin with a suddenly hard expression on her face, which vanished at once as she became aware of their somewhat startled expressions, and looked up at Tilly with her original insouciance. 'So do tell me, dear Aunt, may I be one of your paying guests? I would like it above all things.'

'I – I am not sure,' Tilly said, aware she was stammering and wishing she were a good liar. If she could look this girl in the eyes and announce she had every room full it would be so much easier, but the second floor back on the far side of the house was empty, as

Silas well knew since it was only three rooms away from his own. She could not lie to Sophie anyway. The girl was right. She had never been able to hide her feelings.

'Oh, please, Aunt Tilly!' Sophie jumped up and became all at once a pliant, charming half-child, half-woman that only the hardest of hearts could resist, and she came running across the room and sank to the ground at Tilly's feet, and took her hands in her own gloved ones. 'Do say yes. I had not thought of this until just now, but now I have, it is the one thing I want most in all the world! Please let me come home, Aunt Tilly. For that is what it would be like for me. Coming home.'

Chapter Twelve

DINNER THAT EVENING was a difficult meal for Tilly, although for everyone else it was delightful. There was not a person at the table, it seemed, apart perhaps from Miss Barnetsen who displayed some signs of jealousy, who was not most taken with the charms of Miss Oliver. Even the two American girls who received less than their usual share of attention from Mr Hancock and Mr Cumming hung on her every word as she chattered brightly to all of them and distributed her attractions with apparent artlessness. She turned from one to another with the sweetest of smiles, never paid more heed to the men than to the women but managed somehow always to have the men's attention on her when she chattered girlishly to the female members of the company. And through it all she managed to make an excellent dinner, taking comfortable portions of every dish offered to her by the very attentive men who appointed themselves her guardians as they hurried from sideboard to table (for this was the normal practice on Eliza's cold collation nights) and loaded her plate with delicacies.

'What a pity dear Duff could not be here tonight!' said Miss Fleetwood. 'I remember, don't you, dear Priscilla, just how devoted he was to our little Sophie when they were small.'

'Indeed, yes,' said Miss Knapp. 'It would be interesting to hear what he recalls as well.'

Tilly looked at her sharply. Miss Knapp had said little since Sophie had joined the table, only acknowledging that she remembered her from the old days and now she looked back at Tilly with a blank expression on her face that to Tilly seemed to say far more than it hid.

When they had dined and repaired to the drawing room, to which Rosie had single-handedly fetched the tea and coffee, for Lucy too had her evening out tonight, Sophie somehow communicated to the company, without actually boasting, that she was much in demand as a pianist and singer at evening parties, which action resulted in a pretty little display of eager invitation (by the men) and bashful refusal (by Sophie) and Miss Knapp watched with a slightly sardonic eye as, at last, Sophie yielded to their demands and made her way to the piano.

She did indeed play and sing very pleasantly, her voice being a throbbing and slightly husky one that clearly captivated the men and had Mrs Grayling and the American elders sitting happily bobbing their heads in time to her song, a sprightly tale of wistful love.

'Everyone seems very captivated by Sophie,' Tilly murmured in Miss Knapp's ear during a particularly energetic chorus of the song which covered their conversation. 'She seems to have grown up very sweetly.'

'Hmm,' said Miss Knapp. 'Sweet is as sweetly does.'

Tilly lifted her brows at that. 'Now why do you say that, Miss Knapp?'

'I have a better memory than some,' she said. 'Better than Miss Fleetwood's, and she should know better. We had the teaching of Miss Sophie, you will recall, when she was small and my memory is of a most wilful little minx who demanded her own way in all things. And in my experience, as bends the twig so grows the tree.'

'But there is no sign that she is being wilful or demanding her own way tonight,' Tilly said, not sure why she was defending Sophie, but feeling a need to argue with Miss Knapp. Perhaps for her own sake? she wondered briefly and then fixed her attention on her companion again.

Miss Knapp held out her cup for more tea and shook her head. 'You must not be beguiled,' she said. 'She is at present having what she most desires. Everyone's attention. If for any reason the party stopped being so taken with her music and conversation I think you would find her in a very different humour.'

'She wants to come and live here again,' Tilly said abruptly and Miss Knapp turned and looked at her closely.

'Does she, then?' she said after a long pause. 'Well, well. And her mother?'

'Well, no. It seems they do not live together. I have the impression Sophie has her own income and largely runs her own life.'

'At her age?' Miss Knapp was scandalized. 'I believe strongly in women's education, Mrs Quentin, and the right of girls to show their capabilities as well as do their brothers, but that does not mean I countenance hoydenish behaviour. And for a girl of eighteen – for that is her age, is it not? – to live alone seems to me to be quite shocking.'

'I find it odd, too,' Tilly murmured as the song finished to a spatter of applause and somewhat noisy demands were made for an encore. 'But it is difficult to know what to do. She tells me she has disagreeable lodgings in Covent Garden and had intended to move herself in the not too distant future. She says she came to Brompton by chance and called on me only for old memories' sake and – and now she wishes to remain here.'

'Hmm,' Miss Knapp said and sat and brooded, watching the people clustered around the piano as at last Sophie insisted on giving way at the keyboard and her place was taken by Mr Cumming and Mr Hancock, who offered to sing a comic duet.

'It must not be outrageous, now, gentlemen!' said Mr Lampeter in a jocular tone. 'It would never do to see us on our way to Paris tomorrow with the refrain of a bawdy song in our ears, now would it?'

'I am sure,' Sophie said, 'that no guest of my dear Aunt Tilly would ever sing any song that was not perfectly respectable. That is what is so delightful about this house. It clearly offers all the comforts of a well-conducted residence with none of the drawbacks of the usual sort of accommodation that is offered to those who lack a home of their own. Isn't that so, Mr Geddes?'

'Very much so,' Silas said and smiled at her, and then at Tilly. He was sitting in a chair not too far from the piano, almost a part of the group around it and yet aloof, but his attention, Tilly had not been able to help noticing, had been fixed throughout on Sophie. 'That is why we are all here, after all.'

'Well, I have to say,' Mr Lampeter said in his easy American way, 'it's suited us down to the ground! A real home from home – only sorry we have to leave tomorrow for Paris, as this charming young lady would have been so nice a friend for our two young ones here –' His comprehensive gesture took in Miss McCool as well as Miss Lampeter, both of whom simpered a little. 'But perhaps we'll try to stop by with you on our way back home, Mrs Quentin, so that we can all meet up again.'

'It will be delightful to have you here among us, Miss Oliver,' Mrs Grayling put in eagerly, 'if you will always sing so charmingly in the evenings.' And she beamed happily at Sophie, who smiled sweetly back.

Not to be outdone, the two young men, now sitting side by side at the piano and waiting to start their song, nodded and cried, 'Yes, indeed, yes!' and, 'The sooner the better, Miss Oliver!' Sophie cast a glance over her shoulder at Tilly as if to say, 'You see how it is? What can I do but come here? You cannot refuse me.'

'And think how pleased Duff will be when he returns from Leicestershire to find so old a friend ensconced in his home,' Mrs Grayling twittered on. 'Oh, it will be so delightful for him! And for us – as I am sure will your song, Mr Hancock,' she added hastily as Mr Hancock turned and looked at her a touch irritably as he struck a note on the piano.

They all settled down to listen to the comic song, which was a tolerably respectable although noisy one about a young man who was too bashful to speak his heart to his young lady and so constantly used words that could be misunderstood, and as the sound rose and with it the appreciative laughter of the listeners, Tilly was again thrown into confusion.

Duff. Never mind what her other guests said, never mind that they all took it for granted that from now on Sophie Oliver was to be one of their number; if she chose to tell Sophie it was out of the question then indeed she would, she told herself. But Duff –

She tried to dismiss her freshly aroused doubts, but it was not easy. Miss Knapp, sitting there beside her and watching the group at the piano with small evidence of approval had made her even more unsure, and yet –

I must start at the beginning, she thought then and did so, very deliberately. Why is Sophie Oliver here? Because I sent Jem to look for her. Why did I send Jem to look for her? Because I was worried about Duff. What is it that worried you about Duff? Why, that he was making unsuitable friends and becoming involved in – well, let that be. You wanted to feel sure that he met suitable girls and recalled his close attachment to this particular girl, when he was a child. And of course, Duff himself had in a sense chosen Sophie by saying that that wretched Lord Patrick reminded him of her. That was why Tilly had thought of her at all. And why she had set Jem on to finding her.

Oh dear, she thought, looking across at the piano where both young men, while singing heartily, were directing all their attention towards Sophie, have I made matters worse rather than better? Will Duff, once he sees her again, recall her with affection or will he remember only being angry when she went away? And if he is interested in her, will there be jealousy and unhappiness in the house because of Mr Hancock and Mr Cumming? If Duff competes with them for Sophie's attentions –

And apart from all that, she thought as her ideas went sliding away from her like inexperienced skaters on a winter pond, what is Sophie herself like now? Miss Knapp sees her as a minx, and yet perhaps that is unfair. Everyone else here finds her delightful. Just see how they are all happy and amused in her company; and not just the young men who might be expected to behave so. Mr and Mrs Grayling, and the Lampeters and McCools, and even Mr Gee, seem to enjoy her company. The evenings are always congenial but I can't remember it ever being quite so enjoyable for them all as it is tonight. And if a new vivacious girl amongst them has this effect, how can that be anything but good?

'It is clear that she will be moving in very soon,' Miss Knapp said in her ear and Tilly came back out of her reverie with a start and glanced at her. Miss Knapp was looking at Sophie who was now sitting beside the two American girls and giggling with them. 'Everyone has taken her to their heart, have they not? Perhaps we are being less than fair, Mrs Quentin. It was her mother I found to be, shall we say, not precisely the sort of person I would regard as a friend. It was most wrong of me to tar her daughter with the same brush, however. You say they no longer live together. Then, I suppose that could be a recommendation for Sophie, if we are honest. If she has found a way to live respectably alone without her mother at her age, that has to be to her credit. The girl deserves a secure and respectable home in which to live, if that is the case. It seems to me, on mature reflection, that it is no less than your Christian duty, Mrs Quentin, to agree to her joining us. I would have no objection, certainly, now I have had time to think.'

Miss Knapp, who had as the first ever guest a certain standing in the house in her own and everyone else's eyes, including Tilly's, spoke so firmly that Tilly wavered even more. Miss Knapp, she recalled, together with Miss Fleetwood, had been set against there ever being male guests in Quentin's but had given in to the suggestion from Tilly when Mr Gee had first requested a room, albeit with great concern. They had agreed only because Tilly had assured them he would be quiet and well mannered, and had been most generous in their admission that their fears of the house being ruined by masculinity had been unfounded. So now, if Miss Knapp wanted Tilly to accept Sophie and gave such good reasons for doing so, shouldn't Tilly be equally magnanimous? And hadn't she too been wondering whether she had unfairly tarred Sophie with her mother's brush?

'Oh dear,' she said aloud. 'It is difficult sometimes to know just what is right.'

'Then I think in that case you should give way to others' counsel,' advised Miss Knapp. 'I shall speak to Miss Fleetwood and see what she says and let you know.' She got to her feet magisterially and shook out her skirts.

'And to Miss Barnetsen?' Tilly asked and Miss Knapp frowned.

'Not at all. She came here after we did and has no voice in the matter,' she said stiffly and went across the room to speak in a low voice to Miss Fleetwood, who had been sitting observing Sophie with as much absorption as everyone else.

Tilly watched them as they whispered together, as much in a state of confusion as ever. It seemed absurd that someone as sensible as she thought herself to be, who ran this large and very busy household with very little trouble, should be confused by so simple a matter as whether or not to accept a particular guest for a room she had to spare, but there it was. Her own emotions were entangled in this decision through Duff and her memories of Dorcas and that made it hard for her to think sensibly.

Now she would, she told herself, be sensible and listen to her oldest guests, who would be as concerned as she was to maintain the happiness and health of the house, for their interests were her interests. And vice versa. I shall do just as they say, she promised herself again, as Miss Knapp straightened her back and returned to the chair at Tilly's side.

'And that is how it happened,' Tilly said to Eliza, as they stood at the front door watching Rosie and Lucy bring in the many boxes and bags that comprised Sophie Oliver's luggage. 'I was, I cannot deny, in a great lather about it. You were not here or I would have spoken to you too, although of course, the decision has to be mine.'

'Of course, Mum,' Eliza said woodenly and stood there with her reddened hands carefully crossed on her blue gaberdine gown. Above her neat white collar her face had the round redness of a new apple, but there was none of the usual good humour in her expression. She looked, indeed, almost as though she were scowling.

'Really, Eliza, I did not decide in haste!' she said, now irritated. 'I was, I don't deny, in some confusion about whether or not she should come to us, but as Miss Knapp pointed out, we must not regard her except as herself! To feel she is but an extension of her mother, and bears her faults in herself, is hardly just!'

'Miss Knapp said that?' Eliza said and swivelled her eyes sideways to look at her.

'Indeed she did,' Tilly said firmly.

'Hmm,' said Eliza, who held Miss Knapp's opinion in high regard. 'I s'pose she should know, Mum.'

'Indeed she should, for she taught Sophie just as she taught Duff! And Duff of course will be delighted, won't he.' She tried to make the last a statement rather than a question and seemed to succeed, for Eliza nodded.

'Well, there's no question of that, Mum,' she conceded. 'When Mr Duff gets back, he'll be well pleased, I'm sure. I dare say I'm not being fair at that. It's just that I remember so well, Mum, the way that Mrs Leander treated me and the way that Dorcas put airs on and –'

'The sins of the parent – and grandparent – are not necessarily those of the child,' Tilly said, and again was very firm. 'We must be *fair*, Eliza.'

'We don't have much choice now, Mum,' Eliza said with a flash of humour as Rosie toiled up the steps with the final box and at last the cab went bowling away, leaving Sophie to pick her delicate way up the steps, her skirts held high out of the dust to display a very pretty pair of kid boots encasing the most elegant of ankles. 'Seein' as she's here. I'll be off to my kitchen, Mum, if you'll excuse me.' She turned to go. 'Though I have to say there's somethin' botherin' me still about this whole business, only I can't put my finger on it, like. But I dare say I'm just being foolish.' And away she went in a rustle of crisp gaberdine as Sophie arrived in the hall, smiling up at Tilly as she stepped over the threshold.

'Well, this is nice, dear Aunt Tilly,' she said. 'I feel so happy to be returning home! I have the first of my payments ready so we shall settle that before we do anything else –'

'Oh, no!' Tilly was mortified. 'I present the bills at the end of each month.'

'But I insist,' Sophie said. 'It would not be right not to pay in advance. I feel that most strongly. It is asking too much of you, even though you knew me in childhood, to take me on trust. So, if you please, we will settle this now. I will have to take my bags out at once and move on if you refuse me!' And she smiled at Tilly.

'Oh, for heaven's sake!' Tilly said and turned away. 'Such a fuss! Of course you may pay in advance if you choose – some people do on occasion, of course, if they are to stay only a short time, so it is not all that – anyway, come along to my room where I deal with such matters.'

It was not until she had put away her books, locked in her box the sovereigns that Sophie put into her hand and given her a receipt, and sent Lucy to take her to her room and assist her in settling in, that Tilly realized what she had done. She had been given the opportunity to turn Sophie away at the very last minute. If she had refused to take her payment in advance Sophie had said that she would take her boxes and leave, at once. And Tilly had taken her money.

Clearly, she thought, this was inevitable. I don't know why I made such a fuss. Sophie is home, as she says, and here to stay, and why should she not be? She can do no harm to anyone.

Chapter Thirteen

'I BELIEVE ALL is going well,' Tilly said carefully. 'It would indeed appear that I worried needlessly, so forgive me for seeming to have been ungrateful to you, Jem. I was nasty –'

'Well, I did warn you that there might be trouble,' Jem said. 'So I was quite prepared for your doubts. And you were not nasty. I have never known you to be so, and don't think you could be. Ever.'

She did not look at him, not wanting to encourage him to make any more declarations of approval of her; they all too easily turned into declarations of affection and she suffered enough guilt over Jem as it was. Instead she concentrated on the sewing she had in her lap, keeping her head down.

'She is most charming about the house, I must say. At breakfast she keeps everyone cheerful and starts the day off for everyone most agreeably. There are some new people here, since the McCools and the Lampeters went – they are from France, and they have a young daughter of about Sophie's age. She is, I am afraid, sadly plain, but she seems to be on excellent terms with Sophie and they go about together and shop and so forth and chatter away in French. Sophie seems very glad to have the opportunity to improve her grasp of the language.'

'And is that all she does?' Jem said, leaning back in his chair. He had been sitting forwards, a little eagerly but at Tilly's rejection of his warm words had accepted his *congé*, just as he usually did. 'Has she no other occupation?'

'Oh, she rides in the morning with Silas,' Tilly said, her head still down over her needle.

'Silas?' Jem's voice sharpened a little.

Tilly felt herself redden. 'Mr Geddes.'

'You have become good friends, then.' Jem's voice sounded as usual, but Tilly was not deceived. He was hurt that she should be on first name terms with a man other than himself, and now she lifted her chin and looked at him.

'It was impossible not to,' she said. 'He has been – well, he was very kind to Duff, you know. Took him riding when he was so miserable the day after – when he drank too much, you remember, and generally helped him greatly. I tried to insist we remain a little aloof, but when a person is your son's friend, you know, it is difficult to be formal.'

She knew she was being mendacious, but it had been worth it, for now Jem relaxed again, content with her explanation.

'Ah, I see,' he said. 'Of course, if he has become Duff's friend then there is every reason that – tell me, when will Duff return? It will be most interesting to hear of his experiences in Leicestershire.' He looked around the drawing room where they were sitting so comfortably on this warm afternoon, and shook his head in a sort of awe. 'Who would have thought that I, the son of a shopkeeper, would be so comfortable to visit in such a room as this? It is beyond possibility that I will ever spend time in a duke's house, but to be so warmly acquainted with people who do, and to be able to hear about it from their own lips is most –'

'Oh, pooh!' Tilly said vigorously, glad the subject had been turned and therefore being a little more vigorous than she might have been. 'I will not be impressed by grandeur, and nor should you, Jem. You are worth as much as any duke, I do assure you and your home is as elegant as his, in its own way, and no less special than this one. You must not let notions such as these hold you down.'

He lifted his brows at her. 'Well! You speak like Daniel Carter, who keeps the farrier's shop up near Knightsbridge Barracks! He is a republican, he swears, and yearns for the day when we have a Commonwealth again as in Cromwell's time and wants an end to lords and ladies. Are you such a one? I never thought so.'

'Well, the new thinking, you know, is most interesting. I have been so busy about running my house that I have not thought as much as I might about wider affairs, but I am now remedying that. I have been to a couple of meetings of the Society for the Propagation of Scientific and Philosophic Knowledge and learned much. It is not inevitable, you know, that there should be those who have all the wealth and others who suffer poverty, any more than it is right that one class of person should always be regarded as subservient to another. Are we not all of the same species? Do we not all develop from the same source?'

'Darwin,' Jem said with an air of discovery. 'You have been hearing the ideas of Darwin.'

'And why not?' Tilly looked at him sharply. 'They are very interesting and show the way to an understanding of the world that I never had before.'

Jem looked troubled. 'Well, as to that, I cannot deny that widening one's understanding is a good thing, but is it a good thing to set the world upside down? And it can't be anything but upside down to take the world as God made it and seek to find new reasons for it.'

'Well,' Tilly said, knowing she would shock Jem sorely but feeling a little reckless, 'as to God making the world, precisely – we cannot even be sure of that. The story told in the Bible is an agreeable one, to be sure, but hardly likely, in any scientific way. I find Mr Darwin's ideas much more acceptable.'

'Dear me!' said Jem, staring. 'You have indeed learned new ideas, Tilly! I am quite amazed.' He was silent for a while and then went on, 'And did you just go to these meetings because –' He stopped, leaving the question hanging in the air, looking at her anxiously.

She had to answer it. 'Mr Geddes invited me,' she said, her head still down over her industrious needle. 'He thought I might be interested and as I told you, I find that I am. Now, Jem, will you take some more Malmsey? I have this bottle set aside just for you, since I know it to be a favourite with you.'

'You're very kind,' Jem said abstractedly and accepted his refilled glass from her hand. 'These meetings –'

'Well, if you wish you must come sometime,' Tilly said and put aside her sewing. 'Now, if you will forgive me, my dear friend. I must go and deal with the matter of tonight's dinner. As you know, Duff will return this afternoon, in a couple of hours or so in my estimation, and we must welcome him home properly!'

'Yes, indeed,' Jem said. 'Shall I be on my way then?' He sounded defeated, prepared as always to do as she asked him, but far from happy and she leaned forwards and patted his hand affectionately.

'Oh, Jem, of course not! You stay here as long as you choose and rest and drink your Malmsey. I wish only to check matters with Eliza. She is the one who is doing all the work, of course. She and Lucy – if I seek to join in today I fear she'll be most put out! But there may be stores she needs and I have the keys. I shall return in a few moments.' And she escaped.

It was true that she would have at some time to dole out Eliza's special stores, but her main concern had been to be free of Jem for a little while. It was her own fault that he had become so heavy all of a sudden; she should not have mentioned the way her mind was moving under Silas Geddes's prompting and certainly should not have mentioned Silas Geddes's name. Jem's affection for her was too deep and true and constant to be so abused, she thought as she went downstairs, her skirts whispering on the steps behind her. To let him know that there is another man whose attentions are not unwelcome to me is hardly fair.

Not unwelcome to me. She stopped in the hallway, just before the green baize door that led to the kitchen stairs and pondered. She had been trying not to think about the matter this past few days, but without success. Since Sophie had arrived, somehow she had been forced to think about it. And she did not like what she discovered in the depths of her mind and heart.

Silas Geddes had become too interesting to her. She found his conversation absorbing, his company deeply enjoyable, his physical presence exciting. When he came into the drawing room in the evenings she knew it even if she was not actually looking at the door to see him; it was as though a new lamp had been fetched in to make the whole room brighter. If he lingered to talk to other people before coming to sit beside her and talk to her, she became restless and irritable. And worst of all, resentful.

It was that which perturbed her most. Life had changed at Quentin's since Sophie Oliver had moved in. Now, rather than everyone scattering about their own affairs in the evenings or going to their rooms, they all congregated in the drawing room for at least an hour after dinner, often longer, while Sophie and the young men played and sang and made jokes. There was much laughter and jollity and it was clear that the social atmosphere in the house had risen considerably. 'Every night is like a party,' as Miss Fleetwood had said with an odd mix of waspishness and approval and everyone liked it that way.

Including Silas Geddes. He would come into the drawing room after everyone else, as a rule, having the habit of taking a brisk walk along the road after meals, 'for the sake of my digestion', as he would say, and Tilly would be there in her usual chair, presiding over the coffee and tea trays and waiting for him. She tried to pretend she was not, tried to avoid noticing when he arrived, but it was impossible. She was, every evening, on tenterhooks until he arrived, tense with a sort of animal excitement that startled her, but which she had to admit she enjoyed.

And he would stop beside the piano to speak to Sophie and make a jocular comment of some kind, and every time it felt as though someone had pushed a sharp pointed stick into her ribs and made her breath catch. Usually he would come to sit beside her almost immediately; he rarely lingered by the piano among everyone else for longer than a few moments, but it always disturbed her to see him with them.

Am I jealous? she asked herself bleakly, staring at the green baize on the door and her hand on the fastening. At my age, am I jealous of a slip of a girl young enough to be my daughter? One I have known since her infancy? How can that be?

'Very easily,' she murmured aloud and bit her lip and glanced behind her to see if anyone had overheard. She must be more careful; her habit of introspection and speaking aloud to herself had always been a part of her. But now it could betray her deepest feelings and they had to be secret.

I shall ask Silas to take Jem to a meeting as well, she thought then as, at last, she pushed the door open and went down the stairs into the kitchen. That will reassure Jem that I am still his good friend and will show Silas that he is not alone in finding my company agreeable and will somehow help me to understand how foolish I am being. For I am too old and too set in my ways to even consider a new attachment to a man. Is it not bad enough I have been married twice? I cannot possibly wish to change my situation now.

In the kitchen it was clear that Eliza was in one of her rare takings. Generally a sweet-tempered woman of great capability, there were times when she did become ruffled and less in control of matters than she might be, and when that happened to Eliza, everyone around her, with the exception of Tilly of course, suffered it. Her tongue became razor sharp and her speed of work quite terrifying. She would whirl about her domain like a dervish, getting through a vast amount of work, and expect her minions to be as fast and capable as she was herself. Since no one could be, the result was Eliza in a rage with them and they in tears and sulks. Tilly now walked into the middle of just such a scene.

Dora was standing by the scullery door with her apron thrown over her face, in a flood of tears, and a scatter of broken shards of a dish at her feet. Lucy was standing shrinking against the dresser, while Rosie could just be seen peering over Dora's heaving shoulders from her place of safety in the scullery. Eliza was standing with both hands balled into fists on the scrubbed wood of the kitchen table and her face was scarlet with fury.

'You clumsy limb of Satan!' she was roaring as Tilly came to the top of the stairs. 'If there was a scratch on the floor you'd trip over it, you clumsy creature! That's the third plate you've broken this month and this time you pay for it, Missy, and pay hard. I won't have you breaking the china over our heads like this for want of a bit of –'

'Eliza!' Tilly said, lifting her voice above the hubbub. 'Eliza, what *is* going on?'

Dora lifted her head from her apron, peered at Tilly and went off into another even louder paroxysm of weeping, and Lucy at the dresser began to whimper as Eliza whirled and glared at the stairs.

'This – this lump of idiocy don't know she's alive, Mum, and so I tell you! She wanders around in a dream all because of some stupid notions of her own and breaks your dishes and wastes my time and I won't have it, you hear me? I won't have it!'

'I am sure we can sort this out,' Tilly said soothingly and came down into the kitchen. 'Now, Dora, you tell me. Why is Eliza so angry with you? What have you done?'

'Done?' Eliza said wrathfully. 'What has she done? So busy whispering to Madam out there that she lets the best big platter we got go sliding out of her hands and there it lies, as much use as she is, and I wish it was she who was in pieces at my feet, for she's no more use than a pile of broken pottery at that and fit only to be swept up and thrown out!'

'Eliza,' Tilly said and looked at her directly. 'I am speaking to Dora, if you please.'

Eliza opened her mouth, took a breath as if to speak and thought better of it, and set to work on the pastry that was lying on the table in front of her, beating it to submission in a way that made Tilly think at the back of her mind that tonight's pies might lack their usual lightness of texture. Tilly turned to Dora and said quietly, 'Now, Dora, stop that caterwauling at once and speak to me.'

Dora gulped, snorted, sniffed and managed to obey and Tilly put a hand on her shoulder to push her out into the scullery, nodding at Rosie to leave them. Rosie went with alacrity, scuttling out to the kitchen to set to work with ostentatious busyness, turning the handle of a mincer fixed to the other side of Eliza's table, nodding to Lucy to come and help her feed the pieces of meat she was grinding into the hopper. And Tilly went and leaned against the shelf at the back of the scullery and said quietly to Dora, 'So?'

Dora snivelled but managed to speak. 'I spoke out of turn, Mum. I shoul'n ha' said nothin', but it was only meant as a joke, like. I never knew she'd get into such a takin'.'

'What did you say?' Tilly was patient. Sorting out servants' squabbles was a necessary part of a day's work for any lady running a household and she was luckier than most; it was a rare enough happening at Quentin's. But she still knew how to cope. 'You had better tell me, for if you don't I cannot know how to deal with the matter at all. I need to know whether it is right that you should pay for the broken dish, you see. If you were indeed at fault, then of course you must. But if it was not entirely you to blame –' She stopped invitingly.

'Oh, Mum!' Dora said, looking as though she would start wailing again, given the least encouragement. 'I only said to Rosie as Eliza was looking tired and not surprising seein' what time he went last night and all.'

Tilly tilted her head in puzzlement. 'Who went where last night?'

'Why, her follower, Mum. Her Mr Reagan, Mum, what visits here. He stayed till gone three last night, creeping out up the area steps like a burglar! I saw 'im on account I woke up when I 'eard 'em whisperin' out there.'

Tilly was dumbstruck. She had never attempted to control Eliza's friends in any way, and had over the years been most concerned that she might be missing her chances of marriage and motherhood because she made so little effort to meet potential sweethearts, but Eliza had always stoutly denied any interest in such nonsense. To hear now that she had a follower and one who visited her late at night was a revelation.

'He left at –'

'Yes, Mum, three o'clock. I got a clock o' my own, and I checked.' There was a little glitter in Dora's eyes now, as though she was beginning to see that she might have her own back on the hectoring Eliza. 'It ain't the first time neither. My room sees right over the area steps on this side of the 'ouse like and I always 'ear people come and go. And he comes late, after you've all had your dinner, like, and we've cleared up and gone to our beds, and stays late, too. But never so late as last night. And I just said to Rosie –'

'Yes,' Tilly said; trying to accommodate this information about someone she had always known so well and never doubted to be anything but totally honest in every way was difficult, to say the least. 'And I must tell you that it is none of your affair. Such visitors as Eliza chooses to have are her own affair and the hours she keeps are also none of your business. She is my housekeeper, not a cook or maid only, and as such is entitled to privileges you may not have. So you must stop spying on her from your room – and if you do not then I shall see to it that you are moved to the other side of the house, which as you know is not so agreeable since the outlook is not so pleasant, and then you will not be able to meddle at all. I am not surprised that Eliza was angry and especially so if your silly gossiping made you clumsy. You must pay for the plate if Eliza says so. She is in charge of such matters and I will not interfere. Now, go and apologize to Eliza for being so ill-mannered as to gossip about her and then be about your work.'

Dora's face crumpled as though she were going to weep again, but Tilly looked at her so sternly she thought better of it, and wiping her nose on the back of her hand, she went up to Eliza at the kitchen table.

'I beg your pardon, Eliza,' she muttered. 'Like Madam says, I'm sorry I gossiped about you.'

'Hmph,' said Eliza, not looking up as she slapped a round of pastry over a pie dish and with expert fingers trimmed the excess away to leave it neat and ready to be filled with the meat mixture which Lucy and Rosie had now finished. 'That's as may be. Now, get on with your work. There's the dinin' room waiting to be set and the drawin' room to be checked and hot water jugs for the evenin' to be prepared. Be quick about it, now.'

Gratefully the three maids escaped and Tilly stood waiting till they had all vanished past the green baize door and then looked at Eliza.

She finished the pie, having filled it and poured in the gravy and seasoning, and then set the last trimmings in place on the top before sliding it into the oven behind her and straightening her back to stand without turning, staring down at the range.

'Dear Eliza,' Tilly said gently. 'Why did you not tell me you had a follower? I am so happy for you – I wouldn't have you think for the world that you need keep such a matter a secret from me. I rejoice for you, indeed I do!'

'Oh, Mum,' Eliza said. 'Oh, Mum,' and turned and looked at Tilly and then did something that amazed and alarmed Tilly in equal measure.

She burst into tears.

Chapter Fourteen

TO SAY THAT Tilly was aghast was to put it at its very lowest. She had never seen Eliza so distressed. There had been times in her very early days in the household, as a child of little more than thirteen years or so, when, in a state of almost overwhelming heroine-worship for Tilly, the young Eliza had been exceedingly emotional. But never like this, Tilly was sure.

She sat in the chair beside the kitchen range, rocking herself almost frantically and weeping copiously into her hands, which she held over her face, in the main silently, though the occasional tearing sobs escaped her. Tilly could only crouch at her feet and stroke her knee and murmur at her and wait for the storm to pass, while at the same time attempting to control the great wash of anxiety that overcame her.

Eliza was her prop and stay, the centre of the house and therefore in many ways the centre of Tilly's life. Duff was her best beloved, Jem was her good friend, and she was dealing as best as she could with her current fascination for Silas Geddes, but Eliza – Eliza was Eliza, as much a part of Tilly as her hands or her head. To see her in such a state of unbridled misery could only be an occasion of great agitation in Tilly herself.

Not that she showed it. She just remained there beside Eliza until the storm at last washed itself out and the tears dwindled and Eliza let herself be gently persuaded to lie against the back of the chair, exhausted and drained, her eyes closed, the puffy lids red and painful to look at above the streaked round cheeks.

'Please to tell me what it is, Eliza!' Tilly said at length. 'I can't help you if I don't know.'

At last Eliza opened her eyes painfully and looked bleakly at Tilly. She looked so desolate that Tilly felt her own eyes sting with tears of sympathy.

'It's a sorry story, Mum,' Eliza said at last. She was very hoarse from all her weeping. 'I'd thought to have different news to tell you – difficult in one way, perhaps, but – well, not this, Mum. I never expected this.'

'Expected what, Eliza?' Tilly was as gentle as she knew how to be. 'Please to start at the beginning.'

'The beginning –' Eliza said and then, extraordinarily, managed to twist her face into a sort of smile. 'You could say it was the parson learning me to read at home in the village what begun it all, Mum. If I'd never learned to read I'd ha' been better off.'

'Eliza?' Tilly said, puzzled and fearful now. Was the poor girl losing her mind in some way?

Eliza shook her head. 'Oh, it's just a stupid fancy of mine, Mum. It's the reading circle, do you see.'

'Not entirely,' Tilly said candidly. 'I can't imagine what could happen there that would make you so very – so unhappy. It is but a church meeting, after all, as I understood it, well supervised and run by the vicar.'

Again Eliza's lips twisted in a sort of ghastly smile. 'Well, so it is, Mum, as far as what happens there in Cottage Place goes. But it's where you meet people, 'n't it? You thought it was all for females, Mum. But it wasn't. Like I said, we had gentlemen visitors from time to time –' She swallowed hard. 'Some of 'em every time.'

Tilly began to understand. 'What's his name, Eliza?' she said gently.

'Reagan, Mum. Octavius Reagan. Irish o' course, but I didn't – I mean, I was never one to hold things against people. A person can't help bein' what they are and he was born into popery, I said to myself, so it's no blame to him – especially as he was coming to our church now. I mean, I thought he'd left all that. So I didn't fret over it. And like I said, he seemed good enough for them at St Paul's to have him there and he went to services and all. The vicar seemed to like him – oh, so good looking, Mum! So very good looking!'

Clearly Eliza was not speaking of the vicar of St Paul's and Tilly sighed a little at the yearning note in her voice.

'You were beguiled, I think, Eliza.'

'Well, Mum, he was such a gentleman and read so lovely and wasn't a bit insolent when he was about me, the way some men are. I got used to the silly ones, what makes eyes at you and calls it making love when it's nothing of the sort. It's only trying to be clever. He never tried to be clever, do you see, always the perfect gentleman, quick to take off his hat and bow, and ever so carefully spoken. A lovely voice, and very good at talking real long words. I thought I'd found my special one, like it says in the stories in my magazine, Mum, I really did.'

'Has he been unkind to you, Eliza?' Tilly thought she could probe a little now, for Eliza was beginning to recover. Some of the swelling about her eyes had gone down and her face was less woebegone. She was sitting up more erectly, too.

'Unkind? I s'pose you could call it that.'

There was a long silence then, as Eliza sat staring over Tilly's shoulder at the window with glazed eyes. Tilly gave her a few moments and then said a little more briskly, 'Well, Eliza?'

'He – he said as we'd get wed. I told him, very direct, I told him, as I was a good woman, and wouldn't have no nonsense from no one as wasn't man enough to do the proper thing. So he said we'd be wed, but then I said as I could never leave you, no matter what and he said that would be no trouble, we could still be wed and live close by and I could come and work here with you in the days, as long as he had the nights, and I thought, well, it seemed all right, Mum. I knew he had only a little money got from his dad or so he said, and was looking about him for employment as a farrier which was his trade he said, in Ireland, though I have to say he looked more of a gentleman than that, but he loved horses and knew about them well enough, so I thought, well, we can get him a nice berth hereabouts and I can go on lookin' after you and Quentin's and it'd all be lovely.'

Her eyes filled with tears once more but they weren't the desperate ones of a while ago, and Tilly said nothing, knowing it would be better for Eliza to shed them. After a while Eliza blew her nose and wiped her eyes on the corner of her apron and started again.

'I should ha' guessed, I s'pose. A man what's got no occupation and always dressed so smart and has time to read so many books – he's read more'n me and you know how I reads night after night, Mum – I should ha' known he did more sitting about than anything else, but there it is. I suppose I wanted to think well of the man I was to wed.'

'But you are not to be wed, now, Eliza?' Tilly was trying not to let her heart sink at the thought of losing Eliza to marriage, for she knew perfectly well that whatever scheme Eliza devised for working at Quentin's by day, it would never really serve. Tilly would lose her for good and the thought was a painful one. But she wanted to be fair to Eliza, and if her feelings were engaged and she wanted to wed this man, however unsuitable she, Tilly, might think him, then wed him she would and with Tilly's aid and blessing. She would do all she could to see that this man married Eliza, if that was what Eliza wanted.

The tears spilled over again and tracked down Eliza's cheeks. 'No, Mum,' she said huskily. 'Here you are – it was – I found it this morning under my pillow when I made my bed.'

She pushed a piece of paper at Tilly, who took it and sank back to sit on her heels on the hearthrug.It was a sheet of writing paper, thin of quality but dressed with fancy scroll decoration that bled through to the other side. It was the sort of cheap showy stuff sold by door-to-door pedlars to cooks and housemaids and offered in fairgrounds as prizes on the shot-gun ranges. Tilly glanced up at Eliza.

'You'd best read it,' Eliza said drearily. 'It's all there.' Obediently Tilly bent her head and began to read, though it was not easy, since the handwriting was rather like the scrolls on the notepaper, over elaborate and very showy.

'My dear Eliza, it is with regret that I pen this missive, my dear heart, as I did not wish to hurt you, not at all. When I started our friendship, I do not deny I thought it all a great gas, you are very merry and funny. But I did not intend it to be more than a gas. You see, dear Eliza, not to beat about the bush, I have a wife in Belfast. It was agreed with her I should go and set us up in England or in America if I could not find the right opportunities in London, and I have not found those opportunities, as I will not be any longer a poor farrier, to that I have sworn. I have better things in me than that. So I shall be sailing off to Canada on the next ship out of Liverpool for a ticket to Montreal is a better buy than a ticket for New York or Boston, and I can always work my way south and anyway I do not wish my wife to know where I have gone for she is no great shakes to me and I know you would not tell her even if you knew her which you do not. By the time you read this letter, I shall be well away on the train so do not seek to find me, not that you would I think, for all you said you loved me, as did I love you, as far as I was able, but you should not have spoke of weddings, my dear Eliza, for it alarms a man powerfully, does such talk. Especially when he is as I am, with three small ones already on his quiver at home in Belfast who even if I do not see them again are of my blood and quite enough too. I trust that you will remember always that I thought you a fine bonny girl and a fair armful of joy. I hope you had joy of me as I of you. I bid you good luck and say you need not worry more about leaving your good mistress, on account of you do not have to. I hope you will wish me well in my journey to Canada which they tell me is a wild country but good in opportunity. Yrs. v. obediently. Octavius Aloysius Reagan, Esq.'

There was a long silence as Tilly gave the letter back to Eliza, who sat and stared at it for a long while. Then Tilly said with real care, 'Oh dear, Eliza. I am so sorry.'

'Not as sorry as I am,' Eliza said harshly. 'That I should have been so beguiled! It makes me sick, it does. It makes me fair sick.'

She looked down at the paper in her hand and then with a vicious twist of her wrist hurled it into the firebox of the range. It lay there in the embers for a moment and then flared into life, making a sudden vivid picture of Eliza's face before it curled and died in a heap of ash that could not be seen against the coals. They both watched it and then at last Tilly moved and got to her feet, wincing a little at the way her limbs had become numbed by her prolonged crouch beside Eliza.

Eliza became aware of that and at once jumped to her feet and made Tilly sit in the rocker. 'Oh, Mum, I should be ashamed to worry you so! I would never have said a word if it hadn't been for – well, if Dora hadn't – I thought no one knew, do you see, and it never entered my head that nasty creature was spying on me. I'd take it kindly, Mum, if you let her go. She's not that good at her work and I could do with someone with more sense, I truly could. You can give her a good enough character to get a new situation and then we can see her away. I'd not be able to keep up my head, you see, with her watching me and knowing.'

'Yes, I think you're right,' Tilly said. 'I shall help her find a new place and seek another girl to help Lucy and Rosie – but Eliza –' She looked at Eliza for a moment and then let her glance slide away. 'All I can say is I am sorry. It hurts dreadfully to be so used by a man – to be lied to and – I do wish you to know that I have every sympathy for you.'

Eliza went out to the scullery and came back with a jug of milk from the larder. She set it on the table and then with her usual methodical movements, took cups and saucers and a teapot and the caddy from the dresser, and set to making a pot of tea with the kettle which was, as always, sitting on the range and just at boiling point. Then she gave Tilly her tea and took her own and sat with it on the little coal box that stood at the side of the fender. They sipped in silence for a while and then Eliza took a deep breath and lifted her chin to look at Tilly.

'I had best tell you all, Mum,' she said, still with that husky note in her voice. 'Or all that might be –' and Tilly looked at her encouragingly her head to one side, but saying nothing.

'He said we was to be wed,' Eliza said after another long pause. 'Soon, he said, and I believed him. Why should I not?'

'Yes, I understand, Eliza,' Tilly was soothing. 'But he lied, so you aren't to blame for –'

'I am to blame for being such a fool as to believe him,' Eliza said passionately. 'To believe his talk about the high holiness of love and how a man has to be a man and a truly loving woman proves her love and never thinks there is anything wrong in what passes between man and woman when they are husband and wife. Or about to be –'

She was not looking at Tilly now, but down into her cup, and Tilly looked at her and understood all of it. And she took a long slow breath.

'Oh dear,' she said. 'Oh dear.'

'Indeed, Mum, oh dear is all you can say, ain't it? I should ha' known better, and I'm ashamed and – oh, it's got me to thinkin', Mum, as I'm no better than my old mother who was just like that – I mean, men could – they could tell her anything and she always believed 'em and that was how it was that she – well, there was a lot of us, and for all I know she's still at it. I could have a dunnamany brothers and sisters,' and no Pa to show for it.

'Yes,' Tilly murmured, not knowing what else she could say.

'And suppose I'm like her in every way?' Eliza said with sudden heat. 'She allus said a man had nobbut to look at her and she fell. Suppose I'm just such another? I shall have to go, Mum, if I'm in the pudding club. I'll be out on the street with a little one and –'

'I never heard such nonsense in my life,' Tilly said strongly, her face bright with anger. 'You out on the street? Not while I have breath in this body, Eliza Horace, and never let me hear you suggest otherwise! It is wicked even to consider it possible that I would show such uncharitable behaviour to anyone, let alone to one who has stood my good friend these many years!'

Eliza put her cup down in its saucer with a clatter and leaned forwards and seized Tilly's hands.

'Oh, Mum, I knows that! I didn't mean to say it'd be you as would send me there, but me as would go. It may be as I'm frettin' too soon, and I ain't in trouble, but I got the notion so firm in my head that I am that I can't think of nothing else. And I've got to think about it, ain't I? I can't just pretend to myself there's nothin' to fret over on account of there *might* be. And I couldn't stay here with my head up if I was to – if I'm like my ma and been caught by that heap of – well, if I'd been caught. I wouldn't do it to this house, Mum. I'd have more respect for you and your guests. But I've been thinking all morning, all day really, and I know one way out of it, Mum. I do, I really do. If you'll agree, Mum.'

'I'm not sure what you –' Tilly began, staring down at Eliza, startled now. She had never seen Eliza like this. Her eyes were wide and glittering and there was a dampness over her forehead and a row of beads of sweat along her upper lip. She was breathing rapidly and looked so different it was almost as though she were another person entirely.

'Hear me out, Mum, oh please, do hear me out before you says anything. Here you are, a respectable widow lady with a son near grown but still very young – if you was to be a philanthropist and adopt a baby what had no parents, why you'd be regarded by all your neighbours as the good woman you are. They need never know it wasn't a true orphan but one that – well, they'd not know. I'd be here to care for the baby, but he or she would have a name and a respectable home and a future. If I can't do that, well, out of here I'd have to go to fettle as best I might and it's no start for any child. The best thing I could do for any baby of mine is to ask you to have the care of him – with me to help the way I did for Duff. And oh, Mum, we could manage lovely, I know we could. My name'd be respectable still and the baby'd be better off – and I'd work myself to death for you for the rest of my life, Mum, that I would. Please say you'd do it for me, Mum, if it's needful? Please to say you'll think of it!'

Chapter Fifteen

ELIZA WAS THE one who first noticed the clock, in spite of her misery, and leapt to her feet in a state of near panic for it was far closer to dinner time than it should be for the amount of work she still had to do. Although her steak pies were baking nicely and filling the kitchen with a rich savoury fragrance she still had to make the hollandaise sauce for her poached halibut, and carve and arrange on a platter the boiled mutton in capers that was simmering on the top of the fire and of course check that the damson tarts, Duff's favourite, were ready to go into the ovens as soon as the meat pies came out. There was the vegetable soup to be strained and sieved, the autumn green beans to be boiled, the potatoes to be beaten to a mash, and various other side dishes fetched from the cold larder and dressed fit for the table. She was in a clamour of busyness and begged Tilly to leave her to get on with it with the help of the maids who would be down soon to join her endeavours, and above all to worry no more.

'For there's little enough we can do about my situation tonight,' she said, with a return of her usual practicality. 'And I would never have spoken of it now if that Dora hadn't – well, let be. If you'll keep her above stairs, Mum, and remember you said you'd find her a new place and see her off, I'll be fit enough. Don't you look so fretful, Mum, for I can't bear to see you upset by me – just you go and dress ready for Mr Duff.'

All of which Tilly had to agree made sense. So after saying a rapid farewell to Jem, still alone in the drawing room, she put on her newest dinner gown, a confection of velvet and faille in rose pink and black with a low round neck that almost displayed her shoulders though not quite as much as full evening dress would, and ruffled sleeves to the elbows in the style that was currently high fashion, and dressed her hair with a less exuberant but equally attractive version of Sophie's high plaits and curled tresses. She looked at herself critically in the mirror, noting the way the black velvet set off the pallor of her throat and how the pink braiding in the trimming at the bust and over the hips matched precisely the shade of the rose faille underskirt. Duff would have been seeing ladies in the most costly and modish of toilettes this past week and she was determined, a little childishly she feared, to show him that even ladies who took in paying guests to make a living could be elegant and good to look at.

But when he actually arrived she forgot her gown and her hair and her appearance altogether at the sound of a four-wheeler clattering to a stop at her door, and went flying down the stairs like a child to throw open the front door and welcome him home.

He came in like a small cyclone, clearly bursting with health and frankly in need of a bath, for he smelled tired and sweaty, and looked less than half as elegant as when he had left a week ago. He hugged Tilly close and laughed when she made a small grimace.

'Oh, Mamma, am I all countrified and stuffy? I would not be a bit surprised if I were, for I must tell you that taking a bath at Paton Place is even worse than it is at school, where we must all share the space. At school at least it was tolerably warm in summer but at Paton they are very Spartan. Cold water most of the time – there is always a shortage of hot – and the most draughty bathroom I have ever been in. I have yearned for a little comfort, Mamma. It's clear to me that dukes and their families have no feelings, or not the sort we have. The hardest and lumpiest of beds and always chilled to the marrow even in this pleasant weather – now do take care, man.' He whirled as the cabbie came toiling in with an assortment of bundles and boxes, including the handsome game bag that Tilly had bought him.

'Here you are, Ma!' he said cheerfully, thrusting it at her. 'I've fetched you three brace of plump birds – I can't pretend I shot 'em for I brought down hardly any, but they had a good bag and this is my share. I imagine Eliza will enjoy dealing with 'em though do warn her that they're fairly full of lead. I nearly broke a tooth eatin' a roast partridge last night!'

She looked at him closely and her heart began to lift a little. There was no sign of lugubriousness, no shadow behind his eyes that might suggest his visit had brought him anything but pleasure. But, she thought as he once again dived at the cabbie and supervised the unloading of his luggage, so that he might tip him, if he and his wretched Lord Patrick, or whatever his name was, had been indulging in – well, whatever it was that Duff had hinted at, would he not be just as cock-a-hoop with himself as he clearly was now? Or if not, would he be displaying signs of grief at being parted unwillingly from his intimate? It was very difficult to judge, and she thought with a certain inner sinking sensation – I shall have to ask him. And I don't know how to.

'So, Ma, have you missed me?' he demanded as at last he was ready to follow Dora upstairs with his luggage after Rosie, who was also hovering, had taken the game down to Eliza. 'I hope not, on the one hand, but on the other –'

'Of course we missed you. Just as we did all the time you were at school. I love to have you here by my side.' She held his arm closely tucked into hers as they went side by side up the stairs. 'I think I need not ask you if you enjoyed yourself.'

'It was very fine, Ma,' he said. 'I had no idea shooting could be so enjoyable. Though seeing so much blood on some of the birds was disagreeable – but Patrick says it's much bloodier when they hunt, you know, and wants me to come and try my hand at that. But I am not so sure – the gear, you know – after all, all this was costly, was it not?'

They had reached his room where Dora was already unpacking his bags, sorting out a fairly monstrous heap of soiled linen for Mrs Skinner, and he indicated his shooting clothes and guns that were laid out on the bed to one side; Dora was avoiding them with some trepidation, clearly afraid they would go off and kill her at the least touch.

'The guns are but hired, of course, Duff,' Tilly said. 'And as for the rest – well, your needs are of prime importance to me, but I had not expected you to develop the – ah – tastes of a country gentleman of the sort your friend is. I had expected you to continue to be a town person. We must discuss at some point the sort of career that will be suitable for you and set about arranging matters so that you may pursue it. And country recreations may not fit in well with whatever it is.'

He did not precisely scowl, but he looked a little less pleased with himself. 'Yes, I suppose so,' he said after a moment. 'I dare say I was getting a touch high flown in my ideas, thinking I might hunt at Paton this winter. From all accounts, though, it's a spiffing good thing to do and I should enjoy it above everything, Patrick says.'

'Ah – you – ah – were you very happy to be with Patrick again?' she ventured as Dora, with a little bob and an armful of soiled linen, at last left the room and they could be alone.

'Happy? Well, I told you Mamma. I had a most excellent time, the shooting was –'

'I was not asking about the shooting but about – the other entertainment,' Tilly said carefully and he glanced at her sharply and then away.

'Well there were a lot of people there, don't you know. Some of the fellows from school – not all the ones I quite liked, but one or two of my own set and that was agreeable. Oh, and some girls.'

He said it almost disparagingly and she looked at him sharply, trying not to be hopeful. 'Girls? Did you not enjoy their company?'

'It is difficult to do so when generally speaking they sit with their heads together giggling over nonsense. Or spend all their time making eyes at chaps they know to have titles or to be rich.'

She smiled involuntarily. 'Does that mean none of them made eyes at you, my dear?'

He reddened. 'Well, actually there was one who – but since she also seemed interested in Patrick, simply because he is a lord, I did not find her company at all to my taste. I regard such snobbery as quite beyond the pale.'

She let her lips quirk again, forbearing to remind him that he had himself been quite content to be snobbish over her means of keeping herself and him in comfort. There would be small value in doing so; it would only make him irritable, and she much preferred him agreeable. Was she spoiling him, letting him have too much leeway? she wondered briefly. Perhaps. But then he was her only child, and likely to remain so. At which thought a vision of Eliza's anguished pleading face rose into her mind's eye: 'Please say you'll do it for me, Mum! Please say you'll think of it!' Not now, she told herself, not now, and fixed her attention on Duff again.

'But you had a happy time in all,' she said to Duff and he smiled and stretched and pulled off his jacket as Dora came back into the room, this time bearing a jug of hot water.

'It was a most agreeable time,' he said. 'But never fear that I am not happy to be home again. For I am.' He came and hugged her and she pulled back and made a face at him, laughing.

'Dearest Duff, you must take a bath at once! The hot water, Dora, may be taken to the bathroom and a bath filled for Mr Duff. He'll be there directly.'

'Am I so farmyardish, Ma?' Duff said and grinned. 'Well, as I say, it is not surprising. So, how are things here at home?'

'Oh, very well,' she said. 'We have had some changes you know. The Lampeters and McCools have gone and we have a Monsieur and Madame Salinas with us together with their daughter Blanche. She is shy but – well, she is teaching another of our guests French. A charming girl.'

'Who is? The French teacher or her pupil?' Duff said it almost abstractedly as he collected his sponge bag and soap and other impedimenta ready to go to the bathroom.

'As to that, you must wait and see,' Tilly said with a sudden moment of inspiration. 'I think you may be surprised. You may also be pleased.'

'Oh?' He lifted his head. 'Why?'

'Wait and see!' she said almost coquettishly. 'And now do go and make yourself civilized again. We have had quite enough from you of country air, if I may call it that. I shall be in the drawing room when you are ready. We will wait to sound the dinner gong till you come, but make haste. We must not keep the guests – or the kitchen – waiting too long, must we?' And he laughed, and went, leaving her thinking how clever she had been. Surely once he saw Sophie again, he would finally forget any attachment to Patrick Paton?

They were almost all waiting in the drawing room by the time Duff joined them. Only Silas Geddes and Sophie were still absent when he presented himself, looking resplendent in his velvet-collared dress coat in the deepest black superfine over a white ruffled shirt with a fashionably high collar supporting his elegant whiskers. He had the freshly scrubbed look that Tilly had always found so adorable in him when he was small, and looking at him now she had her usual difficulty in seeing him as a man almost full grown. To her he would always be her darling little Duff. But she was alone in such a view, for she saw Mademoiselle Blanche Salinas's eyes widen perceptibly as he came in and went to kiss his mother's cheek before turning to greet the rest of the company, and to be introduced to the Salinas family.

The Misses K and F and even Miss Barnetsen positively cooed over him – if one with a voice as commanding and contralto as Miss Fleetwood's could be said to coo – and demanded all sorts of details about his stay in Leicestershire, and even the young men clustered round him to hear how the shooting had been, and whether he had achieved a reasonable bag. He dealt with all their questions with relaxed charm, admitting with disarming honesty to being a very bad shot indeed (to which Miss Barnetsen said in her high twitter, 'Oh, what a good man you are, to be sure! To kill those dear little birds, our feathered friends, so cruel!' which gained her a disdainful glare from Mr Cumming), and giving Mrs Grayling lots of very satisfying detail about such matters as ducal drawing-room curtains and carpets and ducal dining arrangements and –

daringly – ducal sanitary accommodation, a question delivered gruffly by an earnest Mr Grayling.

Altogether, he was enthralling and was himself so absorbed in talking to the people clustered around him that he did not notice when the door opened again and Silas and Sophie came in. Silas held the door for her and she smiled up at him with a little flick of her eyes in a way that made Tilly suddenly irritated, and came in quietly to stand for a while, watching what was going on.

Had she known Duff was to come home this evening? Tilly wondered. I cannot recall if I told her. If I did, is that why she has dressed herself so very charmingly? But then she sighed softly and admitted inside her head that Sophie always looked delectable, whatever she wore.

Tonight she had chosen a gown in very simple cream lace which probably cost a good deal; certainly the lace looked good and was shown to great advantage by the simplicity of its presentation, for there were few frills or trimmings; just a little cream braid around the low neck which showed off the delicate colouring of her shoulders to perfection, and a deep frill of darker lace around the hem. Her hair tumbled in artless curls about her ears and on her shoulders, as well as being piled in its usual way on her crown. Clearly she had very thick and long hair that she could deal with most skilfully. Tilly could hardly take her eyes from her and nor, she noticed with a little stab of annoyance, could Silas.

But all Sophie's attention was on the group in the middle of the room and after a few moments it was Mademoiselle Blanche Salinas who looked across and broke away to come running prettily on her tiptoes and with her hands outstretched towards her. She was wearing a sadly over-fussy confection in no fewer than three colours – green and blue and yellow – with a large number of rainbow beads sewn on to the bodice, all of which accentuated her plainness. When she was standing beside Sophie the comparison was almost pathetic, and Tilly forbore to look at Mademoiselle Salinas's parents, who were the only people not standing beside Duff, but sitting together on the far side of the room.

'Ma chère amie!' Mademoiselle Salinas cried. 'Je suis enchantée – I am 'appy zat you are 'ere. It 'as been so exciting, I cannot say 'ow much. 'Ere is Monsieur qui est – 'oo 'as returned from a visit to Monsieur le Duc and it 'as been of ze most exciting to 'ear –'

Duff had turned at the sound of Blanche Salinas's high little voice, and the unusual sound of her accent, and the sentence he had been halfway through died on his lips. He stood and stared, and then slowly moved away from the group with a murmured apology and came across the room towards Sophie.

'I don't think –' he began and then stopped. He looked at Sophie closely, and then glanced over his shoulder at Tilly who got to her feet and came to help him.

'Well, now,' she said wanting to sound as light as possible. 'I did say you might be surprised. You recall who this is, Duff?'

'Unless I am quite mad, I do indeed,' Duff said and held out both hands. 'Is it you? I mean are you the person I suspect you are?'

Sophie laughed, and her eyes crinkled and her short upper lip lifted to display her perfect teeth. The effect was almost overwhelming and, Tilly thought with a moment's acuity, she is well aware of it. I pray I have done the right thing, bringing this girl back into Duff's life. I am sure he needs a nice girl to help him find his way as a man, but is this the right girl? Watching her now sparkle up at Duff, her eyes wide and amused and her smile confiding and sweet, Tilly had, again, a moment's qualm.

'Indeed I am,' Sophie was saying. 'I am precisely who you think I might be, I hope. I will be most put out if you imagine I am anyone but myself, for that would mean you had quite forgotten me! You look very fine and exactly as I remember you. So eager and excited – just like a dear little puppy. Only not so little now. Rather large in fact!' And she let her eyes slide across the width of his shoulders in their approval and then looked up at him again.

'Sophie,' said Duff and took a deep breath and exhaled noisily. 'Sophie! I can't believe it. When I remember how –' He caught his breath again, becoming suddenly aware of the people in the room who were silently watching him. Sophie had clearly been aware of them all the time, and paid them no attention, but Duff now looked over his shoulder and blushed and returned his attention to Sophie.

'Well, we have much to talk about,' he said to the room at large, sounding more than a little stilted and uncomfortable. 'Old recollections, you know and so forth.'

'Indeed we have.' She turned on her heel, and sweeping her skirt aside with a little kick that displayed embroidered cream silk evening shoes and clocked stockings in cream and gold, tucked one gloved hand into his elbow. 'Do take me in to dinner, dear boy, and we shall gossip to our hearts' content. I am sure we will be forgiven by everyone if we don't join in general conversation tonight. After all we haven't seen each other for so many years and we were babies together!'

She looked over her shoulder at the rest of the company, who were now surging to their feet as the gong in the hall below began its loud call to the table. 'You won't mind, will you?' she called and then turned her radiant face up to Duff and led the way out of the room.

Chapter Sixteen

'I RIDE WITH you?' Tilly said blankly. 'But why? Don't you usually ride with Miss Oliver?'

'Hardly usually,' Silas said. 'We have ridden on a few mornings, but only a few. She has hardly been in the house long enough for any of us to use the term "usually" about any of her activities.'

'Every day since she arrived is sufficiently usual for me,' Tilly said in as neutral a tone as she could conjure up. 'And anyway, I had particular cause to assume you were riding with her this morning, for I passed her on the stairs in riding habit on her way out.'

'Oh,' he said easily, 'she has gone with Duff,' and turned away to the window to look out into the street. The weather had changed, with the late summer they had enjoyed for the past weeks being replaced by a cooler, cloud-blowing windiness. The first of the autumn leaves were skittering along the gutters and he watched them as Tilly sat back in her chair and looked at him.

'Ah,' she said, amused. 'So you are feeling spurned by the charming Sophie?'

He looked at her now and laughed, a comfortable easy sound. 'Spurned? Not in the least. She has the company of someone far more to her taste – her young playmate. They are of an age and have so much to share, of course she prefers him to someone who is twice her age, as I am! I suggested we ride together when she first came here to provide a charming child with the opportunity to take some healthy exercise under a safe and watchful eye. She told me she intended to ride, and I could not in all conscience, imagine allowing her to go alone. It would not have been right.'

'I think Sophie Oliver would be able to take care of herself in most circumstances,' Tilly said dryly. 'She has contrived very well so far, living without a parent's watchful eye as she does.'

'I think, having talked with her in these last few mornings, that I have discovered as much for myself,' he said and smiled. 'She made me feel positively antique in my notions of protection. She lectured me on the way the modern young woman is her own person and far less in need of chaperonage than stuffy elders think, and quoted John Stuart Mill at me on the rights of women! I found that most disconcerting, considering the radical nature of my own views and the way I have been reprimanded for them in the past. To be regarded as a stuffy elder by a miss of just eighteen was the outside of enough! I told her so, too, but she merely laughed indulgently at me and begged me not to worry myself on such matters. I must say it was a most humbling experience.'

She looked at him, her lower lip caught between her teeth, thinking hard. Had he really only taken Sophie under his wing out of some sort of avuncular concern for her well-being? Or had he done so because she was so charming and alluring and had aroused in him feelings that were far from those he professed? She could not be sure; even though he stood there smiling at her in his usual easy fashion. And, she thought, I want to be sure, for he really is a most interesting man.

'Well,' she said briskly now, to cover her thoughts from herself as much as from him. 'Whatever the reason for your invitation this morning, I really feel I cannot –'

'Oh, please, don't be put out!' He came to lean on her desk so that he could look down on her from close quarters. 'I am not, I do assure you, treating you as an alternative to Miss Oliver's company. Far from it. I have been chafing a little at the way she has – well – not precisely clung to me, but obviously regarded me as the person she would most like to be with here, which is a dubious compliment, I fear, when I look at Mr Gee and Mr Grayling. Mr Cumming and Mr Hancock who would, I know, give their eye teeth for the opportunity to dance attendance on her, are occupied with their work during the day, so the duty fell to me. But now Duff is here, and able to take over the burden, why, I can relinquish that burden and be free to do as I wish. And I wish to spend time with you. You're a most interesting person, one with a mind to which I can respond, and with a response to the matters which fill my mind that is most refreshing. So, please, will you ride with me? I think it will be healthy for you too, for you're looking a little peaky, you know, and I feel sure you are overworked. Eliza can deal with your affairs well enough during any short absence in the park.'

She blinked at the length and intensity of his speech and held up one hand to stop the tide of words.

'Dear Mr Geddes, you really must –'

'Oh, I beg you not to be so formal! We are friends, you and I, surely? Please to call me by my given name. I insist on the right to address you as Tilly, after all!' He smiled at her and his face was now so close to hers that it made her absurdly breathless.

'Oh, names –' she said. 'That is a matter of small importance.'

'I agree. But your health is not. So let me beguile you out into the air. Riding will be very good for you.'

'No,' she said firmly. 'I have no riding habit, and anyway have not ridden for years. I did when I was a girl, a little, but I am far from being a horsewoman. I am a town person in every way, Mr – oh, very well, Silas – and one who works for her living, to boot. You really cannot drag me away from work at a whim like this. I must beg you to leave me to get on with my bookkeeping now.'

'Oh, pooh,' he said and straightened up. 'You know you can do it later! If you don't wish to take a saddle horse, then we can take one of those fast little phaetons and I will drive you – that will be great fun, I think, and carriage exercise can be excellent. Now, please do fetch your bonnet and be ready for my return. I shall go and fetch a phaeton from the livery stables. What do you say? I can see you are nearly finished here –' and he indicated her desk with his head. 'We wouldn't stay out too long – we would be back in ample time for you to preside over luncheon in your usual agreeable way and you will have a much improved appetite for it too. Do be persuaded!'

She couldn't help it. She wavered. He was quite right; her

paperwork was indeed almost done, for she had been hard at work since before nine, not wishing to join her guests at breakfast. She had asked Rosie to fetch her some coffee and a sweet roll to take on her desk and now had almost completed the month's figures and it was only just half past ten o'clock.

He seemed to be aware of her wavering thoughts and pounced. 'That's decided then. Splendid! I shan't be above a quarter of an hour, I promise,' and he was at the door and out of it before she could protest. By the time she had jumped to her feet to follow him, she heard the front door slam and saw him through the window as he emerged into the street outside to set off at a fast lope in the direction of the livery stables.

She knew when to give up, sighed and set to work to put in the last two or three minutes of tidying her desk which were all that was necessary, setting aside a couple of minor tasks that could safely be left for the next day and closed and locked the desk and went down to the kitchen.

Eliza was sitting at the table, her newest cookery book open in front of her as she pored over it, while the new maid, Susan, peeled potatoes under her eagle eye. Dora, now banished to the upper parts of the house to work, would be leaving to take up a new situation in Knightsbridge at a doctor's house at the end of the week, to Eliza's rather grim satisfaction.

'I am to go for a ride in the park with Mr Geddes, Eliza,' Tilly said. 'I can't pretend I want to, but he can be so insistent.'

'I'm glad to hear that, Mum. You need some exercise and a bit of air. You look right peaky, you do.'

Without thinking Tilly reached up and pinched both her cheeks in an attempt to bring some colour to them. 'He said that –'

'Well, he was right. You go and enjoy it, Mum. I'll have luncheon ready directly you get back. Half past one sharp.'

She lifted her head to look at Tilly and Tilly was alarmed by what she saw and frowned even more deeply. Eliza's cheeks had a higher flush than usual and her eyes were heavy. She looked weary and Tilly said, with a swift glance at the girl peeling potatoes, 'Susan, would you be so good as to go up to my room and fetch me the bonnet you will see on my dressing table? A chip bonnet, very light – and the small shawl you will see hanging at the foot of the bed.'

The girl bobbed and dried her hands on her apron and went, and as she disappeared Tilly sat down in her place and leaned across the table to Eliza.

'Never mind how I look,' she said bluntly. 'You look far worse than I possibly could. Are you ailing?'

'Worryin',' Eliza said. 'It's enough to make anyone look poorly.'

'Hmm,' Tilly took Eliza's hand in hers. 'Let me look at you. I remember how it was you first told me that Duff was to be – you saw my hands and said I had blue veins.'

Eliza's hand was red and strong and capable and there were no signs of enlarged blue veins that Tilly could see, and Eliza laughed and pulled her hand away.

'Oh, do give over, Mum! It was different then. I was still a country piece, didn't know when to hold my tongue.'

'You still don't,' Tilly said and took the hand back. 'Are you showing any – is there anything to tell me, Eliza?'

Eliza shook her head gloomily. 'Not that you could call definite, Mum. I ain't 'ad my usual course this month I don't deny, but it's only out by three days and that don't signify, on account I been much more all over the place than that in my time. I don't usually notice anyway, not having cause, and this time I'm worrying myself fit to be sick, so if I sets the whole business awry, it wouldn't be surprising, would it?'

There was a hopeful sound in her voice as she looked at Tilly and it was as though she had said aloud, 'Tell me it's all right – tell me I'm imagining it – tell me it's not true.'

Tilly shook her head. 'I dare say it can be so. I recall times when I too – when I have been particularly anxious, I have found my system behaving in different ways, but you cannot deceive yourself so, Eliza. You know that. You have cause to doubt.'

Eliza again withdrew her hand and nodded heavily. 'I suppose so,' she said and bent her head again to her cookery book.

There was a short silence and then Tilly said, 'Have you been sick, Eliza?'

Eliza sat silent and then looked up miserably. 'I thought it was all the worrying, you see,' she said and Tilly grimaced and shook her head.

'Oh, Eliza, how can it be so? When you know that – no, my dear, I fear that matters are as you suspected they might be. How long is it now since he went away? And how long since – since you started with him and –' She stopped again, delicacy forbidding her to go further, but Eliza had no such qualms.

'We lived as man and wife near on a month, Mum,' she said baldly. 'It don't matter when he last was 'ere so much as when we started, don't it? And that was a full six gettin' on for seven weeks ago, I think.'

'And you say your normal courses are stopped.'

'Three days or so late, Mum, no more,' Eliza said with a slightly desperate air, but again Tilly shook her head, and got to her feet as Susan appeared at the top of the kitchen stairs with her shawl and bonnet.

'I think we must stop conjecturing and think sensibly, Eliza,' she said, not attempting to lower her voice, for she made sure her words would mean nothing to Susan. 'We must talk again.'

'There ain't a lot to talk about, Mum.' Eliza too got to her feet. 'I'll see you to the door then, Mum. Susan, you get on with those potatoes and cut 'em proper, mind. I don't want half the meat of them left on the parings, and don't you forget it. Make sure you get all the eyes out too – we can't have anything but the best of everything sent to table here.'

'Yes'm,' said Susan nervously and Tilly smiled at her reassuringly and patted one shoulder.

'It's all right, my dear,' she said. 'Eliza hasn't bitten anyone yet, so you need not look so fearful. But she teaches everyone very well, so listen to her.' The girl glanced at Eliza and then smiled gratefully and went back to her laborious work with the potato knife, as Eliza led the way up the stairs to hold the door open for Tilly.

They went to the front door and stood on the step as Tilly tied her bonnet strings and set her shawl about her shoulders, glad she had chosen to wear her green merino today, for it blended well with the Indian shawl and its many colours and offered a necessary warmth, for the air was brisk and quite chilling, though agreeable after the sultry weather of the past weeks.

'I suppose I've got to think the same as you, Mum,' Eliza said quietly. 'And reckon I've been caught. There's not a lot I can do to change that, bitterly though I regret it. Now the only chance there is, is if you –'

'I know,' Tilly said. 'You needn't repeat it, my dear Eliza.' She looked down the street at the few hackney carriages that were clopping past and the delivery vans with their dispirited horses, watching for Silas and the phaeton. 'I have thought a great deal about what you told me last week, even though I have been busy with Duff and so forth. Never think I haven't been concerned, for I have. But it is a difficult idea you have and one that I am not sure –'

'I tell you this much, Mum,' Eliza said, and stood there with the wind lifting the strands of hair that had escaped her cap, and her hands folded neatly on her black housekeeper's gown. 'It's the only way. I'll not stay here under any other circumstances. I'll have to be away and hidden somewhere when I starts to show, though I think I can do well enough for a good six months or longer. I can get more commodious gowns and use a small crinoline. No one'll care when someone like me goes about in outdated fashions, and it'll suit me well enough to have full round skirts. But if you can't do as I ask, Mum, then there it is. I'll have to be on my way. I couldn't hold my head up otherwise.'

Tilly looked at her almost helplessly as at last the phaeton with Silas on the box, looking very rakish with his whip held at a stylish angle, appeared round the curve of the street. 'Oh, my dear,' she said. 'Do you know what it is you are asking? That you and I live the greatest possible lie – and not just for a few days but for the rest of our lives?'

'D'you think I haven't thought as hard as may be, Mum?' Eliza's voice was harsh. 'D'you think I ain't yearnin' to carry a child as'll call me mother and treat me as a mother should be treated? D'you think I wants to go through all the trouble and pain only to deny who the child is as soon as I've borne him? Or her, of course – No, Mum. Believe me, I ain't being captious. It's truly the only answer – not just for me but for the babe. It'll do a sight better in the world as your child than mine – now, sir!'

She lifted her voice and turned with a smile to Silas as he drew alongside with a lively flourish of his whip and then jumped down to hold the horse's head. 'See to it you takes good care of Madam, now!'

'You needn't worry, Eliza,' Silas promised. 'I'll treat her like gold dust. Here, hold this animal's head for me, will you?'

Eliza obeyed and Silas came and opened the little door of the phaeton, which was very smartly painted in dark blue with a frieze of flowers and curlicues of seashells in yellow along the sides, and upholstered inside in matching blue leather. Tilly could do nothing else but accept his invitation to get in. She stepped forward and took his hand and let him lift her into place before he jumped up beside her and reached for the reins, which Eliza fetched to him, patting the horse's nose so that it turned its head, and watched her go.

'There you are, sir. I shall be sure that your vegetable pie is crisp and ready for your luncheon at half past one sharp.'

'I take that as an instruction not to stay out too late,' he said and looked at his pocket watch. 'Very well then. I accept your orders, Madam Eliza. Come up now!' And he whistled at the horse as he flicked the whip over its back and tossed the reins. The animal shook its head, snuffled and obediently moved, turning the phaeton round in response to Silas's pull on its right.

Eliza walked alongside as the phaeton turned, looking up at Tilly, and after a moment Tilly leaned over and said quickly, 'I promise you, by the time we return I shall have reached a decision. I will do the best I can to find an answer, I promise.'

And they were off, spanking along the road with the horse stepping high and elegantly. Tilly looked back to where Eliza stood on the kerb, her gown and her hair blown a little in the lively breeze and her heart ached, for she still didn't know what she could do to help Eliza. It certainly was not possible, she told herself, that she could do as she asked. It would be impractical, for a start, to take on the task of rearing another child, even though such rearing would be a shared occupation, just as it had been with Duff. But she had poured her heart and soul into Duff. He had been her beloved child, the son of her own body, and even though she had not conceived him in love but in shrinking pain and even in terror, for his father had not been a good man, he had been her baby from the start. Loving him had been easy. But how could she love another woman's child, even if the other woman was her dear Eliza? She could not imagine it no matter how hard she tried.

Her spirits were very low indeed as the phaeton rolled on its jingling clattering way and turned into the park gates just past Knightsbridge Barracks.

Chapter Seventeen

IT REALLY WAS a glorious morning and even though she was so preoccupied with Eliza – and to an extent, Duff – Tilly could not ignore that fact. The sky was a bright scrubbed blue, for it had rained last night, and clumps of clouds were scudding busily across it in the high wind. The park sparkled green and fresh as the last of the raindrops were blown away and everywhere people strolled or rode and held on to their hats; and in spite of herself her spirits lifted a little.

'There,' he said, as though he were a mind reader. 'I told you it would make you feel better. Carriage exercise may not be as vigorous as riding, but it still shakes one up most agreeably.'

'Indeed it does,' she gasped and put her hand to her bonnet as the phaeton jolted sharply on a particularly rough portion of the road. 'I feel I must use every atom of strength I have to make sure I remain inside the phaeton and am not hurled out completely!'

'Don't you fret,' he cried. 'I won't let any such thing happen!' And he cracked the whip and flicked the horse's rump and it broke into a sharp trot, tossing its head in some irritation. And then it veered sharply to the left and sent the phaeton almost rolling, though it recovered itself swiftly on its high, well-sprung wheels, as a small figure darted out almost beneath the animal's hooves.

Silas swore loudly and held on to the reins as Tilly let go of her bonnet, and grabbed for the sides of the phaeton and held on grimly. Her bonnet ribbons unravelled and flew free and with them so did the bonnet, dancing away across the grass like a thing with a mind of its own.

Somehow Silas pulled the horse up and it stood still at last, quivering between the shafts and Silas leapt down and ran to its head to soothe it, muttering in its ear to ensure it did not take off again. Not until he was certain it had settled did he return to Tilly's side.

'My dear – are you all right? I had to soothe the brute first for it might have taken to its heels again and taken you heaven knows where. My dear, I am mortified – I promised to keep you safe and now –'

'It's all right, Silas,' she managed and took a deep breath and smoothed her thoroughly disordered hair with slightly shaking hands. 'It was not your fault and there is no harm done – I have but lost a bonnet.'

'Wretched creatures!' someone shrilled and Tilly lifted her head and looked over Silas's shoulder to see a man wearing a top hat held firmly in place with a hat protector tied to his frock-coat, and a warm muffler wrapped round his neck.

'I beg your pardon, sir?' Tilly said and the man, now visibly elderly from the greyness of his somewhat scanty whiskers, snorted.

'Beggar children, Ma'am, beggar children! See them? They run everywhere like the vermin they are, and cause such havoc. Some fool in the carriage that turned in through the gates just before yours tossed a coin at them, and this ragamuffin ran to obtain it. Could have killed you, Ma'am. I trust you are recovered.'

'I am very well – what children, Silas?' she said, for at the old man's words Silas had turned to look, and she too turned now and saw a little knot of figures in the middle of the path a few yards away, at the point where their horse had swerved. 'What has happened?'

'Stay there,' Silas said sharply and moved towards the group, but she was not to be prevented and at once scrabbled at the fastening of the door and managed to swing it open and jump down, though it was difficult, for she had not let down the little steps, so her gown flew about her ankles – indeed almost to her knees – and made the elderly man step back in a state of strong disapproval.

'Well, bless my soul, Ma'am, I trust that you – Madam!' But she had gone, running after Silas.

She caught up with him just as he reached the group and she peered round him to see what was going on. A boy who looked to her maternal eye to be about thirteen, though a very scrawny and ill-grown thirteen, was sitting rubbing a bloody knee with a very dirty hand and biting his lip ferociously, clearly determined not to cry. This determination was not shared by those around him, however. Several of them were bawling loudly and sniffing and gulping in a very unappetizing way. There were perhaps four or five of them, one of them a girl who seemed a little older than the others. She was crouching awkwardly beside the boy, muttering at him and trying to see what his injury was, and every so often roared at the other children to be silent. But they ignored her completely, and snivelled on.

'Now then,' Silas said with authority. 'What's going on here?'

The injured boy looked up with a sudden gleam in his eye. 'Your 'orse, Mister, that's what, your 'orse knocked me down and me just walkin' quiet in the park, like. You done this.'

The other children stopped bawling as though someone had held up a whip in threat and looked at Silas and also at Tilly behind him, and for a moment Tilly felt as though five pairs of eyes were slicing into her, so intense were the stares.

'You ran in front of my phaeton,' Silas said firmly. 'This gentleman here –' He looked over his shoulder for the old man, but he had stomped away in high disapproval; in his book, clearly, people who actually spoke to these children were quite beyond the pale. 'Well, you were seen. The horse swerved and nearly took the bit between its teeth and bolted because you ran under its hooves. What have you to say to that, hey? What have you to say?'

'I say as you ought to pay us for what you done to 'im, that's what!' The girl spoke now, still crouching beside the injured one, and glaring up through a tangle of very dirty hair. Her face was pale and thin, and dirtier than her hair; it might have been a pretty face, Tilly found herself thinking, if it had been washed and fed. 'It ain't right as ladies and gennelmen should run down the likes of us and not 'ave to pay for it.'

'But you ran under my wheels!' Silas began again, but Tilly gave him no chance to go on. She pushed past him and crouched beside the boy.

'Let me see,' she said and the firmness in her voice and perhaps the quietness of it made the boy stop rubbing his leg and Tilly reached forwards and with her own handkerchief, which looked absurdly white against the dirty flesh, mopped and peered.

'It is happily a very minor injury,' she said to Silas at last. 'No more than a large graze. Duff had many such when he played in the garden as a boy. This will form a scab and then heal well enough – can you stand?' And she put out a hand and the boy, a little bemused, it seemed, at his own obedience, took it and let her pull him to his feet.

'There, you see?' Silas said. 'No harm done, glory be. It might have been quite dreadful – you could have killed yourselves and overturned us and –'

'Well, we didn't.' The girl, moving awkwardly, got to her feet and stood there scowling at him. She seemed oddly out of shape, Tilly thought; her face and hands, which were visible round the edges of the large and ragged shawl that was pulled about her body, were very thin, but her body looked bulky. Tilly frowned at her, thinking hard.

'Come on, you.' The girl jerked her head at the boy, now standing with the other children behind her. 'All of you. We'll go some place else where we won't get so 'ard done by.'

She turned but Tilly said softly, 'Just a moment.' The girl turned back, suspicious, but with a glint of hope in her eyes as Tilly put out her hand, and put her own forward, clearly expecting money; but Tilly moved faster and tugged at the shawl the girl was still clutching in place with her other hand, and set it aside. And found herself looking down onto the face of a sleeping infant.

It was almost as dirty as the other children and certainly as thin. It lay there in the curve of the girl's arm, its eyes not quite closed, so that a rim of white could be seen beneath the almost translucent eyelids, and breathing, as Tilly could see clearly, with rapid shallow breaths. That it was a sick baby was very obvious.

The girl snatched her hand back, covered the baby's face and turned to go, marshalling the other children, but Tilly held on to her and pulled her back.

'My dear girl,' she said gently, 'that baby is ill.'

The girl looked at her contemptuously. 'D'you think as we don't know that? It's been sickly since it was born. I been lookin' after it since its ma died and trying to raise it myself, but it won't do.' She looked down at the bundle in her arms and then lifted her chin to stare pugnaciously at Tilly. 'Well, that's the way of it, I dare say. It'll be one I won't 'ave to fret over.'

'Oh, my dear,' Tilly said, as distress lifted in her. 'How can you speak so? Is the baby your – a relation?'

''Alf brother,' the girl muttered. 'Not that that's none o' your business.'

'A sick baby is everyone's business,' Silas put in. 'Now, it is clear you need help.' He became businesslike suddenly. 'I can arrange for care of you and this infant – you say your mother died?'

'Not my ma,' the girl said, still truculent but staring up at him with what might have been a spark of hope in her expression. ''*Is* ma –' She jerked her head at the older boy. 'She took up with our pa and then she 'ad this baby and died and then my pa got took to prison for stealin' food for us – so –' She said no more, just shrugging her shoulders and looking back at Silas.

'How old are you, my dear?' Tilly said.

'Fourteen,' the girl said and then, clearly losing hope of any sort of financial aid, turned away. 'Come on, you lot.'

'Wait,' Silas said and reached into his pocket. 'Do you know where St George's Hospital is? Just down there, by the Marble Arch – at the end of the park –' He pointed. 'Take this card with you.' He had taken a card from his pocket book and was scribbling on it with a pencil. 'Ask for Mr Cumming and say I sent you. Tell him I will settle any costs necessary for the care of this infant and for your brother's injury and tell him also that he is to seek through the almoner for better care of you all. Again I will be responsible for reasonable costs. Children should not have to run under horses' hooves to get their living.'

'There ain't no other way,' the girl said, and hesitated, looking at the card.

For a moment Tilly thought she would not take it, and then one of the other children, who looked to be a very undersized ten or so, began to whimper and she looked back at him and her shoulders seemed to sag even more.

'All right,' she said. 'I'll take 'em there. Can't do no 'arm, I don't s'pose. Worst as'll 'appen is we'll never come out and I don't care one way or the other, sometimes, and that's a fact.'

She took the card and slid it into her shawl somewhere and as she gathered the others under her eye, Tilly also reached into her reticule.

'Here, my dear,' she said hurriedly and quietly. 'A little something to help you on your way. Don't let anyone steal it from you –' and she gave her a half sovereign. The girl looked at it glinting in her filthy palm, and then up at Tilly. Her eyes were glazed with surprise.

'My dear Tilly, anyone seeing that will think she stole it!' Silas said. 'She will never be able to change it. And it would get her into great trouble. Let us at least make it smaller in denomination. She has a better chance of keeping it for herself then.' He shook out change in his pocket and picked through it. 'Give the half sovereign back to the lady, and take this instead. It will give you less trouble.' And he gave her a handful of coins.

''Ere,' the girl said, in some wonderment, 'you lot, you're all right, ain't yer? All right.' And this time she did manage to go, shooing her brood in front of her and they went off across the grass in the direction of St George's Hospital as fast as was possible, the biggest boy limping a little, and the girl hunched over her bundle.

They watched them go and then gently Silas touched Tilly's elbow and led her back to the phaeton. The horse had wandered to the side of the roadway and was cropping the grass contentedly enough and Silas checked the steps for safety, handed her in and then climbed up himself and pulled the horse's head round.

They rode on in silence for a while at a respectable walking pace and Tilly stared out at the passing scenery and the people walking and riding along Rotten Row, seeing little but the memory of those starving, dirty children. And then she turned to Silas and said impulsively, 'I am so glad I was with you when we met those children. Silas – I fear that most people would have been like that old man and shown only concern for our skins and not for those poor children, But you –'

He glanced at her and his expression was unsmiling. 'It makes me so angry to see it, I can barely speak,' he said. 'I spend my time busy about philosophical and scientific matters when what a real man should do is concern himself with these – did you ever *see* such misery, Tilly? How can civilized persons allow such things to occur?'

'Well, you will not, clearly,' she said and put one hand on his arm. 'You did something practical, sending them to St George's – and we will of course be able to find out from Mr Cumming what befalls them and if necessary make other help available to them – it was very good of you.'

'Not good at all,' he said bracingly. 'I would hope anyone would do as much –'

'That old man didn't,' Tilly said. 'He didn't even go to see what had happened to the boy. Nor did any of the other people who were about. I saw them. They just walked past and some looked disgusted that we were speaking to such children at all.'

'Well, they are perhaps inured,' Silas said. 'There are, after all, so many beggars about. We see them all the time. But children – they do reach into one's feelings in a most painful manner.'

'They do indeed,' Tilly said and then took a deep breath as the phaeton turned into Rotten Row proper and began to bowl along gently beside the railings where there were more people, many of them dressed in the first stare of fashion, strolling to watch the passers-by and the horseback riders. 'Well, we have done our best so far and tonight I will speak with Mr Cumming. We will see what more can be done for that sad little party.'

'And I will give some thought to what more I might do to deal with the problem of poverty in our world,' Silas said and seemed to liven up visibly. 'I think a meeting of the society might usefully discuss it as a phenomenon of our times – yes, I think that would serve very well. I shall arrange it as soon as I can. You will of course wish to come to such a meeting, Tilly? I'm sure you will.'

Tilly looked at him and opened her mouth to say she would probably prefer to deal more directly with the children they had sent to St George's and then closed it again. He was right, of course. It was necessary to waken others to such matters and certainly those like the old man with the hat protector. So she contented herself with saying only, 'Of course, if I am able. Silas,' and turned to look at the people riding by.

'Well, that is settled then,' Silas said with a full return of his usual good humour. 'Now, we must settle ourselves to enjoying the rest of our drive, for I would not dare to be late for Eliza's cooked luncheon!'

Eliza, thought Tilly. Oh, Eliza, what am I to do for you? There is much more to think out still, but I think I have a better view of what to do than I had when we set out. When we return, I shall tell her.

'Why, there are Duff and Sophie!' Silas said, and lifted his whip to indicate. 'There, do you see? Coming this way. We must make sure they see us.'

She lifted her chin to look and indeed there they were, riding so closely side by side that their stirrups almost touched and their horses tossed their heads close together, as though they were set between the shafts of the same carriage. Both riders were leaning towards each other too, although it was Duff who was almost sliding out of his saddle in his eagerness. Sophie was sitting more erect on her side saddle, the skirt of her riding habit well thrown back to display her ankles in their well-fitting riding boots, but her head was inclined towards Duff in a most confiding sort of manner.

She looked splendid. Her waist was very small and neat in the habit which fitted like a second skin and the veil that held her hat in place invested her face with a wistful softness that was very appealing. Many people turned to look at them as they rode by, clearly admiring them, and Tilly had to admit that they made a handsome couple.

And also that there was no doubt that Duff was thoroughly

besotted with his companion. At home, when other people were about, he was a little more circumspect. He talked to her and was always there at her side when she played the piano and sang, and often sang duets with her; he handed her to her place at table at dinner time, and played spillikins and so forth with her and the others whenever he was asked. But he was sensible too. He was polite to Mademoiselle Salinas and all the other guests and behaved impeccably carefully with them. But here in the park when he thought himself unseen by people who knew him, he let his heart out to show itself off. He did not take his eyes from Sophie's face, did not notice any other person or sight around him, and was totally absorbed in her, his face positively alight with adoration.

Tilly took a deep breath of sheer relief. She had been right after all to seek out Sophie. She had turned Duff's attention away from Patrick Paton; she, Tilly, had fretted needlessly and thought ill of her boy, and should be ashamed of herself. And she smiled delightedly as Silas beside her pulled on the reins of the phaeton to bring it nearer to Duff and Sophie's horses so that he could hail them.

It was not until the phaeton and two riders were side by side that Tilly looked at anyone apart from Duff, but then as Silas called cheerfully to them and she saw Duff's face change as he looked at Silas, she too turned to look at his companion's face. And was startled to see the oddly triumphant expression that was there, as Sophie lifted her chin and said softly, 'Why, Mr Geddes! Imagine seeing you here! Have you been following me? Fie on you!'

Chapter Eighteen

THE JOURNEY BACK to Brompton was not an easy one. They agreed without precisely discussing the matter that they would return together, with the two horses following the phaeton, and that Sophie and Tilly would be delivered to the house, while the men took the animals and equipage back to the livery stable.

'I dare say you require more time to change out of riding clothes than I,' Silas said cheerfully to Sophie when they arrived and he turned to help her down, after seeing Tilly safely to the pavement level. He reached her side faster than Duff could, for his horse needed a moment of gentling after he dismounted, and by the time he came round to take care of his companion, Silas had done the honours, much to Duff's obvious chagrin. It was clearly getting more and more difficult for him to disguise his feelings. Ever since they had met in the park, while they had paraded side-by-side with the phaeton along Rotten Row, Silas had monopolized Sophie's conversation – or perhaps she had monopolized him. It was hard to tell for certain which. But whoever had been the prime mover in the conversation between Sophie and Silas, it was clear that Duff was unhappy about it. Now, as she stood on the pavement watching Silas, it seemed to Tilly that she knew as vividly as if she had the thoughts for herself why he was so put out. He had looked forward all through the ride to the moment when he would take Sophie's hand in his and then set an arm about her waist to help her down. The physical contact had been something he yearned for, and Silas had robbed him of it.

Duff had also to stand impotently on the kerb watching Silas hand his mother and Sophie up the steps to the front door, for someone had to hold the horses' heads – both were restless, well aware of the hot mash that awaited them at the stables – and it was obvious Silas had no intention of doing so. Tilly looked back over her shoulder as she went into the house and saw Duff's blank expression, the one he always used to hide his real feelings, and some of her delight in his renewed affection for his childhood playmate evaporated. Was he going to break his heart again over her, because she preferred someone else? 'And someone you find interesting too,' her treacherous inner voice whispered in her ear, but she ignored it.

Eliza was waiting in the hall as they came in and Tilly smiled at her and asked her to send one of the maids up with hot water for Miss Oliver as well as herself, and Eliza nodded, but before she turned to go frowned as she looked again at Tilly.

'Where's your bonnet, Mum?' she demanded.

'Blown away!' Tilly said, trying to make it sound gay and amusing, but Eliza was not fooled.

'Just blown away? Or somethin' more? It's not like you to let your bonnet go untied, all messy, like.'

Sophie had reached halfway up the stairs by now and stopped to look down on them. 'Oh?' she said. 'I hadn't noticed that you had no bonnet – How absurd of me.'

Tilly looked up and managed a smile. 'Well, you were so deep in conversation that I am sure you had no thoughts for such unimportant matters as a missing bonnet,' she said. 'It was good to see you both so interested.'

'Interested?' Sophie said. 'Oh, yes, I suppose so – ' and then went on her way. Her voice had been cool and her glance a little sharp, Tilly thought, as Sophie's light footsteps receded; is she suggesting she was not particularly interested in Duff's earlier conversation? Or in Silas's after they had arrived. Because –

'Shall I help you change, Mum?' Eliza broke into her thoughts. 'It's getting very close to time for luncheon.'

'It's all right,' Tilly said absently. 'The men have to return yet, and change out of their riding clothes.' She stopped then and nodded. 'But yes, it will be an opportunity to talk. If you can spare the time from the kitchen.'

'Rosie will manage well enough,' Eliza said. 'I'll send up Lucy with the hot water then and come up myself directly.'

By the time she came to Tilly's room, Tilly had climbed out of her gown and into a wrapper and was brushing her hair, ready to pin it up. Generally she wouldn't disturb her hair once it had been dressed in the morning until it was time to prepare for dinner, but the wind had made a sorry tangle of it, and she had to brush it hard to tame it again.

Eliza came and wordlessly took the brush from her hand and she let her, grateful for the assistance. It had been a difficult morning, both physically and emotionally and she was more tired than she might have expected.

She watched Eliza's absorbed face in her mirror for a while and then sighed. There were lines she had never noticed before, a droop to the usually cheerful mouth that was saddening, and she knew she could not let her go on being so unhappy.

'Eliza,' she said abruptly. 'I must tell you what happened in the park this morning.' And tell her she did, leaving out no detail of the ragged, dirty children, and her encounter with them, and Eliza listened, absorbed, while her fingers busily dealt with Tilly's hair, and said not a word to interrupt.

'So there it is.' Tilly got to her feet and went across the room to her washstand and poured the hot water which Eliza had brought with her after dispatching Lucy to Sophie's room, and began to wash her face and hands. 'I shall ask Mr Cumming for news of what has happened to those children when he returns tonight, and in the future, when the need arises, and we find a baby from – in such a situation, we will make a home for him. Or her – here.'

'Oh, Mum!' Eliza said after a long pause. 'Oh, Mum, dear Mum!' And she came across the room and took Tilly's wet hands in hers and held them to her cheeks and kissed them. Tilly, deeply embarrassed, tried to pull her hands away but Eliza held on, weeping now, and Tilly felt her own eyes prickle in sympathy. But she managed not to cry and at length also managed to extricate her hands.

'Please don't distress yourself, Eliza,' she said. 'It wouldn't be good for you or your baby.'

Eliza began to laugh at that, twisting her tear-streaked face into quite another grimace and Tilly said sharply, 'Now, Eliza, just you sit down and take a deep breath and be still. I will not have you going off into hysterics. Not so near luncheon, certainly. It would be most inconvenient.'

Eliza laughed again, shakily, but this time there was no hysteria in it. Just real amusement and a deep relief. 'Oh, Mum,' she said. 'It'll be all so easy now – you'll see. People'll know as the baby's yours on account of you've adopted it, and that'll make 'em treat the child just as a child should be.'

'I am not certain yet about adoption, Eliza,' Tilly said firmly. 'Now, don't look so worried. There will be no problem, I do assure you. It will be clear to all that I am taking an interest in babies without families, and no one will think it at all odd when we have yours here, because by that time I shall have been seen to be very busy about such children. After today it is my intention to take an active interest in the welfare of beggar children. It is not enough just to send that poor little family to St George's Hospital. There must be more I can do. By the end of the next six or seven months people will be very used to seeing children here. For I tell you, it is my intention to seek out those children we met today, and fetch them here and feed them up and see if good care can't be arranged for them. I'm determined to do something – I can't just spend all my time and energy on the work of Quentin's.'

Eliza lifted her chin. 'Mum, you do whatever you think's best. I dare say when the time comes you'll see the sense of taking my baby to be your own adopted one – but if you wants to bring poor children to my kitchen in the meantime, why, I'll be there to help you! I think it's as good a thought as any you've ever had and you've had your share of them. I do my best to run an economical larder and kitchen but with the best will in the world it isn't always possible to use up every scrap of food I prepare. There has to be more than the guests can eat at every meal, or otherwise they'll think themselves on short commons, won't they? So to have a child or two about the place to clean up the plates, well, it'll suit me fine. I've the experience after all.' She looked wistful for a moment. 'I've never been anythin' but happy in your service, Mum, but I won't deny there's been times I've thought about my sisters and brothers at 'ome and wondered over 'em.'

'I told you many times to go and visit them, Eliza,' Tilly began, but Eliza interrupted her.

'No, Mum, not after what happened with that Mrs Leander and my ma – I swore then I'd never go back and never will I. But I missed the little ones and I won't deny it. So havin' some beggar children here'll be a pleasure, Mum. Until our own arrives.'

She smiled suddenly, a great wide gleaming grin that lit up her face and made her look as though a dozen years had fallen from her.

'Oh, Mum, 'n't it wonderful? I know 'e was a bad man, that Octo-'orrible-avius Reagan, and treated me disgraceful, but oh, Mum, 'n't it wonderful to be carryin' a baby? I never felt so good, Mum, as I do at this moment and it's all thanks to you. Oh, Mum, I do –'

'That's quite enough, Eliza,' Tilly said loudly and very firmly, knowing that Eliza was about to do something she had done once before, when she was very young, and declare an undying love for her, something which she, Tilly, would find impossible to deal with. 'I am happy that you feel better, and happy to know that you will assist me in my determination to do something for those children we saw. Now, I think I will dress myself quite easily. You go and see to it that the table is all ready and that the men are back. I think I heard them on the stairs a little while ago – and call everyone to luncheon. We really mustn't be late.'

Luncheon was an agreeable meal. Few of the guests were there; just the Graylings who, of course, never missed any meals at all, and Sophie, Duff and Silas as well as herself, for everyone else took their luncheon at their place of work, or were, like the Salinas family, much too occupied with their sightseeing to return to Brompton in the middle of the day.

At first the conversation was general, in an attempt to include the Graylings, but Mr Grayling, uncharacteristically, was feeling a little unwell and in consequence spoke less than usual and the pair retired to their own room immediately after eating the excellent milk pudding Eliza had sent up, leaving the four of them together.

Silas and Duff sat on each side of Sophie on one side of the table leaving Tilly in slightly isolated splendour at the top of the table. She could join in the conversation, but it was not entirely natural to do so, since there were spaces between herself and Silas, so she contented herself mainly with listening and, above all, observing.

The conversation was light and frivolous. Sophie was speaking teasingly about something Duff had said regarding the news in the *Morning Post* and Silas joined in with his banter too. It was clear that Duff did not particularly like what Silas said, for his face became a little wooden again and Tilly looked at him and wanted to deflect Silas, and then thought – but if I do, then Sophie will think the less of Duff. He must be free to behave the man, and if I meddle, then how can he? To me he is but a boy but he wants to play the man in Sophie's eyes and I mustn't make it harder for him. And she held her tongue.

And was glad that she had, for Duff found his feet again. He said something sharp that made Sophie laugh a great deal and now it was Silas's turn to look put out and that pleased Tilly. She watched him now, rather than Duff, and when he looked up and caught her eye and smiled broadly at her, a wave of warmth filled her. What a very good person he was, she told herself. He can't be flirting with this girl at all; he said himself he's too old for her, though I have to admit there have been many matches with such an age difference. But he thinks himself too old, so surely he can't be in any sense Duff's rival? See how kindly he changed the subject a moment ago and gave Duff a chance to say something clever?

'Did your mother tell you of our adventure in the park, Duff, before we met you?' Silas said and Duff looked up and then at Tilly. There was a small frown between his eyes.

'Adventure?' he said carefully, seeming anxious. 'Not a disagreeable one, I hope.'

Tilly smiled. 'No need to look so put about, my dear boy! It was a small matter. No need to make a fuss.' And she threw a warning glance at Silas, but he ignored it and launched himself into a lively account of their drive to the park and the beggar children's encounter with them.

'How horrid!' Sophie cried. 'It really is too bad that such children should be allowed into the park at all! I believe the authorities should clear them out. I have heard it said, and fully believe it to be true, that many of them are sent out by unscrupulous parents or masters to beg in a professional manner. They make vast amounts of money that way – it is quite disgraceful! It is dreadful in some parts of London, you know. You can't move for beggars dogging your footsteps, and very nasty and abusive some of them are. Throwing themselves at one's carriage to overset it is the least of it. Why, I have seen them in Covent Garden hanging on to the shafts, driving the horses nearly mad till their eyes roll and they slaver like crazy things, just to persuade the driver to give them money to get off! They are a menace – and giving money to them just encourages them.'

'They are poor,' Tilly said. 'If they have no food nor money to get any, how else are they to survive but by begging?'

'I am sure they can find work of some sort,' Sophie said. Her eyes were glittering with energy; she looked interested in a way Tilly had rarely seen her before. 'It is always possible for people to find some means of keeping themselves without resorting to such behaviour as these beggars do! They revolt me and terrify me. You must not go out in the park, ever again, dear Aunt Tilly! I should worry dreadfully if I thought you were –'

'You are kind to be so worried,' Tilly said a little tartly. 'But there is no need. I can't see these children as dangerous. Only as pitiable. I intend to do whatever I can to make their lives more tolerable.'

'Oh,' Silas lifted his head and so did Duff. 'What is that, Tilly?'

'Why, I am not yet quite sure!' Tilly said lightly. 'I shall wait until I have had the opportunity to talk tonight to Mr Cumming and we will see after that. Perhaps they may find a home here, below stairs, of course. But we must wait and see. Would anyone care for more coffee? I have ample here.'

They refused coffee with a shake of their heads and Duff said, 'You mean to become a philanthropist, Mamma?'

'I told you,' Tilly said, 'I'm not precisely sure what I shall do. I know only that I cannot rest until more has been done to take care of these children. I can't bear to think of them living in such a dreadful sort of way.'

'I am afraid, Aunt Tilly, that your good heart overwhelms your good sense,' Sophie said. 'You cannot care for all the beggar children in London! There are thousands and thousands of them. I tell you, I have seen them – they are the outside of enough, driving ordinary citizens to despair with their constant wheedling and prodding, when we all know they are lazy and dirty and could work for a living if they chose.'

'However importunate those you have seen may be, dear Sophie,' Tilly said, 'and I dare say you may be right that they are not all as poor as they seem to be, I am still concerned about these particular children we saw today. I have no intention of seeking a remedy for all. Just for them.'

'I am the one who is seeking a remedy for all,' Silas said and smiled at Sophie. 'I am quite determined to start a new branch of my Society to consider the welfare of these pathetic creatures. We shall make a story of the cause of their poverty and indigence and see if we can't offer some sort of thoughtful remedy for the conditions that create them and enable them to survive as they do. It will be the best way of controlling the menace, as you express it, Miss Oliver!'

'Well,' Sophie said and put down her napkin and rose to her feet. 'I dare say you think me unfeeling, Aunt Tilly, but I must say I believe that Mr Geddes's way of dealing with beggary is by far the best. To study social conditions and so arrange matters that beggary does not occur – now, that makes sense. But taking in filthy children who are probably verminous and diseased – well, I cannot see what good that does.'

'Except to the children,' Tilly said. 'And they will not remain verminous and diseased – if they are – once they are here. I shall see to it that they are clean and well fed, and undertake that they will be no discomfort to you, or any of my guests. I will, of course, explain to all of them my wishes and assure them they will not be discommoded in the slightest. I have no doubt they will look kindly on my efforts. What do you think, Duff?'

He was silent for a moment, looking from Sophie to Tilly and she could almost feel the tug he was experiencing from both directions. Then he shook his head and smiled.

'I shall try both methods and assess them, Sophie. I shall join Silas in his Society's meetings, if you'll have me, Silas, and also help Mamma with her plans. There! I cannot be fairer than that!'

Tilly laughed. 'Indeed you can't. Nor more diplomatic. I congratulate you! Now, I must be busy. If you will all excuse me, we shall meet again at dinner, I imagine?'

'Unless you have time this afternoon to discuss the manner in which I might start my new branch of the Society, Tilly,' Silas said and smiled at her. 'And perhaps you too, Miss Oliver?'

Sophie chuckled softly. 'Oh, no, Mr Geddes! I must be about something of much greater importance to me. I have a new book to read, and I shall sit in the summer house and read it, if that is permitted, Aunt Tilly?'

'Of course it is!' Tilly said. 'The summer house has been scrubbed and equipped with comfortable chairs for that very purpose. Duff, perhaps you will take out one of the long chairs and arrange it for Sophie? You will be more comfortable on one of those, my dear!' She smiled sweetly at the two young ones, as Duff, moving with alacrity, led the way to the dining-room door.

'I'll see to it at once,' he said. 'Sophie, may I join you in the summer house then? I could bring some cushions for you too, if you want them.'

She said nothing, just dimpling at him as she left the room and he followed, leaving Silas still at the table.

'Hmm,' he said after a moment. 'So that is your plan? I must say it sounds to me to be risky. Some of these children are, I am told, sadly debauched by their elders. They may be used as burglars' aides, ready to creep inside respectable houses and let the robbers in.'

'I shall risk that,' Tilly said. 'It will be better than doing nothing. Don't you feel that, in your heart?'

'Of course I do. Why else am I so determined to find a remedy for the cause of beggary? I just wish I could persuade you to devote your efforts to the matter in that safe sort of way, rather than – '

'Well, Silas, I must tell you that my mind is quite made up!' Tilly said and made for the door. 'I shall take care of these children we met this morning, no matter what. Now, if you will forgive me, we must allow Rosie to clear the table. We are holding her back in her work, you know, and that would never do.'

'No,' Silas said and sighed. 'Some things would never do.'

Chapter Nineteen

'PLEASE BE ASSURED, Mrs Quentin,' Mr Cumming said earnestly. 'The best arrangements have been made. We have much experience of these matters at St George's, for we draw on all the beggar population from Piccadilly as well as this side of the Town, and long ago sought measures for helping them. We have a most active committee of gentlemen who are concerned for their Christian welfare and the boys' cases went to them this very afternoon, since happily, they were having their monthly meeting.'

'But it seems so cruel to split a little family that way,' Tilly said and Mr Cumming lifted his brows at her.

'Little family, Mrs Quentin? Why, there are six of them! That is big enough in all conscience! While I applaud your notion of giving succour to the girl here, I cannot see that it would be of any value to your household to take in four boys and a baby, beside.'

She looked at him in some surprise. The ebullient young man, much given to flirting with the younger lady guests and making a great deal of noise guffawing with his friend Mr Hancock, seemed very different now he was speaking of matters to do with his work. He had become, she thought, almost as pompous as she knew some senior physicians to be, and she sighed a little. She had hoped to find him more sympathetic to her plans than he had turned out to be; now he was looking at her with positive disapproval.

'Let me explain a little more carefully, Mr Cumming,' she said. 'I am not proposing to take these children into my house in order to use them as servants. I believe they are too young for such things – they need care and feeding and a healthy life.'

'Your philanthropic nature is a credit to you, Mrs Quentin, but it is not a very practical matter you're suggesting. How long can such children be kept in idleness? They must earn their bread for the rest of their lives, if they are to have any, and the sooner they start to discover how to do so the better their chances. Boys generally start work on farms at the age of ten or thereabouts, you know, and these four boys are older than that. The youngest is already eleven and the others are in steps and stairs a year older. The fourteen year old will benefit most from being placed on a good farm, you know. There are some farmers who refuse to take a boy as old as that who has had no earlier experience of the work. To be too old is to handicap them. I repeat, your good heart does you credit, Mrs Quentin, but do let me assure you that you will do these boys a disservice if you bring them here and try to rear them as though they were children of your own class. They are not, and never will be. So do at least allow them to be reared to the station in life to which they are best suited.'

She sat and stared at him, her lower lip caught between her teeth, trying to think how she could argue with him. Then Silas, who had been sitting silently beside Mr Cumming, listening carefully, leaned forwards.

'I fear he is right, you know,' he said in a serious tone. 'I have listened to all your discussions, as you so kindly asked me to do, and as you are fully aware I was in total sympathy with your aspirations when we started. You did not have to convince me that your plan was a good one – but now I have heard all that Cumming here has to say, I must admit that I see the force of his argument. To take such boys and keep them here in London when they can go and live and work on a farm and regain some health and where they will be excellently fed, for country people do eat well, is hardly an act of generosity. Sooner or later they will return to the streets if they live here, will they not? You could not intend to apprentice them out of your own pocket to a city trade – and even if you did, and it would be a costly business for four of them, who would take them? They are of such poor background, I cannot see any city tradesman being at all interested in them, not when they can have their pick of better reared boys. If the hospital has this group of good men who are willing to take these boys to reliable farmers, why, I do think you should agree that they are wisest. There is much work to be done regarding children such as these – in prevention, you know, and education and so forth – but filling your home with the trouble such boys are all too likely to bring is not the right work for you.'

'But –' she began and then stopped. She could not argue with them, for what they were saying made clear, if unpalatable, sense, and she lifted her chin and said, 'I may visit them on their farms and see they are well?'

Mr Cumming looked relieved. 'Of course,' he said heartily. 'The members of our committee are eager to obtain all the support they can get, and it pleases them greatly to have ladies who are willing to take an interest in the children they rescue. It is vital they have good caring ladies like yourself to support the goodwill of the farmers, who, excellent Christians though they all are, and acting out of the love of their religion as they do, still benefit from the approval of their betters.'

She sighed deeply, dispirited. 'I would have wished to do more with my own hands,' she murmured and then lifted her head sharply to look at Cumming closely. 'If I agree that I will not seek to take the boys into my home, but will visit them regularly and be their friend, what of their sister and the baby? You cannot be putting them to farm work.'

Mr Cumming looked down at his hands, which had been resting on his knees which were akimbo. 'As to that,' he said after a moment, 'I fear the problem with one of them will be solved for us. The infant is very sickly. I cannot see him surviving much longer.'

'But surely not?' Tilly cried. 'While there is life all efforts must be made to –'

'But who will make such efforts?' Mr Cumming said reasonably. 'The infant is an orphan. It would take a most devoted mother's care to give the child the smallest chance of survival. And he has no mother –'

'He has his sister,' Tilly said heatedly.

'But she will have her own living to earn!' Mr Cumming said. 'This infant will need constant care by day and night if it is to live.'

'And it will have such care!' Tilly said strongly. 'From his sister. She seemed to me a sensible girl and much aware of her responsibilities. I shall take the girl and the baby and she will devote herself to getting him well. Then, in time, when the child has recovered – and I am determined he shall – we shall consider what we are to do for her in the future. How old is she?'

'Fifteen,' Mr Cumming said. 'Hardly a child any longer, of course.'

'Half starved as she is, you cannot call her a woman,' Tilly said. 'I never saw anyone in greater need of care.'

'I grant you that,' Mr Cumming said. 'A poor specimen altogether.'

Tilly opened her mouth to protest at such a term used of a living person, but closed it again. Clearly, she thought, Mr Cumming was too imbued with the attitudes of the surgeons and physicians with whom he spent his working time to see matters as she did; a man who could speak so dispassionately of a fellow human being as a 'specimen' was hardly one who would comprehend the way her own mind bent; and she stood up and folded her hands on her gown and looked at him as firmly as she could.

'I will ask then that you arrange tomorrow for the girl and her infant brother to come here,' she said. 'Or shall I come to fetch them?'

Mr Cumming looked at her and after a long moment shook his head. 'You're a very good, caring lady, Mrs Quentin,' he said. 'I knew myself to enjoy great comfort in your house and I had thought it all due to the efficiency of your manner of housekeeping, but I now see that much of it is due to the innate generosity of your spirit. I fear it will cost you dear one day, but I must admire it. Very well, I shall tell the hospital that the girl and the baby are to come to you. They will be glad enough not to have the responsibility, I dare say. They would have had to keep the child till it died, and to find a place for the girl. It is generally hard to get employment for beggar girls – people are unwilling to take them on, you know! They have no education in domestic matters, and hardly keep themselves clean, and often their morals are sadly low, because of the way they have lived on the streets. That is why your good heart does you so much credit –'

'Please,' she said and turned away. 'It is not specially good. It is surely only that any person with eyes in their head must see what needs doing. Thank you for your efforts, Mr Cumming. I am much obliged to you.'

He got to his feet and thrust his hands into his pockets, and stood there grinning at her, looking now much more like the young man she was accustomed to. 'My pleasure. Ma'am. Only one thing I'd ask –' He winked largely at Silas. 'Make sure the infant's housed well out of earshot of m'room! The bawling of the creatures goes on in my ears all day as it is.' And he laughed heartily and turned to go, leaving Tilly standing beside her fire and staring down into the flames, with Silas sitting quietly in his chair watching her.

They were in her private morning room and it was warm and quiet in there and after a while he got to his feet and came to stand beside her.

'My dear Tilly,' he said and there was great warmth in his voice. 'I will not embarrass you as that rather noisy young doctor did by expatiating on your virtues. I don't need to, for they are there for all to see. But I must say how grateful I am to whatever fate it was that led me to make my home in this house. I had intended my stay to be a short one, while I looked about for something more permanent, but there is no question in my mind now that this house is my home and will be so as long as you inhabit it. For you lend a fragrance to the very air that we breathe here.'

'Oh, pooh,' she said after a moment, painfully aware of the way her colour had deepened, and to cover her confusion she bent over and seized the poker to attack the coals in the grate and send them flying into sheets of flame. His nearness was something she was very aware of and, she had to admit, liked. It was a strange way to feel, she told herself, very strange; while her secret private voice jeered at her and told her it wasn't strange at all, but the most natural thing in the whole world.

'You really must not speak so!' she said as lightly as she could. 'It is quite absurd in you!'

'Not at all absurd,' he said gravely. 'I am a free speaker as I am a free thinker, Tilly, and I demand the right to say to you what I believe and feel. And I want to tell you that –'

She caught her breath and turned and replaced the poker on its hook among the other fire irons with as much clatter as she could and cried, 'No! I really would beg you, sir, to say no more. I have much to do in planning the arrival tomorrow of these children – and they are both children, no matter what Mr Cumming may say – and I really cannot stay here and chatter in this fashion. Do, please, return to the drawing room and amuse Sophie who must be languishing for some attention.'

He laughed, a little tightly. 'Miss Oliver, I think, will be far from languishing, at least while your son is about to entertain her! But all I wanted to say was –'

'No time!' she cried, with an attempt to seem merry. 'No time at all! Do please, go and entertain the others as well as yourself. I shall be about my business – thank you so much for joining me in this discussion with Mr Cumming. I wished you to be here because you, of course, were with me when we first met the children, and so knew of their pathetic situation. I needed you to encourage Mr Cumming fully to understand – and you were a great help, indeed you were.' And she picked up her skirts and sailed for the door, almost forcing him to walk ahead of her to open it and let her escape.

She almost ran out and turned for the baize door that led down to the kitchen and Eliza's domain; and gave him only a quick glance over her shoulder as she opened it and went through. He was looking after her with a quizzical expression on his face that she could not fully read, but she feared it meant more than she could bring herself to think about at the moment. Or did it? Perhaps she should not have reminded him of Sophie? Oh, she thought then with awareness of her own daring in even thinking in such language, damn the man! damn me and my nonsense – I have more important things to do than think of him. So, for heaven's sake, go and do them!

Do them she did. She and Eliza spent the remainder of the evening planning precisely how the house would be arranged to accommodate the newcomers. Eliza was particularly happy to hear the news of who was to come and when, admitting with the greatest of candour that her heart had quailed at the thought of boys coming.

'For I remember all too well what varmints my brothers was and I didn't relish the notion at all,' she said. 'Even our Mr Duff gave us a fair bit of runnin' around when he was a lad, and imagine that multiplied by four and no sensible training from a good Mamma to stand them in good stead! No, I ain't sorry and that's the truth and I hope as you don't think me selfish, Mum.'

'No,' Tilly said. 'Not selfish. Just sensible, I suppose. I wish I were always the same. However, this time it has been forced on me. We shall have just the girl and the infant. Now, I thought that if we took the big attic room at the back, in the old house, and set the new maid to the one on the other side where the wall is extra thick and she need not be disturbed if the baby cries in the night, we could take in the spare bed from the third room on the other side.'

The following morning, by the time Tilly set out in a closed carriage, fetched from the livery stables, to collect the girl and the baby from St George's Hospital, the room was ready.

They had furnished it, she and Eliza, simply enough, finding some old chintz curtains for the long attic windows, and a strip of red drugget for the wooden floor. There was a bed, a small and narrow one, but well found enough and well supplied with blankets and a pair of coarse linen sheets and a ticking pillow. There was a crib, the one that had been Duff's and which had lain unused in the loft ever since he had graduated to a bed when he was five, also well found with blankets and specially cut sheets that Tilly discovered tucked away in the loft too, and a small table and a cupboard. Once a wicker chair with arms had been added, there was space for little else, but the room looked snug enough and was indeed warm, for the heat of the house rose to it and kept it very cosy.

'She's a lucky girl,' Eliza said, when the room was finished and she stood there admiring it. 'To go from the streets to this – why, she'll think she's died and gone to paradise.'

And to an extent that was precisely what the girl said when at last she spoke at all. When Tilly arrived at the hospital, to stand in the big central hall with its black and white floor tiles, trying to ignore the stink of the place, a queasy mixture of human dirt and blood and the ominous sickly sweetness that she knew denoted death, the girl was sitting waiting for her. The baby was tucked inside her shawl and could not be seen, and she had a small basket at her feet. She had been washed since her arrival, and her hair could now be seen to be a straggly pallid brown and her complexion pale. Her eyes were a deep green and she might have been handsome, Tilly thought, if she had had a better start in life. She stood up when Tilly came towards her and just stared at her mutely. Tilly held out her hands to her and said heartily, 'Well, my dear? So you are to come to us! Are you pleased to do that?'

The girl nodded and then turned her head as Mr Cumming appeared at the other side of the hall and came hurrying across.

'The baby is far from well today,' he said in a low voice for Tilly's ears alone. 'If he lives another week, I'll be amazed. I've given the girl instructions as to its medicines but I should not trouble it too much for it will hardly benefit so will lose little if it has none, to be truthful. If you can get it well fed, that will be a start.'

He turned to the girl then and said with a hearty brightness that grated in Tilly's ears, 'Well, Polly, are you not a fortunate creature? To have this good kind lady take you in? You must be very obedient and good, and mind all she says. She will do all she can to help you with the baby, but remember I told you it is not likely to make old bones. But Mrs Quentin will help you, whatever befalls. And you be grateful, now!'

The girl bobbed at the knees, still silent, and Tilly took her away, putting her into the carriage, where she sat very upright, still clutching the invisible infant beneath her shawl. Tilly sat beside her as the coachman called up the horses and they set off, and said softly, 'May I see the baby, Polly?'

Tilly essayed a smile and the girl looked back at her, her eyes deep and suspicious, but after a moment drew back the edge of the shawl. The baby, like herself, had been washed, and Tilly found herself looking down on the most pinched and wizened features she could ever remember seeing on an infant. He looked to be old, very, very old, older than time itself. The eyes bulged a little in the deep sockets, and still showed that rim of white where the lids had not fully closed, and the temples seemed to have collapsed. The small mouth was pursed in what could have been taken for a thoughtful moue, but there was no other sign of any life there. He was breathing, fast and shallowly, but that was all. There was no other movement, no other sign of any awareness, and Tilly leaned forwards and slid her gloved finger into the small fist that lay curled on the infant's breast.

At last there was a reaction. The fingers relaxed as she put her own finger there, and then tightened around it, and suddenly it was long ago and she was sitting with Duff on her lap and letting him grip her finger in just that way; but Duff had been round and rosy and full of life, making faces, chuckling, crying and snuffling, as unlike this sad creature as it was possible for a baby to be; and Tilly sighed and extricated her finger and leaned back in the corner against the dusty squabs. Had she done the right thing? How would she help this girl beside her when the baby died, as inevitably he must? She could not imagine. And she too sat in silence all the way home.

Eliza took the girl's little basket as soon as she arrived, and peered inside it. 'Good,' she said heartily. 'They gave you some bits for the baby, then. I've found a few of the things our Mr Duff wore when he was a baby, Mum, and washed 'em up ready, but it helps to have some that'll fit this one. Mr Duff was a much bigger child altogether.' And she looked at the baby in Polly's arms and then at Tilly, a swift expressionless flash of her eyes that said all there was to say. She, too, clearly knew that this child could not possibly live.

They led the girl upstairs, stomping along between them and

Tilly heard her breaths come shorter and thinner and thought – she needs feeding up, poor thing. She has no strength in her – and at last they reached the very top and the attic that had been prepared.

It was Eliza who opened the door and showed the girl the way in and Tilly followed her. Polly stood in the middle of the little room and stared and then turned round slowly, looking at everything. And still she said nothing.

But then she unwrapped the baby and set him down on his back on the counterpane and knelt down beside the bed so that she could bring her lips close to his ears, and peered into his waxen and expressionless face.

'There, Georgie,' she said softly. 'See? I told you it'd be all right, didn't I? You'll get well here, won't you? O' course you will. You'll get better for your Polly, now. It's all safe now, Georgie. Ain't it all lovely, then? Ain't it?'

Tilly was never sure which of them started to weep first, she or Eliza. Certainly they both had wet cheeks when they left Polly murmuring over the dying baby, Georgie, there in their small attic room at the back of the house.

Chapter Twenty

BUT GEORGIE STUBBORNLY refused to die. Despite all the gloomy prognostications from all around him – Mr Cumming, Eliza and, because of them, Tilly, too – he clung to life like a barnacle, silent, stubborn, but there. Polly sat with him for day after day beside the kitchen fire, tucked into the big rocker and, patiently and laboriously, dripped food into his half-open mouth from a china pap boat. At first the food dribbled out of his mouth to drip down his chin, but she would mop away the mess and try again and again, and after a while less of the pap was rejected. He did not precisely swallow but seemed almost to absorb the food through his mouth; and then one day he actually did swallow, and opened his eyes a little and then closed them fully. Polly lifted her face to Eliza who was, happily, watching them at the time and said simply, 'You see? I told you he'd get better.'

After that first hopeful reaction, which came five days after the pair had moved into Quentin's, he seemed to speed up his progress. He swallowed as much as a dessertspoonful of pap at a time, though it took him close on an hour to do it, and Eliza decided that no matter what the hospital had said – they had given instructions that the baby was to be fed only on bread pap, which was white bread soaked in water and squeezed out to leave a thin, cloudy liquid – that he needed 'somethin' a bit stronger than that'. She showed Polly how to make a richer bread and milk mixture with sugar in it and a little butter, and squeezed it through a muslin sieve to make a thicker, richer feed. And Georgie seemed to like that, for certainly he swallowed more and more of it.

It was a week later that Tilly came down on her way to breakfast to find Polly crouching by the baize door, just inside the hall, her skirts pulled close to her knees, and her chin tucked in so that she could peer out over her hands which were clasped round them, looking as though she was all eyes. Tilly stopped at the foot of the stairs when she saw her and her belly lurched. Had something happened to Georgie in the night?

'What are you doing there?' she cried, sounding brusque in her anxiety and for a moment Polly's face crumpled.

'I was waitin' for you,' she muttered and got awkwardly to her feet. 'Didn't know I weren't supposed to be 'ere. It's the way wot you brought me into the 'ouse, and I 'as to come down the stairs an' all and through 'ere to get to the kitchen so I didn't think it mattered.'

'Of course it doesn't!' Tilly said, still a little sharply. 'I was not complaining because you are in the hallway, silly girl! I was just surprised to see you there. Is there – have you trouble with Georgie?'

The slightly sullen look which had appeared on Polly's face smoothed itself away. 'No, Mum. It's what I was waitin' to tell you. 'E cried in the night.'

Tilly looked at her blankly. 'Cried in the night? To be sure, Polly, all babies cry in the night.'

'Not Georgie,' Polly said. ''E did when 'e was first born, o' course, when 'e was still what a baby oughta be – but since 'e was ill 'e's 'ardly cried at all. Not 'ad the strength for it, see? But 'e cried last night –'

At last Tilly understood. 'Oh, my dear!' she said and held out both hands to Polly. 'How splendid! Of course it is a great sign of his increasing strength, and we must delight in it! Was he hungry, or was it because he was soiled?'

'Hungry, Mum,' Polly said. 'I come down and got some food for 'im an' I 'ope as that was all right, Mum.'

'Of course it was all right,' Tilly said warmly. 'Come. We must speak to Eliza about this, and see to it you've a boatful of food to take up each night so that you need not come down in the dark.'

She hurried down to the kitchen where Eliza had now emerged from her own room and was busy supervising the preparation of the hot dishes for breakfast.

'Kedgeree,' she was instructing Rosie, 'needs to be really hot, you hear me? It can't be one of your half-and-half dishes, so be sure to set it in the chafing-dish with the spirit lamp. It don't matter so much that the bacon goes in a plain one, so long as it's covered and well warmed to start with. That'll keep it nicely hot, whereas a chafing-dish'll go on cooking it and turn it into a crisp and ruin it. But the kedgeree don't hurt none if it goes on cookin' – brings out the flavour of the curry, like. Put a bit o' extra butter on top and stir it in before you takes it to the table, that's all. And Rosie, don't you start those coddled eggs till I gives you the office, you hear me? Yesterday Mr Hancock said his was downright hard and no coddled egg should ever be anything but nicely tender – Good morning, Mum! Oh, there you are, Polly! I thought you'd gone off to the privy, seeing Georgie there like that. Next time you have to leave him, tell one of us and we'll watch him. I don't hold with tying babies to chairs – one of my brothers nearly hanged himself because of that.'

'I shall obtain some leading reins for him,' Tilly said. 'And then we can fasten him to a chair safely if Polly needs to be away from him. Eliza, he cried last night. From hunger. Is that not good news?'

Eliza looked at her and then at the baby who was sitting in the big rocker, slipped sideways a little and fast asleep. Then she peered at Polly.

'Are you sure? Not just wishin' it?' she said. 'He don't look all that bright to me and I won't say otherwise. Still as scrawny as a skinned rabbit.'

'He cried,' Polly said stubbornly. 'Cried real loud. Woke me up! I came and got some pap for him and 'e took it all. Half the boat full.' She snickered then. 'Got into a right mess too, this morning. 'E ain't shit like that since I dunno when.'

Across the kitchen beside the fire Rosie, who was busily turning sausages in the big pan, snorted in disgust and threw a sharp glance at Polly. That the other servants did not like Polly or her baby brother was no secret, but they had done nothing worse than mutter at each other and treat Polly with silent contempt, which seemed to suit her well enough; certainly she showed no sign of minding what they did or said, and did not do so now.

'Well,' Tilly said as dampeningly as she could. 'That is another good sign, no doubt, but we will not discuss it here. Now, while he seems happy enough, and Eliza is here to watch him, go and have your own breakfast.'

'No,' Polly said. 'I'll see to 'im first,' and went and picked up Georgie, who woke and lay there in her arms blinking up at her, and Tilly went over to him and touched his cheek. He had lost some of the thick pallor that had made him look like a waxen effigy rather than a living creature, and though he was still desperately thin, his eye sockets looked less deep, and his temples seemed less hollow.

'You have made a superb task of caring for him, Polly,' Tilly said, 'has she not, Eliza? I don't scruple to tell you, my dear, that when you came here first I was quite certain, as was everyone else, that he could not live more than a day or two. You have confounded us all.'

'Not me,' Polly said gruffly. 'It's 'im. 'E'll confound all of us one day, you see if 'e don't.' And suddenly she lifted him to hold his cheek against hers and began to rock him, with a fierce possessiveness that made Tilly take a step back. ''E'll show everyone one day, you see if 'e don't. 'E'll grow up to be richer an' cleverer an' stronger than any of you. Just you wait and see!' And Georgie let out a sudden wail of protest at the strength of her grip, which sounded like a kind of repetition of his sister's outburst and across the room Rosie laughed incredulously. But it was an uneasy sound.

After that, Georgie came on apace. As the autumn days shortened and the air got crisper, he seemed to grow before their eyes. His appetite became voracious and soon he was clamouring for more food so loudly and so often that Eliza advised abandonment of the pap boat and a transfer to bowl and spoon. He wolfed as much buttered bread and milk and honey as Polly gave him and still seemed to want more, so Eliza added eggs which were beaten into the mixture. That seemed to please him for a while and he became more active and it was no longer safe to set him in a chair, for he would roll out at the first opportunity. Tilly obtained the promised leading reins from Jem's shop, and Georgie spent his time either sitting on the floor beside his sister, attached to her wrist by the leather straps, or perched on her scrawny hip as she moved about the house.

Then he got hungrier again and bad tempered with it, crying so much that even Eliza got irritable, and she assured Polly it would be perfectly all right to feed the child on stronger food and added mashed fish and even scraped beef to his diet. And at last Georgie stopped crying and became more like an ordinary baby. He slept a lot and ate a lot and played a lot and soiled himself a lot, and he looked well. The eyes and temples filled out as fast as his cheeks. His skin lost its sickly pallor and took on a lively rosiness. His hair, a soft brown like Polly's, curled vigorously about his ears and he began to develop bracelets of fat around his wrists as Eliza, now quite besotted with him, added a few dollops of cream to his bread and milk and as much honey as he would take, which was considerable.

Within eight weeks of his arrival at Quentin's, he was crawling everywhere. Tilly had not thought too much about his age and was startled now to realize that he was as old as he was; fully fifteen months, according to Polly.

'I allus knew as 'e was born to be a bigun, like my pa,' she said as she sat crouched on the rug beside him, her favourite position. 'My pa's ever so big. Or 'e was when times was better.' She seemed to brood for a moment. ''E got ever so thin when 'e couldn't work no more.'

'Why could he not work any more, Polly?' Tilly asked and the girl shot a sideways glance at her.

'Done 'is back in, di'n't 'e? Fell off a ladder on account it was all busted, and 'e 'ad a big load o' slates up and when 'e went up to the roof, the 'ole bleedin' thing come down and 'im with it. Couldn't walk at first, 'e couldn't, but after that – well 'e could walk but 'e dragged one leg an' no one'd give 'im work. So 'e did 'is best and stole food, but 'e couldn't run fast enough to get away so –' She shrugged. 'Gone to clink 'e 'as. Won't never come out, I reckons.'

'How can you be sure of that?' Tilly cried. 'Tell me which prison he is in and perhaps I can –'

The girl looked at her almost contemptuously. 'Which prison? 'Ow should I know? I went to 'ear the beak in court when they put pa up in front of 'im to see what I could find aht, but no one'd tell me nothin'. I just got kicked aht for me pains. 'E waved to me from the Black Maria, but I never saw 'im again nor found aht where they took 'im.'

'Well, I might have more success,' Tilly said. 'Which was the court you say you went to? The one where your father was tried?'

Polly sat very still on the kitchen hearthrug, her skirt of blue print stripes – for Eliza had made up a couple of maid's dresses for her, and provided her with aprons and cotton caps to keep her neat – spread about her, and stared up at Tilly curiously. Georgie, sitting beside her on the rug and playing with a little pile of polished pebbles, which he was putting into and taking out of the battered tin mug which Eliza had given him and which he regarded as his own special treasure, made the sort of contented babbling sounds well fed babies do make, and then, oddly, turned and looked at her too, so that both seemed to be regarding her with an air of puzzlement.

Tilly leaned back in the rocker; they were alone in the kitchen because Eliza had gone out to Charlie Harrod's to deliver the monthly order. Tilly had sent Eliza on this errand rather than go herself as she usually did, because she felt the need to talk to Polly about her history, and had therefore created an opportunity to speak to her alone. But now she felt oddly embarrassed, as though she had been prying into matters that were none of her concern. Yet surely, she thought a little defensively, she had a right to ask questions of her own protégée?

'I do not ask out of any morbid curiosity, Polly,' she said. 'I only wish to be of help to you.'

'That's what I was wonderin'' Polly said. 'Why?'

'I beg your pardon?'

'Why? I mean, why should a lady like you go to such a bother over the likes of us? I got a bit o' time to think now, what with Georgie bein' so much better.' And she turned her head to look adoringly at Georgie, who blew a spit bubble at her and tried to put one of the smaller pebbles in his mouth, which she took from him, much to his annoyance, for he let out a sharp squawk of protest. ''E's the way a baby ought to be now, an' it's all been to do with you. I mean, I never doubted, not fer a minute I didn't, as Georgie'd be all right in the end –' There was the now familiar fierceness in her voice again. 'But now 'e is an' I'm that much better too, bein' fed proper for the first time since I can remember, an' gettin' right fat on it,' – And indeed she has plumped up a little, Tilly thought, and looks much the better for it – 'well, I took to wonderin'. Why should you bother? Is it all on account of church, like?'

'Church?' Tilly said, diverted. 'How do you mean?'

'Got used to them we did,' Polly said. 'Comin' down round where we lived and tellin' us they could save our souls for us, and givin' us bibles, us what couldn't read and needed food for our bodies a sight more 'n' we needed bleedin' preachin' – an' if we didn't say as we was mad about God an' all that, they didn't show no more interest. But you've never once mentioned God or comin' to church or any of that stuff, so I was wondering. Why? What are we to you, me and Georgie? We got nothin' –'

'Do you know,' Tilly said slowly. 'I really have not the least idea. It's just that – well, there you were, in the park and when I saw you I felt so sad for you. And so bad about you. It seemed all wrong that you and your brothers should be so – should have so little that he had to run under a horse's hooves and – well, there you are.'

'You gave us money that day. You di'n't 'ave to do no more,' Polly pointed out with an air of great reasonableness. 'So like I says, why? All this, I mean. Givin' me and Georgie an 'ome.'

'I wanted to take your brothers, too, you know, but they – well, I was told they were better off on a farm. I shall be going to visit them, though, and I shall take you and Georgie to see them too, but –'

'See what I mean?' Polly said. 'Don't make sense, do it? I knows you're a lady an' all that, an' got more money and vittles than you can ever use, but all the same it ain't the sort of usual run of things to do. To go an' take on the likes of us, I mean – not if you're not goin' on about church an' all that.'

'I just don't know why!' Tilly said, rather put out now. She had not expected, when she set out to question Polly, to be put through quite such a catechism on her own account. 'It is, after all, my affair, anyway. There is no reason why I should explain to you.'

'I don't see why you shouldn't,' Polly said. 'I mean, it's me and Georgie an' all, 'n't it? It's our lives an' our doin's as you've got yourself all mixed up in, so I reckon we got a right to know why. That's all. I wasn't bein' pert, you know. I ain't trying to misbehave to me betters. I was just *wonderin'*.'

'So you said,' Tilly said a shade tartly. 'No need to go on about it. Let us just say I chose to take an interest in you and your family and that I trust I may have your permission to go on doing so!' And she could not help allowing a note of sarcasm to creep into her voice.

Polly smiled then, and Tilly realized with a stab of surprise that she never had before. Her teeth were broken and clearly unhealthy and her smile creased her face awkwardly, but it lit up her eyes in a way that made the child look almost pretty, and Tilly smiled back involuntarily.

'Course you can,' Polly said. 'I just thought I'd ask, like. Not that I'll ever understand the ways of the quality, I dare say. Georgie, you put that down right away!' For Georgie had picked up his tin mug and was attempting to batter his sister with it.

'We must find him some better plaything than that,' Tilly said, glad to change the subject. 'I am sure that we have some of Duff's oddments still put away somewhere.'

'You was asking about my pa,' Polly said. 'It was at Clerkenwell they put 'im up in front of the beak, on account 'e never did no stealin' near 'ome. 'E thought 'e 'ad a better chance o' not gettin' caught if 'e went where no one knew 'is face, so 'e went down

'Olborn way. But there, like I said, poor bugger couldn't run, could 'e?'

'You should not use such words, Polly,' Tilly said, needing to reprove. 'It is not proper.'

'Oh, lummy, if you want me to talk like you, you've got some fine 'opes!' Polly said and again produced that endearing smile. 'What's wrong with what I said, anyway?'

Tilly sighed. 'Never mind. I'll leave it to – well, never mind. Clerkenwell, you say? Well, we could enquire there and see what befell your father, if you wish me to.'

Polly looked down at Georgie. 'E don't make no nevermind,' she said, with a return of her old sullenness. 'I don't reckon 'e's around any more anyway. It was a dunnamany months ago now and 'e wasn't strong anyway. They dies like flies in clink, don't they?'

Tilly did not doubt the girl spoke from a wealth of knowledge of the sort she herself would never have, and so did not argue with her; but she decided privately that enquiries should be made. If the father was alive and could be redeemed and fetched safely from jail, perhaps he could be helped to some sort of occupation and the chance to make a home again for his children? It seemed to her that if she could arrange such a thing, it would show Mr Cumming and Silas that she was as aware as anyone of the need to deal with the causes of beggary. Loss of a father must surely lead children to beg; therefore fetch a father back and all should be well. So she told herself, and decided to speak to Silas that very evening on the issue, and now turned the conversation with Polly to Georgie; and since he was Polly's favourite subject it was not difficult to fix her attention on it.

So for the next half hour Polly chattered about how it had been for her and her brothers when Georgie had been born, and how her stepmother had suffered, and slowly Tilly built up a picture of the life this girl had led. A life of semi-starvation with an ever-increasing brood of brothers in a couple of cold, wet rooms which were plagued by bedbugs and cockroaches, sharing a midden with the fifteen other families who lived in the same ramshackle house, and struggling day by day just to stay alive. Polly had clearly tried not to love the baby her stepmother had produced and then left her to care for, dying within a week of his birth from loss of blood and some unspecified fever. Listening to her Tilly could see how it had been, how she had done what she had to do for Georgie because she had no choice at first, but how she had been drawn closer and closer to him.

The day she, Tilly, had first met them in the park, Polly had been at almost her lowest ebb. Her father had been gone a full year, and she had been coping somehow with food they begged and an occasional sixpence given to her, she said, 'as a present, like'. And Tilly, knowing perfectly well that such presents were not given to girls without strings attached to them, made no effort to ask how often she got such 'gifts', or how she felt about them. That bright autumn morning over two months ago, Polly had been fit to die, so she told Tilly in a matter-of-fact tone that was chilling in its detachment, and had not even cared whether Georgie lived or died.

'I think I wanted 'im to,' she said now, staring down at Georgie. 'May I be forgiven, that was what I wanted, because I thought then I'd be able to die and it wouldn't matter to no one. The bigger boys'd manage well enough, and with Georgie gone I'd be free. But then you came along.'

She lifted her chin and threw a glance at Tilly that seemed to glitter, so sharp was it. 'And sent us up the 'ospital, what wouldn't 'ave took us without that card from the gentleman, and there it is. I'm 'ere and Georgie's 'ere and it's goin' to be all right.' And she leaned over and hugged Georgie close suddenly and passionately, and the baby laughed and kicked and Tilly touched Polly's shoulder and said nothing.

And then Eliza came in, in a gust of cold air from the street outside, bustling and chattering about the newest line in preserved peaches that Charlie had offered her at a ridiculous price, and how much better her own preserves were than any he would sell; and the moment of tension melted away. But it left Tilly feeling an even greater need to look further into what could be done for Polly and her brothers and if that meant enlisting Silas's help, and therefore company again, well, so be it. And her secret voice whispered, 'And won't that put Miss Sophie in a pet, then!' But Tilly ignored that as too shameful for her even to consider, and smiled at the girl. 'It's all right, Polly,' she said quietly under cover of Eliza's chatter. 'I will always take an interest in you. That's a promise. You and Georgie really needn't worry any more.'

Chapter Twenty-One

'DON'T YOU THINK you have done enough for the girl, Mamma?' Duff said, and took from her the coffee cup she had just filled and delivered it punctiliously to Miss Fleetwood, who was sitting on the other side of the fireplace. 'I can't pretend I like the idea of your hanging about prisons and the like, even for the best of motives. Have you not enough to do without becoming the Elizabeth Fry *de nos jours*?' And he smiled over Miss Fleetwood's head at Sophie, who was sitting on the sofa holding a fan between her face and the flames of the fire, over which she peeped beguilingly at the company. Silas was leaning over the sofa behind her and he lifted his brows at Duff's words.

'To emulate Miss Fry would be no mean ambition, Duff,' he said, and smiled at Tilly. 'If you wish to visit there, I will gladly accompany you, both to be of assistance to you and to reassure Duff.'

'Dear me,' Tilly said, a little nettled. 'I need no protection from anyone, including you, Duff! I don't intend to wander where I should not, you know, amongst people in the prisons! Merely to visit the court at Clerkenwell and see what I can discover about Polly and Georgie's father. There is no great effort in that.'

'All the same, I would be most interested to accompany you if you would permit,' Silas said. 'I am quite determined we must do more at our Society to combat the problems of poverty in London today. The two meetings we have had on the issue were well attended, but it seems too little to me. I need some hard facts to deliver to them so that I can ginger them up a little. They're very –' He sighed. 'I should not speak so of the members of my own Society, I know, but they can seem a little too comfortable, you know. They listen but they do not *feel* –'

'By all means,' Tilly said. 'If you are interested to seek facts, then of course, as long as you know that I am fully capable of dealing with Polly's affairs without help – except perhaps from you, Mr Cumming.' She smiled up at him, for he had joined the small group by the fire, leaving Mr Hancock happily talking to Mademoiselle Salinas for whom he was developing a decided *tendresse*. 'Your care of them both has been excellent.'

'Thank you, Ma'am. I must say it is amazing how that girl has dealt with that baby. I thought he was meat for the graveyard, and had no hope of life, but I saw him this afternoon, and examined him, you know, and he's amazingly well. Still needs to grow and his teeth are in a sad state – as indeed are hers, but it is always so with these gutter children. They never have anything better. It's like the rickets they are born with –'

'Born with or suffer from because of their poverty, Doctor?' Silas asked. 'I am convinced that with proper care and feeding these children could be as well made as any of us.'

Mr Cumming looked amused. 'I know your theories, Geddes. I have heard you propound them often enough. But I take leave to assure you that you are wrong. If the health is not in the germ, then it cannot be in the ear – that is to say, these people are of inferior stock. We must do the best we can for them but they can never be anything other than what they are – creatures of the gutter. Some – the superior sort – are able to pull themselves out and live tolerable enough lives and earn their keep, but the rest of them –' He shook his head. 'If you saw as many as I do at St George's, Geddes, you would not have so rosy a vision.'

Silas opened his mouth to protest, but Sophie, clearly bored now, broke in. 'Duff, my dear friend, shall we discuss our plans with Aunt Tilly? I am sure she will be most interested.'

Duff looked a little put out and his cheeks tightened, but Sophie smiled at him and he melted.

'I had intended to do so later this evening,' he said, 'after – well.' He laughed a shade awkwardly. 'If the rest of you are not too bored by the talk of private plans.'

'We are agog!' Miss Fleetwood said promptly. 'So tell us what they are. It all sounds very exciting.' And she looked archly from one to the other and then at Tilly, her brows raised.

Tilly, who had felt a lurch of anxiety at Sophie's words, but was determined not to show it, looked at Duff. 'What plans, my dear?'

'Well, I have received an invitation to hunt from Patrick,' Duff said, a little gruffly.

'Lord Paton, you know,' Sophie said brightly and beamed beatifically at Tilly. 'And I begged Duff to write and ask if I might be one of the party and he did, and the letter arrived this morning, did it not, Duff? I am invited! Is that not the greatest fun?'

There was a short silence as the company digested their amazement at Sophie's breathtaking impudence; to propose herself to a lord she had never even met, and to do so as the companion of a young man? Had she no idea of the proprieties? Miss Fleetwood opened her mouth to speak, but mercifully – since it was clear she was about to say something blistering – Sophie spoke first.

'I know perfectly well that it is quite outrageous of me to make such a suggestion or will seem so, but you see, I met the duke some time ago.' She dimpled. 'Such a charming man, I thought. He said then that I must come to visit him, but the opportunity never arose. And I would never wish to go alone to such a party. To have Duff as my chaperone, as it were, will be such a comfort!'

'Where did you meet him?' Tilly asked and looked very forcefully at Sophie. Since her arrival at Quentin's she had foreborne to question her about her past and had not been able to bring herself to ask questions about her mother, Dorcas; to hear now that at some time the girl had hobnobbed with a duke was startling indeed.

'Ah, well, as to that,' Sophie said airily, 'it is a long story. It was at the theatre, in Covent Garden one evening. We had been doing the opera, *Faust*, as I recollect – he had enjoyed it greatly and was most complimentary about it. And that was when he asked me to visit.' She looked very directly at Tilly as she spoke, her chin up and her eyes seeming to challenge her.

Miss Fleetwood's mouth was now actually open in amazement. 'You had been –' she began and then as Tilly attempted to interrupt her, held up her hand. 'No, I shall not be stopped! What were you doing at the opera, young lady, talking to a *duke*?'

Sophie looked more charming than ever. 'Why, I was earning my bread, Miss Fleetwood,' she said with an air of great simplicity. 'You cannot think I am able to live on air alone? You teach children in order to earn your bread, and I too have an occupation.'

'What sort of occupation?' Miss Fleetwood said in an awful tone. 'Am I to suppose that –'

'You may suppose what you will, my dear teacher,' Sophie said. 'But it will be simpler if I tell you, will it not? I was dancing in *Faust*. I am an excellent dancer, and I had the main role. That was what the duke had so enjoyed. And why I am able to propose myself – with Duff's aid, of course – to Paton for the hunting. So I hope, dear Aunt Tilly, you will have no objection to Duff accompanying me? For I, of course, shall go, no matter what!'

Silas, as he had promised, accompanied Tilly on her visit to the court at Clerkenwell and she could not deny that she was glad to have his company. Even though he was on the silent side.

He had indeed been so ever since Sophie had dropped her most effective little bombshell into their company. In the two or three days that had elapsed the house had buzzed with it, and with little else. The guests murmured to each other and looked sideways at Sophie as she swept by, and even the servants seemed to have found out, for they looked at her with a sort of awe, and Eliza, when asked about the matter, told Tilly with some complacency that of course she'd known it was something like that all along.

'I knew soon as I set eyes on her again that there was *somethin'* more I remembered than just her being a little girl here. I've seen her picture in my magazines, that's the thing of it, lovely drawin's they was. I knew I knew that dimpled chin from somewhere! Imagine – our little Miss Sophie on the stage!'

Which was small comfort for Tilly, for she herself had been, to tell the truth, somewhat shocked by the revelation. She had never thought much about the theatre; she had attended performances from time to time of course, but very few, for most of her entertainment was found within her own four walls in the company of her guests, who were, she told herself with a stab of wickedness, sometimes as good as watching a farce. If she had ever thought about actresses and dancers at all it had been in the same terms as the generality of her neighbours, that actresses were in some way disreputable. No decent lady, surely, would permit herself to be displayed on a stage. And yet –

The thing of it was, she had to admit, Sophie was so beguiling. If other guests peeped and gossiped for the first day or so, they were soon won round and became as eager for her company as they had ever been, and in some ways even more so. She had now an added sheen to her person, it seemed, and this made her glow and they all basked in it. The servants too seemed willing to treat her with extra respect rather than less. It was as though the power of her own character quite overwhelmed any rascally connotations of her occupation. So why should I feel so put out? Tilly asked herself as reasonably as she could, and receiving no satisfactory answer, took the route she had so often in the past, and went to talk to Jem, finding him, as usual, in his shop, busily arranging the winter fabrics.

He listened as she told him of Sophie's newest piece of news and then nodded seriously.

'I'm not at all surprised,' he said simply and returned to his fabric which was not settling itself entirely to his satisfaction. 'She was always a little madam, wasn't she? Showing herself off and expecting people to admire her. It makes sense she'd be on the stage. And I wondered where she had her money from. Unless her mother had died and left her a legacy, I couldn't see it.'

'She hasn't said her mother has died,' Tilly said doubtfully. 'She never speaks of her and somehow I have never brought myself to ask her.'

'Perhaps you should,' Jem said reasonably and stepped back to admire the thick green silk that now hung in perfect swathes from the bar above the counter. 'There, if that don't sell out inside the week, then I know nothin' about this business or the taste of my customers – isn't it a fine piece of stuff?'

'Indeed it is,' Tilly said and then laughed. 'In fact, you may let me have a length.'

'I've already cut it for you,' he said. 'I thought you'd like it and it'll suit you fine. As to Miss Sophie – she has her own reasons for telling you now and not sooner. I'd not cater to her taste for attention by letting her see you're all that concerned, if I were you.'

Which, she decided, was wise advice and went home comforted, to concentrate instead on the matter of Polly and her father; and sought out Silas and told him frankly she would, after all, welcome his company on the visit to Clerkenwell.

'I beg your pardon?' He looked blank for a moment, dragging his attention from the street which he had been staring into from the drawing-room windows. 'To Clerkenwell? Oh, the court – of course, glad to be of service, Tilly. Very glad.' And he had smiled at her a little vaguely. 'Er – the young ones off to Leicestershire then?'

'Next week,' Tilly said and looked at him sideways. 'Does that perturb you?'

'Oh, not in the least!' he said, a little too quickly. 'Ah – tell me, were you – I mean – were you surprised – oh – that is to say –' He stopped awkwardly.

'Surprised that Duff should be invited to return to Leicestershire?' Tilly said a little wickedly. 'Oh, not in the least. I suspected that he would return – he enjoyed the shooting so much that it is natural he should now consider hunting, I suppose. And I am no longer at all perturbed by his friendship with Patrick Paton. I was an unduly anxious mother to be concerned in the first place. Now I have seen how attached he is to Sophie, how can I deny my own foolishness?'

'Yes,' he said. 'I am sure you are right.' And lapsed into silence to remain so, apart from necessary comments regarding their travel, until they had almost reached the courts.

'I am sorry if I am boring you,' Tilly said a touch sharply just as they entered the City of London and the horse drawing their cab was whipped up to turn northwards for Clerkenwell. 'I would not have asked you to accompany me if you had not offered, you know, and although I said I was perfectly able to make this journey on my own I have to admit I quaked a little at the prospect. But now I see I should have suffered the quakes and left you in peace.'

'Oh, no!' he protested and roused himself. 'I do beg your pardon, Tilly. It's just that –' He shook his head. 'I feel such a fool, you know. I had convinced myself over the years that I was an excellent judge of character. I prided myself on it. And I had Miss Oliver down as a person of independent means who because of her sprightly nature and high intelligence found it possible to live her life independent of any maternal care or support. To discover how wrong I was – I have to confess to being quite put down in my own estimation.'

'That must be painful,' Tilly said and leaned back in the corner of the cab so that her face fell into the shadows and she could study him without close observation on his part. 'Your feelings are engaged with Miss Oliver, I believe?'

He turned his head and peered at her. 'Engaged? Decidedly not!' he said vigorously. 'Or not in any – in any loverlike sense! She is a child and I enjoy her company, for she makes me laugh with her prattling, just as children do. And she is so very pretty that she is a pleasure to the eyes. But my feelings are not engaged further than that. I am a man, Tilly, not a boy like Duff. You may ask him if his feelings are engaged – and I strongly suspect that they are – but for my part – no.' He smiled then a little crookedly. 'If I seem put out by young Miss Oliver, believe me that it is the wound to my *amour propre* and my intellect that causes suffering, not to my heart.'

Does the gentleman protest too much? Tilly wondered, still in the shadows, and then as her spirits quite unaccountably lifted, wanted to laugh. It didn't really matter, did it? He didn't care for Sophie and she had been feeling those stabs of unbecoming jealousy for no reason. How cheering that was! It even helped her pretend she was not concerned about the other comment he had made, regarding Duff and his feelings. She'd think about that some other time.

The courts, when they reached them, were alive with human

activity, and Tilly felt greatly comforted to have Silas's large protective shape beside her. The entrance hallway, which was surging with people of all sorts, lawyers as well as clients – many of the latter looking decidedly the worse for wear, even at this hour of the morning – smelled foully of dirt and bodies and tobacco smoke and the alcohol which had had its damaging effects on the people she saw around her, and she lifted her handkerchief to her nose as unobtrusively as she could as Silas led the way in to stand beside her, looking about.

'I think I must seek out the clerk of the court,' he said in her ear. 'I shall go and make enquiries and return to you swiftly. You be so good as to wait here while I check where he is to be found – I think that will be best, so please don't stir from this spot.' And before she could object he was gone, pushing his way through the crowd, leaving her feeling very isolated and conspicuous, for she was much better dressed than most of the other women in the big vestibule.

There was a uniformed man at the door, and she caught his eye, and he came across to her, his brass buttons winking in the thin sunshine that came in through the high windows.

'Can I be of 'elp, Madam?' he asked heavily, looking at her in an avuncular manner.

She caught her breath and said gratefully, 'Indeed, I am seeking information about a man who was – he was before the court here a year ago and was found guilty. I employ his daughter in my household and seek to gain information about his welfare for her peace of mind.'

'O' course, Madam,' he said as though it was the most commonplace request in the world, and one he regularly heard each day. 'This way.'

'Oh! There is a gentleman with me,' she said. 'He has gone to seek where we should be and –'

'I'll find him and send him to you, Madam,' the man said heavily. 'It ain't suitable for a lady like you to be standin' here in the middle of all this.' And she shrank back as a man a little more drunken than the rest came reeling across the hallway and nearly bumped into her, only being held back by the buttoned one's hefty arm.

She didn't argue after that, and gladly followed the buttons in the opposite direction to the one in which Silas had gone, and let him deliver her to a small room at the back of the building.

'There,' the man said. 'Here's the register of all the people what's been in and out of 'ere this past year. When did this case come up?'

'It was just over a year ago,' Tilly said and the man nodded.

'In that case, you look in this ledger 'ere. Start from the back, see? It'll be quicker than going through for the whole year. You know his name?'

'George Robert Mitcham,' Tilly said. 'So his daughter told me. Of Postern Court, High Holborn.'

'Then you should find him easy enough. Now, the name of the gentleman what's with you? I'll go seek him for you,' the buttoned giant said and she smiled up at him gratefully.

'Mr Silas Geddes,' she said. 'And thank you for rescuing me so kindly.'

'It's no more'n my place, Madam,' he said with an air of vast superiority and turned and went, leaving her with the big leather-bound ledgers. Some of them were set on a sloping desk in the middle of the small dirty room, and the rest were on the shelves which lined the walls in serried rows of well-tooled leather, a series of accounts of felons and thieves of all sorts, going back to the end of the last century, according to the dates carefully engraved at the foot of each ledger's spine. She shivered at the thought of the years of wickedness contained therein, and with a strong effort of will, opened the pages of the ledger the man in buttons had indicated.

It was heavy and the pages smelled of damp and ink and newly released dust, but she riffled them through her gloved fingers, not quite sure why, but needing to become accustomed to the sight of the pages, all of them covered with names and addresses written in perfect copperplate, though in rather cramped lines. After each name was a laconic account of an offence, such as 'pickpocket' or 'horse thief' or, in some cases, 'murderer and batterer'. She saw the words 'hanged at Newgate' appear several times in a final column and shuddered and hurried on, riffling harder and faster.

And then she caught her breath, staring down at the name that leapt off the page at her, almost as though it had shouted to attract her attention.

It was not Polly's father's fate she had found. It was Sophie's mother's. Dorcas Oliver, she read. And slammed the book shut.

Chapter Twenty-Two

'I DOUBT IT will come as so much of a shock to her,' Silas ventured after they had travelled halfway back to Brompton again, and she roused herself from her reverie and looked at him.

'I beg your pardon?'

'Polly,' Silas said. 'I have no doubt she has guessed that his fate was as we found. She said as much to you, you told me. That he was an ailing man.'

'Oh, Polly,' Tilly said. 'Yes, I dare say.'

'So you need not be so sad for her,' Silas went on, watching her as closely as he could in the dark interior of the rocking cab as the driver whipped up his tired horse to send it careering along the Strand on its way westwards, 'need you? It does your tender heart credit, of course, but you should not be so very distressed.'

She bent her head to look down at her gloved hands on her lap. She had not given more than the most perfunctory thought to the way Polly might react to the news that her father had died within six months of his imprisonment, as had been recorded in the ledger; it had been her own feelings about finding Dorcas Oliver's name that preoccupied her, and it was shameful to have Silas thinking so well of her concern for Polly when she was, in truth, being thoroughly wicked, wondering how it would be possible to handle this piece of news about Dorcas in a way that would benefit her, Tilly, and more importantly, Duff.

Ever since she had allowed Sophie to move into Quentin's and had watched her conquer Duff's heart, her feelings had been mixed.

On the one hand she was deeply grateful to discover that her fears regarding the nature of Duff's attachment to his friend Patrick Paton had been unfounded. Clearly, she had decided, watching her son positively mooning over Sophie, he was every inch a woman's man. Whatever adolescent feelings had been involved when he was at school, now he was out in the world all that had been forgotten. She had not even been particularly anxious when Duff had made it clear he had every intention of accepting Paton's latest invitation; she had actually permitted herself to think such a connection could do her boy nothing but good, in a world where the quality of one's friends was of such importance.

On the other hand, her feelings about Sophie were sometimes less than kind. She seemed to Tilly to be altogether too charming to be trusted. Every one of the guests in the house adored her. Even the usually acerbic Miss Fleetwood had come under her spell; and more significantly so had the servants. In Tilly's now wide experience they were a class of people who were very good indeed at seeing through pretension and deceit. There had been previous guests who had seemed charming and likeable to their fellows, and to Tilly herself, but who had been loathed and despised by Eliza and all her staff, and Tilly had learned to see their reaction as a very accurate measure of people's true character. There was Mr Greenwall who had decamped one night by the window of his room, bag and baggage, leaving three months' bills unpaid, and Miss Carter, who had been discovered to be the root cause of the disappearance of several pieces of other guests' property. The servants had not been taken in by those two at all, when those above stairs had been quite hoodwinked.

Yet now, here was a guest she distrusted, yet they did not. Could she be behaving in a most unfair way, tarring Sophie with the brush not only of Tilly's own memories of her mother, but of her grandmother? Tilly had hated and feared Mrs Leander, Sophie's grandmother, who had been her father's mistress all those years ago, a jumped-up housekeeper who had abused her position in the house to – well, Tilly would not think about that again. Think instead of Dorcas, who was still very much to be thought about, going by that entry in the ledger at Clerkenwell Magistrate's Court. Imprisoned for two years for the separate crimes of common prostitution and obtaining money by trickery, she would soon be released. The dates on the ledger had made Tilly shiver with anxiety. Another month, that was all, and Dorcas would be free.

And what had Sophie been using for money in the meantime? She had been but a child of sixteen when her mother was imprisoned. Had she really left her mother's care because she chose to, which was the impression she had given Tilly? Hardly, not at that age. Her mother must have left her to survive as best she could, and find money where she could. Yes, she had worked as a dancer, but why had she only now admitted this fact? Why had she not told Tilly sooner? The questions came thick and fast, and the hardest for Tilly to consider was, had Sophie been living on ill-gotten funds?

At that thought Tilly had felt herself go white. Had she herself been taking, as rent, money Dorcas had filched in some unspeakable manner? It was all too confusing and painful and it was small wonder that now she sat in the cab with Silas's anxious eyes on her, thinking her upset about Polly. She would have to make herself a better dissembler, she thought with some panic, and managed to smile at Silas.

'I am sorry to be so distrait,' she said. 'It is all so – that place was a great deal more unpleasant than I had expected. And the news of George Mitcham's death and all – well, forgive me.'

'There is nothing to forgive,' he said. 'I just didn't wish to see you anxious unnecessarily. I do agree with you. It was quite dreadful to see so many unhappy people, most of whom I am certain are in the difficulties they find themselves because of poverty rather than because of any inherent wickedness.' He brooded for a while. 'I took as many notes as was possible before that officious creature turned us out –' He almost snorted at the way the lordly being in buttons had shepherded them out of the building. 'And I hope it will be enough to convince my Society that action must be taken for these poor wretches.' He threw himself back against the leather padding of the cab and glowered. 'It is a little short of disgusting that some of our fellow creatures should have to suffer so much when out here –' and he gestured out of the window at the handsome new stucco-fronted houses which had been built along the road that led to Brompton '– out here is comfort and decency and every incentive to live a virtuous life. I am fast reaching the conclusion that virtue is entirely to be bought. It is certainly hard to come by for those who lack enough to feed and clothe themselves.'

'Yes,' Tilly said and leaned across and touched his hand. 'You are a good man, Silas, and I must thank you warmly for your help this afternoon. I have been less than gracious in being so preoccupied with my own concern. It is good of you to spend so much time on my behalf and on that of the poor people for whom you show so much compassion.'

'Oh, it is no effort at all,' he said and smiled at her. 'Caring for you, that is. To take care of and to help you, Tilly, is a privilege. It is one I hope to enjoy for as long as you will permit me. For always, if you will consider it.'

She drew back. 'Really, you must not –' She stopped. 'I mean, I was complimenting you on your work for the poor through your Society as much as – well, I am sure they appreciate you.'

'I don't do the work for appreciation,' he said and drew back into his corner. 'But because it needs to be done. Ah, here we are. Another few yards and you may rest a little before you talk to Polly.'

The moment had passed and she wasn't at all sure how she felt about that. Had be been about to declare himself, to make a proposal? It had seemed so, and she was startled at how fluttery such a thought made her. Did she want him to do so? If so, why had she choked him off so quickly? She was a little old at thirty-five to behave like a foolish girl; a widow such as herself should surely be a little more worldly-wise. And one who had twice been widowed – well, it did not suit her at all to behave in so missish a fashion. She was quite ashamed of herself.

He handed her out of the cab with his usual punctiliousness, and she smiled at him tentatively. 'I cannot thank you too much,' she said. 'You have been –'

'Please take it as read,' he said a touch brusquely. 'There need be no more mention of it. Will you speak to Polly at once? Or accept my advice and rest in your room for a while first? It may be an emotional experience for her and therefore wearying for you.'

'Of course I shall accept your advice,' she said, feeling it was the least she could do and in truth glad of an excuse to escape to be on her own for a little while. It would soon be time to busy herself about the normal work of the late afternoon, supervising the preparation of dinner and the arrangement of the dining room, and after that there would be no time to do anything until she fell into bed at night, once the last guest had sought his or her room. No time for anything – not even thinking about Sophie. Or Silas.

In her room she rang her bell, using the code she had devised to tell Eliza it was she who was wanted and not one of the junior staff, and then kicked off her boots and her gown and stretched herself on her *chaise longue*, wearing a wrap.

Eliza arrived rather red in the face, and buttoning her cuffs as she came in. 'I was choppin' fish for the dumplings, Mum. It's a receipt as I was given by Madame Salinas and we're tryin' it for the first time. Five kinds of fish – hake and halibut and a bit o' cod and bream and so forth – all to be chopped together till it's like dough. It does take time.'

'I hope they will enjoy it and warrant all your work, Eliza,' Tilly said, knowing better than to try to deflect her when she was embarked on a description of a dish.

'Oh, Mum, they'll enjoy it and don't you doubt it! I've the almonds ready pounded – it does take a lot – and a fine fish souchy to cook it in – I had far more o' the broth than I needed from the fish I cooked this mornin' – and once I get it all mixed, a few eggs you know, and some fine chopped onion and the souchy'll set to a nice jelly, for I used some bones of sea bream to give it a bit o' body, why, it'll taste fit for the Queen. Madame Salinas, she'll come and check I got the balance right in the seasoning – a bit of garlic you know, they do like their garlic, these Frenchies – and it'll beat the rest of the dinner tomorrow hands down.'

'Oh, this is for tomorrow?' Tilly said. 'Then what are we having tonight? Is it not as we planned? Have you changed it?'

'No, Mum, not at all.' Eliza was shocked at the very suggestion. 'Julienne soup and some oxtail, removed with the fish I cooked in the souchy this morning – that's perch and eels and flounders, the best Jerryman had – and for the third course there's that cold game pie and a haunch of mutton with caper sauce and boiled fowl pudding. Before that the entrées, you remember, like what we said. I have a ragout of lobster and a riz of veau and some sautéed mushrooms and then there's the wild duck which I shall have removed by apple pies with cheese and blackberry creams and a vanilla charlotte.'

'Well, that all sounds very satisfactory. Sit down, Eliza.'

'What?' Eliza stared. 'Me sit down in here, Mum? Whatever for?'

'Because you are working too hard, considering your condition, and I must speak to you, and it will be easier for me to do so while you are in a chair so that I don't have to crane my neck. And because I ask you to,' Tilly said a little impatiently.

Eliza sat down and folded her work-reddened hands in her lap. 'As to my condition, Mum, I'm fine and hearty,' she said. 'I don't never feel sick now, and I'm as well set up as ever I was, though fattening up nicely.' And she patted her belly proudly. 'But that's as it should be, I shall start wearing my bigger gowns soon, but there's not a thing else to fret over. I never was better.' She grinned suddenly. 'Country girls like me, we take it easier, this baby business, than you city ladies. We're bred different.'

'Not at all,' Tilly said sharply. 'Aren't we all the same –'

'In the eyes of God. That's as may be,' Eliza said tartly. 'But in the world like what it is, it's different. And there's no escaping it, you're more delicate than what we are.'

Tilly chose not to argue the point; there were other things to talk about. 'Eliza, Polly's father is dead. He died six months ago.'

'Well, I'm not surprised to hear it,' Eliza said. 'And nor will she be. She's talked a little to me, and I know the girl well enough. She'll be all right as long as she's got that baby to fret over –' Eliza shook her head. 'Is he to stay here for always, Mum?'

Tilly looked at her and made a grimace. 'To tell the truth, Eliza, I hadn't thought about it.'

'P'raps you should, Mum. That child – well, she's more of a girl now than a child – she's all set to stay 'ere. She knows as 'er dad won't never be back and the brothers are off to farms and all –'

'And I must take her to visit them soon,' Tilly remembered and put her hands to her head. 'Oh dear. There's so much to think about. I promised I would and I must. And then there's – well,' she had been about to speak of Dorcas but changed her mind for the present, 'so much,' she ended.

'Well, Mum, let me say this. If we're goin' to have another baby here –' and again she patted her belly, almost absentmindedly, 'maybe it's no bad thing to let young Georgie stay on. I can teach Polly to be a fair sort o' nursery worker, I don't doubt, and the child'll do well enough. Then when there's two of 'em, Polly can be nursemaid, d'you see. As long as she's as devoted to ours as she is to Georgie, we won't have no arguments. Anyway, I'll be there all the time to keep an eye.'

Tilly looked at her, and then shook her head and began to laugh, and Eliza looked back at her with her brows raised and with no laughter at all.

'I don't see what's so funny,' she protested. 'Really I don't, Mum. I been thinkin' and it strikes me that with Polly here to take care of both babies –'

'That's why I'm laughing, Eliza.' Tilly managed to catch her breath. 'It's just so – well, so pat! We seem between us to have a way of looking at problems and finding answers to them that are as neat as – as neat as the pies you make. All the gravy and such that might make a splash and a mess tidily tucked away, and the pastry golden and neat on top, holding all trouble inside. The whole tasting quite splendid and no sign to anyone of the work that's gone into it.'

Eliza looked doubtful. 'I think that means you're pleased enough, Mum?'

'Of course I am. It is what I intended – an excellent plan, though perhaps I should not be so boastful! I laughed only because it is all so *pat*. You make it sound even more simple than perhaps it is.'

'I know,' Eliza said with a flash of annoyance. 'The likes of me don't think as deep as ladies and gentlemen do. Well, we don't always have the opportunity. Life's hard for our sort, so we look for the simplest ways to make it easier.'

'Oh dear, I've offended you,' Tilly said. 'Forgive me! I meant only to – well, let it be. I want always that you should be content, Eliza. Are you? Are you happy, quite recovered from Mr Reagan?'

Eliza sat and stared over Tilly's head for a while, her eyes glazed and then she focused on Tilly and let a smile lift her round cheeks.

'Well, you could say, Mum, I got the best of the bargain. I had a bit o' fun and though I liked it well enough, I don't think it was worth gettin' yourself all upset for. Certainly not worth having a great smelly man lumbering about in your bed for ever and a day. I had the bit of fun, like I say, and I won't go to my grave not knowing, if you see what I mean, which would ha' been a pity. I didn't fancy dyin' as a virgin, never did. But to go on with it all the time – no, I wouldn't care for that. And he left me a bit of 'imself –' Again the belly pat. 'And if God was a woman, Mum, why I dare say she'd ha' arranged it always like that.'

This time they both laughed and felt better for it, and then as Eliza made a move to get to her feet, Tilly made a gesture and bade her sit down again.

'What I actually wished to speak of was something quite different,' she said. 'Now – I – oh dear, I hope this is the right thing I'm doing.' She pondered and Eliza watched her, the laughter fading from her eyes, and her face becoming serious again.

'Don't say nothing you don't want to, Mum,' she said. 'But be assured that whatever you says to me stays with me. No one else knows anything – or ever will. Sealed like the grave an' all that.'

'Yes,' Tilly said consideringly and then gave a decisive little nod. 'Very well. When are Duff and Sophie going to Leicestershire?'

'On Friday, Mum. They said next week, first go off, but Miss Sophie's in such a lather of excitement it's been agreed they go sooner. She wanted to take Rosie with her but I said she had to ask you.'

'Take Rosie?' Tilly stared. 'Whatever for?'

'She said as the great ladies'll all have their own maids,' Eliza said, 'and she don't want to look different. But I did say as we were very busy here and I didn't think we could see our way clear to letting her go.'

'And quite right too!' Tilly said angrily. 'Where does she get her notions? I shall have to speak to her after all –' She shook her head. 'I had hoped to avoid doing so but – oh dear Eliza, I'm in such a taking!'

Eliza looked alarmed. 'Whatever is it, Mum?'

'It's Dorcas,' Tilly almost snapped the name out. 'Sophie's Mamma. I have found out that she will be free in another month and –'

'Free? How do you mean, free, Mum?'

'Oh dear!' Tilly looked at the amazement on Eliza's face and shook her head once more. 'I shall have to explain properly, shan't I?'

And she did.

Chapter Twenty-Three

TILLY WALKED BRISKLY along Brompton Grove towards Charlie's shop, her hands tucked into a muff for the first time this season, for it had become suddenly very cold indeed considering it was still but November, and her eyes were watering against the bite of the wind. She could have let Eliza make the journey, for she had offered and was as capable of leaving the order and paying the bills as Tilly herself, but Tilly had chosen to go. She needed the time to think, she told herself. And perhaps to call in at Jem's shop to talk to him.

She had felt a slight stab of guilt as that thought came to her; she treated Jem so much as a convenience, calling on him for aid when she had need of it and hardly thinking of him otherwise; it was not kind when he loved her so dearly. And she wondered idly for a moment what life might have been like had she accepted Jem's earnest proposals of marriage all those years ago, when Duff was still small and she had been so uncertain of life in her new venture at Quentin's.

But even as the thought came to her, an image of Silas Geddes lifted before her mind's eye, his face so concerned and his approval of her showing in the way he looked at her, and she felt even more ashamed. To be thinking so at her age and when there were so many other problems to concern her was quite ridiculous.

But for all that, she stopped at Jem's shop, ostensibly to buy some linen to make new glass towels for the kitchen, and was quite cast down when the shopman told her that Mr Leland was away from the premises at the moment and not expected back until much later in the day; and she bought her glass cloth stuff and carried the parcel away with her, declining to have it delivered in the usual manner and, now she knew she could not discuss matters with Jem, was forced to consider for herself whether she was right to take Eliza's advice.

She had listened with great care to Eliza's reactions to the news that Dorcas was likely to be free in a month or so. Eliza was a sensible woman who had, after all, known Dorcas as well as she had herself, or almost, and it had been Eliza's considered opinion that she, Tilly, was worrying unnecessarily.

'She won't come round here sniffing and prying and bothering us,' she said stoutly. 'For why should she? She hasn't bothered us these dunnamany years so why start now? Not when she left us a lady riding high on the hog's back, and would have to come back skulking like the jailbird she is. It stands to reason – and anyway, why should she know Sophie's here? Mark my words, Mum, Miss Sophie came here to you on account she wanted to escape from her mother altogether, and had to be away well before she come out of prison. She wants no part of her, not after what she done, and Miss Sophie so pretty and nice.'

'A dancer?' Tilly had ventured and Eliza had looked quite indignant.

'What's wrong with being a dancer and making people happy? I read about the theatre ladies all the time and they're not so black as they're painted. The poor girl had to make her living some road and why not down that one? If I'd 'a' had the looks and the power to do it, why Mum, I'd ha' been proud and glad of it. And,' she ended triumphantly, 'she must be a lady for why else would a duke ask her to stay?'

Perhaps because she is a dancer and anything but a lady, Tilly found herself thinking but she did not say so aloud.

Eliza had got to her feet and brushed down her gown, ready to return to her kitchen. 'Take my word for it, Mum, we don't need to do nothin',' she said confidently. 'That Madam Dorcas won't come back here, no matter what. Say nothing, that's my motto on this one. Least said, soonest mended, and the less Miss Sophie in particular knows the better for her and for all of us.'

And although Tilly lacked Eliza's high opinion of Sophie and her ladylike qualities, Tilly had to admit the strength of her argument. It was not logical to fear that Dorcas would suddenly appear like one of the genies in the operas Sophie danced in. If she, Tilly, had not gone to Clerkenwell to look for news of Polly's father she would never have known about her imprisonment at all, nor have feared her reappearance at Quentin's. There was clearly no need to do so now.

She had almost reached Charlie's shop, when she passed a saddler's with a fine window display of whips and leather boxes and harnesses, and she paused, her eye caught by a dressing case in green leather, well fitted with crystal bottles with silver stoppers and tortoiseshell-backed brushes. Duff, she thought, and after a moment went into the shop.

Why she did it she was not quite certain afterwards. It was not as simple as wanting to give her son a gift, just for the delight of doing so. She wanted to send him to Paton so well equipped that no one could fail to think highly of him, she decided; that was why she spent so much on so luxurious an item. She knew he had spent most of his allowance on hunting clothes to take with him, and that he carried his toiletries in a simple sponge bag; if he arrived at a ducal residence with so splendid a piece of equipment as this case, then he would show all of them just how elegant and well found a young man he was.

It is time, she told herself when she emerged from the saddler's fifteen minutes later, having arranged for the case to be delivered to Quentin's that afternoon, that we spoke about his future, Duff and I. I wanted him to have some peace and amusement in these first months after leaving school, but he cannot spend all his days riding and dancing attendance on –

She stopped then, and bit her lip. That was really what was distressing her, she knew. He spent too much time with Sophie, and whatever Eliza said and however much the other guests loved her, Tilly didn't feel comfortable about her. But am I not being ridiculous?

she asked herself as slowly she began to walk towards Charlie's shop once more. I fretted over his friendship with Patrick Paton, and wished him to make one with a young lady. And now he has, I dislike that too. Am I no more than a jealous mother, unwilling to let go of her only beloved child? Is that my trouble? If it is, then I must mend my ways, Duff will not tolerate my views if I am unjust to him and try too hard to prevent him from living the life of a young man.

It was a relief to walk in through the familiar entrance to Charlie's shop, for it banished her thoughts and she stood, her hands still muffed, and looked about her as the cold air from outside was excluded by the shop boy who seemed to have the task of closing the door behind her, having opened it to welcome her.

Now she could see that much of the work that had been going on all throughout the last months was finished. The shop was larger than ever, and seemed to be extraordinarily full of staff and customers, and she smiled at the sight of the goods piled high in handsome arrangements on the broad mahogany counters and the way the shopmen were so carefully dressed and had such very snowy aprons tied round their neat waists.

A man in the same black as the other shopmen, but without an apron, came over to her in a posture that was only just short of obsequious. 'Good day, Madam. Can I be of service to you?'

'I was looking for Charlie,' she said, looking at him with her brows raised. 'Er – Mr Harrod, that is. I don't believe I have seen you here before?'

'No indeed, Madam.' The man spoke rather carefully, his words clipped and nasal. 'I have joined Mr 'arrod – Mr Harrod – as his floor manager, so that he can be relieved of anxiety on those occasions when he is dealing with customers on our upper storey.' He said it with great pride. 'And of course Mr Harrod has to be very busy dealing with the builders as they extend our departments. Now, to which department may I direct you, Madam? Teas and coffees are all together over there, and here we have the sweet biscuits and chocolates and nuts and other such materials and over there –'

'Mrs Q!' a voice said and Tilly turned gratefully to where Charlie had appeared beside her. 'I'll look after this lady, Mr Lansdown. But make sure you know her next time, for she is one of our most valued customers, is Mrs Quentin. I take it you're well?' And he looked at Tilly with some anxiety. 'I've seen Eliza here this past three or four weeks or more and though she tells me all's well, I like to see for myself.'

'I'm very well,' Tilly said and Mr Lansdown bowed and took himself off to talk to another customer who had just come in. 'I'm sorry not to have been in the shop for a while, but I have been very well. It does look remarkable. You seem to have something new every time I put my head around your door!'

'Don't I just!' Charlie cried delightedly. 'Come and look!'

She could not have argued with his insistence that he show her every part of his enlarged shop, even had she wanted to. He was so very determined that all she could do was walk along beside him as, with his bowler hat pushed to the back of his head and his shirtsleeved arms flailing (for although he insisted his shopmen were always dressed completely *comme il faut* his own daily uniform never varied; Tilly could not recall seeing him without his hat for a very long time now), he displayed his pride and joy.

And indeed it had developed very well since she had last come in. Parts of the shop that had then been shrouded in dust sheets were now proudly on display. There was the patent medicines counter (and very busy it was, she noted with a little amusement; Charlie had been right, as usual, in his shrewd estimation of a line of goods that would give him a handsome profit, even if it had been his nephew who had first suggested it) and the section labelled in large flowing and heavily decorated letters 'Perfumery' and the stationery department, well supplied with a bewildering range of writing papers and cards and pens and inks, looking wonderfully inviting. All these new departments were on the upper floor, and he led her up the stairs to them with such transparent satisfaction that she could have laughed aloud. But of course she didn't, contenting herself with admiring murmurs and nods.

'Now,' she said, when at last he had exhausted his tour. 'I really must pay my bill and give you the new order. If you are too busy I will gladly deal with one of your men – you seem to have enough of them.'

'Sixteen,' he said proudly, 'now I got Mr Lansdown. Ain't he the goods? I like to give a bit o' extra class to the place and he does that. Not that he don't work for his wages, mind you. He can cut a ham as well as the next man and bag up sugar 'n' tea faster 'n you can look at him and correct to a penny weight too. But he's got a winning way with 'im that the ladies like and I think he's worth his money. I'm paying out fifteen pounds a week in wages now, you know!' He grinned at her, again suffused with pride. 'Delivery boys – two of 'em – and someone to haul the stock about and all that, and a dozen shopmen in here – oh, just you watch me!'

'Then I mustn't keep you longer,' she said firmly, knowing he would keep her there for the rest of the day listening to him boasting of his success if he could. 'I shall pay my bill and –'

'Please to come to my counting house,' he said, and laughed. 'It's a comfortable place to stop, if you know what I mean, not that I have that much time for comfort! And I can see old friends there. Come along in and see what's what.' And without waiting for her response he led the way downstairs again to the very back of the shop and a small curtained door in the far corner.

Beyond the door there was indeed a cosy room with a fire burning brightly in a highly burnished grate and a scatter of good chairs about and a tall desk in the far corner. The windows were curtained in green damask against the dimness of the late afternoon and the room was well lit with oil lamps, and she was happy to release the fastenings of her fur-trimmed mantle as she came in and met the blast of warm air.

It was perhaps because she was concentrating on wresting the buttons open that she didn't at first realize there were other people in the room and was startled when she heard Jem's voice.

'Why, if it isn't Tilly! How pleasant to see you! I don't seem to have done that for a few weeks, now.'

She lifted her chin and smiled in genuine pleasure to see him. 'I called at your shop not half an hour since!' she retorted. 'But since you were not there, obviously I can't be blamed for not seeing you! I trust you are well?'

'Very well,' he said with an odd emphasis in his voice. 'Very well indeed,' and he looked over his shoulder at the other chair beside the fire and someone who had been sitting there stood up and came to join him.

'Well now,' Charlie Harrod said heartily and rubbed his hands together. 'If this ain't downright cosy, I don't know what is – We shall take a glass of ratafia and some of my newest Madeira biscuits to go with it, that's what we'll do, just to warm us, shall we? Now, don't you shake your head, Mrs Q! Determined I am that we shall, for you haven't met my Caroline's cousin before, have you? And here we are with news for you, as well. Couldn't be a better moment to share a glass. And it couldn't be a better moment that you of all people should walk in today, for are we not all old friends, if I may be so bold?' And he beamed at her and then at the young woman standing beside Jem. 'Mrs Q, may I present Miss Frances Goodall, who is my Caroline's first cousin on her mother's side, as they say. Fanny, this is Mrs Quentin who has long been a good friend to me and my business and indeed to Jem.'

'I know that,' Miss Goodall said and held out a hand to Tilly. 'I have heard much about you, Mrs Quentin, and am most happy to make your acquaintance.'

Her voice was pleasant if a little countrified and she had an equally pleasant but rather plain face with slightly bulging eyes beneath pallid thin brows. Her eyes were a mild brown and her complexion rosy, and she looked as wholesome as a currant bun. Tilly stared at her and then at Jem, puzzlement rising in her. Jem had an expression on his face that was quite remarkable, she thought, and one she could not remember seeing there before. He looked pleased and yet a touch alarmed, puffed up with a sort of pride he had certainly never displayed to Tilly, and an almost childlike beam creased his mouth.

Fanny looked at him and she too smiled, a quite different expression. Hers spoke of calm certainty of ownership, of assurance that she knew what was best for the man beside her and had every intention of seeing he obtained it. She did not touch him or pet him as Tilly had seen other women do with men on whom they had set their sights, but had she had him tied to her side with a leather leash like a pet dog, Tilly found herself thinking waspishly, she could not be displaying ownership more clearly.

Fortunately she did not have to speak, for Charlie chose this moment to come fussing over with a tray of small glasses filled with the deep amber of ratafia and a plate of round yellow biscuits and chattered as he distributed them, giving Tilly time to untie her bonnet and remove her now burdensome mantle and sit down. And all the time she looked covertly at Frances Goodall, trying to understand what was happening here and certain, in a sick sort of way, that she knew perfectly well.

Miss Goodall was wearing a simple gown of fawn faille trimmed only with the minimum of brown braid, and her hair was dressed in the simplest of modern modes, parted in the centre and brushed back over a pad at the back of her head from which depended only one small coil. It was undoubtedly her best feature, being thick and flaxen pale and with a deep rich sheen which the simple style showed off to full advantage. She had soft cheeks which were already settling into incipient jowls, but she smiled so much they hardly had time to show themselves. And it was clear that Jem approved of her highly.

'Well, let me propose a toast to us all, and waste no time over it,' Charlie said jovially and held up his glass. 'Here's to new friends and old, to new business and old, to the future and the past – and let the best part of it all be to come!'

Jem said heartily – more heartily than Tilly could remember hearing from him before, 'Amen to that, Charlie!' while Miss Goodall smiled brightly and Tilly herself just smiled, and they all sipped, Charlie managing to make his sip empty his glass by fully a half.

'Agreeable though this is,' Tilly said as carefully as she could, 'I really cannot stay long. I must return to my own business if your kind toast is to come true for me. It cannot prosper in my absence for very long!'

'Oh come, Tilly!' Jem said. 'With your Eliza there? How can you be so mistrustful of her? She will handle any problems while you stay half an hour with old friends, surely!'

'I was not being mistrustful!' Tilly said with a sudden flash of anger. 'I was, rather, saying that I have much that must be done. And excellent though Eliza is in every way I would be a poor mistress of an establishment if I did not treat my servants with some consideration!'

'To my certain knowledge, you've always treated everyone with the utmost consideration,' Charlie said owlishly, and sipped again, this time so depleting his glass he had to refill it. 'You've shown it to me since I was just a young lad under my father's thumb when this shop wasn't much bigger than this room here!' And he looked fondly round the tiny chamber and chuckled, and even Tilly, irritated though she was by all that was being said – and not said – around her, had not the heart to point out what a severe exaggeration that was.

'I didn't mean to suggest any lack of care on your part, Tilly, in asking you to stay a while,' Jem said, and some of the joy had gone from his face and he looked a little anxious. 'I wished only to – well –' He glanced sideways at Miss Goodall. 'I thought it would be agreeable for us all to get to know one another, don't you know, Miss Goodall being new to you, if you see what I mean.'

His discomfiture was obvious and so uncharacteristic that Tilly could not help but stare and Charlie burst out laughing.

'Oh dear, oh dear, isn't he making a sorry fist of it? The thing is, Mrs Q, our Jem here is about to take the plunge. I thought he might do so many times in the past –' And he looked at her roguishly for a brief second and then away, 'but it wasn't to be. But now he is, and what's more he's joining my family! Affianced, that's what they are, Jem and Fanny here. Now, isn't that worth half an hour of jollity among old friends like us?'

Chapter Twenty-Four

TO CALL IT a difficult half hour was to understate the situation to the point of absurdity. She smiled and congratulated them. She beamed with apparently the same pleasure as Charlie when Jem looked at his bride-to-be in what Tilly privately considered a disgustingly mawkish manner and she looked back at him in what Tilly interpreted, much more sinisterly, as a possessive manner. She was angry and hurt and, worst of all, she knew that she was being totally unjust.

She accepted a second glass of ratafia, though she managed to refuse the biscuits, a new purchase of which Charlie was inordinately proud, and listened with all the interest she could pretend as Jem and his Fanny prattled on about seeking a house and a new shop in one of the quieter and pleasanter London suburbs, and tried to be pleased for them. She failed totally.

'We thought of Holloway,' Jem said. 'It's most green and charming and there are many handsome new houses and excellent shop properties there. We should deal very comfortably.'

'But your shop here,' Tilly managed to say through rather stiff lips. 'How will you care for that if you move so far away?'

'Sold it to me, ain't he?' Charlie said in a high good humour. 'Oh, I got plans I have, and Jem here's helping me with 'em! I've bought his premises and I shall rent 'em to some suitable well-set up tradesman, and then wait till I can buy all the property twixt me and him. And then I'll break the lease and I'll join all of the places together and won't I have a handsome establishment then!'

'But Charlie,' Tilly protested, glad to have something different to think about. 'How big a shop can you have? You already sell all the groceries there are in the world, and have added such things as perfume and stationery and medicines. Why should you want the burden of so vast an emporium?'

'Burden?' cried Charlie. 'How can a business ever be a burden? I wish it to grow and grow! Like a tree – and just as trees have leaves and fruit as well as twigs, so shall I have many different sorts of goods as well as groceries and patent medicines. I can sell silks and linens and fashions, like Jem here – only he'll be selling his over in Holloway or some such spot so we won't be in competition – and I can sell children's stuff and dresses for funerals and millinery – anything that that there William Whitely sells over in Westbourne Grove, I can sell here in Brompton! Do you know he's put in a Refreshment Room? So he has! I ask you – and a house agency – there's no stopping the man. Well, I shan't be put down by such a one as that. So I'm taking Jem's premises until such time as I need 'em, and he'll be my cousin-in-law and all very nice too, ain't it? Don't you think so, Mrs Q?'

'Oh, yes indeed,' Tilly said, and then spoke no more as Miss Goodall, with the minimum of prompting from Charlie, launched herself into an account of the sort of furniture she hoped to put in her new home and the plans she and Jem had for making a garden if they could find a house nice enough, and what sort of wedding trip they would take. Listening to it all was almost more than Tilly could bear.

Yet why should she be so ungenerous? she asked herself as she walked home when, at last, Charlie could be persuaded to let her escape. Charlie had wanted to send one of his men with her, since it was almost dark and not safe, with some of the streets she had to pass so unsalubrious. But she had managed at last to choke him off by being almost ill-mannered which she much disliked, but he had been overflown with ratafia and she hoped would forget all about it by the time they next met. So, alone and walking briskly, she thought hard.

Why should she be so set down by the news of Jem's approaching marriage? Had she not refused him many years ago and persisted in refusing him ever since? The poor man had been her devoted admirer for so long now, and so often she had told him firmly that he mustn't waste his time on her. That she would be his friend and no more.

And now he had taken her at her word, she should be glad for him, glad he had found his sensible Miss Goodall, glad she was his best friend's kinswoman, glad that his lines were falling in pleasant places. But all she felt was bereft, almost desolate at the thought of losing him. She had relied on him and his good opinion more than she realized, she told herself as at last she reached her front door, and let herself in. He was my best friend and I did not value him as I should.

All through dinner she remained remote and silent, thinking her own thoughts about Jem, and her guests seemed to pick up her mood for there was less talk at table than usual, excellent though dinner was (and the special recipe for fish dumplings à la Madame Salinas met with unanimous approval, and provided the only short period of animation of the entire meal). Eliza too became aware of Tilly's mood and said less than she usually did, and indeed vanished immediately after dinner, leaving the coffee service to Lucy's charge, feeling, she told her deputy – who later told Tilly – a little less well this evening, and fit only to go to her bed early.

Even hearing about that didn't rouse Tilly. Normally she would have gone to Eliza's room to see if there was anything she needed, but she contented herself with sending Rosie, who reported that Eliza was asleep and seemed to want nothing. So Tilly felt able to vanish into her own little morning room after dinner, leaving her guests to the drawing room and their own devices. She had much to think of, and much to do – including finding the right moment to speak to Polly of her father – but the news of the afternoon had left her curiously limp and weary.

She sat in her private morning room as the fire there died down – she could not make the effort to feed it with coals – and listened to the house around her going its usual evening way. There was the tinkle of the piano from the drawing room; Sophie entertaining the company, she thought. Then there was Silas's light tenor and after that Duff's easy baritone followed by a general joining in of all of them. But the jollity there did not seem to be well based, for the evening broke up early. She heard them leave the drawing room one by one, as she sat there in her favourite high-back chair, the fire dying at her feet, the Salinas family bidding shrill goodnights to Mr Hancock and Mr Cumming; the Graylings calling on Rosie for some more hot water for Mr Grayling's nighttime grog; Miss Fleetwood rumbling away to Miss Knapp as they climbed the stairs with Miss Barnetsen giggling shrilly behind them.

Slowly the footsteps ebbed away into silence and the green baize door swung, creaking on its hinges a little for the last time, as the servants went upstairs to bed. She heard the soft whimper of Georgie's voice as Polly went by her door and thought – I must tell that child not to keep Georgie up so late; he should be put down to his cot at the same early time each evening, whether he is teething or not. And I don't think he is having any trouble in that direction anyway, for he eats like a horse and grows like a weed.

The house slid into silence at last, broken only by the occasional creak of a timber as it relaxed in the cooling air as the fires in the drawing and dining rooms were allowed to die. Her own had gone out long since, she realized and wondered if she had in fact been dozing, for the room was suddenly very cold, and her eyes felt hot and sandy.

She looked at the little clock on her mantle and was surprised. Two in the morning. She had indeed dozed off. How foolish, she thought drearily. Now I must go to my room and undress and wash in cold water and probably not be able to fall asleep again when I do get into bed.

She extinguished the oil lamp, once she'd set a light to the candle she would use to see herself upstairs and then stretched a little, very conscious of her stiffness and the way her bones ached. She felt flattened and miserable and somehow drained of all energy, and it was an effort to make her way heavily into the hall, closing her door quietly behind her and then making her slow journey upstairs in the thick darkness, which was barely touched by her single candle.

She reached her room without mishap, and managed to light her oil lamp from the wick of her candle at the second try only, which was a comfort, for her bedroom lamp was a capricious one that sometimes sulked and refused to accept a flame without considerable coaxing. She had been meaning to replace it with a better one and kept forgetting; had it been in a guest's room, of course, it would have been dealt with months ago. But it's only mine, and who cares about me? she found herself thinking. Duff is the only relative I have and he is quite obsessed with Sophie. My friends are few and the only really trusty one has turned his back on me for a Miss Fanny Goodall, and I have an inferior lamp in my bedroom; her self pity was well in evidence as she pulled off her gown. She managed to unlace her stays and step out of them with a breath of relief and finally to leave her chemise and drawers on the *chaise longue* without actually weeping at the sorry state of her situation. She would sort out fresh clothes in the morning rather than tonight, in her usual careful manner. All she wanted now was to get into bed and see if she could recapture sleep and perhaps wake up next day in a healthier and better frame of mind.

She had put on her nightgown and brushed her hair in a perfunctory manner and was about to extinguish her lamp when she heard it, and lifted her chin sharply.

An extra creak outside her room. A door opening softly and then closing. She stood there listening, trying to hear, and frowned. Memories of Mr Greenwall, who had crept out of the house with all his luggage without anyone noticing, came rushing back to her. Surely there wasn't anyone in the house now who would behave so? She tried to think of who might. The Graylings? Mr Cumming? The French family? None of them seemed likely, and yet –

The only way to find out was to see for herself and after a moment she deliberately lowered the wick on her oil lamp and taking it in her hand, moved very softly to her door. She set the lamp down on the floor behind it and then very slowly, opened it.

Outside it was all very black, and she knew she would be unable to open the door fully and see out properly as long as there was any light at all from her own lamp, and so decided to extinguish it completely. Her eyes would soon accustom themselves to the darkness and if there was anything to see or hear she would know it. So she bent, blew down the lamp chimney, and the light vanished in a tendril of acrid oil-scented smoke, and blackness enclosed her like a blanket.

She stood upright again and listened. Still nothing, and now she slid out of her room. This time she did hear something; a faint hiss of breath and a soft burring that could have been speech, or even laughter. Whatever it was, she thought, with fear running icy fingers across her shoulders and filling her belly with even colder sensations, that was no timber contracting in the coolness of the night. That was people wandering about in her house. And it was now – it must be – close on half past two in the morning. A ridiculous hour for sensible, honest people to be about. And she buried her fear in a conscious wave of anger that anyone should dare to behave so under her roof, and moved along the hallway.

She followed all her senses. She could not only hear but feel there was someone near; there was added warmth in the air, and smell too, a rich scent which she knew but could not quite place. She actually pulled back her ears to make it possible to pick up every hint of sound, and stretched her eyelids and even her nostrils as she moved slowly and carefully towards what she believed to be the source of the sounds that had first attracted her attention.

It all happened very quickly. One moment there was just herself and her suspicions pushing her forwards across the dark hallway of her second floor and then there was hubbub. She found herself entwined with other bodies, arms and legs and yielding softness and hard muscle, and she yelped in surprise as someone pinched the soft flesh of her right upper arm shrewdly and a voice deep and half whispering said words she had never heard before but knew to be very powerful swearing indeed.

A match flared and then a candle wick kindled and she was standing blinking in the suddenness of the light, feeble thing though it was, staring at the source of the sounds that had brought her from her room. And as she looked, her still confused feelings about Jem's news mixed with weariness and a sense of deflation and the fear that had come when she had first heard the sounds in the hall, became a shriek deep in her throat. She opened her mouth to let it out; but before it could, a hand came down over her shoulder from behind and clamped itself over her face.

Chapter Twenty-Five

SHE WAS TO try often, in the times that were to come, to remember all that happened then, but never could. There was so much confusion, so many mixed feelings inside her, of anger as well as fear, excitement as well as terror, that she was barely aware of what was going on outside herself. But she did at last recognize and understand the voice that was speaking so urgently into her ear and managed to nod her head in acquiescence.

'Please, Tilly, there is no need to be so alarmed, please, do not make a great din – we don't want the whole house woken, do we? Please, it's just me – Silas, only me – and there is no harm done, after all. Please Tilly – be quiet so that I might let you go.'

Once she had managed to nod her agreement the hand was taken from her mouth and she lifted her own to rub tentatively at her lips, which felt numb, and he was at once all compunction.

'Oh, I do so hope I did not hurt you, Tilly, but it was imperative, I thought, that I keep you quiet. I knew you would be mortified if you woke everyone and they all came out and saw – well, perhaps not saw, but understood –'

'Understood what?' she hissed, instinctively pitching her voice to the same level as his, for he was whispering. 'What is going on here?' And she turned her head and stared about her. The candle that had been lit was still burning, sitting in a small china candlestick on the floor, tilted a little drunkenly so that wax dripped on to the polished boards, and her housewifely eyes noted that and were angered; but there was little to see by the light of that single flame.

The door before which she stood was firmly closed, and she peered, to each side and at once identified which door it was: Sophie's; and she caught her breath and closed her eyes as she tried to remember what she had seen in that brief movement before that hand had come down over her face.

Sophie, indeed, and in the darkness inside her eyelids Tilly could see the fine cambric nightgown she had worn, one shoulder slipped halfway down her arm in a fashion that showed far more of her breast than it covered, her hair in a luxuriant tumble about her neck and her arms up and –

Tilly's eyes snapped open and she stared at the door in front of her. Duff. He had been there too, with Sophie's arms about his neck and his head turned towards Tilly, his mouth half open with shock. And – she swallowed as she remembered – he had been wearing nothing at all as far as she could see in her memory. Certainly his chest had been bare, as Sophie's creamy round arms set against Duff's darker skin made very clear.

'I don't –' she began but Silas set two fingers to her lips and jerked his head to move her away.

'Please, not here,' he breathed, and in one swift movement took her by the elbow while bending to pick up the candle in its stick, and started to lead her towards the top of the stairs which led down to the drawing room.

But before they could reach the stair head, there was a click as somewhere along the hallway a door began to open and in a trice he had blown out the candle and had pulled her sideways to stand close to the wall. In the heavy blackness Tilly held her breath as she heard Miss Knapp's voice, thin and reedy with uncertainty – a rare sound indeed from that usually formidable lady – calling out, 'Is anyone there?'

Behind her, Silas too was holding his breath, and for some reason she took her lead from him. There was no reason why she should not have called out that it was she, Tilly, who was wandering about her house in the middle of the night, which no doubt Miss Knapp would have accepted without question, for who had a better right to wander about than the owner of the house? But by the time Tilly had thought that through it was too late to answer, for Miss K was still standing suspiciously at her door. It was almost possible to see her as a thicker blackness against the pervading darkness of the hallway. If Tilly had spoken now it would have seemed exceedingly odd, she decided. So she still held her breath; and just when she was certain she could do so no longer, but would have to gasp for air in a most audible manner, Miss K at last took a deep breath of her own, and went back into her room and clicked the door shut behind her.

They stood still for a second longer, and then Silas tugged on her elbow and before she realized what he was doing had pulled her into her own room and closed the door silently behind him without so much as a snicker of sound from the lock. And as she stood there in amazement, he moved further into the room with the sureness of a cat which could see in the dark and again lit the candle he was still holding. He must have had a match in his pocket, she thought absurdly, blinking a little as the candle flame lifted and dipped wildly, sending shadows leaping alarmingly over the ceiling, and then the light became richer and stronger and steadied as he found her oil lamp, still sitting on the floor behind her bedroom door, and bent and picked it up and lit it, without, to her chagrin, any difficulty whatsoever.

He stood there holding her lamp high and staring down at her and she took a deep and shaky breath and said, still speaking quietly, but with definite anger in her voice, 'You have no right to be in this room, sir! Please to leave at once!'

'Oh, Tilly,' he said and smiled, a rather bleak smile but one with genuine amusement in it for all that. 'Please, don't be so absurd! Can you not imagine how Miss Knapp is now? She will have woken Miss Fleetwood and they will both be lying there listening with their ears out on stalks. If I leave now they will certainly hear me and they will be out of their room like jack-in-the-boxes and staring about them. Do you wish them to see me emerge from your door? We had to come in here – but now we are here it will be best if we stay for a while until those two old besoms fall asleep again.'

She glared at him, non-plussed. He was, of course, right. Both the

Misses K and F were inordinately curious. There could be no doubt they would be peering about for some time, and the thought of what their reactions might be if they should suspect that she and Silas – her heart quailed and with it her legs seemed suddenly to become jellies and she almost tumbled across the room to land on her *chaise longue* in a little huddle.

At once he set down the lamp on the small table that stood at the foot of the *chaise longue* and was on his knees beside it. 'Oh, my dear, are you overcome? You are fully entitled to be, for this has been a dreadful ten minutes for you.'

'Ten minutes?' she said and glanced up at the clock. It was indeed just a quarter to three and she took a deep breath and shook her head. 'Only ten minutes.'

'Well, not much more,' he said. 'Are you all right?'

'A little bewildered, perhaps,' she managed. 'That is all.' And she put her hands up to her head to smooth her hair, suddenly very aware of the fact that she was wearing just a nightgown and a thin silk wrap and that her hair was tumbled about her shoulders. 'I am not sure what is happening here.'

He smiled again but more warmly this time. Because he was still kneeling beside the *chaise longue*, his face was on a level with hers and also very close and she could see clearly that there was a small quirk in the corner of his mouth and found herself thinking, he must have been dimpled when he was a child. A ridiculous thought to have in such circumstances and her awareness of that made her sharp. She drew back from him against the corner of the *chaise longue* and said. 'So, what were *you* doing wandering about the house at such an hour?'

'The same as you were, I suspect,' he said and seemed to take the message from her, for he sat back on his heels, leaving more space between them. 'I heard sounds and was alarmed. I do not believe that every night we are surrounded by would-be robbers, yet one hears so many tales of barefaced burglary that – well –' He shrugged. 'I felt some concern.'

It made sense, she thought, looking at him. There had indeed been recent tales of local houses being broken into by robbers in the boldest manner possible; had she not herself thought that she was being robbed, though perhaps by an insider rather than an outsider?

'But why creep about so, like a robber yourself?' she snapped. Her strength and self-control were returning to her now. 'If you thought there was trouble abroad, why not come out with a light and call out as any sensible person would?'

'You did not,' he pointed out with sweet reasonableness, still smiling. 'As I recall, you too were creeping along the hallway in the dark trying not to be heard.'

She flushed. 'I was not sure – it might have been – I did not know –' she began and he lifted his brows and nodded.

'Precisely. I felt the same way. It might be a robber bent on stealing – or it might have been some persons showing a greater interest in each other's company than – well, we have an interesting household here, after all.' He quirked an eyebrow at her. 'Have we not? Mr Cumming and Mr Hancock and Mademoiselle Salinas – after all, people are but human –'

'Not in my house!' Tilly said with a snap in her voice. 'I would not permit – I mean – this is a respectable lodging. I would not have among my guests such as would misbehave in such a way that –' Her voice faltered and she looked down at her hands, which were twisting and untwisting in her lap.

'Yes,' he said after a moment, his voice grave, and he got to his feet and sat down on the end of the *chaise longue*, not too close to her but near enough for her to be very aware of him and feel the heat of his body. He was wearing a thick silk dressing-gown and beneath it she could not help but see his bare ankles and feet in leather slippers. Clearly he too was in his nightshirt beneath the gown, and no more, and there was something so intimate in that thought that she found herself getting flustered again.

'I hope – ' he began and then stopped and thought for a while before trying again. 'I hope you will not be too perturbed by tonight's events,' he said at last.

'Perturbed?' She too was thinking, remembering the way those two faces had looked in the gleam of the single candle in the split second in which she had seen them, before Silas had put his hand over her mouth and she had closed her eyes automatically as she struggled to escape his grip. Duff, looking rather foolish if the truth were to be told, with his mouth half open and his eyes set so wide with shock that she could see a line of white above the pupils, and Sophie's own face, for she had stood there with her cheek pressed to his and also staring at Tilly. But she hadn't looked foolish in the least. The expression on her face had been a complicated one, a half smile curling the lips, the eyes seeming modestly shaded by the lids but gleaming in a way that showed they missed nothing – she had looked more like a satisfied cat, Tilly thought suddenly. A cat with cream on its whiskers.

'I'm not sure what you mean by perturbed,' she managed to say and put her hands up to her face again. Her eyes were feeling hot and sandy and her lips were tight and dry. She licked them in an effort to be more comfortable but that seemed to make the dryness worse.

'It is not easy when a mother – when young men grow up,' Silas was saying carefully. Too carefully, she thought; he sounds like an adult talking to a child and I am not a child. 'So he and the delectable Sophie are enjoying a little amatory adventure? You should be happy for him that he has so much pleasure in his life rather than – '

'You do not need to lecture me, Mr Geddes,' she said icily. 'I am well aware of the responsibilities and problems of a mother of a young son. I have after all, been such a mother for some years. You have not.'

He looked taken aback. 'Well, no, I have not. But –' He seemed to gather his composure, 'But I have been a young man like Duff, and I can only commend his good taste and applaud his good fortune in finding a young lady so willing to dally with him.'

'In the middle of the night? In a hole in the corner fashion? Dressed like a – like a –' She could not say the word that had come into her mind and she suddenly remembered those words she had heard out there in the dark hallway; words she knew were curses, even though she was not certain of their meaning. Now she thought of it, they had been said not by Silas or Duff as she had supposed, but by Sophie. 'I have been wickedly misled,' she said with sudden passion. 'I believed Sophie to be what she seemed, a respectable, well-behaved young lady. I set aside my doubts about her living alone at her age, even set aside my concern when she admitted to being a dancer on the stage, but I should not have done so. I should have sent her away immediately and never have let her anywhere near Duff.'

She felt sobs choking her throat and could not stop her eyes filling with tears. 'It was all my fault. If I had not been so anxious – if only I had – oh, I am wretched! Quite wretched.' And the tears overflowed and began to run like a tap. So did her nose. She was sobbing bitterly and her face was wet and she had no protection for it but her own two hands.

He moved closer and set one arm about her heaving shoulders and with his other hand set a large handkerchief to her face. She seized it gratefully, and mopped her cheeks and blew her nose and tried very hard to stop the tears, but it seemed beyond her powers to do so. The weeping went on and on, her shoulders enveloped by his warm grasp and her nose filling yet again. She seemed to consist entirely of head; there was no sense of any other part of her body. There were just her eyes and nose and ears and face, all melting away into thick, scalding, horrible tears.

But slowly the storm subsided until she found herself clutching the sodden rag that was Silas's handkerchief in one wet hand and lying with her head resting on his shoulder. He was rocking her gently and crooning into her ear and it was agreeable in the extreme. She sat there staring sightlessly ahead of her and making no effort to move at all.

How long she might have gone on so, she could not know. She was, in fact, becoming sleepy. The excitement and the great rush of emotion added to her existing fatigue had almost overwhelmed her. She should, she knew in a vague sort of way, be concerned with the fact that she had surprised her innocent young son almost *in flagrante delicto* with a girl who was, she was now certain, no better than a slut at heart, but somehow there was no emotion left in her.

It had happened and that was that, and she felt her eyes slowly closing.

Silas moved beside her, putting his head forwards so that he could look down into her face and without thinking she lifted her chin and looked up at him, her eyelids heavy and blinking. She wanted to say something; that she was appreciative of his care; that she was sorry to have made such a cake of herself; that it was time for him to go, please, and thank you for your interest and just leave me be so that I can go to sleep – I am aching to sleep –

But he seemed to see something else in her face for suddenly he bent his head and put his mouth on hers and her eyelids, hitherto seeming totally out of her control, flew open in amazement and then, as he became more urgent, pushing her lips apart with his tongue, closed again and now she had no control over them whatsoever.

Or indeed over anything else, it seemed. It had been many years since she had been this close to a man. In the days when her first husband, Francis, had been alive, his attentions had been more frightening than enjoyable, more painful than pleasurable, but this was different. Sensations were moving through her body that amazed her. It was as though there was sitting beside her and watching her with a sardonic eye another Tilly who was observing and recording all that happened and saying in an amused sort of voice, 'Well, well! Dear me! Imagine you, Tilly Quentin, behaving in such a manner! And enjoying doing so, what's more. And there were you criticizing your son, or rather Sophie – well, well, dear me.'

But she ignored that cool and critical watcher and let herself sink into the sensations she was so enjoying, sensations which filled her belly with heat and tightened her chest and made her breasts ache. Her nipples felt hard and very sensitive against the fabric of her nightgown as he pulled her closer and began to caress her back with both hands, and she thought the hurt was wonderful. There was nothing for her but the here and now and feeling, feeling, feeling.

Chapter Twenty-Six

SHE WAS VERY tempted not to go into the dining room for breakfast but to send for a sweet roll and coffee in her morning room; but she found a shred of pride somewhere deep inside and refused to behave in so craven a manner. She dressed carefully, getting up as soon as Rosie brought her morning tea and her jug of hot water, and went to considerable trouble to make herself look as presentable as she could.

It was not easy. Her head ached dully, and her eyes were reddened and the lids were swollen. She bathed them in cold water which helped a little, but all the same, even when she had put on her newest day gown, a crisp russet-coloured gaberdine with handsome green braid, in which she knew she looked particularly fetching, she looked the way she felt. Drained, pallid and bone weary.

She had slept eventually, but the sky was already paling by the time she did so. The first thought to come into her head when Rosie rattled her curtain rings was not the earlier part of last night's extraordinary events, but what had happened with Silas Geddes. She had come to, as though from a faint, when his kisses had started to become more urgent, and his hands had moved from her back further forwards, all of which she had found herself liking, but somehow she had managed to dredge out of her depths a few shreds of constraint, and was able to pull herself away and say in a cracked and gasping voice, 'No – please. No –' He had stopped at once, pulling back from her to sit in the corner of the *chaise longue,* staring at her with wide eyes and an expressionless face.

'I think,' she had said after a silence, 'I think I would like you to leave now, if you please. I am very tired – and I think I would like you to leave.'

He did not move. 'Are you angry with me?' he asked softly.

'Angry?' She considered that carefully. It was difficult to think; her head felt stuffed with feathers, and ideas had to push and claw their way to the surface. 'No, I do not think I am angry precisely –'

'Then what are you?'

'Tired,' she had cried, almost piteously. 'I am desperately weary and I must, I really *must* ask you to leave me. I cannot cope with much more, indeed I cannot!'

At once he had got to his feet and stood there, his head a little bent as he looked down at her.

'Then of course I shall go! I want you to know, though, before I do, that I regard you – with – with the greatest respect and behaved as I did only out of – out of an impulse which I did not have the strength to put down. It is not an ignoble impulse, however, and is based, I am most anxious you should know, in only the deepest of regard for your character, your charm, your intellect –'

'Oh, please!' she cried, unable to take another moment of his careful speech. 'No more, please. Just go – I cannot take another word – goodnight – *goodnight*.' And she had turned her head away from him and put up her hands to her face and stayed resolutely so until she heard the door close softly behind him.

She had collapsed into bed then, and had been certain that she would fall asleep immediately, but of course she had not. The remainder of the night, short as it was, seemed endless, and when at last she did sleep it was to dream dreadfully vivid dreams which she could not remember when she woke. Which made them harder to be rid of, for the menace in them seemed to hang over her.

But she did the best she could and came downstairs in what was, she hoped, her normal composed manner. Polly was at the foot of the stairs, a duster in her hand, rubbing the bannisters, and Tilly stopped when she saw her and frowned.

'What are you doing there, Polly?' she said sharply. 'Why are you not in the kitchen with Georgie?'

'He's had his breakfuss, Missus, and he's asleep, in the corner, Missus, so I asked if I could do somethin' useful, and Mrs Horace, she said I could do this.' She scowled a little then. 'If I'm doin' it wrong then I'll 'ave to be taught 'ow, won't I? I can't know from nothing, can I? I never lived in 'ouses like this before.'

'It's all right, Polly,' Tilly said, her voice softer now. 'I did not mean to sound harsh. I was just surprised. Afraid that Georgie –'

The child's face split into an unlovely grin. 'Georgie's fine, Missus, real fine. Why, carryin' 'im's making my arms ache, I swear to you, 'e's that 'eavy now. No need to fret over 'im.'

'Good,' Tilly said and made to pass on. 'Don't worry about the stairs. I dare say you are doing them well enough. If Eliza is happy, I shall be.'

'Please, Missus,' Polly said as Tilly reached the dining-room door. 'Did you find out anythin'? Did you go to the beak's?'

Tilly stood with her back to the girl, her bottom lip caught between her teeth. Heaven forgive her, she'd totally forgotten the matter of Polly's father. It seemed an eternity now since she had gone to Clerkenwell Magistrate's Court to find out about him and had discovered so much more than she had expected. Dorcas – there too was unfinished business she would have to give some thought to, surely –

Slowly she turned and looked at Polly. 'Yes, Polly. I have been there.'

'And did you find out anythin'?'

'Yes,' Tilly said and stopped.

Polly looked at her very directly, and then with an odd gesture pushed her hands through her hair, setting her cap askew. 'Oh, well,' she said and her voice was harsh, as though she had swallowed some caustic substance that had abraded her throat. 'I said as 'e was dead, didn't I? I knew it. It 'ad to be.'

'But I didn't say –' Tilly began but again Polly made that odd gesture and then shook her head.

'You didn't 'ave to, Missus,' she said, and now her voice was normal again, a little thin, pitched rather too high for comfort. 'Seen it in your face. 'E's six foot under, 'n't 'e?'

'Yes, Polly,' Tilly said gently. 'I'm afraid that's the case.'

'Well, it'll suit 'im well enough,' Polly said and turned back to the bannisters. 'It'll be peaceful now, any road, and 'e won't get cold and 'e won't be 'ungry or in a takin' over us. Better off, really.'

'Oh, Polly, I am so sorry,' Tilly said and without stopping to think reached out to the girl and put her arm around her. For a second the girl stood rigid, and then she softened and for just a moment leaned against Tilly who held her close.

Then she stood up again and pulled back. 'It's all right, Missus,' she said equably. 'Don't you fret none for me. I've got Georgie, see, and the boys is all right, or so I'm told, and as for pa, like I said – 'e's comfortable enough now, I got no complaints. I'm better off 'n I ever thought I could be, and I'm grateful to you for that, Missus. So don't you fret none over my pa dyin' an' all.'

'I shall take you to the country this very Saturday, to see your brothers, Polly,' Tilly said on an impulse born of guilt. 'I should have done it long since, but there has been so little time – but we shall make some. I shall order a carriage from the stables and we shall go into the country and see them this very week.'

The girl's face lit up and again that wide grin appeared. 'Oh, Missus, Georgie'd like that,' she said. ''E ain't never been in a carriage, not Georgie, or not so 's 'e'd notice much.'

'Then he will on Saturday,' Tilly promised, her heart sinking a little at the thought of a long journey with a baby. 'I won't forget.'

Mr Cumming came down the stairs at that point and greeted them both with a cheerful 'Good morning!' and Tilly seized her opportunity.

'Mr Cumming, I am planning to take Polly to see her brothers in the country this Saturday coming,' she said. 'I would be glad if you could let me have full directions of where they might be found.'

'Oh, that is a pleasure, Mrs Quentin,' Melville Cumming said heartily. 'I shall collect that today. It was somewhere in Kent, I believe. Edenbridge, perhaps? Somewhere like that. I shall obtain all you need to know this very afternoon.' He peered at her a little more closely. 'Some country air will do you no harm either, Mrs Quentin,' he pronounced, suddenly every inch the doctor. 'You are looking a trifle peaky, Ma'am!'

'Oh, I am well enough,' Tilly said quickly and went into the dining room, with Cumming close behind her, still talking.

'Well, you may believe so,' he said. 'But there are signs that are clear to the expert medical eye, and I can see that you are not as well as you might wish to be. A touch run down, you know. Nothing a little rest and country air won't cure, mind you. I'll get you that information this very afternoon.'

'What, our Mrs Quentin unwell?' Miss Barnetsen was sitting at the breakfast table with a large plate of kedgeree in front of her. She looked archly at Tilly as she came to her place at table and went on. 'We cannot have that! You are our prop and stay, dear Mrs Quentin, is that not so, Mr Cumming?'

'Indeed it is,' Mr Cumming said heartily. 'Good morning all. Good morning, Hancock. Drat you, I made sure I'd be down before you today, but I was waylaid on the stairs so it does not count towards our totals.'

The two young men had a running wager on which of them left their bed with the greatest alacrity in the mornings; it was a jest that they were all well used to and to which no one else paid much attention.

'As to that, you make excuses,' retorted Hancock. 'Mrs Quentin, I am sure, will give you the lie – will you not, Mrs Quentin?'

Tilly lifted one hand and gave a deprecatory shake of her head but Hancock would not be stopped.

'It's only fair, Mrs Quentin! There's fully three half crowns resting on this wager! You must not be partial now – admit to me that he was not at all delayed on the stairs by you.'

'Not by Mrs Quentin, man, but by her protégée!' Cumming was helping himself to a great deal of bacon and devilled kidneys. 'We were speaking of Mrs Quentin taking the girl Polly and the baby to the country this weekend.'

'Protégée!' squeaked Miss Barnetsen, as the Misses K and F came sailing in to take their places at table. 'That little housemaid with the dreadful teeth who was in the hall polishing the stairs when I came down? Surely she is not a protégée!'

'Indeed she is,' Mr Cumming said. 'And her infant brother.' He shook his head. 'I thought everyone in the house must know by now of Mrs Quentin's kindness in taking in this baby and his sister. Beggar children, yet she has given them a home.'

Tilly threw a look at him that was ice cold in its displeasure. 'I would have preferred this matter was not for general discussion, Mr Cumming,' she said frostily. 'I find it difficult to act always in the bright glare of attention.'

The room was filling rapidly now as more and more of the guests arrived to take their breakfast, and Tilly felt rather than saw Sophie come drifting in. She was scented with Parma Violets and, Tilly saw when the girl passed her, dressed in a gown of beautifully cut silver-grey wool that made her hair seem to flame more vividly than usual.

'A baby as well!' Miss Barnetsen fluted. 'How generous and kind you are. I had seen the infant about but I had considered – well,' she simpered, 'I did not presume to ask what it was or to whom it belonged.'

'Well, it was hardly likely to be mine,' Tilly said somewhat waspishly, and then shook her head. 'I would much prefer we did not discuss this matter.'

'I am happy not to do so as long as there is no interference in our comfort.' Mrs Grayling was sitting very upright, the last of the arrivals and looking somewhat flustered, for she had dropped her reticule on the way in and had only just managed to rescue all its contents. 'All is so very comfortable as we are that I fear any changes in our circumstances must be for the worst, for they cannot be for the better.'

'I will accept that as a compliment, Mrs Grayling,' Tilly said evenly. 'And I assure you that the presence in this house of these two young people – who are not, I assure you, beggars any longer, but well cared for members of my household – will not discommode anyone in the slightest. Has anyone heard the infant cry?'

'I have once or twice,' Mr Hancock allowed, his mouth full. 'But then I dare say once or twice it's heard me snore!' And he laughed loudly and then jumped to his feet and bowed as the Salinas family came in. He was clearly delighted to see Mademoiselle Salinas and Tilly found herself wondering bleakly if there had been or were about to be any more amatory adventures in her lodgings. Was the establishment about to slide into the gutter? Mrs Grayling had, perhaps, more to worry about than she knew, she told herself and got quickly to her feet.

'I must leave you to serve your own coffee and tea this morning if you will forgive me,' she murmured. 'I have much work to do in my office. I shall collect that information from you at dinner time, Mr Cumming – yes? Thank you so much. Good morning, everybody.'

And she escaped to her morning room, grateful that at least Silas and Duff had not appeared. It was only Sophie she had to avoid as she fled, and once she was in the hall she found herself thinking, why should I flee? Is she not the one who should be ashamed to show herself to me? I am the one who has been affronted by misbehaviour under my roof, she the one who committed it –

'And Duff,' whispered her secret voice.

She hurried along the hall to her morning room as though she could run away from her own thoughts, and was about to close the door behind her, safe inside at last, when it resisted and was pushed open again.

It was Sophie who stood there and Tilly let the door go as she saw who it was and walked to her desk, proud of her own steadiness, for inside she was feeling very shaky indeed. The only way to deal with her anxiety was to fan it into something hotter and deliberately she let anger take over, encouraging her own rage so that when she reached her chair she was able to whirl and sit down in a susurration of skirts and then look at Sophie with her head up and say sharply, 'Well, Miss! And what do you have to say for yourself?'

'Why, only that I am leaving for Leicestershire today,' Sophie said and smiled. She looked as lovely as ever, not one of her beautifully arranged tresses disturbed, and her skin even more glowing and peach-like than usual. Did she use rice powder in the mornings? Tilly found herself wondering and then dismissed the idea as one that should be beneath her contempt. As if it mattered, after all.

'And I trust will not be returning here,' Tilly said and lifted her chin. 'It will be better, I think, if you did not.'

'Oh, do you?' Sophie asked and shook her head in apparent regret and then looked about her to select a chair, into which she sank with great elegance. 'I cannot imagine why. Do I not pay my bills regularly? Do I not entertain your guests on every possible occasion? You cannot deny that they all positively adore me and would sorely miss my company. So why should you wish me not to return?'

'Oh, don't play the artless puss with me, young woman!' Tilly cried. 'You know perfectly well! I will not have my house turned into a – a –'

'A bawdy house?' Sophie said sweetly as Tilly stopped, lost for words. 'What an interesting comment for you to make.' She laughed then, the soft tinkling practised laugh that was so musical. 'You may not know how wisely you speak, dear Aunt Tilly. But let that be. Let me say instead that you can hardly blame *me* for what you observed last night, your son seeking to besmirch my honour and my name by making advances to me in the middle of the night – why, if I were to broadcast that fact, imagine the sense of revulsion that would fill your guests' hearts!'

'My son – my –' Tilly almost spluttered it. 'It was *you*! I saw the look on his face and on yours. You looked so – so very pleased with yourself while he – he was positively frozen with alarm!'

'I grant you that he was much the more bouleversé of the two of us,' Sophie said with a thoughtful air. 'Indeed, yes. But then he is so young a boy, is he not? So very inexperienced.' She shook her head in a reminiscent manner. 'Well, he will learn, no doubt. But let us be clear, dear Aunt Tilly, that you have no reason to be angry with *me*. It is your son you should speak to. Whose door was he at? Mine. I was not at his, let me remind you. I do not believe that you are being just in your reactions, and neither would anyone else, given the same facts to contemplate. I know it is painful to discover a beloved child is less than perfect, but please, Aunt Tilly, you must be fair.'

She got to her feet and smiled down at Tilly. 'Well, we shall see what we shall see. For my part, I shall leave for Leicestershire today. I was assured my welcome would be great at whatever time I chose to arrive. I think it will be politic to go now and furthermore it will let the heat die out of dear Duff a little if I am ahead of him as a guest. Then when he arrives he will not be so embarrassed as he might be were he to have to face me here in his own house, under the very roof beneath which he attempted to – well, let be. As I say, I shall make no fuss about what he did last night and I am sure you will see the wisdom of that. Goodbye for now, dear Aunt Tilly. I shall complete my preparations and be away from here in an hour or so. I shall leave my rent for the next two weeks, of course, so that my room awaits my return. Goodbye, dear Aunt Tilly.'

And with the coolest air in the world, she came to Tilly, bent her head and kissed her cheek in a most nieceish manner and went out of the room with her elegant gown swaying almost insolently as she walked. And Tilly could say not a word as she watched her go.

Chapter Twenty-Seven

TILLY HAD NEVER been more grateful for the amount of work she had to do to keep Quentin's running smoothly than she was that day. She had no sooner re-established her composure after Sophie's insolent departure from her private room than Eliza had arrived at her door full of complaints about the delivery from the market garden and begging her to come and arbitrate between herself and the man. The resultant heated discussion of how much of the mud which clung to potatoes could justly be charged in the overall weight of a delivery, and whether or not the outer leaves of the cabbages Eliza wanted were merely crushed or, as Eliza swore, frozen in a way that would indicate the inner part of the vegetable had been similarly damaged and would therefore be uneatable, occupied Tilly's mind totally.

She spent the next hour in the kitchen, planning the meals for the remainder of the week, and inspecting some of the extra preserves that Eliza had put up, including pickled red cabbage and beets, onions and nasturtium seeds (to stand in for capers to dress winter mutton) as well as a special pickle made of large lemons, of which Eliza was inordinately proud.

'I found the receipt in a book of Eliza Acton, Mum,' she said. 'And I followed it that careful, and don't it look good! They'll be fit to eat this time a twelve month, for they take a long time, but well worth waiting for.'

'Yes,' Tilly said, looking at the plump sunshine-bright lemons, scored from end to end and stuffed with spices, bobbing about in their briny vinegar, and tried to show enthusiasm, but it was difficult. It was strange to remember how little Eliza had known of cooking when she had first come to Quentin's; almost as little as Tilly herself. Where would I be without her now? she thought and looked at Eliza, whose face was rounder and whose waist was thickening noticeably under her large apron, and was suddenly afraid. In another few months there would be a baby between herself and Eliza; and although Eliza had sworn she wanted Tilly to adopt that baby and that nothing would change in her attitude after she gave birth, Tilly remembered perfectly well how much her feelings had altered after Duff had been born. She had been concerned for her unborn child, but it had been a pallid concern, a feeble love she had felt when compared with the way she responded when she looked into Duff's infant face lying in the crook of her elbow. Then her feeling had almost alarmed her by its intensity; her need to protect as well as love him had been savage in its strength. Surely the same would happen to Eliza? Surely she would cling to her baby, and decide to move on to make a new life for them both elsewhere where no one would know of the shame of her child's fathering? It was a dreadful prospect, and Tilly could not bring herself to contemplate it. So she hurried through the rest of the kitchen tasks and then left Eliza to get on with her bread baking, while she escaped upstairs to check her linen cupboard and to make sure that Miss McCrasky had finished the new sheets to her satisfaction.

She was sitting on the floor of the cupboard in a manner that was hardly elegant but decidedly convenient, since the new sheets were piled on the lowest shelf, and was checking their hems when a shadow fell across the open doorway and she looked up. Her belly lurched and she felt sick.

Duff was standing there looking down at her and because the light was behind him and rather bright, for all it was a winter morning, she could not see his face clearly. But she could tell by the set of his shoulders that he was in a mood that was both apologetic and truculent. This was going to be a disagreeable meeting.

'Good morning, Duff,' she said as calmly as she could. 'I must check the last of these sheets and then I shall –'

'There is no need to disturb yourself, Mamma.' His voice was tight and a touch high with tension and her heart melted; she wanted only to jump up and hug his unhappiness away, but she could not. And it was not entirely because she was encumbered with a lap full of heavy linen sheets. It was important, she knew, to maintain some air of disapproval until she could be sure. She did not, of course, believe Sophie's version of last night's events. There was no doubt in her mind that it had been Sophie and not Duff who had taken all the initiative in their 'amatory adventure' but she had to be just (or so she told herself with some energy, as she continued to look at the sheets, ostensibly inspecting the stitching of the hems) and give Sophie some benefit of doubt. 'I wished only to say that I regret disturbing you last night.'

'Disturbing me?' She squinted up at him, irritated by the difficulty of seeing him clearly, an irritation that sharpened her tone. 'Is that the best description you are able to make of what occurred?'

'Well, Mamma, what did occur?' he said and his voice was tighter than ever. 'I was escorting Miss Oliver to her door, after we had sat up far too late talking of various subjects. We had not noticed the time – and we did not wish to disturb the household, so that was why we did not have a candle or a lamp. I wished only to see her safe – and then you come creeping along and make such a brouhaha that Silas has to come and – and –'

'Oh, Duff, please,' Tilly said wearily, and put the sheets on the shelf and got to her feet. 'Do not compound matters by creating a tissue of lies – I saw you! You were – were not dressed and she was in her nightgown. I am not such a fool as you think.'

'Oh,' he said blankly and then caught his breath. 'Well, I wished only to save your face. For, after all, Mamma, what does it signify? So, I was flirting with Sophie – is that a crime? You make it all so – so sordid, creeping about so and spying on us and –'

'Spying!' Tilly gasped. 'Oh, that really is the outside of enough! I heard a noise and feared that I was being robbed. I have been in the past, you will recall, by fleeing guests who chose not to pay their bills! I would be a poor sort of householder if I had not come to investigate unexpected noises.'

'Well, anyway, it was all hateful!' Duff burst out. 'You spoiled everything, appearing like that – I was so – so –' He shook his head and now she could see his face it was clear that he was on the edge of tears. 'It had all been so sweet and – and romantic and – and then you were there and it became a shabby business, a scrabbling about in the dark that I – oh, pshaw! We did but talk a little and then I went to bed and slept not at all, and then this morning I am told she has gone to Leicestershire ahead of me and – I am so wretched I could – oh, Mamma, how could you!'

'How could I – oh, now Duff, this really must stop! I will not be blamed and made to feel the guilty party when it is you who should apologize to me for behaving so under my roof. I cannot control all your life and nor would I wish to. I am well aware that as a man you may follow some sort of behaviour that I would not admire – but I think you must learn, young as you are, that there is a time and a place for all things, and this your home is not the place for dalliance with the likes of Sophie Oliver!'

'How do you mean, the likes of?' He almost spat it at her, standing there in the hallway outside the linen cupboard with his hands thrust into his trouser pockets and his eyes glaring at her, a little red-rimmed over a shadow of unshaven stubble. Not a lot, for he had not been shaving for so very long, but enough to make him look rather wild. 'She is the dearest girl in all the world and I will not have you speak harshly of her. I know you hated her mother, but then so does she and –'

'Please, Duff!' She put her hands out and set them on his shoulders. 'We must not quarrel like this. It is not our way, it never has been. I have been distressed by all that has occurred and do not trust Sophie, but we need not quarrel, need we? I hate quarrelling above all things. I – when I was younger I suffered the hearing of so much of it that now I shrink from disagreements with pain.'

'But I thought you were angry with me!' he said blankly, staring at her.

'I was, I am – but it is possible to be angry and hurt and anxious without exchanging hot words, surely? That makes any distress so much the worst, I believe. Let us simply talk as sensible people.'

'I cannot be sensible about Sophie,' he said. 'I do love her so, Mamma!'

It was like a cry of physical pain and she could have wept for him and let her hands slide down his arms so that she could hug him close, and though at first he resisted, he softened eventually and let her hold him. And then straightened up and shook his head at her.

'I shall have to go to Leicestershire early as well, Mamma. I can't let her be there without me to take care of her.'

'She's well able to take care of herself,' Tilly said. 'And no, don't look so stormily at me. I was not making a criticism but speaking simply a fact. She lives without the benefit of a parent's guidance although she is young enough to need it, and –' She stopped then and stared at him. 'What was that you said about Sophie and her mother?'

'Eh? Oh, that you hated her and blame Sophie for –'

'No – that is not quite true. I mean, I don't hate her precisely, but – no, I meant what you said about Sophie and her mother.'

He looked embarrassed. 'I'm not supposed to speak of what she tells me. We are close and share so much and we must be loyal to each other – it is the most important thing. We both agreed it.'

'It is not disloyal to tell me of matters which affect her welfare,' Tilly said after a moment. 'If she has no parent to care for her and lives here, then I must surely take some responsibility for her – and anyway, you said it. That she hated her mother as I did?'

'Something like that,' he muttered.

'Then they parted in anger – it wasn't because of Dorcas going to prison,' Tilly said, almost to herself and he lifted his chin and gaped at her.

'What did you say?'

She bit her lip and looked at him for a long moment and then sighed. 'I had not intended to speak to you of this. Why should I? But now – well, when I was seeking information about Polly's father, I found out that Dorcas had been up before – in the same court and sent to prison for two years. She is due for release very soon – and – well –'

He was silent for a long time and then took a deep shaky breath. 'Mamma, I am going to Leicestershire as soon as I may. I shan't worry about hunting clothes – Patrick will take care of that and lend me what I need, I dare say, for he's a good fellow. But I must be with Sophie. If she does not know this about her mother, then hate her though she might, she will be, I'm sure, desperately unhappy when she does hear of it. I might have to be the one to tell her. I must be with her in case – well, I shall go today, Mamma. I insist upon it. I will not be stopped. It is too important to me.'

'I think you are mistaken to run after her in this way, but I shan't try to stop you,' she said quietly. 'I know I will fail. I say only to you to beware. That I am certain Sophie knows perfectly well where her mother is and why, and that's why she lives alone as she does and why she worked at the Opera House and –'

'I prefer not to discuss her, Mamma,' Duff said with dignity that once again affected Tilly deeply, filling her with a strong desire to hug him again and soothe him but knowing it would be foolish to attempt it. 'I wanted only to say to you – to say, well I am sorry you were disturbed last night, but there, it had to happen, I suppose. After all, if I am to marry Sophie –'

'Marry her?' Tilly said. 'Marry – but Duff, you have no income, no career – you are barely seventeen! How can you speak of marriage?' She could not believe that he had allowed himself to become so deeply embroiled with Sophie; that he was attracted to her and wanted to have, as Sophie had put it, an amatory adventure was understandable, but marriage? The very idea made her feel cold.

'I know that,' he said, his face suddenly red with anger. 'Do you not think I have worried and worried over that? But she will wait for me, I know she'll wait for me. I will think of a career of some sort and work hard and one day – one day we shall be wed. But I have to take care of her now.'

'Oh, Duff, please!' Tilly cried. 'Do try to be sensible. This is moonshine. You can't speak of marriage at your age – you're far too young. And there are other things to take into account and –'

'Well, Mamma, I dare say, but I will not speak of it now.' He set his lips mulishly. 'I wished only to tell you I was going away to Leicestershire and to ask you to – well, I'm sorry if you were upset last night. That's all.'

With which skimpy apology he turned and went, running up the stairs to his room, and she stood there in the hallway, outside her linen cupboard, staring after him without any notion of what to do next.

It was not until just before luncheon that Silas came to speak to her. After Duff had left her she almost ran back to her fastness in the morning room to spend the next hours sitting there ostensibly working on her ledgers but in truth staring out of the window at the dripping November garden, for it had rained heavily in the night, and trying to collect her thoughts.

That Duff would fall in love quite so desperately that he could babble nonsense about planning a marriage had never occurred to her when she had allowed Sophie to return to the house. She had wanted only to provide him with an agreeable distraction from a schoolfellow she deeply distrusted. That he should find the girl as interesting as he had when they had been infants had been the sum total of her hopes; yet now see what she had done with her meddling. Oh, if only she hadn't asked Jem to seek out Sophie. If only he had not been so swift in obeying her. If only he were still there to be leaned upon, her solid comfortable friend who never hurt her or upset her, even though she had not returned his feelings when he loved her as dearly as anyone could – or she had thought.

She dragged her thoughts away from Jem and his new-found happiness, castigating herself for being so ungenerous to him. He had every right to seek his happiness elsewhere when she had rejected him so steadily for so long; and if she had to pay the price of his contentment in missing his support, well, so be it. She would have to cope alone. She had lost her Duff too to another female and that was the size of it. There was no one in the world left for her and her alone.

It was at this self-pitying point in her thinking that the door of her morning room opened, without so much as a preliminary scratch on the panels, and she lifted her head, startled, to see Silas standing in the doorway.

He came in, closing it carefully behind him and came to stand beside her chair, smiling down at her.

'Good morning, Tilly,' he said. 'Or should it be good day, since the morning is so far advanced? I've been looking for you –'

'I've been here,' she said as colourlessly as she could, although her pulse speeded up with his closeness. This was absurd. She should be angry with him, not so ridiculously glad to see him.

'I haven't come to apologize for making love to you last night,' he said then and crouched beside her chair. 'Did you think I had? Did you think I should?'

'I would rather you sat in a chair properly than squatted there like – like a –'

'Like a puppy dog begging favours at your feet,' he said cheerfully and stood up, and brushed down the knees of his trousers. He had, she thought, after a swift glance, gone to some trouble when he dressed this morning, for his checked cheviot trousers were crisply pressed, and his shirt blinding in its perfection under a handsome checked waistcoat and grey cutaway university coat. He smelled of bay rum and his hair had been most elegantly brushed. Oddly enough this circumstance made her feel more relaxed rather than the reverse; if he had taken such trouble over his appearance did this not mean that he felt uneasy about their meeting even if his manner at the moment did not suggest any discomfort?

'Well?' he said and she glanced at him and then away at the floor.

'Well, what?' she managed.

'What do you expect me to say to you this morning?'

'It is not up to me to teach you how to behave,' she said.

'It is, my dear Tilly, indeed it is! It is up to you to teach me everything from now on, just as I must teach you, for I must tell you that I am determined that we shall never be apart again. Last night it was my privilege to – to help you in a dilemma, and afterwards it was my delight to hold you in my arms.'

'I would prefer you not to speak of it, sir,' she cried, and he frowned.

'Sir? Why so formal? Are you telling me that you are angry?'

'I – well, I am not precisely – I mean, why should I not be? Or rather, why –' She stopped. She had to admit it now; there was no avoiding it though she had been trying to, she now realized, ever since she had woken this morning. She had been as much at fault, if fault there was, as he had. She had liked being kissed. She had liked it a great deal, and only when his caresses had begun to be a little more urgent had she made any effort to stop him. And as soon as she had shown that she was less than willing he had desisted immediately. He had behaved like a gentleman in every way, and she couldn't deny it. If anyone had been outrageous it was she, Tilly Quentin.

And that, she knew with a sudden rush of insight was why she had been unable to be as angry with Duff as she was entitled to be. Why, she had blamed Sophie for seducing her Duff, rather than the other way about, which was what most people, given the circumstances, would have done. Tilly knew how she had felt herself, and been only too aware of the power of feminine desire. It was she who had been in control of what had occurred last night between herself and Silas, and she had no doubt that same situation had obtained with Sophie and Duff.

'I think it is I who should express regret,' she said in a small voice. 'I did not behave as a lady should and I can only put my lapse down to the strain of the moment, the lateness of the hour and my undoubted fatigue. I'm sure you will be wishing to seek other accommodation, since it will be a matter of considerable embarrassment to us both to continue under the same roof.'

He laughed aloud at that. 'Oh, dear Tilly, have you learned nothing about me? I am one of the new people, remember? I don't regard it as in any way at all shocking that a woman should have needs and desires of her own and that she should express them. Have you not listened to what I have said about the way people behave, or should? Have you not understood me at all? In common with most of the members of my Society and the people whose opinion I most value, I regard the relationship between the sexes as one that should be free and untrammelled by conventional ideas! There's no need at all for you to be ashamed of what passed between us last night any more than there is for me. We should glorify the fact that we have found each other and can together explore the –'

'I have no wish to explore anything!' she cried and he stopped and stared at her.

'Do you mean that? Truly? Look at me and tell me whether you mean that or whether you are being – well, conventional and making pointless protests you don't in truth mean?'

She lifted her chin and looked at him, stung by the accusation that she was behaving missishly and opened her mouth to speak. And couldn't. The sensations that had crawled in her belly last night when he kissed her were conjured up again just by looking at him; she felt her face get hot as she found it was not just her belly that was feeling the sensations, but her breasts, the small of her back and her thighs, and indeed the most intimate parts of her body. She was bursting with desire and though at one level she recognized it as a delightful feeling on another she was deeply, desperately ashamed of it.

'Oh, dear,' was all she could say, and he smiled a wide triumphant sort of grin and stepped forward and pulled her to her feet and kissed her again. And just as she had last night, she cooperated with every atom of strength she had and enjoyed it hugely.

Chapter Twenty-Eight

SHE WAS GRATEFUL for the peace that succeeded those few days of upheaval. The first week after Sophie and Duff departed was not an easy one; the other guests clearly missed the company of the young people, notably Sophie, and there were a few flares of irritable temper due to the resultant boredom from Miss Knapp, from whom it was only to be expected, and from Mrs Grayling, from whom it was rather surprising. But Tilly managed to soothe them with a flash of inspiration when she purchased one of Charlie Harrod's newest ideas, an exceedingly large and varied compendium of games. There were dominoes and cribbage, chess and bezique, Pope Joan and Nine Men's Morris as well as a wickedly exciting racing game and, of course, draughts. In no time the drawing room after dinner rattled with the sound of dice rolling or counters clicking and the cries of exultant – or disappointed – players. The gap left in their social life by the loss of Sophie and her singing and general sparkling charm slowly closed over and calm and contentment returned to Quentin's.

Or it did for the guests. For the proprietor things were not quite so easy. She went about the business of her day looking as serene and purposeful as she always had, ensuring that every one of her guests had all they required for their comfort, that Eliza was able to run the kitchen economically and the maids were able to keep the house thoroughly clean with the maximum of efficiency. No one seemed aware of the fact that behind her smooth exterior a great deal of confusion swirled; not even Silas, though he spent a good deal of time with her – or at least as much as he was able, allowing for her busyness.

He tried to persuade her to spend the evenings in her morning room in his sole company, but she was adamant that she owed it to her guests to be with them and insisted in such a way that he could not see it as anything but the thoroughgoing concern of a hard-working businesslike lady trying to run her establishment in the best possible manner. For Tilly it was enough always to see Silas in the company of other people; the last thing she wanted was to be alone with him.

His presence continued to make her body react with a degree of excitement that alarmed her; she was continually aware of the hunger that lurked inside her, which only he could assuage, but was determined to maintain complete self-control. She was not going to let anything, anything at all, spoil the life she had built for herself and her son, she would tell herself night after night as she prepared for bed and thought of Silas doing the same in his room along the hallway; allowing loose rein to her feelings for Silas would do just that. It could not be.

And a wicked little inner Tilly would quiz her, asking her if she was *quite* sure? And she knew she wasn't, but still managed, somehow, to maintain her façade. But it was far from easy.

At least all was peaceful below stairs. With the departure of Dora, Eliza had relaxed considerably and looked blooming and happy. That she was fattening was obvious, but oddly no one seemed to be all that surprised by the fact or to draw any embarrassing conclusions from it. Eliza was a cook, and cooks were supposed to be large and comfortable – or the best of them were. All Eliza was doing as far as the maids – and the guests, when they saw her – were concerned was ensuring that she fitted her role properly.

That she was happy was undoubted. She would hum cheerfully beneath her breath as she worked and sit comfortably sewing in her rocking chair in the kitchen or reading one of her beloved magazines, as solid and secure as a lighthouse and giving off the same sense of security to all around her who could bask in her light. She made

Tilly in particular feel better than she would have thought possible, under the circumstances, and certainly the whole house seemed to be in a particularly tranquil mood.

Until the letter came from Duff that removed any possibility of tranquillity for Tilly.

It arrived by the third post one dull afternoon, thick and heavy with many sheets of closely written paper, with a certain amount of scratchings out and heavy underlinings that showed how anxiously it had been written. Tilly, recognizing the hand as soon as Rosie gave it to her, escaped to her morning room with it, and sat down on the sofa to read it.

But she did not read it for a considerable time, finding it easier to sit turning it over and over in her hands, for she was filled with a sense of unease. What was he going to tell her? What horrid news did this thick missive contain? She had no doubt at all that it was horrid; she had been fearful ever since he had gone away, her dear Duff, that he might not come back to her, and now, she told herself, almost in tears at the prospect, that it had happened just as she had feared. Around her the pale walls seemed to leap and dance as the flames that burned so high and briskly in the grate threw light against them and there were glints of rich light reflected back from the curving legs of her pretty fruitwood chairs and tables. After a moment she got to her feet and fetched herself a glass of Madeira wine from the decanter on the corner whatnot. There was always some there, although she rarely drank any. Why she kept it she was not quite sure; perhaps in memory of her mother, whose room this once had been and who had been very partial to Madeira. Too partial, in fact.

With the glass on the small table beside her, she at last smoothed out the pages. And read, slowly and carefully, Duff's effusion.

'Dearest Mamma,' he wrote. 'This is such a difficult letter to write, even though it contains some excellent news because it also brings some that may dismay you, as you will see.

'But let me tell you first that all is well with me here. I arrived in some Trepidation, since I was in advance of my invitation, even though I had sent a letter to Patrick to tell him I was coming a little earlier than planned, but the Dear Old Fellow did not object in the Least, but professed himself Most Delighted to see me, and assured me that he had been deep in Ennui until we arrived.

'I say we, for the same Welcome was extended to Sophie, not that I am surprised by that, since she is so Charming. Patrick's papa, the duke, seems particularly to like her, and spends much time talking with her and laughing at her Witty Comments. Patrick's Sisters seem to be happy to have her company also, although Lady Euphonia, who is the eldest, is a shade waspish at times. But Patrick says she has always been thus, since she is the Eldest Child and feels Bitter that she cannot inherit the dukedom, which is a comical notion, is it not?

'Patrick and I have spent much time about the Estate, and he has shewn me much of country Life, which I find most Agreeable. He says I have a Natural Aptitude for such matters as the Keeping of Game and the Care of Horses, or rather the supervision of those who have such care, and is most most impressed, he is kind enough to say, by my ability with matters pertaining to money. He was always the worst in the school at Arithmetical matters and I often did his Preparation for him when we were boys there together.

'Which brings me to the Excellent news I mentioned. I hope you will regard it as I do, with Approval. In talking one afternoon, I said that I wished I could always live in the country amongst such Agreeable People and with my Friends about me, as here at Paton, and he said in the most casual manner imaginable that perhaps I should learn to be an Agent! I have to confess to you as I did to him that at this stage I had no Notion of the work of an Agent, but he laughed and explained that all he does is oversee the running of the Estate of a Gentleman and take the burdens from the Landowner and see to it that the Income runs well and that the Tenants are Happy and the Hunting and Shooting interests are well protected. He says their present Agent who is a great friend to the duke, Patrick's papa, dislikes Patrick excessively and when his papa dies and he succeeds to the Title, he fully intends to be rid of him. And he said then that I should take his place!

'I gasped but then he rode me over to Little Egton, one of the villages on the Paton Estate, to show me the Agent's house, which is a handsome one indeed, well proportioned and comfortable, being perhaps a hundred years old but with modern conveniences, Patrick said, they have their own excellent Well which never dries up in even the hottest Summer, as well as natural drainage that ensures there is no problem of Middens and such. He said I should have the House to live in as it is part of the Agent's Entitlement as well as an income of some Hundreds of Pounds a year to live on!

'I was amazed by this, but Patrick was quite certain and spoke in the most relaxed manner possible of this plan. He cannot arrange this until he is Duke, but he says, and I dare say he knows, that his Papa is a sick man and is well known in the County to be living on Borrowed Time. I thought that it was sad to speak so of his own Papa but he says his Papa hates him and that it is a tradition in his Family that the Son and Heir is always cordially Loathed by his father and why should they be different?

'Also he says I must stay as his Permanent Guest, learning secretly the work of an Agent so that when the time comes, as he is sure it will inside the next Twelvemonth, to tell the man Oakburton that he must leave, I shall be ready to take up my Duties.

'I have not spoke to Sophie yet of this, for I felt it proper I should Apprise you first of this Excellent Change in my fortunes, but I shall tell her as soon as I hear from you that you are happy for me in my choice of Career – I am sure you must be, since you have mentioned often your concern that I should choose some way to make my way in the world, and that you will see that the future is now most Sunny for me. To live in so handsome a house as Little Egton Hall with an Assured Income must make me most Eligible and able to ask Sophie to wed me, and then we shall be as happy as we may be!

'I await eagerly, dear Mamma, your reply to my letter assuring me that you are as Happy as I am with the way my Lines Have Fallen, and rejoice in my Good Fortune, all of which I owe to my friendship with the Dearest Fellow in the world, Good old Patrick.

'I must hurry to Post this letter, Mamma, which is villainously ill-written for which I Beg your Pardon, and sign myself Affectionately and with all Respect, your son Francis Xavier Quentin.'

And after that he had provided a sort of afterthought, his usual scrawl of 'Duff'.

Slowly she reread the letter, and then folded the sheets with careful fingers, ensuring that she made no new creases and then hid it away in one of the smallest pigeon-holes of her desk, the one with a sliding cover to it that she could lock it with the smallest key on the bunch she wore at her waist. And then she sat down again on her chair by the fire, to try to order her thoughts.

Duff, an agent to a duke? It sounded a great opportunity indeed, but it was as full of holes as a fisherman's net. First of all her boy was a London boy. He had been born in this very house, and had spent his youngest years no nearer to nature than the park, where he had chased sparrows and pigeons and thrown crumbs to the ducks on the Long Water but then had walked home over cobbles through the din and smell of town life. To be sure, he had learned to ride at school, and had found himself able to join a shooting party on a great estate, and now a hunting one, but did that fit him for a life in charge of a great countryside establishment? She tried to imagine it, and could not. The thought of Duff in breeches and gaiters and carrying a gun, in the manner she had seen in illustrations in *Punch*, was absurd.

And then there was the question of the duke. She found it repugnant to hear that her son's friend had spoken so flippantly and indeed hopefully of his father's death. Perhaps in high society of this sort it was normal to hate one's parents and to say so, but to do so as openly as this young man seemed to do shocked her.

She tried to remember how it had been in her own father's lifetime. She had feared him and often disliked him and, indeed, on occasion had found him hateful but she could never, surely, have spoken so cheerfully of his death with such – such – the words 'gloating delight' came into her head and she dismissed them. Duff had not actually said any such thing and she had never met Lord Patrick Paton so she had no reason whatsoever to think in such terms; but there had been something in Duff's account of his conversation with his friend that had created this thought for Tilly. And she shivered at it.

She made herself think about the worst aspect of the whole letter; his desire to remain in Leicestershire to learn how to be this agent at some unknown future time, a time dependent on an old man's death. She shivered again at the thought and shook her head. It could not be. She would write to him at once and bid him come home. He could not stay there, living in someone else's house, however rich and commodious, for a prolonged period. It would not be proper. He would cease to be a guest, surely, and would become a sort of parasite, could even be treated as a poor relation, with all the unpleasantness such an existence made inevitable. She was not rich but she was comfortably off, with Quentin's as successful as it was, and her son did not have to rely on living in a grand house as an object of charity. She would not countenance it! And she got to her feet quickly and hurried over to sit at her desk and kindle a lamp so that she could see better to write a strong letter to Duff.

And then she stopped, the pen in her hand. Was she going to insist he return home? How could she? He would be so desperately unhappy at the suggestion that he might baulk at it. She had seen enough of her now almost adult son since he had returned from school to know he was no longer the biddable child he had once been. This was a young man with strong views about what he would or would not do. To try to force him to do as she said as though he were still a child would avail her nothing. He might – and the thought made her chill as though she had swallowed pieces of ice – flatly refuse to obey her. And then what? Go to Paton herself and drag him away in ignominy? He would never forgive her. They would never deal happily together again. She had to find a better way of dealing with the matter. But the harder she tried to think the worse her anxiety became.

And then, at last, slowly an idea began to form. It might not work, she told herself; it smacked of the most disagreeable dishonesty; it *could* not work; and yet –

She thought hard for some time and then again picked up her pen and a sheet of her letter paper and began to write. But the letter was not addressed to Duff.

'Dear Sophie,' she wrote with a steady hand. 'I trust that you are finding your stay at Paton agreeable. I understand from Duff that he is to stay on at Paton for some time; he will himself explain to you why this should be so, I am sure.

'I have thought a good deal about our last conversation and feel that I was perhaps too hasty –'

She swallowed. It was painful to write such weasel words, but what else could she do? she asked herself almost piteously. Somehow she must lure Duff home and if the only way to do it was to use Sophie, and bend her own head to her, well, so be it. She would do it. She was not anxious to have the two of them together under any roof, but if they had to be, it would be better here, under her own, where she could observe what was happening and perhaps protect her son from a girl she was convinced was avaricious and thoroughly dishonest, than at some far distant duke's house.

She continued with her letter. 'I realize now that you were not to blame for any disagreements we might have had, but that Duff misbehaved. That being so, I believe the least I can do to recompense you for my ill humour is to invite you to stay at Quentin's as my guest in the future. Not as paying guest, you understand, but as one of the family. You are, as you say, known to me from your childhood and I will be happy to include you here as one of us. This will, I hope, release you from anxiety about money, which I suspect you have. I do recall your speaking of the need to earn your living; well, live with me and the need will evaporate and you will never again have to display yourself on the public stage in a way that you must find distasteful on occasion.'

I hope I haven't gone too far, she thought, biting the end of her pen. I don't for a moment think she finds it distasteful to display herself, but she does find it distasteful to be short of money. She will rise to the bait, I'm sure: come to live here free of cost and then return to dancing, just to annoy me, as she will see it, and keep all her money for herself. She will like that very much.

She bent her head and finished writing her letter. 'I look forward most eagerly to reading your response to my invitation, dear Sophie, and do assure you that I regard myself very much as your own dear Aunt, Tilly Quentin.'

So, I can be as devious as you, Miss, she told herself in a flash of amusement as she blotted and sealed her letter. I too can pursue an unpleasant means to an end I desire, as I am sure you have many, many times. Let us see what sort of haul this bait brings ashore.

There was a sudden scratching on her door panels, an urgent anxious sound and she lifted her head and called, 'Enter!' and it was Eliza who stood there, her face redder than usual and her forehead creased in anxiety.

'Oh, Mum,' she said breathlessly. 'Oh, Mum, do come and see. I do 'ope as I'm wrong, but I don't think I am. You'd best come and look for yourself, for if I'm right and saw what I saw, oh dear, oh dear!' And she actually pulled up her apron and wiped her face with it, as though she were still the little tweeny Tilly had taught not to behave in such a way. And Tilly, her pulse thumping a little as she caught Eliza's anxiety, got to her feet and hurried out of the room after her.

Chapter Twenty-Nine

ELIZA HURRIED HER along the hallway and into the dining room, where the long table was already set for dinner and looking very attractive with glossy laurel leaves as the table decoration and the faint glitter of silver and crystal (for the room was unlit, though it received a good deal of light from the hallway). The windows had been shrouded in their dark-green plush curtains, all except for one sliver on the left-hand curve where the dimness outside the windows could be seen; and it was to that point that Eliza took her.

'Look up,' she whispered, even though there was no possible chance that anyone outside the closed windows could hear her. 'I was just drawing the curtains ready to light the lamps and all, and I saw – so I left 'em like this so's I could show you – see?'

Mystified, Tilly went to the sliver of uncurtained window and peered out. It took her a few moments to adjust her eyes and then she was able to see, for it was after all only late afternoon, and not totally dark yet.

There were the steps up to her own front door and the curve of the doorstep behind the pilasters that held up the porch. There were the railings and the pavement. That was all there was to see in the immediate foreground and beyond that there was a repeat of the same as the steps up to the front door of the empty house next door and its matching pilasters and porch echoed her own, and on and on to the end of the street in retreating perspective. The cobbles of the roadway shone a little greasily in the light thrown out by one or two windows along the street as well as from her own drawing room on the floor above, where some of the guests were already congregating to wait for the summons to the dining room and dinner, and beyond those rectangles she could see the shadows of the houses on the other side of the road.

And that was all. There was no traffic at all, not so much as a tradesman's donkey chaise, or a street seller; they had long ago scuttled back to the safety of their own homes, for few people liked to be abroad in the dark in Brompton, even though the village had become much more respectable and, therefore, safer in recent years. Sensible citizens tended to be warmly within their own doors on such a cold and dismal winter afternoon.

'Well?' Tilly said, puzzled, and turned to took at Eliza. Was she having some sort of megrim, due to her condition? Tilly herself had never suffered in that way when she had been carrying Duff all those years ago, but she could remember very vividly how easily she was startled and alarmed by unusual sights or sounds. So she said more gently, 'There is nothing there to see, Eliza. What alarmed you?'

'Oh, pish!' Eliza said a little surprisingly and almost pushed past Tilly to peer out through the crack in the curtains herself. 'I was feared she'd do that the minute I come to fetch you. Maybe she's gone in, then.'

'Who has gone in where?' Tilly said, a little irritable now. Had Eliza thought she had seen some sort of man skulking about, then her fears might be justified; fear of robbers was a commonplace. But she had said 'she'; clearly this was no more than some servant girl misbehaving and Eliza being avid for a bit of gossip. Or perhaps –

'Is it one of our girls you saw? Is someone slipping out when she is supposed to be at work? Rosie?' Rosie was an excellent housemaid, and very good at her work, but undoubtedly pretty and sometimes pert; if anyone had a follower she was sneaking out to meet when she should be working, it must surely be Rosie.

'No, Mum. Would I worry you over such a thing? I can deal with our girls and need never bother you and never you think otherwise – it was just that I thought I saw – and there! You see?' And she almost pulled on Tilly's arm to get her back to the window.

Another rectangle of light had appeared on the cobbles; a softer, wavering one and Tilly thought, that's from a room that is candlelit, and was about to withdraw herself from the window and expostulate with Eliza for fussing over nothing at all, when she realized just what was odd about it, and froze.

'That's from next door,' she said. 'The drawing-room window, isn't it? You see how it matches with the light from ours? Oh!' For now the light had dwindled and vanished as though whoever had been holding up a candle in the drawing room next door had left the room. Tilly straightened her back and said slowly, 'I see. Someone has gone in there?'

'Yes, Mum,' Eliza said grimly. 'It's been empty this twelve month and more and not a sign of no one coming near nor by, and now there was someone – I saw her.'

'Perhaps the house has been sold,' Tilly said slowly and made a little grimace. 'I had hoped it would stay empty so long that the price would come down far enough for me to buy it. I am not quite ready yet to enlarge but I hope the time will come – but if it is taken,' she shrugged, 'well, Eliza, there is nothing we can do about it. Though I must say this is a strange time of day to come looking at empty houses, is it not? Impossible to see anything inside and as for checking the drains and so forth –'

'But I saw her,' Eliza cried again. 'I saw who it *was*, Mum – and it wasn't just someone comin' to look at a house with a view to takin' it. Or I don't think so. I pray it's not so!'

'You're talking in riddles, Eliza,' Tilly said, knowing how much Eliza liked to make the most out of every happening; she had always been a natural dramatist. 'Who are you speaking of?'

'Oh, Mum!' Eliza said, turning back to the window to peer out once more. 'I only caught a glimpse like, and I don't want to – there! Look Mum, she's comin' out.'

Tilly looked out and now she could see that someone was standing on the front porch of the next-door house. She was holding a well-protected candle, using her hand to make a shield against the movement of the air in the street and was standing with her back to Tilly's windows as she leaned and peered down into the area. It was hard to see much, for the person was turned away from Tilly, but there was no doubt of the femininity of the shape: a full skirt of a somewhat old-fashioned cut with a pelisse over it and a high bonnet. Tilly frowned, trying to see some detail which might reveal the figure's identity.

And then the woman turned and looked over her shoulder, towards Quentin's, and the light of her candle, which was guttering a little wildly in spite of that curved hand held in front of the flame, lit the face beneath the bonnet. Tilly caught her breath and stared, trying to be sure of what she had seen as the woman completed her turn and went back into the house and the door closed behind her.

'Well, Mum? Did you see what I saw? I was right, wasn't I?'

'I'm not sure,' Tilly said, trying to recreate that fleeting moment when she had seen the face leap out of the darkness as its owner turned away. 'There wasn't enough time.'

'I'm goin' in there,' Eliza said stoutly. 'I mean, we're respectable 'ere, and we've every right to go checkin' when we sees people goin' in and out of empty houses! I'll fetch my shawl.' And she was gone, pattering across the dining room so fast that Tilly could not stop her.

Tilly was standing at the front door when Eliza returned, her shawl about her shoulders and pulled up over her head. Tilly too had fetched a pelisse from the hall stand and was wrapped up against the cold.

'I'm coming with you,' she said shortly as Eliza opened her mouth to protest and to assure Tilly she could manage perfectly well on her own. 'I too am concerned. Come along.'

She took the lead, going down her own steps in a steady manner and turning immediately left to reach the steps that led up to the adjoining premises. She stopped as she reached them, however, and looked up at the front door.

It was a shabby one indeed. The paint had long ago blistered and in places peeled away and the steps were dull and broken-edged. Tilly's own front door was a far more elegant affair, painted every year into a rich glossy black surface in which her guests could see their own faces and her door step and the steps down to the street were scrubbed and whitened with a stone every single day of the week, including Sunday. Tilly's railings were painted in the same high gloss as the front door and the area they enclosed was clean-swept and neat. The area beneath the rusted railings of this house was a drift of dead leaves and all sorts of detritus (Tilly shuddered to think what might have found its way down there) and the whole house's general shabbiness had long been an irritant to her. If she could buy the place, it would not only rid her of a disagreeable eyesore, but it would also enable her to make Quentin's more successful by providing her not just with space for an extra dozen guests, but also a writing room and a study for those who preferred to spend their evenings in contemplation rather than the busyness and occasional noisiness of the drawing room. It had long been her hope that she would be able to, but the various set-backs she had suffered – including her financial losses over the absconding Mr Greenwall – had made such hopes remote, so she had not given much thought to the house next door for some time.

But all that had changed now. If what she had seen was as she feared –

She lifted her chin, pulled her pelisse closer around her, and went up the steps, moving carefully to avoid the broken edges. The door was closed fast and she lifted the dull knocker and released it twice.

She heard it echo through the house behind it, imagined the waves of sound moving across the dusty hallway and up the naked stairs and through dusty, empty rooms, and she stood there, very aware of Eliza's rather heavy breathing behind her, and listened.

Nothing happened and she knocked again, more peremptorily this time, rattling the iron against its clapper several times; and this time, when the echoes died away she heard it clearly; footsteps clattering along naked boards. She straightened her shoulders and prepared herself.

The door opened and then the gap widened, and whoever stood there, a candle still in her hand, stepped back almost behind it.

'I wondered how long it would be before you noticed I was here,' the once so familiar voice said. Tilly knew it immediately, though it was deeper now and had a roughness about it she did not recall.

'Do come in. I cannot entertain you very well, but you're welcome all the same.'

Tilly sat on a wooden packing case in the middle of what should have been a dining room, looking at the woman sitting on a similar object in front of her. Eliza had gone, after some firmness from Tilly who had assured her she would deal perfectly well on her own and that Eliza was needed in the kitchen at Quentin's, and now they were free to talk.

Tilly looked steadily at the other and said carefully, 'Well, Dorcas? I do not ask you how you are, for I can see that you are far from well. You've become very thin, I fear. I trust it is not a severe illness.'

'If you're asking if I have consumption the answer is no, by some miracle.' When they had last talked Dorcas's voice had had a fluting sound to it, much like Sophie's, but now there was a depth there that was quite marked; and Tilly remembered suddenly how the same thing had happened to her mother. Her change of voice had been due to her intake of spiritous liquors; was this the case with Dorcas? It might well be. 'It's because I've lived on the most vile of slops this past two years, and as little of that as I dared.'

'Oh,' Tilly said, and no more. All she could do was look at Dorcas, and though she tried not to let her opinion show on her face, she feared it was impossible to hide how shocked she was.

Dorcas had been more than pretty when she was young. There had been a vitality about her, a liveliness that clothed every part of her with the sort of allure that the plain and then very timid Tilly had envied sorely. Her eyes, her hair, her teeth, her smile, all had glittered with a raw life and animal energy that had been very attractive. Certainly men had found her almost irresistible. Hadn't Tilly's own husband, Francis, on their wedding day – but she would not remember that, no matter what. She just looked at the wreck of the Dorcas she had known, and marvelled.

She looked like a woman at least ten years older than she was. Tilly could compute it easily. If she, Tilly, was thirty-five, then Dorcas was past forty. But the lacklustre hair with distinct areas of grey in it, the sagging skin, sallow and even yellowish in the light of the candle and the reddened, dull eyes spoke of much greater wear and tear than a mere two and forty years. The hands that were crossed on the lap of the gown she was wearing (which was not particularly cheap, Tilly could not help but notice, but which looked far from clean and certainly was not pressed) were reddened and cracked and the nails broken and discoloured.

Dorcas saw the direction of her gaze and glanced down and then curled her fingers inwards, and laughed. There was no amusement in the sound.

'If you had been picking oakum for two years your hands would be in a similar state,' she said, and Tilly blushed and looked at her face instead.

'I'm sorry,' she said simply. 'I truly am, Dorcas.' And it was true. No matter how cruel and selfish Dorcas had been in her dealings with Tilly all those years ago, however much distress she had caused her as a child – and later – they were still tied by memories of their shared young years, when she, Tilly, had been the daughter of the house and Dorcas but the daughter of the housekeeper, Mrs Leander. To see her now, cast down and destroyed by her experiences, was dispiriting in the extreme, and could not be deserved, no matter what she had done. And on an impulse she tried to say as much.

'I know you were in prison, Dorcas. I found out when – I had to go to the court at Clerkenwell, to seek information for someone, and I saw your name in the ledgers. I am not sure what you did to warrant such a sentence but whatever it was, this cannot be right.' And she reached forward and set her hand over Dorcas's closed fists.

Dorcas sat with her head bent, looking down at her lap and for a moment Tilly thought she was about to weep. But not Dorcas; with a momentary return of her old insouciance she lifted her chin and said, 'Well, as to that, I'm no beak! I can't say what goes on in their minds. If they had to keep body and soul together in a hard world, and had skirts instead of the rubbish that fills their damned trousers, they'd make the same sort of shifts I had to, I dare say. Especially if one of their kind dropped them in the midden as happened to me, the bastard!'

Tilly drew back, chilled. 'I don't ask questions, Dorcas –' she began, but Dorcas laughed.

'There is no need, I shall tell you. I was arraigned for keeping a bawdy house. I have no objection to such establishments, of course – but that had not been my intention then. So I had not made the usual arrangements with the law to protect myself. It was that which landed me in prison, you know! The proper palms had not been oiled, and they were vindictive. But how was I to know? I had planned with that man – a friend, or so I thought him, called Nicholas Rees – that we should run a proper gaming house – and that was risky enough, God knows and costs a fair amount in bribes on its own account. But there it was. He did things behind my back and arranged matters so that – well, let it be. I have no wish to rehearse it all again now. Why should I? Enough that I've spent the past two years in the most stinking place in the world picking that God-forsaken oakum.'

She opened her fingers suddenly and stared down at them. 'Have you any notion what that is like, Tilly? Have you? I had such pretty hands once, did I not? Even when I was washing dishes and emptying slops and the like in your papa's house, I kept them white and nice, with pigs' fat rubbed in every night and lemon juice stolen from the larder – and now look!'

She held her hands up and they were indeed a pathetic sight, with half-healed cuts and sores as well as the roughness and redness that clearly went deep. 'They make you unpick rope, d'you see. Ends of rope soaked in tar and as stiff as these boards here –' she stamped a foot on the floor '– and having to be shredded into tow to use for ships' caulking, and no implements to do it – it was work set aside for the men, but they hated me in there, oh, they hated me, those warders, and made my life such hell and only fed me what little they did if I picked their oakum to their satisfaction and so they wore me down.'

She lifted her chin and laughed aloud. 'But I've defeated them, haven't I? I've shown them they can't put an end to me the way they did the others! Here I am, and I have my house and I shall do as I choose this time and no man shall ever again see me into such straits, I swear it and I mean it, by God I do.'

The words were ordinary enough but the venom with which she spoke them made Tilly want to curl up away from her. She was without doubt the most angry person Tilly had ever seen or heard and the sight made her quail.

But then Dorcas relaxed, set her hands back in her lap and lifted her head from her contemplation of them and looked at Tilly.

'It won't take too long, Tilly! Give me a little time and I shall soon be plump and well again. I shall heal – skin heals, you know. I shall fatten up now that I can get decent victuals again.' She laughed richly. 'That was what made them angriest of all. They knew I had tucked away money and more and yet they could not get their hands on it or make me tell them. I served my time and now I'll have my property –'

She lifted her arms again, but this time in a wide gesture that took in the room around her, which looked huge in the light of one small candle, for the tiny flame threw great shadows in the corners which seemed to stretch the place to infinity. 'And I have the money I hid here and now watch what I shall do!'

'Money you hid here?' Tilly said blankly. 'This is your house?'

'Oh, indeed it is,' Dorcas said and laughed. 'I was not completely taken in by Nicholas Rees, I must tell you, stupid though I was in some things. He thought we were putting all we had into the place in Covent Garden, but I – I always had concerns of my own. I bought this house all that time ago, and hid my treasures here and thank God I did, for otherwise I'd have come out of prison a pauper and died in the gutter. But now – now, my dear, I have such plans for this house! And won't it be jolly that we should be neighbours, eh, Tilly? Just like old times in some ways!'

And it was very much the old Dorcas who laughed in Tilly's horror-struck face.

Chapter Thirty

THE NEED TO talk to someone about her confusion became ever more clamorous as the evening wore on. She had come back to the warmth and comfort and cleanliness of Quentin's from the house next door feeling, as she stepped inside her own front door, that she had woken from a dream. It had been so cold, so very dirty, so very bleak in there, and her conversation with Dorcas so bewildering in all its implications that she did wonder wildly, just for a moment, if she had indeed been dreaming. But of course she knew she had not and went as always, when in need of privacy, to her morning room to collect her thoughts and try to decide what her next steps should be.

Inevitably Eliza came to her within minutes. Probably watching through the kitchen window to see me pass the area, Tilly thought a little wearily, as she came in and stood hovering expectantly at the door. For a moment Tilly thought of sending her away with her curiosity unsatisfied, but then relented. She could not do that to Eliza; not only was she entitled to know what had happened – it would be downright cruel to keep her in the dark.

'She was looking around because she already owns the house,' she said in reply to Eliza's first question. 'Not because she wants to buy it.'

Eliza gaped. 'Owns it? But how can that be? How could she –'

'She bought it,' Tilly said shortly. 'More than ten years ago, when the old man died – Mr Shepherd, you remember? His widow went on living there for a while, paying rent. That was why we did not realize the house had been sold. It has lain empty since Mrs Shepherd died because Dorcas was not able to do anything about it –'

'Because she was in clink,' Eliza said succinctly.

'Yes.'

'And now she's out.'

'Yes.'

'And coming back here to live.'

'I'm not sure.' Tilly shook her head. 'She talked a little wildly – she's had a very bad time, Eliza.' Tilly tried to conjure up again the pity she had felt for Dorcas. It was not so easy now that Dorcas was not here in front of her, showing her scarred hands and battered visage, but she persisted. 'She was stubborn in prison, I gather, and stood up for herself and they treated her badly.'

'I dare say they did,' Eliza said with a certain stubbornness of her own. 'And I dare say she deserved it, the way she behaved. I remember her well enough not to be surprised at anything she did, that one. Nothing at all. It's a miracle her daughter's turned out so good as she has.'

Tilly stared at her and then threw back her head and laughed. It was a genuinely amused sound and Eliza stared at her.

'Oh, I'm sorry.' she spluttered at last. 'It isn't funny at all, in truth – it's just that – I did not even mention Sophie! I did not tell Dorcas she had been living here nor about the letter I wrote to her this afternoon and –'

'Letter, Mum?' Eliza said, mystified.

'Oh, it doesn't matter, Eliza. It's just so absurd that we talked for so long yet never once did either of us mention her child. Yet I would have thought for any woman in her situation that that would be the subject closest to her heart. How could she not ask me? How could I not tell her? You must agree it's funny.'

'If you say so, Mum,' Eliza said soothingly. 'But I wouldn't fret over it, in your shoes. All that I'd be fretting over is what happens to us now. Is she to move in there, Mum? Because I'll tell you flat, I don't trust her one bit. Why, there's no knowing what she mightn't get up to there and what would our people say if she caused any sort of disturbance, I want to know?'

Any remaining shred of humour vanished from Tilly's face. 'Yes,' she said slowly. 'I know.'

Eliza pounced. 'She's told you, Mum. She's said what she wants to do.'

'Yes,' Tilly said. 'She's told me.'

Eliza waited, expectantly, her hands crossed on her comfortable big belly. It did not occur to her, clearly, that she was being impertinent, a servant to be so quizzing her mistress, and Tilly could not bring herself to think ill of her for that. Eliza was more than a servant; she was as much part of Quentin's as Tilly was herself. I might own it, she thought, but she is the one who makes it work, who feeds and keeps them happy. I help her, but she is the engine that drives this machine – she has a right to be concerned, to ask questions.

'Come and sit down Eliza,' she said, and for once Eliza did not argue. She came and sat in a chair beside Tilly's desk and looked at her anxiously.

'First she says she has to get herself well,' Tilly said cautiously. 'The past two years have almost ruined her health, as you saw. But then she says she must use her equity in the house and she has some money she says, to have it set to rights and well furnished. She must use her property to give her a living.'

'No doubt, Mum, but it's a question of how, 'n't it?' Eliza said and then frowned sharply. 'She ain't thinkin' of settin' up in competition to us, is she? Because if she is – well, it won't make no never mind. We'll still be the best place there is. No one as could get a room with us would even think of going to the likes of her, or anywhere else come to that.'

'If it were so simple, Eliza,' Tilly murmured and Eliza, still muttering about the superior quality of Quentin's, looked at her and quirked her head.

'I'm sorry, Mum, I didn't quite catch –'

'It doesn't signify, Eliza,' Tilly said and got to her feet. 'All I can tell you is what I have said. That she is to get herself well, and then decorate and furnish her house before she decides how best she can use it as a form of security against the future. Perhaps she will sell it, or perhaps she will let it, who can say? I doubt she will set up in opposition to us, for I do not think the district will carry another such establishment as Quentin's and we were here first and so have the edge. Anyway it is very hard work to run a guest house and she will not like that – and I believe she is well aware of that. So you need not fret over the matter. Now, I think it must be getting very close to time for dinner and I have not dressed yet, so if you will check the dining room and kitchen for me this evening, I'll be upstairs. You may sound the gong at the usual time, I shall be ready.'

This conversation had made it clear to her that she could not talk to Eliza about her fears and the details of her discussion with Dorcas. She would become much too anxious, she was sure, and anyway there was a shrinking in her at the idea of confiding in Eliza. Much as she loved and appreciated her, she should not be made privy to all matters pertaining to her employer's affairs.

If only Duff were here, she found herself thinking as she presided over dinner. Eliza had found a section in one of her cookery books that discussed cookery *à la Russe,* and for the first course had made a cabbage soup rich with sour cream and a potato gratin and dishes of stuffed yeast pancakes which everyone was exclaiming over so happily that they hardly noticed that Tilly herself was picking at her food. Certainly she had time to think.

But Duff would not help me, she reminded herself. He is madly in love with Dorcas's daughter. How can I speak to him of my fears and doubts about her, any more than I can risk doing so about Sophie? All I will do is estrange him utterly, the state of mind he is in. I must keep my own counsel.

And she found herself thinking yearningly of Jem, and how much benefit she would have obtained in speaking to him. He had known Dorcas too, known her very well indeed. If anyone would have ideas about how to deal with that lady, it would have been Jem. But how could she take herself to him? He was to be wed this coming Saturday. The invitation to the church and the breakfast had arrived last week and she had been in the process of steeling herself to attend; he must be quite enthralled with his Miss Goodall, and certainly too busy about his own affairs to concern himself with hers. No, she could not speak to him.

Rosie was clearing the first course and bringing in the chicken pie and crimped cod and boiled leg of mutton in caper sauce which made up the second, and Silas, who was seated three places down on her right-hand side, with Mr and Mrs Grayling between them, leaned forwards and said across them (they being quite enthralled in a colloquy between themselves), 'Are you ill, Tilly?'

'Ill?' She looked at him in surprise. 'No, of course not.'

'Then why are you not eating?' he asked, and Mrs Grayling became aware of their conversation and looked sharply at Tilly, her wrinkled old apple face curving into lines of anxiety. She hated any hint of illness in anyone. It frightened her.

'Oh, I ate too many of Eliza's coconut cakes at tea time!' Tilly lied hastily and Mrs Grayling looked relieved and returned to her husband's conversation. 'And I would prefer you not to make public remarks on such matters!' Tilly finished *sotto voce* and with some sharpness. 'I am perfectly well!'

'Then eat your dinner, coconut cakes or not!' Silas said and smiled to take the sting out of his injunction and she shook her head at him crossly as Rosie bent over her to enquire of which dishes she wished to partake.

She accepted a portion of chicken pie and let Rosie add some of the creamed spinach that Eliza had said would be the best accompaniment, and was very aware of Silas's eyes on her as she ate it; and was glad she had, for she had indeed been hungry and not known it. Far from eating too many coconut cakes at tea time, she had taken nothing since lunchtime and then had been in no humour for more than tea and a few sippets of toast and honey.

By the time she had eaten her share of the last course, which included a most delectable bread and butter pudding, which was one of Eliza's specialities, she felt a little less anxious. She had let Dorcas's old ways and her memories of them cloud her judgement, that was the problem. The woman she had talked to in the house next door had not been the Dorcas of long ago, full of energy and, it could not be denied, considerable wickedness, always determined to do as she pleased rather than what was good and proper. This was a woman who had suffered and had been punished for her bad ways, who had learned a lot. She would not connive and be cruel again as she had used to. Tilly was worrying for no reason.

But she thought, it still would be nice to have someone to talk to, and she looked consideringly at Silas as he came as usual into the drawing room and sat beside her to help her with the coffee equipage.

It was strange, she thought, how differently she felt about this man than she had felt about Jem, whom she had once intended to marry. Jem had been kind and gentle and good; a man to be relied upon, one she trusted completely; but he had not aroused in her that sense of need and delicious desire that Silas made her feel. Yet Silas, who could create that feeling just by sitting beside her as he now was, did not give her that sense of security and comfort she used to find with Jem.

I want the impossible, she thought as, with slightly tremulous fingers, she gave Silas a cup and saucer to carry to Miss Knapp. I want a man who is both Jem and Silas. And if I had him, she went on in her thoughts with a sudden shaft of self-understanding, I would probably find him lacking in some way. The truth of the matter is that I cannot trust *men*. I have had such difficult experiences with men that I never think that any one of them can behave well. Yet in truth it is a woman who now alarms me the most and I need a confidant. What shall I do?

When everyone had their coffee (or tea, which she now provided in the drawing room in response to various people's entreaties) and the compendium of games had come out and everyone who wished to play had found themselves a place at a table, she leaned back in her chair and again looked consideringly at Silas.

Usually at this point in the evening he was claimed by one or other of the tables to make up the number of necessary players. But tonight, because the Graylings had declined their usual favourite, which was dominoes, and gone to bed early, there was in fact one space less for a player, since one table had been abandoned completely. Silas had, by dint of great charm and a display of uncertainty about what sort of game he most wanted to play tonight, managed to cast himself as the spare one and settled down next to Tilly in the most natural manner possible. No one looking at him, not even the sharp-eyed Priscilla Knapp, would have guessed that he was deeply content, being precisely where he wanted to be.

'Silas,' Tilly said in a low voice. 'I would be glad of some advice.' She had made up her mind. In the absence of anyone else to talk to, it would have to be Silas. She really could not manage without some sort of discussion of her dilemma.

'Of course,' he said. 'I had suspected you had some anxiety, for I have been watching you and you are like – well – a person struggling to remain still while sitting on an ant hill!'

She managed to smile at that. 'Well, it is not perhaps surprising since it is hard to know where to begin this matter.' She set down her coffee cup, almost regretting now that she had even begun. Perhaps it would be better after all to work this out alone. But she looked up and saw the glint in his eyes and knew that he would not rest until she had spoken of whatever it was; he could be very stubborn, she found herself thinking.

'The beginning is often the best,' he said.

She sighed. 'Very well. Sophie – you know she has been known to me for many years?'

'Indeed. She calls you aunt.'

'Yes. She is not, of course, related. But her mother –' She swallowed and then shook her head. 'I must tell you something of my own history, I think.' And she did, leaving out nothing, finding it easier and easier as the words came out of her. He sat there quietly listening, never taking his gaze from her face, as the counters and dice clicked and rattled around them, and the coffee in their cups cooled.

She told him of her tyrannical father and frightened mother who had shut herself away with her sherry and gin and left him to the wiles of the housekeeper, Mrs Leander. How Dorcas had herself married and run away, and how and why Tilly had gone in search of her, long afterwards, and brought her back to Quentin's. About her own marriages, and why they had caused her so much pain; she left out nothing, except for Jem Leland. For some reason she could not herself understand she felt the need to hide that sad little history from Silas, sitting there looking so handsome and elegant. He could never understand, she was sure, that a lady such as she could accept the attentions of a man who was a very ordinary sort of tradesman. She could imagine how shocked he would be if he thought she had, say, planned to marry Charlie Harrod. And Jem, whom she had almost wed, had been Charlie's dearest friend. Still was, in fact. No, she could not speak of Jem, not because she was in any sense ashamed of him, but because he was important to her, her good friend – or had been.

But everything else she told him, including the way Dorcas had behaved to her over the matter of her second marriage, and how in spite of her, Tilly had inherited the house next door to her father's original home and had had them joined to make what was now Quentin's.

'And now I discover that she has come out of prison and still managed to maintain control over some property. She had bought the next house along the line that lies now to our left and – and –' she swallowed. 'She intends to make it into a place that will earn her sufficient to ensure she is, as she says, never worried about money ever again.'

'What sort of a place?' Silas asked sharply.

'She is not quite certain,' Tilly said miserably. 'But because she was sent to prison for – for running a bawdy house, and though she assured me that she did not, that her then partner so arranged matters that she would be blamed for what he was doing, she thinks she will run one now. She says that there are ways and means of dealing with – with the law that such establishments can be set up and be left in peace and not prosecuted. And since she has the name, she may as well have the game.

'Oh, Silas!' she said then and her face was twisted with worry. 'What shall I do if she does that? How can that not lead to the complete destruction of all that I have worked for here at Quentin's?

For who would come to live as a paying guest next door to a house of ill repute? Would you? Only the most disagreeable sort of people would come – I really don't know what to do!'

Chapter Thirty-One

TILLY SLEPT BADLY, waking early to come down to breakfast with shadows under her eyes, a headache and no appetite. But she was very thirsty and sat and drank her way through three cups of tea, grateful that she was so early that none of her guests had yet put in an appearance.

She had done her best to take Silas's advice. 'There is no point in getting yourself excessively anxious before you know precisely what there is to be anxious about,' he had said soothingly. 'And I cannot believe that it would be so easy for her to flout the law in these matters anyway. She may say to you that it is merely a matter of bribes and so forth, but I am sure that if you have actual proof that the sort of house she speaks of – that it is being maintained, that is – then the law would have to act to relieve you of the resulting nuisance. So please, Tilly –'

'But that could be so – so laborious and so public!' Tilly had almost cried out, only remembering just in time to keep her voice down so that the games players around her in the drawing room would not hear. 'And would probably take so long that by the time it was settled all my guests would have melted away and I should be hard put to re-establish a reputation it has taken me so many years to build –'

'I do not think so,' Silas said stoutly. 'I shall be your eyes and ears, my dear Tilly, and will ensure that whatever happens in that house you shall know of it. Forewarned, remember, is forearmed – yes, forearmed.' He had looked as pleased with himself as if he had said something of great originality and for a moment Tilly was irritated by the hint of pomposity but then had to agree that he was right. She had been warned and that was better than having something happen to her out of nowhere, as might have been the case had Eliza not seen Dorcas from the dining-room window.

Now sitting staring sightlessly out of that same dining-room window at the pouring rain – for it was as grey and disagreeable a December day as it could possibly be – she once more tried to push her anxieties to the back of her mind. There was much to be done; Christmas was barely a fortnight away and though Eliza was well in hand with her puddings and her cakes and various pickles and other seasonal delights, Tilly herself had to see to it that her geese were chosen from the flock in the yard behind Mr Spurgeon's shop, that the baron of beef she had ordered was being properly hung and that the hams that were being pickled in their tubs of brine in the back scullery were coming along properly. There was also the matter of the spruce tree she was to decorate in the manner that Prince Albert had introduced for the royal family at Windsor, which she had thought would amuse her guests if she used it as an exemplar. She really had too much to do, she thought, rattling her cup back into its saucer, to waste time worrying about Dorcas.

She got to her feet and went over to the sideboard to check that the chafing dishes were all as hot as they should be and that the food beneath the covers was properly presented, and moved along the row, lifting one heavy silver dome after another. Grilled bacon, well crimped; sausages from Mr Spurgeon, plump and glistening with their own fat; kidneys neatly arranged with slices of baked tomato between them; and shirred eggs with mushrooms. Silas would like that, she thought as she replaced the dome quietly and turned to go, and then noticed that the lowest drawer of the sideboard was partly open. She tried to close it, only to find it resisted her push and she pulled it wider to find what had obstructed it. And there, at the back, she found a soft roll of leather that had curled open and tucked itself into the drawer's runners, and drew it out.

She took it to the table and sat down, and slowly unrolled the bundle. She knew what it was of course; she had obtained the services of the saddler in Brompton Road, near Charlie's shop, to make it for her when the contents had been so wonderfully restored to her over a dozen years ago, after she had been sure she had lost them for ever.

Her mother's wedding spoons. Beautiful, silver, the bowls covered with the most delicately executed enamel in jewel colours, deepest amethyst and delicate rose, throbbing crimson and burnt orange, irridescent green and burning blue.

She sat with the unrolled bundle before her, looking down on the spoons and remembering. So many years of sadness before the happy ones that had been her lot this past dozen years. Turmoil, fear and loneliness had been succeeded by prosperity and tranquillity. Two distinct segments of her life had been punctuated by those spoons.

That is a silly thought, she scolded herself; of course the spoons had nothing to do with the improvement in her life. It had been sheer chance that she had lost them to Dorcas and equally so that they had come back when they did, and equally a matter of chance that her attention had been drawn to them this morning. But she could not convince herself that there was not some omen meant in finding the spoons as she had. They lived in that drawer and she did not fetch them out from one year to the next; it was enough to know they were there. Yet this morning, when she had been so worried, there they were to reassure her; her spirits lifted absurdly and she wrapped up the spoons again and restored them to their hiding place at the back of the drawer, closed it tidily and went cheerfully down to the kitchen to speak to Eliza.

She was making porridge, very carefully adding quantities of cream and brown sugar to it, and the kitchen steamed agreeably with the nutty scent of it, mixed with coffee and the grilling of herrings. Mr Grayling, thought Tilly. He must have asked Eliza especially to provide them this morning, for he was dearly partial to a herring, and she, dear creature, never forgot anything. Where would I be without her? And Tilly smiled widely at her across the kitchen.

'You're looking better this morning, Mum,' Eliza said approvingly as she heaved the great iron pot on to the table and began to ladle its contents into a chafing dish ready to go up to the dining room. Behind her the herrings sizzled contentedly before the fire and the kettle steamed ready to make the second pot of coffee that would be needed to replace the one that Rosie was waiting to take up to the dining room together with the porridge. Lucy was busy, too, making toast, and the whole kitchen had an air of quiet purposefulness that was very comforting. Tilly breathed it in deeply, feeling better by the moment. She had been worrying for no purpose. There was nothing Dorcas could possibly do to upset the happy rhythm of Quentin's. It was as secure as it possibly could be.

'I am indeed feeling well,' she said, and sniffed appreciatively. 'I thought I was not hungry and wanted only tea, but you know, I think perhaps I shall return to the dining room and take breakfast with the guests. That porridge looks very good –'

'It is, Mum,' Eliza said and held out her ladle so that Tilly could taste it and she did, relishing the sweet nutty flavour and the richness of the cream which had given it a much more agreeable tawny colour than its usual grey.

'Mmm,' Tilly said. 'I shall indeed have a plateful upstairs, Eliza. I wanted to tell you –' She hesitated and glanced at Rosie and Lucy. 'That matter we discussed last night – I have considered it further and I am convinced we have no need for anxiety.'

Eliza cocked a sharp eye at her. 'Is that so, Mum? Well, I'm glad to hear you think so. Me, I'm not so certain –'

'Well, I have thought a great deal, and there are reasons why I will not worry further,' Tilly said firmly. 'I shall speak to you later this morning. I must see Spurgeon about the geese and, of course, the beef. Is there anything else I must talk to him about?'

'Yes, please, Mum,' Eliza said. 'I want to make a liver paste in the French manner and I need extra goose liver for that. If he can contrive to find some – for not every cook wants 'em, more fool they – I'll be greatly obliged, tell him.'

'I will,' Tilly promised, and went back upstairs to eat porridge with her guests who were now arriving, hungry for their breakfast.

The first post had already been delivered and Tilly glanced at the pile of envelopes beside her plate and was disappointed not to see Duff's familiar handwriting and then chided herself. Absurd! He had written to her only yesterday – there could not be another from him yet. And she thought of the letter she had sent to Sophie and wondered how long it would take her to respond. Quickly, she hoped. As long as it was the right response, of course.

The table talk was surprisingly sprightly. On most mornings people ate quietly or read a newspaper as they did so, but this morning they all seemed in a festive sort of mood, perhaps because of the approach of Christmas, and chattered busily. The only silent one was Silas and he waited till most of the others had drifted away about the day's business before he spoke quietly to Tilly.

'I have been thinking of our conversation last night,' he said. 'Trying to think of how I might reassure you that –'

She smiled brilliantly. 'Oh, I know now that I was worried for no reason,' she said. 'Or for very little. In the clear light of day, I feel much more calm about it all, and beg your pardon for so tediously occupying your mind with a minor matter.'

'It was neither tedious nor minor. No conversation with you could ever be so described,' he said and grinned as she blushed and glanced at Mr Gee, who was seated at the far end of the table absorbed in the *Morning Post* while he ate the last of a great deal of toast and boiled ham.

'Hush,' she said. 'You must not –'

'Why not?' He was looking a little wicked, and leaned back in his chair and glanced at her from beneath his lashes with mock delicacy. 'I would have thought that good *close* friends such as we are should be able to speak to each other in any way we wish. Are we not intimate friends now, Tilly?'

She bent her head, again very aware of the physical effect he had on her. 'Well, yes, but –'

'No buts.' He was serious now. 'No buts at all – ah!' He looked up in satisfaction as Mr Gee got to his feet and made his way to the dining-room door, the *Morning Post* held neatly under his arm. 'On your way then, Oswald?'

'Yes. I must be at court in –' Mr Gee looked at his watch and tutted importantly – in just an hour, you know. Must be about my business! Good morning to you, Mrs Quentin! Geddes!' And he went in a bustle, leaving them alone. Rosie had not come up to clear yet.

'I must make the most of my opportunities,' Silas said rapidly. 'I know this is neither the most romantic time nor place, but you give me little opportunity to be alone with you in such circumstances, so I must make the best of what there is. So, here amongst the wreckage of our excellent breakfast, dear Tilly, will you be my wife? There, I've asked you. I never thought I would ask any woman that, so greatly valuing my freedom as I do – not wanting even the trouble of owning my own house, let alone a wife, but you, Tilly, are enough to make any man forget his resolutions.'

She gaped at him, so taken aback that she was breathless. Of all the things she had not expected to happen this morning, this had to be the most remarkable. That he might declare himself one day was a possibility that had, of course, occurred to her and she had tried to think about what her response might be; but this had caught her so much by surprise that she could not think at all.

'Why, Silas –'was all she managed and then had to shake her head. 'I hardly know what to –'

Behind her the door opened again and Rosie came in, bearing her tray.

'May I clear, Mum?' she said, hovering at the door. Without stopping to think, Tilly, ever the careful housekeeper and well aware of the importance of getting out of the servants' way so that the work of the day could be properly executed, got to her feet at once.

'Of course,' she said almost automatically and then stared at Silas, who was looking startled and not a little annoyed. She bit her lip. It must have seemed to him a dreadful snub not to have sent Rosie away for a while, and she said quickly, 'Come to my morning room, please, Silas –'and hurried away, without waiting to see whether he would follow.

Happily, he did and came to sit beside her on her small sofa and took both her hands in his and smiled.

'Well? Now you have ensured that your housekeeping duties have been given due precedence,' he said, 'am I to have my answer? Or will you play the shy miss and insist upon making me wait?'

She swallowed. 'My dear Silas, I am not a shy miss, nor would I wish to ape one, but this is – I am so surprised that I must of course have time to think. And I am not precisely alone in this matter, am I? I mean, if I am to wed again I must – my son – he is part of –'

'Now, Tilly, hear me!' Silas said with a sharp change in his manner. He had become masterful and not at all the easy unruffled man of thought and letters he usually was. 'Your son is a grown man, or as near as makes no matter. You worry too much about him. Indeed, you have let him rule your life to a degree that cannot be healthy for either of you –'

Her brows snapped together. 'What do you mean?'

He spoke more gently now. 'I mean only, dear Tilly, that he must live his life and you must live yours. Of course you will always be as close as mother and son should be, and he will, I know, love you dearly always. But he will wed one day – and you must remember he seems to have made his choice on that score – and to have you left behind alone and lonely may make him most unhappy. If you wish *him* to be happy you will seek happiness for yourself, for the two go together. You don't need to ask his consent to make me his stepfather. You must decide it for *yourself* and then simply tell him of your decision. You must see that, Tilly, I am sure, if you think about it.' He softened then and smiled happily. 'And anyway, are not Duff and I very good friends? I cannot imagine he will have any objection to me as a stepfather. He knows I have his good interest at heart, in his own right. If he knows that I am tied to him by marriage to his beloved Mamma, why, I am sure he will be glad of it. He has no father or brothers, after all.'

She was unable to think clearly at all, and turned her head away. 'I must think,' she said a little stiffly. 'Please to give me some time.'

'Of course.' He was all gentleness now. 'I have been most hasty in speaking as and when I did, but as I say, chance is all. Be kind to me and to yourself, dearest Tilly. Choose well.'

And he bent and kissed her hands one after the other, and then leaned forward and kissed one cheek as well and got to his feet and went, leaving her more breathless than usual by his attentions.

She sat for some time staring at the wall, trying to think, and could not get her mind into any sort of order, and needing some sort of physical action, jumped up only to tumble her letters, which she had carried with her from the dining room, all over the floor. She crouched and picked them up and then noticed that one of them was unfranked. It had not been brought in the post at all, but delivered by hand, for it bore on the envelope only her name, and she turned it in her hands, distracted completely now from Silas and his proposal.

It must be from Dorcas, she thought fearfully, sitting back on her heels, and looked again at the handwriting, but it was hard to tell. The letters were all in capitals, and it seemed had been written with some difficulty and Tilly, remembering Dorcas's cut and reddened fingers, could imagine how painful it might be for her to use those hands to write and was more certain than ever. She bit her lip to control the sudden surge of anxiety that filled her, and slit it open.

'Dear Tilly,' the short letter read. 'I am to go away to recover my health. I shall be back in the New Year at some time, possibly not until February or later. Meanwhile, the house will remain empty and no steps taken.' There was no subscription other than her name, scrawled in large letters, like those on the envelope: Dorcas Leander Oliver.

How odd, she thought staring down at it. Why should she have kept her mother's name in that manner? How very odd.

Chapter Thirty-Two

TILLY'S GREATEST PROBLEM, she decided a few days later, was that she could not sort out the confusion of problems she had to face.

First of all, there was the matter of Silas's proposal. One part of her wanted very much to accept him. That she needed and would greatly enjoy the intimacy of marriage even after so many years of solitude was clear to her now. She had even started to dream about episodes with Silas that made her blush to remember them in the morning. But she could not wholeheartedly go to him and give him the answer he wanted.

The trouble was, she told herself, not only his criticism of her close attachment to and concern for Duff, justified as it was, in part; it was more because of the way he had spoken when he had proposed. She could hear it still echoing in her head: 'I never thought I would ask any woman that, so greatly valuing my freedom as I do, not wanting even the trouble of owning my own house, let alone a wife.'

If she had learned anything about her years as the proprietor of a busy guest house it had been that people do not change. They may put on shows of some forms of behaviour in order to impress new acquaintances, but when they were comfortable where they were, they soon reverted to being themselves. The Graylings, for example, had put on a great performance of being elegant people, well connected and of excellent *ton* when they had first come to her house with a view to taking rooms, but since they had settled in had shown themselves clearly for what they were, ordinary people from a trade background and none the worse for that. There had been many others over the years who had taught Tilly the same lesson. And, she had to ask herself, was Silas now reverting to the person he really was? He made a parade of his free thinking, of his attachment to ideas of equality and the rights of the individual, but he had not spoken so when he had proposed: 'the trouble of owning my own house, let alone a wife'.

Had he meant that he regarded a wife as a possession? Tilly had had enough of that when she had been married to Frank Quentin, just as she had had enough of being her father's possession before that. For more than twelve years she had owed allegiance to no one but her son and herself, and any others she chose of her own free will. Did she want to give up that freedom simply for the sake of passion and the admitted comfort of having a husband to share her burdens? She rather thought she did not.

But that was the least of her problems, she decided. Silas had agreed, the day after he had proposed, when she had not been able to prevent him asking for an answer, that he would wait until she was quite certain she was ready to marry. He seemed to accept her doubts to an extent and said very cheerfully that he was glad they could at least regard themselves as engaged to be married and was quite happy to leave matters at that for the present; there was plenty of time yet to tie the knot. And he also agreed, though less willingly, to keep their decision a secret from everyone else in the house.

'I could not bear the chatter and the way the Misses K and F would go on and on – and Mrs Grayling – and the men would torment you, I've no doubt –' she had said and he had made a little grimace and acquiesced. So, for the time being, all was well. She had not fully made up her mind, even though Silas thought she had, and she had time to think. So that was one problem she could set to one side.

The next was not so easy to sort out. Sophie did not reply to her letter. Nor did she reply to the one that Tilly sent after that repeating her invitation and not even to the one she had sent most recently, in which she hinted that she had news of her mother for her.

Tilly had thought carefully about that and at first had decided it would be better to let Dorcas tell her daughter herself of her plans (if she chose to, and knew of her whereabouts, of course) rather than that she should hear from other lips; but she was so baulked by Sophie's silence that she had almost recklessly thrown the information at her. But it made no difference. She remained silent.

Duff wrote regularly of course. He prattled on cheerfully in letter after letter about the wonderful time he was having learning how to ride to hounds which was 'splendid fun, even though I take far too many tumbles – but it is hardening me nicely, Patrick says' – and his ardent interest in all matters rural as he spent long hours at the farms and in the stables.

He was less forthcoming about Sophie although he did write that she was 'still having a most enjoyable time, and is the Object of everyone's Attention. Patrick's younger sisters take her everywhere, to Parties and Balls to which they are invited, though I am not, and Sophie loves to go of course, and I am glad she has company to beguile her while I am so busy working about the place –'

Tilly had a picture of Sophie leading a life of giddy social excitement with much to entertain her, while Duff was left a little forlornly on the sidelines watching her. But she said nothing in her letters to him about that, nor did she try to persuade Duff to return home even for the Christmas celebrations, however much she disliked the arrangement he had made with Patrick Paton. She had taken Silas's words to heart more than she realized at first. She did try to cosset Duff too much, did try too hard to keep him at her side. He was a man now and had to find his own way in the world, and even though it was one she disliked, she would keep silent on the matter. Silas had taught her that much.

But she did not tell Silas of her change of mind, for she was a little ashamed to admit she had been so wrong in the past and that, too, worried her when she thought of their engagement. Surely she should not wish to hide anything from one she had told she would

– no, she would not think about that. There was plenty of time for that.

And then there was the problem of Polly and the baby Georgie and the effect they had on Eliza. With every day that passed the child became ever more vigorous, and was most active, and Eliza took a great pleasure in him, finding an echo in caring for him of the years when she had looked after Duff and, of course, with her present interesting condition. She taught Polly a good deal about how to care for so large and hungry an infant, gleaning her knowledge from memories of the way she had cared for her own brothers and Duff in his infancy, and told Tilly privately that she was even more convinced that Polly would make a grand nursemaid for the new baby as well as for Georgie. 'It'll all work out beautifully, Mum, you see if it don't,' she said on several occasions, a comment which made Tilly uneasy, for it was clear to her that Eliza had quite made up her mind that her baby was to be adopted by Tilly and nothing she could say would shift that notion.

And behind all that there were her still lingering doubts about what would happen to the house next door. She had almost convinced herself there would be no trouble after all; that Dorcas had spoken when newly out of prison from remaining anger at her two years of misery. By the time she returned from wherever she was, Tilly would tell herself, she would surely have forgotten all that nonsense about turning the house next door to Quentin's into a house of ill repute. Even the thought of having Dorcas living there became attractive in comparison.

All this discomfort and anxiety was hidden, as it usually was with Tilly, behind a façade of busy serenity. The house blossomed into holly and laurel wreaths as Christmas arrived and the tree, a five-foot high rather bushy example of the genus Norway spruce, obtained with some difficulty and considerable expense with the aid of the market gardener, was set up in the drawing room and decked with candles which tended to set the branches alight and make them smell rather powerfully, and ribbons and German baubles bought from Charlie Harrod (who had an amazing array of them, for they had become fashionable this year). The amount of food which Eliza prepared for the holiday was staggering; as well as the actual Christmas Day dinner for which the centrepiece was two huge and beautifully roasted geese, with baked apples around them and a stuffing of prunes and nuts and other delicious things, there was a massive baron of beef, an equally large haunch of venison and two great boiled hams which made the table look fit to groan. There was such a profusion of tarts and pies, jellies and puddings and patties and ices that by the time the flaming plum pudding was brought in no one had any room to eat it – or so they said. But it vanished fast enough once Tilly started to serve it.

And that was not all. They ate almost as vast a supper on Christmas night and the following day started again as though they had been starving for weeks. By the middle of the week after christmas when efforts were made to return the household to normal, everyone was somnolent and a little bad tempered. Tilly had escaped this morning, ostensibly to shop for replacements for all they had consumed, but in truth to be alone for a while.

It was a melancholy trip to do her ordering, and she wished she hadn't made it. Jem's shop was unrecognizable, for the new tenant, whoever he was, had changed everything. Where Jem's window displays had had some elegance and shown good quality merchandise, this new man, Tilly decided as she stopped to look, was all set to sell the cheapest stuff he could find. The window was hung with a profusion of cloths that to Tilly's experienced eye were wickedly wasteful, for cheap as they were, they would wear so badly that in the long run buying them would be an expensive business. The shopkeeper himself, a tall and rather thin man with a drooping set of whiskers and a most unpleasant oily manner, was standing at the door of the shop trying to coax customers inside and Tilly escaped him hurriedly and went on her way to Colonel Nichol's and to Charlie's, glad she did not need to rely on what had once been her shop of choice for materials for sheets and towels and gowns, and tried to be happy for Jem.

His wedding day had not been easy for her. At first she had determined not to attend and then had realized how unkind that would be, for was he not an old and good friend who would be saddened by her absence? So she sat stolidly in church as Fanny Goodall, in a froth of white lace and satin that Tilly privately thought a shade excessive on one of her rather sallow appearance (a sentiment for which she reproved herself sharply), moved happily along the aisle clinging to her new husband's arm and clearly very pleased with herself. Jem had a slightly bewildered look, she told herself as she followed the wedding party out into the street and on to the wedding breakfast; would he have looked so had it been I who had wed him today? Again she scolded herself for such thoughts. Altogether it had not been an agreeable party and she had gone home gratefully after Jem and Fanny had departed on their wedding trip in a shower of rice, and went to bed early with a headache.

Now she felt a touch headachy again and marched on determinedly to complete her shopping at Charlie's, having decided not to seek new flannel for nightgowns for herself at Colonel Nichol's after all. That could wait. She would go only to Charlie's to make all the necessary arrangements to refill her depleted larder and storerooms and then hurry home as fast as she could. It was so raw a January day and the back of her throat was tickling. She hoped she had not caught a cold.

Charlie was full of talk of the wedding and the fact that the happy couple would return from their wedding trip to Ostend – 'Getting very smart ideas, our Jem, ain't he?' he said approvingly – in another week and begging Tilly to consider attending a dinner party he and Caroline intended to give for the newly weds. It took her some time to extricate herself from that; Jem might have been her dear friend, and still was, of course, but she should not have to sit and watch him with his new wife. That would be pushing the demands of friendship too far.

She returned home despondently, painfully aware of the flaws in her own character in a way that was most unpleasant. To feel so helpless in the face of so many anxieties, to refuse to set her wounded pride aside (for that was all she felt regarding Jem, surely?) and to be harbouring the early symptoms of a cold was enough to make anyone miserable.

It started to rain long before she reached home and unfortunately she had come out without her umbrella, believing when she had left the house that the dull coldness would remain long enough to bring her home dryshod, if chilly, but she could not have been more wrong. It was the sort of fine, bitter rain that entered every gap it could find in clothing, and she was disagreeably aware of the fact that she was wearing rather thin house shoes instead of her sensible boots and that her feet were, in consequence, sopping wet. She felt the damp rising up her woollen stockings in a most unpleasant manner and also spreading up her skirts.

She would not stand still in such unpleasant conditions long enough to forage in her reticule for her door key, so as she hurried home with her head down against the driving rain, she decided to enter the house through the kitchen. It would be better, anyway, than dripping all over the freshly polished hall floor. As she pushed open the area gate, registering the fact that it creaked and needed some oil on its hinges, something got into her eye painfully, and gratefully she almost tumbled through the kitchen door to stand stamping her ice-cold feet on the doormat just inside.

The kitchen glowed with the firelight and was warm and smelled pleasantly of new bread, for Eliza had been baking today, and she took a deep breath of relief in spite of the pain in her eye as she pulled off her soaking wet pelisse and bonnet and shook out her hair.

'Eliza!' she called, eyes tightly closed. 'Are you there? My face is wet and I have something in my eye – please to fetch me a towel, will you?' And she reached out one hand blindly.

She heard movement across the kitchen as the chair by the fire rattled on its rockers, and then a towel was pushed into her hands, wordlessly, and she rubbed at her face, and then gingerly tried to open her eyes, though the left one, which contained the intruding object was still painful.

'Oh, Eliza, can you see if there is anything there, and perhaps remove it?' she implored and tipped up her chin and again tried to open her eyes. She managed it, though both were swimming with rainwater and sympathetic tears by now and she could see only a dazzle as careful fingers reached for her face and with a corner of the towel dabbed at her right eye.

'No!' she cried. 'The other one, the other one – ah!' She took a deep breath of relief. 'That's better. I think it's washed itself out – just a moment now.' And she mopped at her eyes again with the towel, and was filled with gratitude at the relief from pain.

'There!' she said and opened her eyes properly to peer at Eliza, still standing silently in front of her. 'Thank you so much –' and then stopped short.

Because it wasn't Eliza at all.

Chapter Thirty-Three

'DUFF!' SHE CRIED delightedly and hurled herself at him, throwing her arms about him and hugging him so tightly that he grunted as she expelled all the air from his chest. 'How wonderful to see you! Oh, my dear, I have missed you so! How is it that you are here? Why did you not write and say you were returning? What has –'

She stopped, turned her head to kiss his cheek and then let go of him and led him to the fireplace.

'I was so delighted to see you I did not stop to think, my dear,' she said. 'Clearly there is some problem. In your last letters you were – well, let's settle ourselves and then we can talk.'

She took her pelisse and arranged it on the small clothes horse by the fire where Eliza usually kept her tea towels to be aired and perched her bonnet beside it. It was unlikely, she found herself thinking inconsequentially, that she would be able to rescue it for future wear, for it looked sadly bedraggled. As if that mattered! And she turned to look at Duff through eyes which still felt hot and sore, especially the left one, but which now gave her a clear vision of all there was to see.

He looked quite shocking. His face was drawn and tight and there was a greyish tinge to his skin, beneath what was clearly an out-of-doors reddish roughness. His chin had not been shaved today, so looked dirty and sad and his eyes looked as her own felt, red-rimmed and painful. There were pouches beneath them that spoke of long sleepless hours spent in tears and she felt her insides twist in sympathy as she looked at the total picture of misery that he presented.

Gently she made him sit down in the rocker and pulled over the low stool that was Polly's usual seat to settle herself at his feet. They sat in silence for a while as her skirts steamed gently in the warmth of the fire, and her hair, too, began to dry and form tendrils around her face. Beyond the kitchen the house was silent, and in here they could hear only the faint hiss of the kettle on the fire and the occasional crackle of the burning coals. It was very peaceful and, had it not been for Duff's unhappiness, which seemed to hang in the room like a fog, it would have been a pleasant interlude for Tilly.

To have her boy back under any circumstances was what she had wanted; but now she did wonder, looking at his ravaged face. He seemed to have aged ten years since she had last seen him and in a surge of maternal anguish she squeezed both his hands between hers and said, 'Oh, dearest Duff, I dare say you would rather I left you in peace, but I cannot bear to see you so unhappy. What has happened, my dear? Why are you here? Is there –? Tell me about it, please. Unless it is really too painful for you.'

When he spoke she realized it was the first time since she had come in and marvelled a little at the way he sounded. His voice was dull and heavy and he croaked rather like a frog.

'That's all right, Mamma. I have to tell someone – and who better than you?'

She said nothing, not wanting to prompt him and after a long pause, during which he stared at the fire, he said abruptly, 'I'm not sure, but I think the worst bit is that I feel such a *fool*. To think I didn't see it, and it was right beneath my nose! Such a fool.'

Still she said nothing, just sitting there and holding his hand. The next pause was a little shorter.

'I mean, the whole thing was so contrived! I thought – I never thought he could behave so to me – he was my friend, you know? I loved him! You remember, Mamma, how much I loved him and how he tried to persuade me to play the stupid – well, be like the other fellows, and I wouldn't? And yet – well, perhaps it was that as much as anything. I mean, I remembered he had always had a liking in that direction and could never have imagined he would be interested in a girl. And anyway Sophie – she was *my* Sophie.'

His head came up then from its drooping posture and he stared down at her and his eyes seemed to bulge a little. 'He knew that! I sat there with him the night I arrived and I told him all. I begged him not to tell anyone else, but he knew how much I yearned to marry her and – and everything. And he seemed so understanding and sympathetic.'

He took a deep shuddering breath. 'And I was delighted to see Sophie so happy as the days went by, you know. Patrick's papa liking her so much and the girls, except for Euphonia –' He brooded for a while then. 'She was the only one who was honest, I think. Patrick was always so hateful about her, and said such cruel things, and called her a she-horse and so forth, for she is rather plain, but she is an honest person, I believe, much more so than any of the others.'

Tilly took a chance and spoke. 'Are you saying that all of the family, apart from this one, were – misbehaved to you?'

He looked down at her miserably. 'Yes. In a way. I mean, I think they knew what was happening. You see, it was his papa – he liked Sophie vastly – he kept saying so, and Lady Euphonia didn't like it above half. She is the lady of the house, you see, since the duchess died. Well, they – the others – they were all so amused by the way the duke fussed over Sophie and only Euphonia didn't seem to like it, and that was one of the reasons I did not like Euphonia either – but I see now –'

The pause was so long this time that she prompted him. 'What do you see now, Duff?'

'I see that I was a dupe, that is what I see!' he said with sudden rage, and she was glad to see it. It was infinitely less distressing than the sodden misery he had been displaying, and into which he lapsed again almost at once. 'I think it was because his papa liked Sophie and fussed over her so much that Patrick tried to – decided to try to – that he chose to cut his father out. I was so stupid. I thought the duke was just being – well, like a father to Sophie. She is much the same age as his own youngest daughter, Lady

Genevieve, after all, but I know now he had much more wicked ideas. And Patrick chose to – to thwart him to amuse himself. To start with. That's why he told me all that stuff about being the agent.'

Tears had gathered in his eyes and they threatened to spill as he went on in a low voice, almost piteously. 'At first I agreed only in order to give myself a – a future, you know, and a chance to obtain a house and an income so that I could wed Sophie and we would be happy for always. But then I learned to like the work itself. I liked the animals and the fields and the – well, it was all so comforting, you know. And all the time Patrick was lying to me, because he just wanted to keep me out of the way while he spent all his time with Sophie, when he could get her away from his father. I thought it was just his younger sisters who took her to parties and on morning visits and so forth but Patrick used to take them, and I did not know. I thought he was about other business on the estate.'

'How do you know he wasn't?' Tilly said, wanting to comfort him if she could.

'Euphonia told me, when it all came out – oh, I was so easily led by the nose, I should be shot!'

'No, Duff, don't you speak so! That is so – if you did not recognize villainy when you saw it, it is because you have a sweet and honest soul yourself. It is a credit to you that he could dupe you as he did, not to your discredit.' She sounded as passionate as he had, kneeling in front of him now and holding both his hands tightly. 'If you have been duped by Patrick Paton, then it speaks ill of him, not you.'

'Thank you, Mamma.' He managed, amazingly, a sort of grin. 'It is sweet of you to try to comfort me, but I know what I know.'

'You do not,' she said stoutly. 'You know only that you set yourself high standards and they do not. So this hateful Patrick wooed Sophie, I take it.'

'Yes.'

'To – to annoy his father? It seems a childish thing to do.'

'Childish?' Duff opened his eyes wide at that. 'How can it be childish to make love to a beautiful girl who is spoken for by someone else? I know of no child who would behave so.'

'Trying to score over your parents sounds childish to me,' Tilly said. 'The duke sounds childish in himself, dangling after a girl as young as Sophie. I am sure she scorned him.' She was sure of nothing of the sort but she knew Duff needed to hear kind words about his beloved. Or thought he did. But she was wrong, for he reddened with anger and snapped at her.

'Of course she did not! I should have seen more clearly from the start. She loved it! She thinks a man who is a duke is wonderful for all he is so disgustingly old, and has a face like a – like – a – so red and veined as to make one quite sick, and yellow teeth and a breath you can smell for half a mile!'

Tilly couldn't help it. She laughed at that. 'Oh, Duff, is he really so dreadful?'

'And worse!' Duff said passionately. 'And I hope his son looks the same in less than a twelvemonth and that she has to watch it happen and remember what might have been. For whatever else I am not – like a lord or a duke – I am not smelly and red-faced and disgusting.'

'Oh, of course you are not, darling Duff,' Tilly cried and hugged him again and wanted to laugh once more for in fact he himself had clearly not washed since his long journey home.

She leaned back then and stared at him. 'I am not sure,' she said carefully, although she was, almost, 'quite what happened. Are you telling me that Sophie and – and Patrick –'

'Yes,' Duff said and his voice was grim. 'They have run away together. Left a set of letters as cool as you please, telling everyone that they have eloped to Paris and will be wed, and when the old duke dies, Patrick says, that will be soon enough to return to Paton, and then he writes to me that – that it is a pity he had no more intention of sending Abner Oakburton away when he succeeds to the title than flying to the moon, for he is an excellent agent who knows all there is to know about the estate, but that I might be able to find a berth as agent elsewhere for I seem to have some small aptitude for the work and might learn how to be an assistant in a few more years if I set my mind to it.' He clenched his fists then. 'If I could reach him now, I swear I would kill him!' he cried and looked at Tilly with tragic eyes.

'So that is why she did not answer my letters,' she said slowly. 'She had already decided she was never returning here –'

'What is that?' he said sharply, and she explained her offer to Sophie. He listened, dully, and then shook his head.

'Patrick made a better offer,' he said simply. 'I hate him – I will hate him till I die –'

She was trying very hard to think sensibly of what to say next; but it was not easy. She was filled – and she had to hide it very carefully – with elation. Sophie, gone out of her darling Duff's life in a way that must surely mean she would never come back. If she did change her mind and not marry this Lord Patrick – which was clearly highly unlikely, for there could be no question that Sophie would find the prospect of one day becoming a duchess deeply gratifying – even if she did return he would spurn her. He was unhappy now, her secret voice was telling her, almost delirious with joy at the back of her mind, but he would forget that horrid minx soon and be glad he had escaped from her clutches. She felt almost giddy with relief.

'I know what you are thinking, Ma,' he said with a prescience that made her flush with embarrassment. 'That you are glad and that we were too young and that Sophie is a bad person. But she is not bad. She is a little silly, I grant you. But I knew that. She is greedy, but I knew that too, and at least she is very honest about it. I prefer her clear delight in things and clothes and money and titles to the pretence some people make of being above such things. In time I would have taught her to be happy enough with what I had to offer. But Patrick has stolen my time from me and it is that which makes me so angry. But one day – you will see, Mamma. One day she'll come back to me. She'll have to. She belongs to me, you see. She has done since we were children.'

He said it with a simplicity that made Tilly's face burn hotly and she touched his cheek with one hand and said as carefully as she could, 'I am sorry, dear one. Sorry that you are unhappy. I will not lie to you and say that I am sorry that – that there can be no wedding at present. I still believe that you are much too young to have made so important a decision, and have to find your way in the world first. But I am wretched to see you so sad and will do all I can to help you be happier.'

'All I ask of you is that you do not – do not force me, Mamma. I will decide in my own time what career I wish to follow. In the meantime I ask only that you let me live here and help you in whatever way I may, and not to speak of what has passed. I will heal my own heart in my own way. I cannot – could not – bear a great deal of prosing in the matter.'

He looked at her sternly and she wanted to laugh again for he looked so like his infant self, so much the four-year-old Duff telling her solemnly of his plans to make a lake in the garden which she must not on any account prevent.

'Not a word, dear one. I shall have to explain to the others that Sophie will not be returning, but I dare say we shall think of some tale to satisfy them and keep them quiet.'

'Say she has gone away to join a new dance company somewhere, and that I am lonely and so they must not speak to me of her,' he said. 'That much I can tolerate. But after that, I beg you, do not speak of me or of her to anyone here. They are but your customers after all.'

She sat back on her heels again, a little chilled. 'Customers? That sounds very – that does not sound at all agreeable.'

'It's what they are, though, isn't it? Customers? We are in the trade of providing board and lodging here, are we not?' He spoke harshly and some of her satisfaction evaporated. Clearly he had picked up more than pain at Paton. He had entrenched his notion of their own lowliness. And that would have to be put right, indeed it would. But all she said now, as she got to her feet and shook out her sadly creased gown, was, 'Well, to me they will always be my guests. Paying guests, undeniably, but my guests all the same. I think I shall see where the maids are and arrange for a bath to be fetched up to your room. When you are washed and shaved and changed you will feel much more agreeable.'

'Yes,' he said wearily, 'I dropped my baggage in the hall, and came straight here in search of you, since you were not in your morning room, and got no further.' But he made no move to get up, still sitting staring at the flames. It was as though the spirit of him had suddenly left the room, leaving only his body behind. She looked down at him for a long moment and then went to the stairs.

In the hall there was clear evidence that Polly had been hard at work, for the bannisters on the staircase shone particularly brightly and she thought inconsequentially, Oh dear! I promised to take her to the country again this week to see her brothers. We stayed so short a time when we last went, and this time it must be for the whole day that we go, and now Duff is home and I wish I did not have to go.

I'll take him with me, she thought then. Yes, that will serve very well – give him something to think of; he can look after us on the train. And she reached for the bell to ring it.

She heard it peal above stairs, on the maids' floor high in the attics as well as down in the kitchen and waited and after a few moments there was a rattling of footsteps on the stairs and Polly peered down at her.

'Oh, Missus,' she said. 'I di'n't know you was back. Mrs Horace, she said to tell you as she wasn't feeling the ticket and was havin' a lie down and all was in hand for dinner and not to fret none.'

'Eliza, not well?' Tilly was immediately anxious. 'She is in her room?'

'Yes, Missus.'

'I shall go and see her. But now, you go up to Lucy or Rosie, I don't care which, and tell them Mr Duff has come home and wants a bath in his room and they are to help him unpack. At once – away with you now.'

'Yes, Missus,' Polly said and her head vanished and Tilly called, as an afterthought, 'And we shall ask Mr Duff to come with us to see your brothers.'

The rumpled head reappeared, the face this time split into a huge grin. 'Cor!' said Polly. 'That'll be 'andsome, that will!' And vanished again.

Tilly, still in a turmoil over her son, was now filled up with even more anxiety as she hurried back to Eliza's room alongside the kitchen to see what was wrong with her. She was past the time of her pregnancy when there was any risk to her or to her child, surely? Tilly's memory was hazy on such matters, but she seemed to recall that the first three months were the hazardous ones, and once past that no one need fret unduly, unless the mother got severely enlarged or had fits, in which case there was very good cause for anxiety. Had Eliza had a fit? Certainly she had been looking more and more enlarged for some time now.

And she scratched on Eliza's door and waited anxiously, her ear to the panels, for an answer.

Chapter Thirty-Four

IT CAME SLOWLY. She had to scratch on the panels twice more and then at last heard a drowsy 'Mmm?' and, waiting no longer, turned the door handle and walked in.

Eliza was lying on her bed fully dressed, but for her boots which were on the floor beside her. She looked blowzy and heavy-eyed as she stared at Tilly, clearly still befuddled with sleep, and then seemed to come to her senses fully and almost leapt off the bed.

'Oh, bless my soul, what time is it? I only laid my head down for a minute or so and then – oh.' She stood for a moment swaying, and then sat down hard again on her bed, and stared at Tilly with an expression of surprise on her face.

'My dear Eliza, what is it?' Tilly cried, thoroughly alarmed, and Eliza shook her head as if to clear it and then did so again before speaking carefully.

'I'm all right, Mum, I think. I just felt a bit light-headed there for a moment or two. Stood up too fast, I shouldn't wonder.'

'Then lie down again at once!' Tilly instructed, but Eliza waved a hand in refusal.

'I'll get over it the sooner if I sit up, Mum. Give me just a second or two.'

Tilly came further into the room, leaving the door open behind her. The kitchen was empty, for Duff had obediently gone upstairs to his room, and there was just the two of them.

'Are you all right, Eliza?' Tilly said sharply. 'You are not suffering from any bleeding or anything that might make us fear?'

Eliza, still sitting with her head held in the awkward manner of one who perceives the world as spinning round her, managed a smile. 'No need to fear for the baby, Mum,' she said and managed to set one hand protectively on her belly. 'That's as firm as a rock. It's my own fault really –' She took a deep breath, seeming to begin to regain her balance. 'I been worryin' too much, and lyin' awake o' nights in consequence. I should have more sense –'

'Worrying?'

'About next door, to tell the truth, Mum. I try to keep a brave front just like you do, I'm sure, but I can't help it. One minute I think it'll all be all right, stop fussing, woman, I says to myself, and the next, well, I keep imagining all sorts goin' on there to spoil our life here. It's all so good, 'n't it, Mum? Us and our guests and all so happy – and there she sits like – like some sort of spider just waitin' and us not knowin' what way she'll jump.'

'Do spiders jump, Eliza?' Tilly said absurdly and came to sit down on the bed beside her. 'You see how foolish you are? She is not, in fact, there in the house, but away somewhere, perhaps even abroad – or so she told me in her letter. I cannot see why you should think of her in such a manner. There is no sense in worrying yourself into illness, now is there?'

'That's as may be,' Eliza said. 'But you do it – I've watched your face and I know what you're thinkin' and it's not possible for me not to worry when you do. We've got all our lovely plans for us and the future and – and this woman and her house – oh, if only somethin' would happen to scare her away! I keep havin' these imaginings, you know? I think – suppose the house was spoiled in some way and made impossible for her to fix up. Wouldn't she be glad to sell it to you then at a low price just to be rid of it? I know you've been careful with money this long time, and we have such good reliable guests, you'd have no problems, I'm sure, in finding the money. Then you could fix it up as part of Quentin's, couldn't you? If you was to buy it as it is, you'd have to pull out the heart of it anyway to make it fit in with us here as we are, wouldn't you? So it wouldn't be a difficulty for you if it was to catch fire inside like, would it? I think about that –' She brooded for a moment. 'I think about that a lot.'

'Well, it isn't going to catch fire or be spoiled inside,' Tilly said firmly. 'So stop thinking such stuff. And even if it were, it is no doubt insured as is this establishment, so it would make no difference to Dorcas, so it is all a nonsense, a childish dream. You are having notions because of your condition, that's all there is to it. I remember when I was heavy with Duff I was much the same. And here's Duff home again and –'

Eliza lifted her head and stared at her, her eyes huge with surprise. 'Mr Duff here? Oh, Mum, has he come home? Why didn't you say? Where is he then? Do let me see him.' She struggled to her feet and pulled at her hair with slightly shaky fingers to smooth it and then scrabbled for her boots. 'Here's me lying here in a foolish megrim and Mr Duff home, what will he think of me? And so much to do for dinner, oh dear, oh dear.'

'Eliza!' Tilly protested as the other made for the door, pulling her skirts neatly in place and shooting her cuffs. 'Please do rest! You're in no state to –'

'I'm very well indeed, thank you, Mum,' Eliza said firmly. 'It was just a momentary thing on account of I let myself fall asleep and ashamed indeed I am of it. I'm well rested now and feeling very bobbish indeed, thank you. And all the better for knowing Mr Duff is here.'

Tilly followed her out into the short corridor that led to the kitchen proper and pulled the door closed behind her. Eliza went ahead of her into the kitchen to check her fire, and as Tilly reached her, was standing with her arms akimbo staring at the grate, which was burning merrily, as Polly crouched beside it, sweeping the hearth with a short brush. Tilly was surprised to see her, too; she had not heard her come into the kitchen.

'Well, Miss, and what are you about?' Eliza demanded. 'Aren't you supposed to be with that young imp o' Satan o' yours? Who's looking to him, I'd like to know?'

'Oh, he's asleep, Mrs Horace,' Polly said and looked over her shoulder and grinned cheekily. 'Just like you was.'

'Mind your tongue, minx,' Eliza said but there was no malice in it. The two of them had, over the weeks, drifted into a comfortable sort of relationship which was marked by such sprightly exchanges. 'You be away to him and see he's all right, now. He's your task, not my fires – where's Lucy as ought to be tending them?'

'Missus sent her to help Mr Duff to unpack,' Polly said and stood up and dusted her hands together. 'I got to fetch up some hot water for 'im, and I was just setting the fire 'igher to get the kettle to boil the faster – ah! There we goes.' And she hauled the kettle, which had begun to rattle its lid energetically, to the hot water jug standing on the hearth and filled it. She went into the kitchen then to refill the kettle from the pump, set it back on the fire and then picked up the steaming copper jug, which looked almost as tall as she was.

'Now, don't you go spilling that,' Eliza said scoldingly. 'Give it here – I'll take it up to him.'

'You'll do nothing of the sort, Eliza,' Tilly said sharply. 'If Polly can't manage it, then she shall go and fetch Rosie or Lucy to help her.'

'I can manage well enough,' Polly said and, indeed, seemed to have no trouble carrying the jug. She had set a folded towel over the top to hold the steam in and was already on her way to the stairs and the upper floors with it. 'I'll be back for another lot as soon as it's boiled.' And she went toiling away up the stairs leaving them both in the kitchen.

'I'll have to wait till he comes down to see him then,' Eliza said, disappointed. 'Is he well, Mum?'

'Not as well as he might be,' Tilly said after a moment, and then went on and told her, as briefly as she could, what had happened. Eliza listened, her face growing darker with every sentence.

'That nasty madam!' she burst out when Tilly had finished. 'And to think she had once so beguiled me with her pretty ways. I thought her a dear, good girl, I did, and now she's gone and done that to our Mr Duff? Well, I hope she may rot in hell for it. As good and loving a boy as our Duff, to be treated so. It's the outside of enough! Oh, is it any wonder,' she went on with sublime illogicality. 'That there Dorcas is such a dreadful, wicked woman as to frighten us so when she's got such a daughter as this one? I hope they both rot, that I do.'

'Eliza, do stop this nonsense about Dorcas!' Tilly said. 'You are in danger of turning her into something a great deal more important than she is.'

'As you have too, Mum,' Eliza said stubbornly. 'And you can't say you haven't.'

'I know,' Tilly said after a moment. 'But we must be sensible. Now, let's see about tonight's dinner, and see if we have time to make something special for Duff. He needs a few creature comforts, feeling as he does.'

Eliza brightened. 'Indeed, we shall, Mum! I've some lovely damsons I put up that'll be fit and ready for a good pie. It won't take me above twenty minutes or so. He loves a nice damson pie, does Mr Duff, and I've some lovely thick cream to send to table with it, for the dairy man came just this morning with the eggs and I took an extra pint of best cream thinking it might come in handy – it's like it was meant, ain't it? The Lord looks after them that looks after themselves.' With which gnomic utterance she hurried out to the larder to get to work. And Tilly sighed with relief and set about her own evening duties, as happy as it was possible to be under the circumstances. At least one of her problems had been solved. Duff was home, and even though he was a mostly unhappy Duff, to have him under her eyes again was all she needed to lift her spirits very high indeed.

Her delight in having him with her persisted for the following days and greatly reduced her shrinking at the idea of once more taking Polly to the countryside to see her brothers as she had promised; for to do so with Duff to keep them company on the journey, and help with carrying the baskets necessary for such a trip, would be much more agreeable than doing so with only an over-excited and nervous Polly.

The first time she had taken Polly to Kent had been an unhappy experience; the boys were very content on their farm, and were clearly thriving in their new lives. They had, like Polly herself, fattened up considerably and had the agreeable weather-beaten look that comes from outdoor work. They did not live in great comfort, it had to be admitted, since they were accommodated in the barn, and slept in hay, but since all the young labourers working there lived under the same conditions (unless they chose to marry, when they were found a cottage) and the barn was snug and dry, this did not constitute a great hardship. Indeed the boys seemed to enjoy the rough and tumble of life with their fellows and had shown only a brief interest in their sister's arrival. That was the first thing that had made the expedition an unhappy one. After their initial huge interest in the basket of good things that Eliza had provided for Polly to take to her brothers – some plum cake and a dozen or so fruit tarts left from the previous day's luncheon service, together with pots of jam and some honey as well as a number of other treats – they had been about their own interests, leaving Tilly and Polly, together with a now tired and fractious Georgie, to wander about the farm on their own.

They had admired the cows and the fruit trees, neither of which had much to offer in the way of interest in these dank winter months, and became very damp and chilled. The farmer had been too busy to do more than welcome them cordially enough and to offer them luncheon at his wife's lavish table, which had quite overawed Polly, for there had been so many people there all bustling and coming and going at different times, and they had made their way home to London in a less than happy state.

This time, Tilly promised herself, it would be better and she assured Polly the same thing.

'You should be glad they are so happy and busy, Polly,' she said. 'If they were weeping and clinging to you as they used to do, that would make you a great deal more unhappy, would it not?'

'Yes, Missus,' Polly said lugubriously. 'I dare say it would.' She brightened then. 'But maybe this time they'll have a bit more time for us? It's dark of winter now 'n't it? There can't be that much to do on a farm when it's freezin' cold, like this.'

It was indeed bitter January weather, and Tilly wore her thickest fur-trimmed shawl mantle and carried a muff as well, and added a soft woollen scarf to protect her ears beneath her bonnet. Polly was bundled into a thick brown ulster coat that had once been Duff's and which served perfectly well for so small a girl, with a pair of thick black woollen stockings and well made boots to protect her feet, as well as a good bonnet and scarf like Tilly's. Eliza had looked at her sharply when she was dressed and stood in the kitchen, very neat and respectable, and bade her to mind her manners and to be grateful for Mrs Quentin's great goodness; at which Tilly shook her head in discomfort and Polly looked sulky. But that she was grateful was undoubted, for she stroked the thick cloth of the coat surreptitiously and with much pleasure.

Duff was silent for most of the journey, ostensibly reading a newspaper as the train they took on the London, Chatham and Dover Railway bore them south-eastwards from Victoria Station, a cluster of somewhat battered wooden buildings at the end of Grosvenor Road, and Tilly was glad of that. Polly was silent too, and the baby Georgie slept, which pleased them all, and the time passed agreeably as the train rattled through the fields of Kent, leaving a great plume of grey smoke on a sky which was not very much brighter on this dreary January day.

At the farm, which lay some mile or two outside Faversham, their welcome was an improvement on their first visit. As Polly had suspected, the farm was less busy than it had been last time, and her brothers were given more time to spend with her by the farmer, who was a cheerful enough man and somewhat garrulous. He bade them take their sister about the place while he entertained Tilly and Duff with some splendour in the heavily furnished parlour, plying them with ratafia and cake in quite the modish manner, as he talked busily about his view of the world and his place in it. His wife, a thin bony woman with a blank face and quite unlike the usual image of a farmer's helpmeet, sat silently, clearly well accustomed to saying nothing.

'It's a great benefit to these boys to get the chance to work on a farm,' Mr Milstead boomed. 'When I recall how they looked when they was brought here, all shivering and white as they was, well, it does my heart good to look at 'em now. It's the third set of such lads as I've had through my hands, Mrs Quentin, and I'm not ashamed to say I'm right proud of the ways they turn out. Two of the first lot is wed now to local girls and living in cottages on our land. One's shaped into a very good cowman and the other's as good a fruit grower as you'll find in these parts, now I've trained him, and you can't say fairer than that. These lads can do just as well.'

Duff seemed to brighten a little and said, 'What sort of cows do you keep here, Mr Milstead?' The question made the farmer's eyes light up with enthusiasm as he launched himself into a panegyric on the subject of good English dun-coloured breeds like Norfolk polled cattle, as compared with Jersey or Guernsey breeds and Friesians which, Mr Milstead avowed, were good milk producers but, of course, gave nothing like as much cream as a well cared for Lincoln Red.

Duff joined in with some animation and Tilly listened, startled by the interest he showed. Oddly, though, she realized as the conversation went on, that it was not so much the cows that interested him as their produce. He seemed to know a good deal about the quality of milk and the cream that was skimmed from it, of the making of good butter and even of cheeses, and equally as much about the way the beef each breed produced cooked and ate and how much hanging it needed to give it the right toothsome tenderness. I must tell Eliza how knowledgeable he has become, she thought. There'll be a lot she can learn from him.

And this was a notion that grew when the discussion left cows and turned to fruit. Mr Milstead had a mixed farm, dairy and fruit ('For which Kentish farmer doesn't grow his apples and pears, I'd like to know?' he said with a great guffaw) and now Mrs Milstead began to show some interest too.

'The best for cooking, in my estimation,' she announced in a surprisingly deep voice, 'is Ribstons. They makes the fairest apple pie you ever set your knife to. But if you wants to make apple butter now, to preserve it, then you wants a good Nonsuch. For plain eating, though –'

'But what about Colvilles for baking and such-like cooking?' Duff interrupted. 'They are excellent.'

'They're good enough,' Mrs Milstead allowed, 'if a shade tart for my fancy. For eating, as I was saying –'

'Codlings and Summer Pearmains,' said Duff. 'Good summer apples, they are. But for the autumn I prefer Dontons and small Russets. And of course, there's the sweet little Beauties of Bath –'

'Yes,' said Mrs Milstead and sank back into silence, but now Duff was well away and Tilly relaxed, grateful to see him animated for the first time since his return from Leicestershire a few days ago.

When it was time to bid them farewell, collecting Polly from the barn where she had clearly spent a reasonably contented time with her brothers and was leaving in a much better frame of mind than she had after their last visit, Mr Milstead shook Tilly by the hand firmly and bade her take his good wishes back to the committee at St George's Hospital.

'For I tell you, Ma'am, they got the best idea about dealing with young beggary. None of us is about to take care of the full-grown beggars, for we have enough indigents of our own and the Poor Law rates enough to cripple a hard-working man like myself, comfortable though I may be, but these children are not past redemption and I'll gladly take more when I can. I works 'em, I don't deny, but you can see for yourself they're happy enough, and well fed into the bargain.'

Indeed they did look well, and were grinning happily enough at their master, and not showing undue fear of him, though undoubted deference.

'If they'd stayed in the city, why, all they'd do is drive their betters to distraction with their pestering and then go crawling into places where they got no right to be and doing all sorts of damage. Why, I heard only last week of a house over Covent Garden way where the owner was away abroad and he comes back and found no less than seven of 'em bedded down in his chambers! That'll never do, will it, Ma'am? So you tell the committee that they can send me their children – boys only, mind – girls makes trouble, if you'll forgive me saying so.' And he cast a sharp look at Polly who stared back at him mulishly. 'And are better off in service to a good mistress like yourself to watch over them. But boys I'll take any time and glad to. Good day to you, Ma'am, and I thank you for your visit and wish you well.'

'Are the boys happy, Polly?' Tilly asked her in the brake that carried them back to the railway station at the end of the afternoon, through the darkening countryside where the ground was developing the silvery sheen of frost under their eyes as the wheels clattered over the frozen ruts of the road. 'They look well enough, but they may have spoken more to you?'

'Oh, they like it very well,' Polly said. 'They has to work and very hard at that, but don't we all? I works too –' She looked at Tilly from beneath lowered lids, a glance she caught even in the dim light of the swinging lantern fastened to the front of the brake as the horse trotted on its swaying way.

'Work never hurt anyone,' Tilly said, a little uneasily. Was she making this child work too hard in the house? She must talk to Eliza about that, for in truth she could not really know.

'I knows that and so do the boys. They ain't complaining. It's just the way he goes on about beggars all the time that frets 'em, they says. It's like we was born to be different, when all we was, my brother says – Tom, the one that got under your wheel that day, Missus – he says we was just unlucky. Our pa was as caring a man as any he's met here, he says, only he was unlucky, so when the master goes on about beggars and the wicked things they do 'e's fair to 'it 'im. Not that 'e would, because that'd prove to old Milstead 'e was right in what 'e says, and Tom won't 'ave that –' She too lapsed into silence and stared out into the blackness of the Kentish night, at the way frosted stars were caught in the naked branches of trees and small rustlings in the hedges showed where frightened animals had been put up by the sound of the wheels.

Tilly said no more about it, either, but was very aware of Polly's uneasiness. That she was happy to see her brothers well was clear, but she was still fretful, and Tilly wondered why. And then put it down to the girl's natural tendency to be argumentative, and since they were on the train and on their way back to Victoria by now, allowed herself to doze off with her head against the dusty cloth of the carriage rather than to make conversation.

Duff saw them all into a four-wheeler cab at Victoria and Georgie woke for a while and wailed, but Polly shushed him back into quietness and they all sat in the rather bemused state tiredness created – for it was now well past eleven o'clock and they had left Quentin's at eight in the morning – thinking longingly of their beds.

Until the cab reached the end of Brompton Road and took the great curve that brought them within sight of their own front door. Tilly, who had started to doze again, was roused by an unusual light or sound; she could not be sure which it was, and then realized it was a smell that had dragged her back to the here and now. She had been dreaming she was in the kitchen so early that no one had set and lit the fire; and that Eliza was crying aloud in distress at that fact as she set a flame to the paper beneath the sticks. The smell of the new fire filled her nostrils agreeably and she tried to tell Eliza not to worry so, it did not matter she was late, they would manage well enough. But Eliza went on shouting, louder and louder; and then Tilly was awake and staring about her in alarm, her heart racing.

Duff had his head out of the window of the cab, staring ahead into the darkness, and the noise Tilly had heard in her sleep changed and became not one woman's dream voice but the cries of several, and she sat bolt upright, just as Polly too woke and stared about her.

'Duff, what is it?' Tilly cried and tried to push him aside so that she could see out, but he wouldn't let her. He was calling to the cab driver who had pulled hard on his reins.

'Driver, get that horse going, will you? That house – it is close to ours – we must get there as fast as we can!' Duff cried but the cabbie shouted something unintelligible back at him and Duff opened the door and jumped out, swearing. Tilly was taken aback; she had never heard him speak so before.

He reappeared a moment later at the window. 'Mamma, I don't know what's happening but it seems the horse will go no further according to this dolt of a driver. He says it's afraid of fire – I shall run ahead and see what's afoot. You remain here safe and I shall return for you.'

'No!' she cried. 'A fire? Oh, Duff, not Quentin's? Tell me it's not –'

'I don't know,' he cried, for now the noise of shouting had increased and there was a roaring sound and Tilly thought, That's burning, I can hear burning, and pushed against the door, still held by Duff, to get out.

'I'm coming with you!' she cried. 'Polly, stay here.' And not waiting to see that she was obeyed, took her skirts in both hands and began to run after Duff, who was haring along in front of her. And as she ran she saw it as well as heard it and smelled it. The sky was a glorious golden and crimson ahead of her, and she was certain, absolutely certain, that it was her beloved Quentin's that was creating that glow.

Chapter Thirty-Five

THE NOISE WAS dreadful as people shouted and the roar of wooden beams and brick walls being consumed by the leaping flames rose higher and higher. The light was lurid, and as Tilly arrived, breathing so hard that her chest felt constricted and her lower teeth ached, her eyes began to sting with the acrid smoke.

On the far side of the road, staring up at the great fire, was a knot of people and she recognized several of her neighbours, some of them in their dressing-gowns and night caps, and then her chest tightened again, for in one cluster of people were her own guests. She could see Mr Grayling holding his wife hard by the shoulders as, her head tied up in a turban, she stared up open-mouthed at all that was going on, and the Misses K and F, with Miss Barnetsen shrinking between them, standing august and severe and almost daring the fireman, who was trying to urge the unlookers to go further away, to move *them* on any pretext. Silas was there too, and she ran across the road towards him, past the snaking leather hoses that stretched from the fire-engine that stood to one side of her own front door.

'Silas!' she cried, and her voice was thick, for she had inhaled some of the smoke that was billowing along the street. 'What happened? Is anyone hurt? Is everyone here? The maids – where is Eliza? And the –'

'It's all right.' Silas took her elbows and held them tight, and bawled in her ear because of the hubbub that was increasing now as a second fire-engine, drawn by four very excited, stamping horses, came thundering along the street. 'It's not Quentin's – it's all right –'

She clung to him for a moment and then pulled back. 'Is everyone out?' she shouted again. 'Have you made sure that everyone is all right?'

'I told you it isn't our house – it's next door. The empty one. There's no need to be worried at all. The guests came out only because the fireman said we should, for safety's sake in case it spreads, but he is doing all he can to prevent it – Oh!'

He stared over her shoulder as the newly arrived engine stopped, spewing out a cluster of brawny men in the uniform of the London Fire Engine Establishment, who pulled their hoses away from the equipage to seek a water hydrant. The light gleamed on the brass and leather helmets and coats, and made them look like emissaries from hell; and they were very fast.

So fast that by the time Tilly was aware of what it was that had alarmed Silas, it was too late to stop it. The man in charge of the second engine, an excitable fellow with a great deal of showiness in his behaviour and a most stentorian voice, had shouted to his men some unintelligible instruction and they had turned their hoses on the front of Quentin's, even though Tilly could now see by squinting through the smoke and shifting light that it was indeed the adjoining house that was the seat of the fire. Dorcas's house.

Quite why the power of the water was so strong she did not know. There had been much rain lately and perhaps the wells and the reservoirs were full. Perhaps the pump on the fire-engine was particularly strong and efficient. Whatever the cause, the first hose snaked, leaped in its custodians' hands and then straightened its kinks rapidly as the water filled it and burst out of the nozzle at a rate so swift that when it hit the drawing-room windows of Quentin's, at which it was pointing, the impact was so powerful that the glass shattered.

Tilly screamed, Silas shouted and several of the guests set up a noise to match, and Tilly turned to try to plunge across the road to stop the firemen with the hose.

'Oh, no!' she was crying. 'There is no fire in my house – it's the other house – no –' But Silas seized her arm and held her back.

'They have to, my dear,' he cried. 'It is essential to make the adjoining properties wet in order to stop the fire from spreading – see? They're doing it on the other side too.'

She turned her head and through eyes streaming with a mixture of irritation caused by the smoke and tears of distress, saw that a third engine had now arrived and was, indeed, dousing the adjoining house, as the first engine went on struggling with Dorcas's house. And then she flinched and sprang back to stand close to Silas as with a great roar the upper part of the front of Dorcas's house collapsed in a great shower of sparks and leaping flames which in any other circumstances would have been regarded as positively beautiful.

A sort of sigh went up from the onlookers, a faint hissing sound as if they had all drawn a breath through their teeth at the same moment in sympathy with the house's pain, as though it had been a sentient thing, and Tilly looked over her shoulder at them, at the upturned faces lit to a vivid orange by the greedy clamour of those high bounding flames and felt her own face crumple.

Silas held her close then and she was glad of it, burying her face in his coat and holding on tight. He started to speak to someone over her head, but still she paid no attention. All she could do was cling to him as the thought pounded and throbbed in her head.

Eliza did this. Eliza did this. Eliza –

It took several hours finally to douse the fire in Dorcas Oliver's house. It was still dark when the firemen at last hauled in their hoses and made their weary way back to their equipages, but there was that lightening in the air that spoke of a new dawn approaching. The people who had been watching had vanished one by one, the residents of the street whose houses had, to their good fortune, not been affected by more than the stench of smoke to go gratefully to bed, and the others to make what shift they could in the dreadful state their houses had been left in by the licking of the flames alongside and the floods of water that the firemen had poured into the houses to save their fabric.

Tilly sat curled up in her kitchen, her feet tucked up beneath her, with Eliza sitting on the stool beside the grate. The fire in the range had been allowed to go down, and now Eliza began painstakingly to find dry coal in among the wet pieces in the scuttle to start it up again. The floor was awash with an inch or more of filthy water, for it had flooded down the area steps and in through the kitchen door and windows which, like the upper ones, had been shattered by the force of the firemen's over-eager hoses. It slapped about the table legs and the chairs like an ill-tempered tide on a sluggish sea; the gay rag rug with its brave colours looked bedraggled and muted as it half floated, half sank in a corner of the room and the smell everywhere was disgusting.

'They must have drawn some of their water from the drains,' Eliza said heavily. 'It'll take all the time we got to get this clean again. Oh, Mum!' And she burst into a flood of tears that shook her sturdy body as though it were an aspen tree.

Tilly sat and stared at her, not knowing what to do. Her normal instinct would have led her to reach over to Eliza and hug her and comfort her, but how could she? How could she possibly when she was so sure that Eliza herself had been the origin of all this horror? All she could do was sit there with lacklustre eyes and watch Eliza as the tears and sobs racked her body, and wait until she had recovered.

She did eventually and also sat there dumb and miserable, staring into the fire which was at last beginning to catch, though it looked as low and as sullen as Tilly felt, for the coal had been wetted very thoroughly.

Silas appeared at the top of the stairs. 'Are you all right?' he called, peering down. 'Stay there and be warm. As soon as I have seen to it that all is well up here, we shall contrive a bed for you, Eliza. Your bedroom is well enough, Tilly. Duff has checked all the rooms and it is the drawing room and dining room which have suffered most, and the big front bedrooms. But the maids have managed to go to bed, and most of the guests, though there has been some doubling up – Mr Grayling has gone to share with Mr Cumming and Mrs Grayling, she's gone to share with Miss Barnetsen. I dare say we should try to get them back to their rooms again tomorrow – they do so fuss over being apart, the Graylings! Are you sure you're all right?'

'Yes,' Tilly said dully. 'I'm all right – oh!' She sat more upright. 'Please, do ask Duff – did he deal with the cab and fetch Polly and Georgie? I left them there at the end of the road.'

'No need to fear,' Silas said reassuringly. 'Polly fetched herself and the baby home and the cabbie, as far as I can tell, chose to do without his fare and took to his heels. No one is hurt, happily.' He had come downstairs now and was standing on the bottom step of the staircase looking across at her. 'I'd come across to you but I've only just changed into these dry boots.'

'It's all right,' Tilly said and closed her eyes. 'I shall stay here for a while. Just as long as I know everyone is safe and comfortable.'

'I'm seeing to the last of them,' Silas promised. 'As soon as all are settled I shall return, minus boots, and carry you upstairs. You must take off your own boots, Eliza, when I come back for you, and wade through barefoot. I am afraid I cannot carry you for you are too buxom for me – but we are arranging a bed for you, Duff and I, in Tilly's morning room. I trust that will be all right, Tilly?'

'Anywhere you choose,' Tilly said, her eyes still closed and at last he went, stamping away upstairs with some impatience to continue his efforts. She should have been grateful to him, she knew; he had set to to help in a very definite manner and that was important, but all she could do now was be glad he had gone so that she could think again about what to do about Eliza.

'I have to say it, Eliza,' she said suddenly, almost surprised to hear the words coming out of her mouth. 'I have to –'

Eliza lifted her head and looked at her. She too had been sitting in silence, miserable and unresponsive to Silas's energy. 'Say what, Mum?'

'You wanted this to happen,' Tilly said. 'Didn't you?'

Eliza gaped. 'Wanted it to – oh, Mum, what a thing to say! To want our lovely house in this state! Oh, Mum!'

Once again there was a sound from above as the door to the main part of the house swung open and voices could be heard coming from the hallway. She identified Miss Knapp's confident bellow, and the more twittering tones of Miss Barnetsen, and then the door swung again and shut it all out. Tilly looked up. But the door remained closed and no one stepped forward into the light of the one lamp they had burning on the kitchen table.

'Who is it?' she called but there was no response and she turned her head back to Eliza. 'Everything is at sixes and sevens, the doors are probably all warped and will have to be replaced. There is so much work to do here now, and what will my guests do while it is in hand? And what will it cost? And you wanted it to happen.'

'Oh, Mum!' Eliza said and burst into tears again, her face crumpling and turning an alarming shade of red. 'Oh, Mum, how can –' And could say no more.

Still Tilly couldn't bring herself to comfort her; all she could do was sit there, curled up in her rocking chair and staring at her and feeling the bitter hurt and anger invade every part of her being.

Again Eliza managed to stop her weeping and at last looked up at Tilly through swollen lids.

'Mum, I know what I said to you that day but I never meant it! I mean, I did wish it to happen to the house next door, I can't say I didn't, but not like *this*. Not with our house hurt so grievous. I wanted to see the other house lose its pull on that Dorcas, that I did want and – and – but to say I wanted all *this* to happen –' she gestured piteously – 'I couldn't want such a thing. How could I?'

'But you made it happen,' Tilly said and her voice was metallic in its coldness. 'Didn't you? It just went further than you thought it would.'

'I made it – Mum, what are you saying?' Eliza jumped to her feet, oblivious of the water that still swirled about the floor, though it did seem to be oozing away a little through the interstices between the stones. The cellar, Tilly thought in a vague sort of way, must be almost full of it. 'I don't deny I said to you as I had this hope as something'd happen to get that Dorcas woman away from us and us left in peace and maybe with a bigger house into the bargain, but

I never would have – I couldn't have! How can you think such a thing, Mum? How can you?'

'What else am I to think?' Tilly cried, staring up at her. 'Do you not think I want to believe you? But if it was not you, what happened? There is a house that has been empty these many years now and never a hint of a problem and then when Dorcas comes back and – and makes us fear for the future – you tell me that you wish it would burn so that she would no longer want to have it and would sell it to me and – then it happens! What else am I to think? Who else could have done it? For I am sure as I sit here that this is no accident, Eliza. And I have no doubt that the firemen will soon find out what happened and how. They will be back tomorrow to inspect the place and I dare say they will know what befell. They are very clever at such matters. I was told that when the insurance was settled for this house – as though they were warning me. As though I needed a warning! Perhaps I should have warned you, however.'

'No!' Eliza said as though it was all she could manage to get out. 'No – no –'

They were both silent then as the fire settled once more in the grate to a dull redness, and the muffled noises from beyond the green baize door disappeared. Tilly sat and stared at the embers and tried to get some sense of order in her weary head; and had to admit she was almost asleep with the sheer exhaustion of it all.

When she heard the gulping start, and the sniffing, she thought, how can she have more tears to shed? Has she not shed them all already? And did not take her gaze from the fireplace. But then Eliza said sharply, in a voice that had quite controlled its own tearfulness, 'Who's that?' and Tilly whipped her head round and stared.

Eliza was again on her feet and had started to wade across the floor to the staircase; and she reached forwards into the darkness when she got there and pulled and then came back; and it was Polly she had by the elbow, a Polly who was weeping as though her heart would shatter into so many pieces it could never be healed again.

*

It took them half an hour to stop the weeping. Silas and Duff came back to the kitchen to report that the household had settled down at last, everyone but themselves in a bed, and were startled to see Polly.

'I saw her into her room myself,' Silas said, somewhat aggrieved. 'Carried the baby up, saw him put to bed and thought she'd settle herself. What are you doing here, girl?' But Polly wept on and could not be persuaded to speak at all.

It was Duff who found the answer. Looking rather absurd with his trousers rolled up and his legs bare from the knees down, he lifted the girl bodily and gestured with his chin at Eliza who at once moved out of his way. Tilly also stood up and after a moment Duff sat down in the rocker with Polly and held her in the crook of his arm and let her weep her misery out on his shoulder.

'She has had a difficult day, to say the least of it,' he said in a low voice. 'The visit to her brothers, and now this. And she is still very young. She will get over it. Perhaps, Eliza, some tea to restore us all? Is it possible on so low a fire?'

'I'll manage something,' Eliza said and seized a poker and went to work, coaxing the stubborn embers into some semblance of life, and then paddling away to fetch cups (she did not waste any effort on saucers) and milk and sugar.

The tea, when she made it, was scalding hot and very comforting to the five wet and bedraggled people, for even Polly was persuaded to lift her head from Duff's now soaking wet shoulder and tremulously take a cup from Eliza's hands.

'Now, Polly,' Tilly said firmly. 'Are you all right? Will you go to bed now? Georgie may wake and need you.'

The eyes that had almost disappeared into the puffiness of the tear-stained face brimmed again and Tilly said hastily, 'There is no need to hurry, Polly. It is just that it is very late – indeed almost morning and –'

Duff bent his head and set his cheek alongside Polly's streaked wet face. 'What is it, Polly?' he murmured. 'What is it that has worried you so? You can tell me, can't you? It is safe to tell all of us

– we're your friends. We won't hurt you.' And he glanced up at his mother over the child's head as though to obtain her agreement.

Tilly gave it at once. All she wanted was to get Polly away to bed and then everyone else. The matter of what Eliza had done had still to be dealt with but not, she knew, now. It was too late, there was too much going on, they all needed sleep. Tomorrow – or later today, rather – would be soon enough. 'Of course, Polly. We're all your friends. No one will hurt you.'

'Or be angry with you,' Duff murmured. 'Tell us what the trouble is.'

'Oh, Mr Duff, sir,' wailed Polly and again her face twisted into an agony of misery. 'Oh, Mr Duff, it was me what made the fire next door, and I never thought, honestly, I never thought nothing like this would happen. But it's all my fault, all of it, and oh, Mr Duff, what are you going to do to me over it? Will you send me to jail? And what will happen to Georgie if you do?'

Chapter Thirty-Six

THE LAST TIME Tilly had spent the whole night out of her bed had been fifteen years earlier, when Duff was three and had so severe an attack of croup that his life had been despaired of; she had sat and watched him, sponging him to reduce his dreadful fever, and filled the room with steam from the kettles which Eliza carried upstairs in an unending relay till the dawn had broken over Brompton, and had not gone to sleep until mid-morning when it was clear he was past the crisis.

Now, sitting listening to Polly, as the unglazed window behind her paled with the early light and the fire in front of her tried to produce some warmth in the bitter chill of the freezing morning – the water at the edges of the kitchen floor showed a dull gleam where ice had formed on it – she had the same odd sensations she recalled from that last occasion. She felt light-headed and remote as though she were not, in fact, herself at all. It was as though she were sitting on a cloud hovering over her own head and looking down on all that was going on, interested but dispassionate, there, but not a part of what was happening.

It was Duff who questioned Polly, gently and carefully, after Silas had almost frightened the girl into another attack of weeping by bursting into loud expostulations, but Tilly had reached out and held on to him to hush him and now he sat on the edge of the kitchen table, with Eliza beside him, staring hard at Duff and Polly with a mulish look on his face, but his mouth mercifully closed. Tilly sat on the small stool on the other side of the fire, her feet up on the fender to keep them dry, and also said nothing. All she could do was listen. It was all any of them could do.

'Tell us from the beginning, Polly,' Duff said in a matter-of-fact voice, neither hectoring nor making any offers of gentleness. 'We cannot answer any of your questions until you have told us all there is that we should know. Are you saying you set fire to the house next door?'

She gaped at him. 'Oh, Mr Duff, not what you could call – I mean – oh, Mr Duff, I don't know!'

'Well, tell us what you do know,' he said and looked at her with an unsmiling face. It was an odd conversation, for she was still sitting on his lap, but somehow he managed to set a distance between them for all that, and she behaved as though she were, in fact, standing in front of him with her hands folded on her apron in the time-honoured manner of servants being reprimanded. He has a great gift for dealing with people, Tilly discovered with a sudden excess of maternal pride. Dear Duff –

'We cannot possibly understand it all until you do. *All* of it,' Duff went on with a slight edge of asperity in his voice, for she had not answered, but sat staring down at her lap.

She lifted her head at that and peeped at him with a scared look in her eyes and bobbed her head and said breathlessly, 'Yes, sir, Mr Duff.'

'Well?' he said, impatiently, and she took a long breath.

'Well, it was like – what Mr Silas said to Missus and what Missus said an' all, and anyway, there was always so much 'ere, and any amount of it wasted, one way and another and no one never noticed if a bit went, so I thought it no 'arm –'

'I said from the beginning, Polly,' Duff said.

'I am tellin' you,' she protested. 'I got to explain properly, don't I?' For a brief moment there was a hint of the old combative Polly there.

'Then be clear about it. It is very late and we are all much in need of sleep, you included. So – what did Mr Silas say to my mother that is germane – that led to whatever it led to?' For a moment Duff sounded very young again, and Tilly wanted to reach out to him. But she managed not to.

'He said as 'ow it was all wrong that some people should be beggin' and some should be so comfortable like. 'E said we all 'ad a responsibility to everyone, in a fair world. 'E said as 'ow –'

'I know what I said!' Silas interrupted wrathfully. 'But what my philosophy has to do with –'

'Please, Silas,' Duff said sharply. 'Let her go on.' Silas scowled and subsided.

'And Missus, 'ere, 'elpin' me and the boys like and the 'ospital and everyone bein' so good about taking in me and Georgie – and me bein' that grateful and – well, I took Georgie for a walk didn't I? Along down the park, pushin' 'im in that old baby carriage, Mr Duff, what Missus said was yours when you was a baby.'

Duff reddened and said stiffly, 'Well? So you took a walk – what has this to do with what happened next door?'

'I'm comin' to it, Mr Duff! Well, I met some of me old muckers –' She saw the look of mystification on his face then and said quickly, 'Old friends, like, people what I knew when we was beggin'. Before you all rescued us like, me and the boys and Georgie.'

'Ah!' Tilly said and her gaze sharpened. She began to have an inkling of what was to come. Hadn't Eliza told her how surprised she was that so much more was being eaten in the kitchen since Polly came? Hadn't they thought simply that the girl was making up for the years of half starvation she had suffered?

She glanced at Eliza and saw the same dawning awareness in her expression and at the same time began to feel sick. Had she accused her own dear Eliza for no reason? Oh, God, please let Eliza understand and forgive me if I did.

'Well, they was most took with the way we looked, me and Georgie. They never reckernized us, first off. I 'ad to speak to them – and then they was that jealous!' Her lips curved reminiscently. 'Specially Joe. 'E was right put about, 'e was –'

'Joe?' Duff said, mystified, and also to bring her back to speech, for she was staring down at her lap again and her expression had become more remote.

'Feller,' Polly said succinctly. ''Bout your age, like. Nice feller.'

'Ah,' said Tilly again, but no one paid her any attention.

'So what did you do when he was jealous of your good fortune, Polly?' Duff said softly and she threw a glance at him, frightened now.

'Well, I said as 'ow – well, I thought, there's all this food 'ere and Miss Eliza and Missus they said I could eat what I wanted any time, just to go an' take anythin', as long as it was a dish what 'ad bin started like, and not a fresh one as'd been made for upstairs, and I thought, Joe an' 'is old man, they looked shockin' thin. An' I said – well – I told 'em if they come late, I'd give 'em some vittles.' She looked at Eliza this time, appealingly. 'I meant no 'arm, honest I didn't. It was just I 'ad so much and they 'ad nothin' and Missus and Mr Silas they talked about takin' care of beggars like, so I didn't think no 'arm to it.'

'There was no harm in it,' Tilly said. 'But you did not need to steal it for them, Polly. You should have asked me. Or Eliza. Could you not have trusted us?'

'I di'n't know if I could, Missus,' Polly said simply. 'I mean, wouldn't you 'ave said well, 'ow many's likely to 'ear of this and all turn up together? Eh? Ain't that what you'd a' said?'

Tilly was silent, aware of the wisdom of Polly's question. Would she have been so willing to feed these people? It was so easy now to say so, but in reality –

'Anyway, it was all right to start with. It was just Joe and 'is old man and I never 'ad no trouble. But then they said as 'ow they 'ad one or two others as wanted a bit of vittles and I said it was 'ard, like, to take so much, but I'd try – and then –'

'Then what?' Duff said. 'You'll have to tell us now, Polly. You've come this far, after all.'

'You won't get the law on them, Mr Duff?' she said, breathless with anxiety, but he shook his head.

'At this stage, Polly, I can make no promises. Just tell us. Then what?'

'Joe saw the 'ouse next door was empty,' she said in a small voice.

'And?'

'And – and 'e said it was bleedin' cold sleepin' out and the old man 'ad the pneumony, 'e didn't doubt, and 'e was goin' to get in and sleep dry and warm of a night – and it'd make it easier for me to give 'em the food if they did. I wouldn't 'ave to come down in the middle of the night and meet 'em 'ere at the back door.'

Eliza drew in her breath sharply and Polly bit her lip and avoided her eyes. 'Well, it seemed all right to me! I never saw no one there, I don't know nothin' about the place. So they got in, di'n't they?'

'How?' Duff said and Polly shrugged.

'Don't know. Never asked. I didn't *want* to know, to tell the truth. I mean, I was gettin' scared. Joe used to be so nice, but 'e was gettin' a bit rough – wanted me to – well, never mind. 'E just got a bit tough, like, and I didn't want to cross 'im. 'E said 'e'd found 'is own way in and I was to leave the vittles, much as I could, down the area. Round behind the steps, like. All I 'ad to do was go out when it was convenient like – early mornin' was good – an' leave the stuff there an' I 'ad to do nothin' else –'

'You're sure?' Silas said sharply, for again she had stopped and she looked at him with that scared rabbit glance of hers and went pink.

'They wanted coals'n all,' she muttered after a long pause.

'Coals!' Eliza cried. 'Coals? Are you telling me that you took *coals* to these beggarmen as well as our good food?'

'Yes, Miss Eliza,' Polly whispered. "E'd 'ave 'it me if I 'adn't. I di'n't dare not to. 'E said he'd mark me so as you'd all see and ask and then I'd get into trouble, wouldn't I? And you'd throw me out –'

'Oh, Polly, of course I wouldn't!' Tilly cried. 'As if I would!'

'I wasn't to know that, was I?' Polly said with a sudden access of passion. 'You've been nice enough, o' course you 'ave and I'm as grateful as I know 'ow to be, what with Georgie doin' so well an' all, but if you'd known as I was givin' your vittles and firin' to beggars next door, wouldn't you 'ave been in a takin'? Stands to reason you would!'

Tilly opened her mouth to answer, but Duff forestalled her. 'How could they risk lighting fires?' he said with a note of amazement in his voice. 'Surely they wouldn't risk someone seeing the chimney smoke.'

Polly shook her head at that. 'They never used the fireplaces, Mr Duff! No one never uses fireplaces when they take over an empty drum like that. You gets a bit of good iron, see, from somewhere like the railway – they sometimes 'as bits lyin' around – and you lights the coals on that. You soon get used to a bit o' smoke in your eyes when you're used to sleepin' out in the cold. You *likes* it. It makes you feel warmer.'

Tilly shivered suddenly, and it was not just the icy chill from the gaping window which could not be defeated by the brave fire that Eliza was keeping going in the grate. It was the glimpse of the sort of life these people lived and of which she had so little understanding that made her feel so cold. In a curious way she was sick with shame and guilt as though she had herself seen to it that this should be their lot. It was an absurd notion, she told herself; but all the same she couldn't be rid of it.

'Oh, no,' Silas said slowly. 'They set a sheet of cast iron on wooden floorboards and burned coals on them. Is it any wonder that eventually they scorched and burned through? The hot coals must have tumbled through to the cellar beneath and set the whole place alight.'

There was a long silence as the five of them sat and thought; Polly, her head down and staring once more at her apron, but seeming somehow more at peace than she had been; Eliza with her face a study of anger and pity; and the two men blank with disbelief. Tilly herself was almost as blank as they were. She could see what had happened and how it had happened and understood Polly's role in its happening. But that no longer concerned her. It was Eliza she was thinking about now. Suddenly she turned and looked at her and seized her hand and stared up into her face.

'Eliza?' she said.

Eliza turned her head and looked at her, and there was no expression in her eyes at all. But after a long moment she seemed to soften and she lifted her other hand and set it against Tilly's cheek.

'There, Mum,' she said huskily. 'Don't take on. There ain't no need. It's all right, Mum.'

'Are you sure?' Tilly said, needing to apologize, but unable to get the words out before this audience. And Eliza seemed to understand and nodded.

'I'm sure,' she said. 'Everything's fine, all right. You see if it ain't. Now we know.'

Tilly slept till almost eight that evening, rolled into her counterpane and sunk in so deep a slumber that she did not even dream. When she woke, with a start, she was ravenously hungry and curiously light-headed. Her house, she recalled with a sort of shock of surprise, was in a state of squalor and upheaval. Her business had been struck cruelly and she had no idea what was to happen to her and her guests in the time to come, or how much permanent damage had been done; but she was deeply content and she lay there blinking at the dimness of her bedroom ceiling.

She tried to understand why she should feel so. And finally did. It was that Duff was home and Eliza had done nothing to hurt her and had forgiven her for suspecting that she might. Whatever had happened, the most important people in her life were safe and secure and as they had always been – part of her and now totally with her. In such a case, she could, she told herself, cope with anything and everything.

It was not until she had dressed and was hurrying downstairs that she realized that, in her analysis of how she felt about her current situation, she had given no thought at all to Silas, the man to whom she was supposed to be engaged to be married, albeit secretly. And she stopped halfway down the stairs to contemplate that thought and decide what she must do.

He would have to be told that under the circumstances she would release him from his offer of marriage. She would be much too occupied in the coming weeks, months even, with cleaning and renovating Quentin's, she would tell him, to be able to pay him the attention a husband-to-be was entitled to enjoy. He must understand that, surely? And she completed her journey downstairs, guiltily aware that the truth had to be faced by both of them at some time.

She did not love him enough to wed him. The need for physical excitement had been a sorry guide, she thought, as she made her way a little fearfully towards her drawing room to see the damage that had been done there; it had led her into a most complicated situation that she really did not want. And the thought came as a relief. At least she now had a full understanding of her true feelings.

She pushed open the drawing-room door with trepidation. Quite what she expected to see she did not know. In her memory she saw the great jet of water from the hoses hit the windows and the glass shatter. The place must surely be awash with water and her heart almost contracted as she thought of her good Turkey carpet as well as shards of broken glass. But look she must.

She was so amazed that she could only stand and stare. The floorboards were not under water, as she had feared, but bare and swept. There was no broken glass to be seen. The boards were somewhat dull for want of polish, but clearly drying, encouraged by a great roaring fire in the twin fireplaces that decorated each end of the long room. The carpet had vanished, but otherwise things looked well enough. The great deep-green curtains had been drawn and all over the room lamps and candles had been lit as usual, so that it looked welcoming and agreeable. It was not its usual elegant self, of course, but far from unpleasant.

She went over to the curtains and peeped behind them and saw that someone had nailed boards over the spaces where the glass had been shattered and she marvelled. She had slept all day. Who had dealt with all this?

She hurried downstairs to the dining room, to find the same sort of rough and ready order there. Here too windows had been broken but the glass remnants were gone and the spaces nailed up and again the carpet had been removed and a roaring fire in the grate was doing its best to get rid of the smell of damp that came from the drying floorboards. The table had been set for dinner in its usual way and she blinked at it. It was not laid for as many covers as usual, but it had been set.

In the kitchen she found the source of all this success in clearing up. Eliza was moving about the kitchen happily, with Lucy and Rosie helping her as usual, and beside the fire, in the great rocker, Duff sat, his head on one side and his mouth half open, snoring gently. He looked exhausted and yet contented. Eliza smiled at Tilly as she came hurrying down the stairs, her skirts billowing up in her hurry, and said softly, 'He's all right, Mum. He'll be fine for his dinner, he said, and then he'll go to bed. I gave up arguing, for he's so young and strong and seemed to be happy to be up and doing it all.'

'But it is all most miraculous!' Tilly said. 'The carpets – where are they? And the windows –'

'Oh, he sent a message to Charlie, Mum. Charlie Harrod. Lucy took it, and he sent round one of his men to fix the windows temporary like, and put in hand the glazing – they're comin' tomorrow to do that – and had the carpets took up to be sent away to be cleaned. He's got a man that does that sort of work, Charlie said, and he'd fix it all up for us, and what was friends for, after all? And Rosie and Lucy, they bustled about and cleared glass and scrubbed out down here, once the water'd drained away, and look at it, Mum! Not so bad is it? We'll soon get it back to its old shine. Polly, she scrubbed fit to bust, she did.'

Eliza sniffed then. 'And so she should, the limb of Satan!' But there was no anger in her voice at all. She seemed to have accepted Polly's role in the disaster with amazing equanimity.

'Poor darling Duff,' Tilly murmured and went and crouched before him. 'Has he not been to bed at all?'

'No, I tried, but the firemen had to talk to him and then there was the matter of the lawyer –'

Tilly stared at her over her shoulder. '*Lawyer*? Firemen? What do you mean, Eliza?'

'Ah,' said Eliza, and bit her lip. 'As to that, Mum, p'raps Mr Duff had better tell you himself.'

And that was the moment Duff chose to wake up.

Chapter Thirty-Seven

'HELLO, MA,' DUFF said drowsily and closed his eyes again, only to reopen them sharply and gape at her. 'Oh! Ma! Are you all right? Are you feeling better?'

'I'm a great deal better than you are,' she retorted. 'I have slept all day – and why no one woke me I cannot imagine – and you have not slept at all, clearly! My dear boy –'

'Ma.' He struggled to sit upright, sending the rocker swaying wildly. 'Ma, there's a deal to tell you – oh, a great deal. The firemen, they came and said as everything Polly said was so. There had been people in there this past two weeks – and they had burned a hole through the drawing-room floor to the ground level. But there were no injured people there – no one was burned – they had just run away and vanished –'

'Thank God for that,' Eliza said piously and then spoiled it. 'Polly'd have not been fit to live with if one of those beggars had got burned up, though it'd have served the varmints right if they had been.'

'Hush, Eliza,' Tilly said. 'I too say thank God. I would not wish such a death on any person and neither should you.'

'No, Mum,' Eliza said, but it was clear she did not agree.

'There is little that can be done,' Duff said. 'To that house, I mean – but I took the liberty, as you were sleeping, to send a message to Mr Collins, urgently –'

Tilly stiffened. 'Mr Collins?'

'He is your lawyer, is he not?' Duff looked a little startled, for her tone had become very cool. 'Or am I –'

'I suppose so, yes,' Tilly said unwillingly. 'It is just that the last time I dealt with him I found him – shall we say, tiresome. I had been considering taking my affairs and putting them into other hands. But then – well, I have been lax. So, you sent for Collins. Why?'

'Insurance,' Duff said. 'If the house next door is to be refused insurance payment – and the fireman told me that he was sure it would be, for it was not a truly accidental fire – then I wanted to be sure that we were safe with *our* insurances.'

Tilly stared at him, amazed. 'My dear Duff, when did you become so – so businesslike? I have never told you much about the business side of Quentin's, not wishing to discommode you, yet you seem to know –'

'I learned a good deal in the weeks I was being kept out of Patrick's way at Paton,' he said grimly. 'And I am determined to see to it that I shall use that knowledge – and gain more – to the benefit of Quentin's. Ma, I have acted without your authority, but as your son should, I believe.'

He got to his feet and stretched and then held out his hand to her, while she remained crouched by the fire looking at him in continuing surprise.

'There is much work to be done here to get the new Quentin's going and I shall be the one to do it. I do not wish you to have to work so hard in the future as you have in the past. I am a grown man now and I must take my share. I acted for us this afternoon and though Mr Collins wishes your comfirmation' – suddenly, he looked very young again – 'for he says I am not yet twenty-one, so he must do so – I am sure you will not argue with what I have done.'

He frowned then with what was an attempt to be severe but which she found touching in the extreme, for he looked as he had as a small boy, telling her firmly what he intended to do.

'What have you done, Duff?' she said as meekly as she could. 'I am all agog to hear. I thought you had done well enough to get Charlie here – which was an excellent thought and I do congratulate you on it – and would have been deeply grateful for that. But clearly you have gone further.'

'Oh, indeed I have!' he said with a sudden excess of glee and behind the unshaven cheeks of the man once again the boy appeared, full of pride at his own achievement and energy. 'I have made it possible for you to enlarge Quentin's quite marvellously.'

'Enlarge Quentin's?' She stared at him. 'What *are* you talking about?'

'Well, Mr Collins assured me that the insurance we will definitely get will cover the repairs here and some more besides. He also told me' – and here the glee almost boiled over – 'that he acts for the house next door! It seems that when Dorcas lived here – I wonder if you know this? It is all very surprising – she followed you to his firm to become a client and after the first two partners died, and he took over, she remained with him. It was he who bought the house for her, and well, to cut it short, Mamma, she gave him full authority to do as he thought best for her benefit while she was unable to do so for herself. She told him this, he said, two years ago when she had to go away for some purpose – he would not say what – and she has not countermanded it. So –'

He stopped and looked at her, for the first time showing a moment of doubt. 'I hope I did not do the wrong thing, Mamma. Perhaps I should have woken you and asked but you know, I was so sure. I thought and – well, I was sure and felt so light-headed and yet so full of energy –'

'Not enough sleep, that's all,' Eliza said sapiently from the other side of the kitchen table, where she was slicing beef for the dining-room platters, but Duff paid her no attention.

'Well, I did it. I told him that the house would get no insurance payments, for we knew the fire not to be accidental, and would make sure the insurers were told of the fact if the firemen did not, which they will. And that means, I said, the house had no value to his client at all and that we would buy its lease. I told him we could give two hundred pounds for it and not a penny more, unless we could have the freehold which would cost us another forty pounds. And he said it was a fair offer and he would ask her as soon as he could find her, but I said he must decide now, for if he did not the offer would be taken away and he would never find anyone else who would take the place but us, for why should they, when it is such a wreck, and he said – he said –' Duff swallowed, 'he said he would consider it.'

'He said he would consider it,' Tilly said, almost stupefied by the turn events had taken. 'I cannot believe that – Duff, I have wanted to take over that house for – well, for some time, but after the affair of Greenwall –'

'Greenwall?'

'Oh, you did not know of him, perhaps. Well, let that be for the present. Let me just say it seemed unlikely I could ever buy the house, for I had managed to save less money than I had hoped. And I dislike going into debt if I can avoid it. Yet now you tell me you have made an offer for a house that – How much did you say?'

He repeated the money terms and she listened intently and then nodded slowly. 'Well, it is a great deal of money, but –'

'Say we can, Mamma! I am determined it will work well for us!'

'I see little point in saying anything before we hear whether or not the offer is acceptable,' she said with a hint of asperity. 'I must warn you, dear boy, that there is more to doing business than merely speaking of offers and so forth!'

'I know that!' Duff said and went a little pink. 'I am not entirely foolish! But it seemed to me important that we strike at once or lose all. Anyway, Collins said he would return and let us know.'

'He is coming himself, the old man?' Tilly said.

'He said to me when I took him out to the door as he'd probably send his young partner,' Eliza said. 'Seeing as how he's too tired to make the journey twice in one day. Not best pleased, he wasn't, I thought. But glad to get the offer from Mr Duff. He stood outside and looked at the mess there next door for a bit before he told his driver to whip up the horses and take him off, and I never saw a man so grim.' She laughed then. 'It's my belief he knows when he's well off, that one. I'll bet you any sum you like Mum, as the answer'll come back that the house is ours for the asking.'

'Ours?' Tilly said and looked at her and then at Duff, and could not help herself. She began to laugh and could not control it, until she was laughing so much that she wept. They stood and stared at her until at last she caught her breath and dried her streaming eyes and managed to speak again.

'My dear Duff, Eliza too, you are both almost too much for me sometimes! You get a notion of what you would like to see happen and then you – you simply arrange matters so that it does! You, Eliza, and your plans for Polly and her baby and – and well, you understand. And you, Duff, with your great dreams of buying houses. I feel like a cork bobbing on the water between you.'

'Well, that's all right then,' Duff said and grinned at her. 'You let us carry you along and all will be well.'

They all stood very still then, as a bell pealed from above and Eliza pulled up her apron and rubbed her streaked face with it.

'That'll be the lawyer,' she said, trying to sound matter-of-fact and not succeeding too well. 'I'll let him in myself, shall I, Mum?' and she went, leaving Duff staring at his mother across the kitchen.

'Is it all right, Ma? Have I done wrong?' he asked and she looked at him and shook her head and then held out both hands to him.

'Dear Duff, I cannot say you have done anything right or wrong until we have talked to Mr Collins, but I will say only that I am happy, indeed more than happy, quite delighted, to see you take such an interest in my affairs. I thought you were ashamed of Quentin's and me with it –'

'Perhaps I was when I was younger and more foolish,' he said, sounding as old as he was able. 'I know better now. I can see the fascination of making something that will grow, of making things happen the way you want them to – it is much better than being in the hands of people like Patrick, who run their lives on whims and notions.' His face darkened for a moment, but then he set his mouth and shook his head as if to rid himself of unwanted thoughts. 'I tell you I will be very content to work here with you.'

She held on to his hands warmly, giving him time to compose himself again, for some of the old misery was back in his face. 'Well, I am quite overcome with it all, dearest Duff,' she said. 'To have you to share my work would be – well –'

'I shall do so very well, Ma,' he said seriously. 'And if we are allowed to buy the house next door, you will need me anyway. It will be a mammoth task, will it not, to –'

Eliza appeared on the stairs above them and they looked up at the sound of her rather elaborate throat clearing.

'I got Mr Lansdown here, Mum. Come in place of Mr Collins,' she announced with heavy deliberation and came down into the kitchen, followed close behind by a tall man who had to bend to negotiate the way without banging his head on the low ceiling. 'This way, Mr Lansdown.'

He behaved as though they were all in the most elegant of drawing rooms in the richest of houses. He seemed sublimely unaware of the cooking smells, of the state of the floors, of the general mess, and bowed politely over Tilly's hand and murmured his greetings and Mr Collins's apologies.

'I am doing most of his work now, Ma'am, since he is becoming more tired and is less able to work as he should like. I would have attended you this afternoon, had I not been previously occupied in a matter that was unavoidable, though happily now complete.'

'I hope it went well,' she said with automatic politeness and he suddenly seemed to change before her eyes. He had seemed at first glance a somewhat dour man with very dark eyes under heavy straight brows, and a saturnine expression, but now he smiled and his whole face lifted into a much younger cast and she felt herself warming to him.

'As to that,' he said with great satisfaction, 'the rogue did not, as he believed he would, get off scot-free, but was dealt with sharply by the magistrate and my client is now a happy man!'

'I am glad to hear it,' she murmured, a little startled and then, as Duff pushed forward a chair for her and then one for Mr Lansdown, was glad to relax into it. This day was becoming more and more bewildering.

'I have all the necessary information you require here,' Mr Lansdown was saying, and he reached into the leather case he was carrying and extricated some papers. 'The deeds are to be re-written and will be available in due course, but at this stage –'

'Do you mean our offer is accepted?' Duff cried, no longer able to contain himself and Mr Lansdown looked up and stared at him.

'But of course,' he said simply. 'I told Mr Collins as soon as I heard of it that it was clearly the best course of action for all our clients, both you and Mrs – um – the vendor of the house. The offer you made was misrepresented to me, I fear.'

He smiled again and once more it lit his face agreeably. 'I suspected Mr Collins had got it a little wrong. I checked the asking price of our – of the vendor, and here are the details. I think you will find them in order.'

He held out the sheet of paper in his hand and Tilly, a little bemused, took it and she and Duff together bent over it.

It was a simple but clear document. The house next door to Quentin's, known as number eighteen, was to pass into the sole ownership of Mrs Matilda Austen Quentin for the sum of two hundred pounds, including the freehold for which there would be no additional charge, the price of the house being deemed to be one hundred and sixty pounds and the freehold forty pounds. It was unencumbered land and property, the paper said, and went off into a great many other lawyerlike sentences that Tilly made no effort to read. She just raised her head and looked first at Duff and then at Mr Lansdown.

'Are you sure this is fair?' she asked.

'You think it too much?' Mr Lansdown looked perturbed. 'I can if you wish go to the vendor and ask her – but – um – it may take time to find her and she may not be willing to drop her price.'

'No,' Tilly cried. 'I did not mean – I was thinking –' And then stopped. Why was she worrying about whether the sum offered to Dorcas was a fair one? Had Dorcas ever shown any concern for fairness in her dealings with Tilly? She bit her lip and looked up at Duff. He was staring at Lansdown with his face quite incandescent with delight.

'Then my offer is accepted –' Duff said.

'Less forty pounds. Yes, Mr Quentin,' the lawyer said. 'It is accepted. If you will arrange with me to have the papers signed and the money paid into the bank within three working days, then all will be arranged to everyone's satisfaction, I hope –'

'Satisfaction?' cried Duff. 'I should say so!' And he laughed aloud in his delight.

'I shall have to seek a loan,' Tilly murmured, looking down at the paper. 'Charlie perhaps –'

'As to that,' Mr Lansdown said smoothly, 'we do have clients who are able to offer some venture capital on loan at advantageous rates. I am empowered to act for them – it is not unusual to arrange matters so – if you wish. I would have to see you from time to time to oversee the repayment of the loan, of course, if that were not too tiresome.'

'Tiresome?' Tilly said and now it was her turn to smile. 'No, it would not be tiresome. We must think about this, of course. Three days, you say?'

'Yes,' Mr Lansdown said gravely. 'You have three days to sign finally.'

'It will be done,' Tilly said and folded the paper and tucked it into her waistband, and then looked at Duff. 'Well, Duff?'

Duff seemed to glow as though a great lamp had been lit inside him. 'Then I did the right thing, Mamma? You will let me work here with you? We could make Quentin's into a glorious hotel, Mamma, better even than the guest house it has been so long. A big and elegant hotel for the *ton* and the –'

'An hotel?' Tilly said and stopped and stared and then repeated slowly, 'An hotel. Quentin's Hotel. Well, my dear Duff, my own darling Duff, why not? We shall indeed have an hotel. You and I together. And Eliza too, of course.' And she held out a hand to Eliza who came round the table to stand at Duff's other side.

'Well, well,' Mr Lansdown said. 'An hotel. What an interesting thought. It would be gratifying indeed to act for an *hotel*. We have none in our practice at present and as one with an interest in and a taste for fine foods and wine, why, I think it will be a pleasure to act for you, Mrs Quentin, Mr Quentin.'

She looked up at him and smiled as the last shred of lingering guilt that she had been feeling about parting from Silas Geddes shrivelled and died. She would still have to see him, talk to him, tell him that she had, regretfully, to release him from their engagement and try to explain why without hurting his feelings. It would be difficult, if not impossible, for how do you tell a man you find him no more than physically interesting, that his tendency to talk rather than do, and to pose rather than be, was too irksome, and a destroyer of affection? A way would have to be found, and soon, but at present it was enough to be where she was, and with whom she was.

'Do you know, Mr Lansdown, I suspect you will be a great asset to us here at Quentin's Hotel. Thank you for your interest.'

'It will be consistent, I promise you,' he said gravely, and then got to his feet. 'I would like, if I may, to see the damage next door. I have not had the chance to look.'

It was Duff who led the way out of the area door and up into the street above, and they stood there in the darkening evening, the four of them, Duff with an arm round the shoulders of both Tilly and Eliza, with Mr Lansdown alongside them, staring up. The front of number eighteen was stained with smoke and soot, and the gaping holes that showed where once windows had been and where bricks and stucco had caved in, seemed ominous and sad at the same time. Beside it the spruce front of Quentin's lifted its head and seemed to glow bravely in the darkness, each of the windows where there was still glass winking cheerfully and the paint gleaming softly.

And Duff said quietly, 'Just you wait. Oh, Ma, Eliza, just you wait. This time next year – well, it will be the best thing you ever saw. Quentin's Hotel! I shall fetch some champagne from the cellar – for no amount of fireman's water down there will have harmed that! – and we and all our guests, our *friends* – shall drink to the future. What do you say? Shall we?'

And they did.